Do Nothing Shadows

Do Nothing Shadows

Robert Laubach

Writers Club Press

San Jose New York Lincoln Shanghai

Do Nothing Shadows

Writers Club Press
an imprint of iUniverse.com, Inc.

For information address:
iUniverse.com, Inc.
5220 S 16th, Ste. 200
Lincoln, NE 68512
www.iuniverse.com

ISBN: 0-595-15086-1

Printed in the United States of America

Part 1

In all probability Freud would have attributed Harry's character defects to his early relationship with his mother, or, to be more precise, to the lack of one.

She hadn't talked to him in a normal manner since shortly after his father died in the war. Instead, she gave him orders. Like when she'd stand in the doorway of his room at 4:30 in the morning and say, "Get up, it's time to deliver your papers, and put your boots on, it's snowing," or, "This is a list of what I want from the store, don't be gone long."

It hadn't always been like that. When his father was alive she was different—the house was different. The three of them were happy and they'd do things together—fun things. Sometimes on a Friday night his father would take them to the movies, and afterwards, for Chinese food and ice cream. In the summer, they would go up to the park and ride the merry-go-round, and his mother would get mad when she'd catch him sneaking a taste of his father's beer.

Holidays were special. On Thanksgiving, the house smelled of pies and roasting turkey. He'd help his mother strip the little peas from their pods and watch that nothing boiled over on the stove. When ice formed on the inside of the kitchen windows, he'd scratch funny faces in it with a fingernail until she told him to stop.

Sometimes in the late afternoon, they went to his grandparents' homes and the eating would start all over.

Christmas Eve, when he was allowed to stay up until midnight, was the best. Neighbors would come to the house with cakes and candies and he would run his electric trains for them. Finally, after exhausting every possible reason why he should be allowed to stay up, reluctantly, too excited to sleep, off to bed he'd go. Almost holding his breath, he would stand behind the bedroom door listening while his mother and father crept up the stairs to get his presents out of the so-called secret hiding place. Up until the time his father went away to the war, those were the happiest days of h is life.

Then everything changed. It was August 24, 1943, and it was his ninth birthday. By 8 a.m. he was up, dressed, and ready to go. His mother had bought him a pair of Flyer roller skates, but she said he had to wait awhile before going out, that it was early, and the neighbors would complain about the noise they'd make on the concrete sidewalk.

At last, it was OK to go out, but just as he was about to turn the knob, somebody banged the heavy brass knocker so hard it scared the daylights out of him. When he opened the door, there was a kid not much older than he standing there. The boy said, "Western Union"; no one had ever sent them a telegram before. Maybe, he thought, it was from his father, wishing him a happy birthday. Wow, wouldn't that be special, he thought.

His mother had been working in the kitchen, so he was surprised when she was suddenly standing next to him. He was more surprised when she pushed him aside and snatched the telegram out of the kid's hand, and without saying anything, disappeared back into the house.

For a moment he stood in the doorway watching as the messenger went back down the stoop and got on h is bike. It was a Schwinn with bright, chrome fenders. Someone had put little lights inside the spokes so at night when the wheels turned, the small things on the ends of them would rub against the tires and they'd go on. If I had a bike like that, he thought, I could probably do two paper routes before school. I could even put a wire basket on it and deliver groceries for Mr. Horowitz. Maybe when Daddy comes home and goes back to work, I can get one.

About to go out, he heard his mother's voice coming from the living room. "Harry, please, would you come in here?" Her face ashen, she was sitting on the couch between the windows, and her hands were shaking so badly, she was having trouble holding the telegram.

"Sit down, sweetheart, here, next to me," she said, brushing the hair back out of his eyes. He started to cry. He didn't know exactly why, but he knew something terrible had happened.

After some fumbling, she managed to get the folded, yellow piece of paper out of the envelope. How funny it looked, he thought. There were narrow strips of paper glued to it with typing on them. It hadn't been folded right either, at least not the way he would fold a letter.

"No, no, no," his mother moaned, her entire body now trembling as if she was suffering an epileptic convulsion. "Please God, not this, not this, please God, please God."

The telegram slipped from her hands and slowly, like she was in agonizing pain, pulled herself up from the couch and left the room. He could hear her in the kitchen crying and calling his father's name. The message read

Dear Mrs. O'Day:

It is with deep regret that I must inform you that your husband John Harold O'Day U.S.N.R., is missing in action and presumed dead.

Commander Vincent S. Lockridge
U.S.N
Pacific Fleet Comm.
By order of the Secretary of the Navy

He read the words over and over until they became just a blur and the tears running down his face started making spots on the yellow paper.

"Harry, would you come in here please and help me?" he heard his mother call from the kitchen. Still holding the telegram, he got up and went to her. Gently, she took it out of his hand, carefully folded it, and put it into the pocket of her apron.

"I think these cookies are cool enough now so we can put them in the box, "she said matter-of-factly. "Go and get the wax paper we bought yesterday. When we're finished, do you think you could take them down to the post office for me? I promised your father. You know how much he loves them. So do you."

"Mom, the post office isn't open today."

"Oh, yes, you're right, how silly of me. What am I thinking about?"

"Mom, the telegram, is Daddy coming home anymore? Did they send it because Daddy's dead?"

She put her arms around him and he could feel how warm her tears were on his face. Sobbing and holding him tightly she said, "No, sweetheart, I don't think so, I don't think he'll be coming home. He told me last night that he had to go away."

Startled he asked, "You mean he called? How could that be? Why didn't you let me talk to him?"

"No, sweetheart, he didn't call. He came in my room last night, but he said he couldn't stay long."

"Mom, I don't understand."

She explained how the noise from the wind in the trees outside her bedroom windows had woken her up. It was 3 a.m. because she picked up the alarm clock and looked at it.

That's when she heard him call her name. He was standing at the foot of the bed, all suntanned and wearing his dress uniform.

"Carry? Don't be scared, it's me. I came to tell you that I have to go away. A lot of the other men are going with me. Don't worry, I'm going to be all right now. Take care of yourself and our son and tell him how much I love him. Remember, as long as you stay in this house you'll be safe. As long as you stay here I'll be with you. I have to go now, they're waiting. You understand, don't you?" Then he was gone.

The one thing she never told her son, was that in the morning, she noticed the alarm clock had stopped at exactly 3:03 a.m., and from that day on, it sat up on her closet shelf.

Harry and his mother stayed in the kitchen together for a long time working on the cookies, but not saying anything. Each could hear the other softly crying, and from time to time, they'd go off someplace by themselves.

Time stopped in that house, on that day and gradually, it became like a cold tomb, and to which, circumstances forced him to return each day. His mother changed. Her face took on a permanent, defiant, stonelike expression, and, as the months and years wore on, they said less and less to each other, until finally, they pretty much stopped speaking to one another at all.

One day when he came home from school, he found her packing whatever was left of his father's things into a box. She had even taken his picture down off the dining room wall. When he asked her what she was doing, she snapped at him.

"It's my business." The only thing she hadn't packed was the little flag with a single star on it that hung in the living room window. Someone at the War Department had sent it to her. There were a lot of houses in the neighborhood with the same kind of flag in their windows.

A few times after that he tried talking to her about his father, and about what was happening to her, but her responses became more and more hostile. Until the day she died, he never again tried talking to her about anything except maybe what she might need from the store, or if anybody had called for him while he was out.

Even when he came home with the consent papers the Marine recruiting officer said she had to sign, Harry and his mother said little to each other. During his four years in the Corps, he could count on one hand the number of times he went home on leave. He'd go someplace, but not home. On his other hand, he could count the number of letters he and his mother exchanged.

After his discharge, he went back to the old neighborhood and got and apartment. The job he found was mediocre at best, so he cut back on the boozing just enough, and just long enough to attend college at night and get a degree in finance. Over time, he moved in and out of several more jobs, each time picking up a few dollars in salary increases, but still, nothing big.

The only important thing that happened was his marriage. Fortunately it didn't last long.

Eventually, a good job did come along, and with it, his nightmare.

Part 2

Komti, Ltd. was one of Japan's largest and most diversified manufacturers. Salvaged from the devastation of World War II by the founder's son, its products included aircraft, supertankers, TVs, toothpaste, golf clubs, stereos, automobiles, and bicycles. In addition the company was deeply involved in research, some of which it was rumored, had military applications.

At the age of 29, he was hired as the assistant credit manager at Santronics, Komti's home electronics entertainment subsidiary. He would be in charge of its Northeastern region, a territory that took in all of New York State, New Jersey, Pennsylvania, and New England.

Accordingly, he enjoyed a position of some authority and prestige, especially since his boss, Ira Senowitz, was such an incompetent.

"If you have a problem, go see Harry," was the word around the company.

For the first time in his life, he had a job of substance, a job he didn't hate, a job that was finally putting some cash into his constantly empty pockets. Only recently he'd managed to buy his first new car.

Unfortunately, the good times were about to come to an abrupt end unless he could force the company to back down. Ira had messed up big time, and since he was considered to be Ira's protegee and the real brains in the credit department, they were probably both going to get fired.

That's why they'd been summoned to a meeting at Komti's corporate headquarters on 34th street at 8th avenue, he was sure of it. First they were going to watch Ira grovel while trying to explain how three crooks had scammed the company for $2,227,000, and then fire him. "Oh! And Ira," they'd tell him, "take your friend, O'Day, with you."

Only Harry had his own agenda. He'd come too far now and knew too much. There was no way he would allow himself to be sacrificed for somebody else's blunders. Nor would he allow himself to be intimidated by the three has-been samurais scheduled to conduct the meeting. Not only was he prepared to tell them what they could do with their termination notices, but he was going to demand that both he and Ira be promoted with substantial increases in salary. They'd get a good laugh out of that, he thought, but by the time he finished explaining the quid pro quo, they would be laughing out the other sides of their faces.

After a series of heart stopping events in his life, including several murders which he knew somehow he was involved with, having both his home and auto broken into, being followed, and almost getting shot, he'd accepted the help of some very bad people. Reluctantly, at first and then eagerly, he had taken their offers. They were willing to lend him as much of their power as might be necessary for him to get what he wanted, providing they got what they wanted.

The need for advancement and money was not the driving force behind the actions he was about to take. It was the letter he'd found in his mother's belongings after she passed away, written in 1947 by a man who'd known her husband during the war. A man who had suffered in the same horrible prison camp and knew the name of her husband's murderer, Col. Sugomu Nagakura who was now the shadowy CEO of Komti, Ltd.

No doubt the fee for using his new acquaintances' muscle would be high, but it didn't matter, he would worry about the cost later. Far from being stupid, he'd given careful thought to what he was doing. His friend, Mike O'Banion Jr., tried to warn him, "Harry, you can get hurt around those people, hurt bad."

As if he's any better, Harry would think to himself. The O'Banion family bar in Rockaway was a hotbed of IRA activities, including the harboring of terrorists—men who thought it politically correct to blow up a truck full of British soldiers and then hop a plane for the States.

The only thing that mattered to Harry was getting his hands on the bastard who'd tormented and butchered his father. He hadn't just died in the war, his father had been executed by a sadistic madman who then ordered the body desecrated. Just as his mother had been forced to live with the knowledge of how her husband had died, Harry was being forced to live with it every minute of the day. His mother, God rest her soul, hadn't been able to do anything about it, but he could.

Whatever anxieties he may have suffered as a result of pledging allegiance to a man who would become his *Machiavellian* mentor, soon dissipated. In fact, swearing loyalty to this merchant of evil would prove to be the best thing he ever did.

*   *   *

No herringbone jacket and slacks today. Given the magnitude of the occasion, he put on a dark, charcoal gray, three-piece business suit, a blue, button-down oxford shirt, and a paisley print tie. Even his penny loafers got a rest. Instead, he put on a pair of new, shiny, black wingtips. After dressing, he stood in front of the mirror and examined his efforts. "Not bad O'Day, not bad at all for a drunk," he said.

Appearancewise, he wasn't bad looking. Standing just over 6' 3" tall and weighing a respectable 225 pounds, he had a full crop of sandy brown hair that matched his eyes, and his stomach was still reasonably flat. Although he kept promising himself to cut down on the booze and greaseburgers, he never seemed to get around to it.

His head may have appeared too large for his body, but when people looked at him it was his rugged, exaggerated, square jaw that caught their attention. His huge hands bore the marks of having grown up in the streets. If it weren't for his nose having been broken more times than he cared to remember, and the faded, four-inch scar under his left eye, one might even say he was handsome. While he'd never admit it to anyone, he liked the idea of the prizefighter nose and scar, he though they made him look intimidating, which they did.

Most of his visible scars were acquired during a street fight when he was 16. On the way home from school one day, he saw two mutts beating on a kid behind the string of garages by his mother's house. He'd seen the boy around the neighborhood, but the punks trying to take his head off were strangers. The kid was on the ground and it looked like he was unconscious, but they were still kicking him. There really wasn't anything else to do except stop them.

Before it was over, he got smashed across the face with a piece of two-by-four, but luckily when he fell, he managed to grab hold of a broken Coke bottle and used it to slash both of his attackers.

Once they saw their own blood and how badly they were cut, they ran. A woman hanging out wash saw the fight and called the cops. They took one look at all the blood and threw him and the boy into the back of the patrol car. One of the cops though the kid might already be dead.

It was his first overnight stay in a hospital and he loved it, especially when the young, good-looking nurse with big breasts took his blood pressure and changed the dressing on his face. Getting meals served in bed wasn't bad either.

They kept him overnight because they wanted a specialist to look at his eye, and to make sure he didn't have a concussion. The kid he'd helped wasn't so lucky. Harry found out later the doctors had to remove his spleen. They said if someone hadn't come along and stopped the beating when they did, the boy would've died.

About a month after the fight Harry's mother got a large bill for the emergency room, the overnight stay, X-rays, and the eye specialist, but it was marked "PAID." She called the hospital's accounting office, but the only thing they'd tell her was that someone had come in and paid it in cash. "Hey, listen," the girl in the office said, "don't worry about it, you must have a rich friend someplace."

The hospital bill wasn't the only strange thing that happened. His mother had saved a few dollars to have badly needed repairs done on the roof, only she made the mistake of hiring some neighborhood jerk-off who claimed to be a roofer. He'd show up around lunchtime with half a snoot full and it would take him the rest of the afternoon just to get a few rolls of tarpaper up to the roof without falling down the ladder.

After three days of that nonsense, several trucks pulled up in front of the house loaded with men and all kinds of roofing materials. Besides sending the drunk packing, within two days they put an entire new roof on the place. They even went into the backyard and put a new roof on the garage. His mother kept frantically trying to tell the boss of the crew that she hadn't ordered all the work they were doing, and that there was no way she could possibly pay for it.

"Look lady," he'd say, "how many times I gotta tell you, forget about it, it's been taken care of."

*   *   *

On a normal workday the trip from his apartment in Queens to his office at Santronics in Brooklyn, would take about twenty minutes. He'd even have time to stop for a doughnut and coffee, or a morning drink depending on which he needed the most. More often than not, it was the latter. This morning however, it would take him more than an hour to get to his meeting a Komti's corporate headquarters in Manhattan because of the traffic in the Queens Midtown Tunnel.

It had taken only three days of working at Santronics to see that a gold rush was in progress, like back in California in the 1840s. Except now Santronics merchandise was the gold, and the company's dealers were the miners. The line had been deliberately priced so far below similar American-made products that in essence, Santronics was simply exchanging it for U.S. currency. The dealers were getting richer by the hour and he could have made them dance naked in the streets just by hinting he might have to hold an order. But that wasn't his style. Nobody made any money that way.

It was a gigantic crapshoot and he took everything he'd ever learned about credit from a textbook and threw it out the window. If there was a problem with an account he'd get in his car; after a free lunch and five drinks, the dealer would be telling him what a great guy he was while writing the check.

By the time he got to within a half mile of the tollbooths, the traffic had already slowed to a crawl.

"Damn," he said, "why the hell didn't I stop for a container of coffee or something?"

But he soon forgot about the coffee when he recognized the car and its occupants ahead and to the left of him. He'd seen them before going through the tunnel and had gotten a good laugh watching their antics.

The car was the longest, ugliest, gaudiest Caddy he'd ever seen. It was bright yellow with swirly, red pinstriping up and down the sides, and the continental wheel extended a good two feet beyond the trunk. Almost as high as the roof, the car's rear fenders looked like they'd been taken off a rocket ship.

As if the car weren't funny enough, its driver looked like an escapee from the Collins Avenue dog track in Miami Beach. Clad in an electric blue jacket and white golf hat cocked to one side of his hairless head, he had a cigar long enough to hit the windshield stuffed in his face.

Next to him was a woman in her 50s, but desperately trying to look in her 20s. Sporting a bleach blond, beehive hairdo, her makeup looked like a $29.95 Earl Shieb paint job that somehow had gone terribly wrong.

When a space opened, he jockeyed his car next to them so the two vehicles would go through the tunnel side-by-side. In so doing, he'd guaranteed himself a front row seat for the Miami Marvin show—that's the nickname he'd given the Caddy's driver after the first time he had seen him.

Blondie's head disappeared from view the moment their cars were swallowed up by the semidarkness of the tunnel. Every so often it would popup only to be pushed back down by Miami Marvin's ham hock of a right hand. It wasn't Harry's practice to watch other people getting it on, except for an occasional porno film, but he made an exception with these two. These were funny people. They looked and dressed funny, they drove a funny-looking car, and they reminded him of a couple of characters he'd seen in an animated Walt Disney movie when he was a kid.

It was a short show. They weren't more than a quarter of the way through the tunnel when the car made a sudden, jerky motion and Blondie's head popped up like a jack-in-the-box. In one hand she was holding a wad of tissues, and with the other, she was trying to push her beehive hairdo back to where it had once been. Dumbstruck, he watched as she looked straight at him, pursed her lips, and blew a kiss.

"Well I'll be damned," he said, "the bitch knew I was watching." Being the gentleman he was, he blew a kiss back and flicked his tongue in and out a couple of times to let her know that he really cared.

While they were falling in love, Miami Marvin was having serious problems adjusting the driver's side power seat and almost put his head through the cloth roof of the convertible. Harry thought that was funny. He also laughed because of how much Blondie reminded him of the way Elsa Langcaster looked in the "Bride of Frankenstein."

As the traffic inched slowly along the tunnel, his thoughts turned to other things, like his recent divorce, and how he was glad that it was finished, except for the alimony payments. He remembered how upset he'd gotten reading the court papers. His now ex-wife's lawyer had said a lot of nasty things about him, none of which were true, as far as he was concerned. When he called to complain, she said, "Oh, don't worry about it. My lawyer said that if we made you look dangerous the judge would grant the divorce quicker. He said we had to make you look bad."

The truth was he'd never once laid a hand on her, nor had he ever verbally abused her. The more he thought about their relationship, the more he realized she had been the one with the problems. Martie had never made the slightest effort to understand that it was important for him to stay out after work with business associates. She'd get mad too when he wanted to go fishing on the weekends, again, with business associates and have a couple of drinks. The same thing would happen when he wanted to use the company's box seats for a football or baseball game. But the thing that got her absolutely nuts was when he had to go on a business trip. The end came when she had the audacity to say he had a serious drinking problem and needed to get some help.

The sound of a phone snapped his attention back to the smelly reality of the tunnel. It was coming from one of the narrow, plexiglas guard cubicles scattered along the tunnel's catwalks. He figured Tunnel Control was calling to see if any of its men were still alive, or if they'd all died from carbon monoxide poisoning.

"How the hell can anybody work in this place?" he asked himself. "It's got to be like living in the men's room at Yankee Stadium." Again, the monotony of the ride, the cars, the repetitive markers, and most of all, the godawful smell, caused his thoughts to wonder.

His mother's death was something he tried hard not to think about, but when it happened, he'd struggle to have only good thoughts, like about the tidy piece of change the sale of her house was bringing. Not once had he ever considered moving back into it, too many memories made that impossible. Located in an Italian/Irish section of Queens, it was in excellent condition because she'd been a stickler for repairs.

Working in the Navy Yard as a welder, his father made good money, so right after marrying Harry's mother, he bought the place for her as a wedding gift. Crimewise, the neighborhood didn't have any. If someone was stupid enough to come into it and cause trouble, they left it real quick, one way or another. The only trouble was the way the Italian and Irish gangs would beat each other up with baseball bats and bicycle chains. Nobody ever died, so it was considered as an acceptable right of passage—training, if you will.

Wanna-be wiseguys and button men were commonplace, but the rule among them was you didn't do bad things to people where you lived. Harry was sure the guy living next to his mother's house was a big shot in the rackets because that's what the papers kept saying. At Christmas time, you could do all your shopping right in the neighborhood out of the trunks of cars owned by men who worked at the airports.

He'd been over to the house several times during the past two weeks trying to inventory its contents, but it was taking a lot longer than he'd imagined. From the first night, it was painfully obvious that she'd never thrown anything out. There wasn't space to walk in some of the rooms.

"Put that downstairs," or, "Put that upstairs, we may need that," she was always telling him.

Fortunately, he didn't have to worry about some little Bob Cratchit bureaucrat from the state coming in and trying to grab up part of her property. Shortly before passing away, she'd taken his advice and allowed a lawyer friend of his to draw up a will. His friend assured him that barring any difficulties, it would clear probate within a few weeks, which was good because even without clear title, he'd put the house on the market. In fact, the real estate agent was breaking his chops to clean the place out. He said he could up the asking price another five grand if he could bring a couple of painters in.

The St. Paul Society operated a chain of secondhand outlets around the city and was always looking for good, used clothing and furniture. Everything in this mother's house had been well cared for so he was sure they'd be interested. On a Saturday morning, he met two of their trucks, and within an hour the house was empty. Two days later the real estate agent called and said he'd gotten an offer—an unusual one.

"Harry, I gotta tell you," he said, "we have a chance to *quadagnare forte*. You know what that means? It means to make some big money. But we gotta be careful, we're dealing with very important people."

The agent said a lawyer had come to his office and told him that his client, a Mr. Ponzinno, lived next door to the property, and was willing to pay a substantial premium over and above the asking price to ensure he'd get it. In addition, the lawyer wanted Mr. O'Day to know that he would have his client's gratitude if he agreed to the sale.

In short, Harry was being asked to, "do the right thing," and, in return, Mr. Ponzinno, the infamous Mr. Ponzinno, would repay the kindness when the opportunity presented itself.

What the lawyer had said wasn't a threat or anything to be misconstrued—it was simple. When a man like Ponzinno asked in a respectful manner for a favor, you would have to be a fool not to accommodate him, because the IOU could prove to be of immense value at some future date.

As a kid, Harry used to pick up extra money shoveling snow and Ponzinno's house would be the first place he'd go. Even the upstairs windows had wrought iron bars as did the heavy, glass screen door, but as least someone had welded little birds to the bars on the door so the house wouldn't look too much like the Bastille.

No taller that 5', a white-haired, wrinkled woman dressed in black always answered the side door. After telling him in badly broken English what a nice boy he was, she'd let him clean the sidewalk, and for that he got ten bucks—a fortune. Afterwards she would ask if he'd like to come in and have something to eat, but he never did. Not that he was afraid, it was just that if his mother found out he'd done it, she would have gotten mad.

Besides the house having bars all over it, he remembered how men would come and go from it until all hours of the morning. Sometimes they'd still be out in front, draped over the hoods of expensive automobiles when he went out at 5 a.m. to do his paper route. Many of the same men hung out up on the avenue by some kind of club next to the pastry shop. His mother used to warn him, "If they're outside, walk on the other side of the street. They're bad people, they're guineas."

As a kid, a lot of what she told him and said about people never made any sense to him. Like when she'd say, "they're gypsies and they'll steal your wash at night if you leave it out," or, "I don't want you playing with them, I think they're Spanish." But the thing about "guineas" confused him the most. The old woman who paid him all the money to shovel snow was Italian and she certainly wasn't a bad person. The cross she wore around her neck with Jesus on it was almost as big as she was, so how could she be doing bad things? The white-haired man who sat outside with her in the backyard during the summer, he was Italian, and he didn't do bad things. The guy always gave him grapes and figs when they were ripe. Half the kids in his classes, maybe more, were Italian and they didn't cause too much trouble, at least not while they were in school.

                    *   *   *

The only things left in his mother's house were several file boxes containing her personal papers which he'd locked in a small room downstairs in the cellar. Now that the sale of the property was imminent, he had no choice, they had to be sorted out. Doing it there would be far less messy than dragging the dusty, dilapidated things over to his apartment in a brand new car.

Armed with a quart of liquor, two pastrami sandwiches, a package of paper cups, and plastic garbage bags, he unlocked the front door.

Incredible, he thought, as he sat on an old, wooden milk case in the basement pouring out a cup of Bushmills. His mother had kept every gas, electric, water, phone, tax, and any other kind of bill she'd ever received. The same was true for junk mail, grocery receipts, Christmas cards, and canceled checks, plus bank statements. Out of an entire box, maybe, there would be three or four items he thought might require a second look. Everything else went right into the garbage bags.

The last box had been heavily tapped shut, so after washing down several mouthfuls of sandwich with another cup of whiskey, he used his penknife to open it. By doing so he'd profoundly changed his life.

Inside were three large brown envelopes, about the size of the ones they used for interoffice mail at work. They too were sealed with the same heavy tape. The first one contained packets of hand-written letters, each small bundle carefully tied with individual strips of red, white, and blue ribbon. Just touching them suddenly made him feel like an intruder. They were his father's wartime letters to his mother. At first he hesitated, not being sure if he should, or even wanted to, read them. But curiosity and the need to once again be part of the family so callously ripped from him as a child, demanded he do so.

In his father's first letter home, he wanted to know how they were managing, and said that he loved and missed them both very much. "I wish all of this could get over with soon," he wrote, "but it's probably going to be some time before we can all be together again. Things are getting ugly even here, so if you don't hear from me for awhile, don't worry, I'll write as soon as I can."

There were parts of the letter, and of others that made it abundantly clear just how deeply his parents loved each other, and cherished him. As he continued reading, the letters began taking on an ominous tone.

Obviously his father had come to the stark realization that his chances of surviving the living hell he was in were growing slimmer by the day, and he'd begun preparing them for such a possibility.

"If it should come to that," he wrote, "and it very well may, at least you have the house and our son. As long as you stay there you'll be safe, and I'll always be with you. I know that you are a strong person and that somehow, should I not make it back, you'll manage to make a life for the two of you. I thank God every day for letting me know you, and for the beautiful son you've given me. Goodbye, I love you both. Sweet Jesus, pray for us."

*   *   *

As he drove through the tunnel, he remembered how it was that night sitting in his mother's cold, dimly lit basement, how with tears streaming down his face, and fighting hard to swallow the lump in his throat, he meticulously retied the bundles of letters. He remembered the agonizing sense of shame he'd felt.

Even now as he thought about it, he was ashamed. Ashamed for all the years he'd failed so miserably to understand what had happened to his mother that day, so many years ago when the boy brought her the telegram. She had died that day too, along with her beloved husband, the only man she'd ever known. Her physical body remained, but her ability to love and her heart had been trampled into the blood drenched sand of a prison camp far away in another world.

He felt ashamed for having thought badly of her when he had come home from school and found her packing his father's things into a box. Again, he'd failed to understand; if she had been forced to look at them day after day no doubt it would have been like a jagged piece of glass ripping at what little was left of her emotions.

He was ashamed for not having realized that only by withdrawing into a protective shell had she been able to deal with her agonizing grief and the tormenting emptiness now a part of her daily life. Only by becoming the person she did, had she been able to survive, not only for her own sake, but for his as well, the way her husband had told her to do.

What he was most heartily ashamed of, though, was that even when she lay dying in the hospital, he couldn't put aside his pettiness and say that he loved her.

There was a small potbellied stove in the basement and he used it to burn the letters. It was his way of guaranteeing what his mother and father had shared so joyously in life, would be theirs and theirs alone for eternity in death.

Emotionally and visibly shaken, he was suddenly uncomfortable being alone in the house. It had always made strange, moaning sounds when the wind rocked it, and he'd heard them countless times as a child, but tonight they seemed louder and more terrifying. Even the floor joists above his head had begun to creak and make stretching noises as if someone were walking around upstairs in the kitchen.

Quickly he loaded the garbage bags into the trunk of his car along with two yet unopened, brown envelopes. Too much was happening there—he had to get out. It was like the place was moving and breathing with him in it.

As he went back up the stoop to lock the front door for the last time, he heard laughter, he heard the sound of a man and woman laughing and it was coming from inside the house. To this day he would be willing to swear before Christ himself that on that night, as he locked the door, he heard a man and woman laughing inside his mother's house, and the smell of something baking was as strong as it was so long ago in the kitchen when he helped his mother bake his father's favorite cookies.

It was their house and always would be. No matter who owned it, or lived in it, his mother and father would always be there, together, the way it should have been.

The next several days were busy ones, and he was glad because it helped blot out the events in his mother's house. Boston was a one-day affair. He spent another entire day with Gimbel's accounting people trying to straighten out returns, and he finished out the week by spending a couple of twelve-hour days at his desk catching up on paperwork.

On Sunday morning he woke up, which in itself was a medical miracle, considering the amount of booze he'd consumed the night before. Not that he had planned on a staying out, but as usual, he ran into some of his heavy-hitting friends on Queens Boulevard and it was off to the races.

A prolonged shower and a couple of mugs of coffer laced with whiskey got him back into the world of the semi-sober. On his way into the living room to watch football highlights, he spotted the two brown envelopes from his mother's house. They were sticking out from under a pile of newspapers and unopened mail on the hall table.

"How long could it take to finish this stuff?" he asked himself, so along with his whiskey coffee, he took them and sat down on the living room couch. "Again with this damn tape," he growled, giving the strip on one a good yank. When he did, the envelope came apart, spilling its contents. An icy chill ran up his arms and across the back of his neck. There, right on top of what had fallen was a telegram. Instantly he knew he'd seen it before. A boy had delivered it to his mother's house at 9 a.m. on August 24, 1943.

Besides the telegram, there were letters from the Secretary of the Navy, the office of the President, and the State Department, all addressed to his mother. There was also a hand-written letter from a Mr. Jeffery V. Prior, 27 Montrose Lane, Van Nyes Calif., postmarked September 8, 1947, and it was six pages long.

Mr. Prior explained that he knew her husband before the war, they had worked together in the Brooklyn Navy Yard as welders. A week after the Japanese attacked Pearl Harbor, the Navy came around asking for volunteers to join the Seabees, a branch of its service comprised of heavy equipment operators, welders, engineers, and general construction workers. He joined on the spot, and since her husband was a chief petty officer in the Reserve, they activated him. A lot of the other men working at the yard joined up at the same time.

After two weeks of learning which end of a rifle to point, they were shipped out, but they weren't assigned to the same battalion. In March of 1943, he was part of an engineering group trying desperately to keep an airstrip on some island operational. The place was so tiny, Prior said, it didn't appear on most of the Navy's maps. But they were told the strip was of vital importance because it gave fighter pilots either wounded, or flying shotup planes, a place to set down if they weren't going to make it back to their carriers.

It was an impossible task. Besides daily attacks by enemy planes, his unit was in desperate need of heavy equipment operators and welders. Most of theirs had been either killed or wounded. He himself was working twenty hours a day. Finally, a relief unit of Seabees came ashore, and much to his delight, her husband was among the men.

Not long after, Prior went on, the senior officer of the Marine garrison defending the island called the construction people together, and told them plans were being made to evacuate them immediately. Navy intelligence had intercepted Japanese radio traffic indicating a large enemy force was about to attack the airstrip, and that any further attempts to hold the island wold be futile.

The intelligence wasn't good enough. At 3 a.m. the very next day the Japs attacked. Those Americans not killed outright were taken by landing craft out to transports lying off shore. After six days at sea, they were herded out of the holds, taken ashore, and forcemarched through the jungle to a prison camp. About half the men originally taken prisoner survived the trip, the rest either died from their wounds, or were murdered and thrown overboard by drunken guards.

One morning, Prior's letter continued, he noticed a commotion in the main yard involving her husband and a guard. A young Marine had died while sitting up against a wooden shack and he was trying to explain to the guard he wanted to take the body away. Laughing, the guard spit on the dead Marine's face, and that's when it happened. Her husband tried to grab the rifle. On a direct order from the camp's commandant, a Colonel Sugomu Nagakura, the guard, along with two others, bayoneted him. Nagakura ordered both bodies be left there as a warning to the rest in the camp. After five days, a chaplain was allowed to take them outside the wire for burial. Prior said in late November of 1944, the entire island came under increasingly heavy attack by American fighter-bombers and one morning the Japanese were simply gone. Somehow they'd managed to sneak off, undetected during the night. A day later, American reconnaissance patrols came ashore with doctors. Even the most battle hardened of the Marines wept when they saw what was left of their tortured, and emaciated comrades.

It was only by the grace of God he himself managed to survive the hellhole for as long as he did. As a result of the horrendous beatings he'd taken, it wasn't until the summer of 1946 that he was discharged from the Long Beach Naval hospital. After being home for a while, Prior said his head started to clear and he began thinking about her and her son. He said her husband always carried a picture of them and never missed an opportunity to show it to others. Personally, he never got tired of seeing it because it reminded him of his own family and home.

Prior said he was sure she had received the initial telegram advising her that her husband was missing and presumed dead because his wife had gotten one. But he wasn't sure if she'd ever been officially notified about his actual death. Navy intelligence did know about it because they had debriefed everybody when they were taken off the island. He was hoping that someone had contacted her to explain everything. It was customary in such cases for the deceased's spouse or next of kin to receive an American flag along with any honors and medals that were due.

The possibility, for whatever the reason, they hadn't contacted her, nagged at him for a long time, he said. He couldn't remember how many times he'd picked up a pen and started to write only to change his mind.

"God help me," he would say, "if the poor woman doesn't already know the truth, I'll be starting her pain and suffering all over again."

It was his wife who finally convinced him to go ahead and write. "Look," she said, "it's the woman's husband. If anyone has the right to know what happened to him in that godforsaken place, she does. At least she'll know where his body is."

The letter ended by Prior telling his mother that he had only good thoughts about her husband. "You can be proud of him, he was the type of man who was always ready to help a fellow worker, and even though I only knew him for a short while, I never once saw him back away from adversity. For what little comfort it may bring, both you and your son can be proud of the way he conducted himself right up to the end. May God bless the both of you and keep you, and if there is ever anything I can do for either of you, please, it would be an honor."

It wasn't until the light coming in the living room windows began to fade, making it hard to see, that he realized just how long he'd been sitting there. All the time reading the letter over and over, turning the handwritten pages, sometimes not seeing the words through his tears, and smoothing their yellowing, bent edges.

His mother had made copious notes on the backs of the letters from the Navy and State departments. She'd sent them both a copy of Prior's letter and demanded to know why they hadn't notified her about her husband's death. She also demanded to know why they'd never made any effort to recover his body. "At least you could have had the decency to give him a proper burial," she wrote.

Their responses amounted to nothing more than a lot of dumb sounding, bureaucratic bullshit, just a lot of stupid, disrespectful, meaningless nonsense.

Carefully he refolded Prior's letter, and along with the so-called answers to her inquiries, put them into a desk drawer. The telegram he placed in the back of his mother's Bible he now kept on top of it, slowly closed the cover, and held it against his chest.

"With God as my witness," he said, "no matter how long it takes, no matter how much it costs, I'm going to bring him home. I want the flag, I want the medals, and I want the bastards to explain why they wouldn't tell her the truth."

Part 3

For a moment the blaring noise of a car horn and gruff voice yelling, "Move it, you jerk. What are you, drunk or something?" startled him. He'd fallen behind in the line of traffic and the Neanderthal in back of him wasn't too happy.

"God, how I hate this tunnel," he said to himself, picking up the pace. On any other day he would have said something to the ass with the horn, but getting to Manhattan, and to his meeting was far too important.

In just a few years, Komti, through its Santronics subsidiary, had practically taken over the rapidly growing home electronics entertainment business in America. In the process it had built enormous warehouse/office distribution centers in New York, New Orleans, Atlanta, Boston, Chicago, and San Francisco.

Every Santronics expansion had cut deeper and deeper into the profits of its American competitors. Not a day went by without articles appearing in most of the major newspapers about how the Japanese were deliberately underpricing their goods and dumping them into the American marketplace.

The U.S. manufacturers were spending millions lobbying their already bought and paid for politicians, but nothing seemed to be happening. Some changes in the import and tariff laws were proposed, but in almost every instance, they were either stopped in committee, or vetoed by the President. Someone, somehow, always had enough juice to maintain the status quo.

On day, halfway through a liquid lunch, one of Harry's more flamboyant dealers told him an insane story about what he thought was going on. Supposedly the CIA and the Pentagon had told the President that it would be good if he helped certain people in Japan with their import problems.

"Now why the hell would they go and do a thing like that?" Harry asked, motioning to the waiter to bring another round of drinks.

"Because," the dealer said, "the CIA was told through back channels that if he didn't, these very powerful people would make sure the Japanese Government threw our military out of some of the bases over there."

"Abudi, you better have another drink, either that, or loosen your turban a little. You got too much pressure on your brain."

"No, I'm not kidding, Harry. The CIA told him if they lost the bases they wouldn't be able to protect his queer friends in Hollywood in case the communists attacked."

"You're a sick man Abudi, here, have another drink."

"But it is true, Harry, listen to me. The spy people said if he didn't, they were going to tell everybody he was screwing around in the White House."

Harry sat for a moment sipping a water glass of whiskey and then smiled. "You know Abudi," he said, "in this country they have places for guys like you—they're nice—nice and quiet. They teach you how to make things with clay and if you're really good, sometimes they take you to the zoo."

"No, Harry, I swear, it was written in the papers."

"Yeah, sure, the only problem Abudi, is it was written in those papers you get from back home in tent city. I'm tellin' you, you're puttin' too much brown stuff in your water pipe."

After ordering one more round of drinks and the bill, he told the dealer, "Look the only thing that should be written is a check to cover the past due invoices on your account which now total $143,578. Can you handle that?"

"Sure Harry, sure, whatever you want, you know there's no problem with money. Here, I'll make it out for an even $200,000, this way you can ship me a little extra. Please, just do me a favor, tell you sales department to ship some of those stereo headsets. I got a lot of people asking for them. Well, thanks for lunch. I better get back to the store before my cousin starts stealing from the registers again."

There wasn't any doubt in his mind that a lot of what Abudi had said about the President's antics in the White House were true. The guy had the reputation for being a womanizer even before he was elected to his first term. But all the other garbage about the CIA and everything was just that, garbage, or so he thought. Even if some of it was true, so what? Also, he could care less about the whinings of corporate America. God knows how long most of them had been selling things to the American people knowing full well that some of them could, and did, make the people sick, or even kill a few. Now that the Japanese were giving them a run for their money, they were pissing and moaning to their friends in Washington.

If the truth be known, Harry wasn't the least bit interested in anything political. His main interest had always been, and always would be, himself. He'd never voted and had no plans to start. On a scale of one to ten, he ranked all politicians at a minus two. And as for the sleazebag in the White House running for reelection, the guy would do just fine without his vote. There were plenty of jerks around who thought his marital infidelities cute, and dumb enough to put him back into office for another four years. Having him there probably made them feel less guilty about messing around themselves with their sister-in-law, or with their brother-in-law, or whoever else it was they were screwing on the side.

As far as he was concerned, the American voters had always gotten exactly what they allowed themselves to get. The first clown that came along and gave them a ten cent flag to wave and a free barbecue on the Fourth of July got their vote, along with power of attorney over their checkbooks.

*   *   *

The only time he ever allowed himself to be drawn into a serious conversation about politics, the alleged intrusion by the Japanese into American business, and the shortcomings of the White House was one night when he ran into Peter Longdon, a drinking enthusiast like himself. Peter had recently been transferred from D.C. to replace the credit manager of one of Santronics' American competitors, a man who suddenly had gotten sick and had to retire. A man who had bragged to Harry on numerous occasions how he'd never been sick a day in his life.

One of Harry's favorite after work watering holes was a Bavarian-style restaurant in Ridgewood, Queens. Their sauerbraten was excellent as were the humongous Manhattans they served. If you weren't in the mood for a regular sitdown meal, you could snack at the hors d'oeuves steamtable in the bar.

Besides the food and drinks, Harry liked the way the female help were required to dress. In keeping with the Bavarian theme, they wore short, dark, flared skirts, with colorful, wide suspenders, and black net stockings. Their blouses were off the shoulder and, undoubtedly for the benefit of the male customers, some of the lacing up the front was left undone. Harry was sure that when the owner had to place a help wanted ad for a waitress, he specified "Large breasted women only need apply."

One night when he decided to stop for a few, he spotted Peter sitting at the end of the bar stuffing his face with Swedish meatballs and shrimp. Peter wasn't exactly a friend, but he could drink like Harry and anybody who could do that, Harry considered to be a friend, at least for the time they were drinking together.

The bar section of the restaurant had high, red leather captain's chairs, but woefully inadequate to support Peter's 300 pound-plus body. Whenever the owner saw him come in, he'd go in the back and bring out a special, oversized, padded stool for him to sit on.

Longdon made some very disgusting sounds when he ate, loud enough to cause people around him to throw disapproving glances in his direction. Also, he sweated profusely, like he was in a sauna, especially from the face and scalp. So what people saw when they first looked at him was a fat, sweaty person with bad table manners who ate and drank to excess.

However, after a closer examination they began noticing other things about him. To begin with, they noticed his impeccable dress. Even in the dim lights of the bar, you could tell from the way his expensive looking suit fit that it had probably been tailor-made, which it was. All of his clothing was tailor-made. His white-on-white shirt with French cuffs and silk tie matched the suit perfectly, and the small handkerchief carefully fluffed in the outer pocket of his jacket was made from the same fabric as his tie. Harry had been tempted a couple of times to ask him if he also had his socks and underwear specially made.

Peter's jewelry consisted of a gold ID bracelet, a gold watch, and a gold ring that had a stone in it the size of a large marble. When he spoke, he did so in a slow, but yet, crystal clear voice, like he was choosing every word carefully so there shouldn't be and misunderstanding about what he'd just said. To Harry, it sounded more like Peter was giving ultimatums when he spoke. He sounded more like a cop or a lawyer than a credit manager.

"Well, hello, Harry, pull up a stool and have a meatball. I haven't seen you for a while. Busy?"

"Yes, very. The animals keep screaming for merchandise. How about in your place?"

"I wish. You and your little friends are making it difficult for us Americans to make a living."

Harry was just about to say that the people he worked for weren't exactly his buddies when Jerry, the bartender came over and asked what he was drinking.

"I'll have a Manhattan rocks, please, Jerry, and see what my poverty stricken friend here is drinking."

"Mr. Longdon, sir, would you have a drink with this gentleman?" Jerry asked.

"Certainly, just don't let him pay for it in yen."

"Oh, there she is again," Peter said, leaning over real close. "Harry, turn around slow and look at the Heidie standing next to the kitchen door." That was Peter's name for all the waitresses because of the way they dressed.

"You mean the tall one with the long legs and ponytail?"

"Yes, boy, would I like…" but before he could say another word, the young lady looked directly at them and started walking toward where they were sitting.

"Jesus, Harry, she's coming over here," Peter gulped. "You don't think she knows that I'm talking about her, do you?"

"I'm sure she does, and now she's gonna come over here and slap you silly in front of all these people."

"Hi, Harry. I saw you when you came in before," the women said bending to kiss his cheek.

She was in her early 20s, and even in the bar's artificial light you could see how white and soft her skin was. Her hair was a natural fire red and hung down her back in a ponytail to her waist. Her only makeup was a neutral lip gloss that gave her mouth a pouting, sensual appearance and her perfume had the scent of a woman who'd just showered and dusted her body with bath powder.

"Peter Longdon," Harry said, I'd like you to meet Miss Diedra Agnes Shannahan."

Longdon hadn't heard a word Harry said because he was too engrossed with the nearness of the beautiful woman's body.

"Hello? Peter? Are you with us?" Harry taunted.

"Uh, oh, yes, please, excuse me. It's nice to meet you," Peter stammered. He'd been caught with his eyes in Diedra's cleavage jar and he was embarrassed.

"It's nice to meet you too," she replied. "Are you a friend of Harry's from the office?"

"Uh, uh, no. Not from the office. Just a friend—a business friend."

As they spoke, a busboy carrying a tray full of dirty dishes came down the narrow aisle behind the long row of bar stools. In order for him to pass safely, Diedra had to wedge her body between the two men, causing her thighs to rub against their legs and placing her breasts just scant inches from Longdon's face. Harry fought to keep from laughing as he watched his friend nervously squirm around trying to put some distance between himself and the two things that just minutes earlier he would have given anything to touch.

"Well, I'm in the way here," she said, "besides, I'd better get back to my tables. Harry? Could you call me? There's some things I need to talk with you about." She leaned over and kissed him again, this time, almost on his lips. "It was nice meeting you Mr. Longdon, I hope I'll see you again." And with that, she turned, walked back into the main dining room and disappeared into the kitchen.

Anticipating his friend's question, Harry said, "No, I'm not sleeping with her, and yes, she certainly does have some body on her."

It was true, they weren't lovers, at least not yet. But when they were near each other, both could feel their growing desire, and they knew it was just a matter of the right time and place.

"How long have you known her?" Longdon asked, wiping the streams of perspiration from his face.

"A long time. I knew her husband before he killed himself."

"What was the guy, some kind of schmuck? A wife like her and he commits suicide?"

"No, it wasn't like that. He was a cop and he got killed on the job." Harry explained that he'd grown up with him and six months after Diedra made the mistake of marrying the mutt, he got called off the waiting list for the police academy. He'd always been a motorcycle nut so he got his father, a retired captain, to pull strings and get him onto the highway patrol unit. The only problem was the kid was a nasty drunk like his old man.

One night he was chasing a couple of skells in a stolen car on the Grand Cental Parkway and cut his head off when he crashed into a concrete construction barrier. There wasn't any autopsy, at least not officially, but scuttlebutt had it there was enough booze in him to croak a small herd of elephants.

"Wow," Longdon said, "that must have been devastating for her just having gotten married and all."

"Yeah, for awhile it was. She doesn't have any of her own family, but she's better off without the scumbag."

"My, my, talk about speaking disrespectful of the dead."

"You think so, Pete? You really think I'm being disrespectful? Did you happened to notice how she kept turning her head from side to side when you were talking to her? That's because she's deaf n her left ear. She got that from the very first beating. You happen to notice the scars on her face and chin? He did that one night when he went after her with a broken beer bottle. He said if she wasn't so pretty, other men would stop looking at her. Sometimes she'd come to our apartment in the middle of the night and she would be so badly beaten my wife couldn't figure out where the hell all the blood was coming from."

"My God, Harry, I had no idea. How could a man do anything like that to such a beautiful woman?"

"How? Because he was a scumbag just like his old man, that's how. May his soul rot in hell."

Just then, Jerry the bartender walked over and said, "You two look like pallbearers with those faces. Here, this round is on the house. My boss is very insistent that I give away his profits."

Diedra's late husband wasn't the only cop Harry knew. When he was growing up, going on the job was a popular choice of occupation among the non-Italian kids in the neighborhood. The Italians thought the Department of Sanitation had a good future, or they got jobs in the same line of work as their father's were in.

Every so often he would read in the papers about somebody from the old neighborhood either getting a promotion on the force, or getting himself stuffed into the trunk of a car out at the airport. It got to the point where watching the news on TV and reading the papers, was like thumbing through his grammar school yearbook.

He knew a lot of good people as well as a lot of very bad ones, and he got along with all of them. Each group had its own hangouts and after-hours spots and he moved in and out of all of them with no problem. That's because he followed the rules. You came in, you had a good time, you spent your money, and when you left, you didn't know anything more than you did when you first walked into the joint.

As the evening progressed, he and Peter enjoyed their usual activities which consisted of drinking, laughing, and drinking some more. Nothing of any significance was discussed until Longdon asked, "So what's with all these warehouses Komti keeps putting up?"

"What about them? Warehouses are warehouses," Harry answered. "They've got to have someplace to put the stuff after it comes off their ships. You have any idea how much merchandise we move just here in the New York area? I have dealers coming to my office begging me to take on-account payments because they're afraid of getting short-changed on inventory. That screwball, Crazy Phil, up in Beachaven, he calls me up today and says he wants to start buyin' trailer loads and can he get a discount."

"You know, Harry, you and your company are putting a lot of Americans out of work."

"Me!?" Harry shot back. "How the hell do you figure that?"

"Well, I shouldn't say you personally, I mean your company is. The field isn't level anymore and it's getting worse. People are starting to say that Komti has a rabbi someplace."

"Oh, here we go again with the bullshit, " Harry said, sounding irritated. "OK. Tell me where they have a rabbi."

"Maybe in Washington, maybe even in the White House. Maybe they even have more than one. You know, people do some bad things if there's enough money involved. So what do you think?"

"About what?" Harry snapped back, annoyed by the direction Longdon was making the conversation take.

"About how maybe your company has gotten certain people to look the other way. About how maybe they're into something besides just selling stereos and TV sets."

"What do I think? First of all, I think you've been pulling your pudding too much and it's starting to affect your brain. Secondly, I couldn't give a rat's ass if Komti had a rabbi, a priest, a mullah, or one of each. If someone in the White House is getting greased—so what? That's life. You show me one American CEO that isn't spreading a little bread on the water when he's trying to sell something to the government, and I'll show you a guy who's going to be dumped by his board of directors. It's called *baksheesh* and it's a way of life in half the world, maybe more, who knows?

"Besides," Harry continued, "that clown in the White House isn't any danger, except to himself. He can't get a blow job without someone catching him."

"Still," Longdon persisted, "we'd all be a lot better off without him. Wouldn't you say?"

"All I know is that I gotta get my ass out of here," Harry answered as he stood and stretched.

"Yes, me too, I have a meeting in the morning, and then I have to fly down to D.C. for another one."

They left the restaurant and walked around back to the parking lot.

"Harry? Have you been in all of Komti's warehouse centers?"

"Again with the warehouses? What's with you tonight? Forget about warehouses, you'll have bad dreams about them."

"Yes, but I'm just curious about something. Are they all designed the same? Do they all have those research and development rooms?"

"For God's sake Pete, yes! They're all the same. Exactly the same. And yes, they all have research centers. They've always used the same design. Now, would you please give it a rest?"

"Hey, that's a nice set of wheels," he said as Longdon unlocked the door of a new, expensive looking sedan. "Poverty seems to agree with you. I like the color, beige, isn't it? Only how come you didn't get white-walls?"

"I was going to," Longdon said, "but I changed my mind. They're such a pain in the ass to keep clean."

Harry asked if he could take a look at the interior. Obligingly, Longdon leaned over and unlocked the passenger side door.

"This is real leather, right?" asked Harry.

"I hope so, I paid them for leather."

"You know, when I was shopping around for a car, I looked at this very same model," Harry said as he got in. "But the problem I had was the way they put the heater core and fan motor inside here on the firewall. It takes up too much space."

As he spoke, he was moving his hand around under the dashboard until it touched something. It was a gun and from the size and shape of it, he knew it was a .45.

Trying to be nonchalant, Longdon smiled and asked, "Did you find my little friend under there?"

"I sure did, Pete, and it's not so little. What the hell are you doing with a cannon like that taped up under your dashboard?"

Longdon explained when he worked in D.C., a large number of his accounts were in bad neighborhoods. One dealer in particular, an elderly man who was about to retire, had the gun. He'd never registered it and now that he was selling the business, he didn't know what to do with it. Longdon said he gave the guy a hundred bucks for it, no questions asked.

"You have a carry permit?" Harry asked.

"Of course. It's all legal."

"Well, personally I think you're crazy for keeping it like this, bit it's your business."

Longdon said he had tried carrying it, but the damn thing was so big and heavy, the bulge it made under his jacket was too noticeable and he was bulgy enough. He said he couldn't remember the last time he'd touched it.

"OK, look, I gotta get going," Harry said, "be careful going home." And with that, he got into his own car and drove out of the parking lot.

When he stopped for a light he unwrapped a new Tony Bennett cassette he'd bought and slipped it into the tape deck. The car immediately filled with the smell of something burning. "Damn. What the hell?" he said.

At first he thought it was the tape, or maybe even the radio. Pulling over to the curb, he pushed the ejection button and brought the little plastic cartridge up to his nose. The smell was more on his hand, and there was an oily substance on his fingers as well as on the steering wheel. It was his right hand, the one he'd touched Longdon's gun with.

Right away, he knew what it was. It was a combination of cleaning solvent and oil, the same stuff he used each year to get his rifles ready for hunting season. And from the amount of it, Longdon had recently serviced the .45, maybe not more than a day ago.

"Why did he lie about the last time he'd touched it?" Harry asked himself.

For the rest of the trip home he kept asking himself, "Why the gun? Why lie about the last time he'd touched it? Did he lie about buying it from the old man? How can he afford to dress like that? Why all the questions about the warehouses, and what business are they of his any-way? How does he know Komti has research centers?"

Now that he thought about it, awhile back Longdon had asked him how Santronics got their merchandise from the piers and airports to their warehouses, and whether or not he knew any of the truckers.

He would get answers to all his questions very shortly, none of which he would like.

Part 4

Three quarters of the way through the tunnel he saw the pulsating reflections of the tow truck's lights as they bounced off the roofs of the cars in front of him. It had backed in from the Manhattan side.

"Son of a bitch," he growled, his patience now wearing thin. "If it's not one thing it's another."

As he watched the truck's operator hooking his chains onto the stalled vehicle which, of course, was in his lane, he started squeezing over to his right. "Son of a bitch," he repeated several more times. He'd wanted to talk to Ira before the meeting, only now that might not be possible.

Ira had been one of the first Americans hired by Santronics, and in those early days he was the entire sales department, credit department, and official interpreter for the Japanese. Not that they couldn't speak English, on the contrary, most of them spoke several languages fluently. But they were having difficulty understanding some of the ethnic colloquialisms and business practices of their fledgling New York dealer organization.

Back then Santronics' entire line consisted of just six items which Ira literally carried around to the small momma and poppa appliance stores in an old, black, cardboard suitcase left over from his Fuller Brush days. His god smiled upon him one evening when his sister came home and said she was getting married. It just so happened that her intended was the head buyer for Price Right Appliances, a chain of fifteen stores located in Queens and Brooklyn.

After nagging him nearly to death her fiancé agreed to give Ira a small order. Much to his surprise three days after being delivered to the main store, the merchandise was sold. He gave Ira a second order for several times that amount and again, the same thing happened. Realizing there was money to be made with "this Santronics stuff," he gave Ira a distribution order covering all fifteen stores. It totaled just over $78,000. Two weeks later the individual store managers were on the phones to him looking for more.

Once the other chains, and especially the department store buyers, got wind of the line's low price and high markup, everybody was off to the races, and to the banks with healthy deposits. While the merchandise was selling itself Ira was being rewarded. Almost over night, he became the fair-haired boy at Santronics. From being the company's only salesman, he became the sales manager in charge of ten other men. Then he became the sale/credit manager, and finally, he was promoted to director of credit for the entire Northeastern part of the U.S.

The only problem was he didn't know a thing about credit, and he certainly didn't know how to collect the company's receivables—he was too nice of a guy. Analyzing even the most basic of financial statements was a problem, and when it came to understanding any kind of legal document, he was lost. Overwhelmed by the volume of business Santronics was doing, Ira consistently failed to make monthly collection quotas and his bad debt write-offs mounted dramatically.

His immediate boss, a terrible little man named Max Kiedleman, who bore an amazing resemblance to Heinrich Himmler, had been looking to dump him for some time. Kiedleman couldn't stand him ever since he found our Ira still received an end-of-the-year bonus based on sales in the Northeastern region. Also, Kiedelman thought he was going behind his back and bad-mouthing him to the Japanese, which wasn't true. But now Ira was playing right into his sweaty little hands.

At the eleventh hour, knowing he was in trouble, Ira went directly to the real power in Komti, Mr. Yamatoki. While there were others in the Japanese corporate hierarchy who, by virtue of their titles should have been his superior, it was Yamatoki who unquestionably ran the show. Even the most senior of them snapped to his feet and bowed obediently whenever he entered a room.

It was Yamatoki who originally hired Ira. He told Yamatoki he was in the process of hiring an assistant, a credit and collection "specialist," a crackerjack systems man that knew the home electronics business like the back of his hand. A maven who was going to put everything right. The only problem was the person Ira was describing didn't exist. He'd concocted the story out of desperation that very morning at the breakfast table while lamenting his woes into his wife's apron.

Strictly out of a sense of obligation for Ira's past service to the company, and not wanting to lose face himself, seeing how he'd brought him in, Yamatoki gave him one month to get his act together. Now all Ira had to do was go out in the street and find his savior.

Ironically it would be Yamotoki who would eventually order Ira's execution.

Ira had met Harry on several occasions while attending electronics shows. Although characteristically at the opposite ends of the spectrum, they'd taken a liking to each other. After making some inquiries, the word came back that while Harry O'Day was no diplomat and that he was known to be a heavy drinker, he was also one of the best, young credit/collection men in the industry. College educated, street smart, and aggressive, he enjoyed the respect of his peers when it came to work.

That's how it all started, that's how Harry ended up having lunch in Komti's executive dining room, and how he got involved in murder.

Max Kiedelman was one of a number of people Ira introduced him to that day. Like Ira, Kiedelman had been with Santronics from the start and Harry took an immediate disliking to him. When they were introduced, Kiedelman pretended he didn't see his offer of a handshake. If that weren't insult enough, he suggested they might want to come back later in the day when he wouldn't be so busy.

Kiedelman's value to the company was that when it came to statistical analysis and cost accounting, he was a genius. He lived for numbers, and for charts and graphs. In addition, he was the company's premier yenta, stool pigeon, and bloodhound especially when it came to uncovering the theft of a pencil or some paperclips by an employee. It was his obsessive-compulsive nosiness that eventually caused him his final problem.

Harry saw a lot that day at Komti, but he didn't see the shadows. They had been there watching him, watching everybody. They were in every department at every Santronics' warehouse center in the country. Superimposed on the legitimate Japanese executives and workers, they were like an elite guard of SS. The only thing they feared was the madman who gave them their orders, a man who once willingly helped plunge half the world into Armageddon, and who was planning to do it again.

These shadows, these young, zombielike men in business suits were his soldiers, willing to die if necessary to carry out his insane scheme. No better than thugs and murderers, he'd charged them with the responsibility of seeing that others, innocent, unsuspecting men, put into place the machinery that would ensure the success of the next holocaust. Handpicked by a fanatic and indoctrinated to become fanatics, they had no god, no souls, and placed no value on human life.

They had an array of impressive titles yet their desks never had any papers on them. They attended every meeting, yet they never spoke, and contrary to custom they were openly disrespectful, even to the majority of the senior Japanese executives. The only thing they, and the rest of the Japanese steered clear of was the credit and collection departments; calling a dealer and saying, "send me a check you son of a bitch, or you don't get any merchandise," was too repugnant for them to be involved in.

Part 5

In their case opposites did attract, and from day one Harry and Ira liked working together.

Ira kept a Kosher home like his parents had when they were raising him in the Brighton Beach section of Brooklyn. To placate their incessant nudging, he'd studied to be a cantor for several years, but gave it up after they died. On rare occasions he would have a drink, but only one, and if someone told a dirty joke in his presence his face would turn a bright shade of red. On Fridays he left work early to attend prayers before going home to be with his family. If he had a fault it was the black suits and ties he wore that made him look more like an undertaker than a business executive.

In contrast, Harry came from a single-parent home in a tough Irish/Italian section of Queens, and had raised himself in the streets. Thinking it a waste, at 15 he stopped going to mass. Instead, on Sunday mornings he would take the black, leather case containing his custom-made cuestick and head for Barney's Billiard Academy. While not having an official police record, by the time he joined the Marines the neighborhood cops had caught him more than once borrowing parts off of parked cars. They knew where he lived and that his father died in a prisoner of war camp, so the worst they ever did was give him a good kick in the ass.

At one point he'd used his bicycle to work for a local policy bank after school and on the weekends.

Later, in the service, he liked to kid people about his old neighborhood, especially about the junior high school he'd gone to.

"The place was so tough," he'd say, "that when the girls went to sewing class, the guys when to Zip Gun 101, at least the ones who'd made bail the night before."

Besides his poolroom expertise, another early life accomplishment was his ability to consume enormous quantities of alcohol without getting too drunk, a feat considered by his street peers to be a badge of honor.

Ira's immediate benefit from hiring Harry was that it saved his job, and in the not too distant future, it would keep him from being assassinated. Right off, Harry made changes in the way new accounts were investigated, the way collections were handled, and the same with troublesome dealers. He made it a face-to-face thing between him and whoever was causing the problem. The results were immediate. Bad debt write-offs slowed, collection quotas were being made, fewer orders were being held, and the company was happy.

At first he didn't mind all the work, there was plenty of action—just the way he liked it. He was making three times his old salary, the company had given him an unlimited expense account, and he was driving a brand-new car. The twelve hour days didn't bother him, nor did the ten or twelve drinks he'd have each night on the way home. For all practical purposes he was the credit department as Santronics. In time he thought, Ira would learn something from him and start carrying some of the load, but it wasn't happening. He was teaching but the jerk wasn't learning, and he was getting annoyed.

Not that he was big on compassion, but he'd taken a liking to Ira and just going to him and saying, "You're worthless," would've been like kicking a sick puppy. Instead, he figured out a way to take his friend out of the loop and make things easier for himself.

While driving Ira home one night, which he did periodically when one of Ira's kids had borrowed his car, he mentioned his idea.

"Ira, it's been a long day, how about I buy you a drink? Besides, there's something I've been meaning to talk to you about."

"Oh, I don't think so Harry, my wife is expecting me. Maybe some other time. Thanks anyway."

"Come on, just one drink, it's important we talk. Look, how about I call your wife and tell her you're with me? She likes me, she doesn't like you, but me she likes."

"No, Harry, I can't, it's getting late."

"Ira, I don't know how to tell you this, but your wife called me today. She said to tell you that she doesn't want you anymore, so I either let you out at the next corner, or you come have a drink with me. How's that grab you?"

"Well, if you put it that way," Ira said with a smile, "I don't have much of a choice, do I? But just one, and I have to call."

They drove to a small restaurant in Sheepshead Bay opposite the fishing docks and parked along side the building. The owner, a man accustomed to having his name in the papers, had to show the Internal Revenue Service at least on legitimate source of income and this was it.

While Ira called, Harry paid the mandatory respects to his friend. Over the years they'd gotten to know each other through mutual acquaintances, and from time to time he'd done certain favors for the guy, no questions asked.

Ira finished his call and they took a table in the small alcove at the end of the bar. For the comfort and safety of some of his more notorious customers, the owner had painted over the four, narrow windows in the rear dining room and put iron bars on the outsides of them. Too bad because Harry couldn't see the beige, four-door sedan that had double-parked next to his car on the now dark side street. Nor could he see one of its occupants using a jimmy-bar to open the driver's side door.

Harry's idea was to create a Key Account List, and put Ira in charge of it. All of the other accounts, he'd handle himself. He would also take over the setting up of all new accounts. He told Ira that the Key Account List would be made up of the department stores, major chains, and all of Santronics' distributors, "All of the important accounts." It was only natural given Ira's vast experience, he should be the one to handle it.

His ego soaring, Ira thought it a marvelous idea and that they should do it immediately.

"You're right, Harry," he said, "it would be best if I handle it."

From a credit standpoint there wasn't a problem account on the list. They were like money in the bank. When the customer received invoices their computers simply matched them to warehouse receiving records and forty-five days later, printed a check. The big problem was claims for returned or damaged merchandise.

Sometimes Harry would spend an entire day sequestered in the bowels of one of these places with a clerk pouring over reams of paperwork trying to straighten things out. Now Ira would have all the fun. Now he could stand by the Xerox for two hours taking care of the "If you send me a copy of the invoice," requests.

"You know, Ira, it wouldn't hurt for you to start getting out more, maybe get to know these accounting people who run the computers. Maybe even start taking them out to lunch. You could do it on the day a check was being cut. Just think how good you'd look coming back to the office with all that dough."

Ira was sold. Without realizing it, Harry had made him his bagman. Not only that, he'd moved him out of the way, someplace where Ira could feel important while taking care of unimportant things. Someplace where he couldn't get himself into trouble, or so he thought.

"Well, I gotta get going," Harry said. "I promised somebody I'd do them a favor and he's not too far from here. How about I drop you off?"

"Good, I should be going. My wife likes to worry."

They finished their drinks and walked around the corner. The weather had turned nasty and a light rain was beginning to cover things with a thin coat of ice.

When he bent to put the key in the lock, the door was ajar, and Harry could see the light in the open glove compartment.

"Son of a bitch, they broke in," he yelled.

"What! How can you tell?" Ira shouted excitedly, startled by Harry's outburst.

"How? Because this fuckin' door is open, that's how. And look, the glove compartment is open. Son of a bitch, doesn't that beat all? A brand new car and already the pricks break into it. Well, that's the end of this crap. The guy told me when I bought it to put an alarm on it, but no, I didn't listen. I'll be a little late in the morning, maybe they can do it while I wait."

"I'm sorry, Harry."

"Hey, listen, it's not your fault. I'm just surprised they had the balls to boost a car in this neighborhood. You get caught touching the wrong guy's stuff down here and you could end up over there with the fish."

The stereo radio was still in the dash, and his expensive London Fog raincoat was on the backseat where he'd left it. "What the hell were they after?" Harry asked. "Well, like I said, first thing in the morning it goes to the dealer."

As calm as he was going to get without having a few doubles, he asked, "Ira, is it 65th Street, or 65th Avenue you live on? I can never remember."

"65th Street, right up from the boat channel."

"Tell me, what happens if your Jew neighbors see you getting out of a goy's car?"

"What happens? Well they come to my house on Sunday morning and take me up to the shopping center. You know what a *Brith Milah* is? That means they do another circumcision on me, but this time they don't leave anything."

They laughed. Harry couldn't believe it, Ira had actually said something funny.

After dropping him off, he went back down to the Shore Parkway. It was the quickest way to his friend's newsstand on Kings Highway. Joe Joe, a/k/a Joseph Cosmo Bonaveddia, and his family had been neighbors in Queens until he got the stand in Brooklyn, and had given him his first after-school job delivering envelopes to people on his bike.

"You're gettin' paid to deliver them kid, not to be stickin' your nose in 'em. *Ci siamo capiti?* We understand each other?" Joe Joe would say in such a way that made him afraid one might get opened accidently and he'd be murdered. But that didn't happen, and he kept making good money up until the sad day Joe Joe moved his business to Brooklyn, Harry made more money in one afternoon delivering the little, white envelopes than he made in a week doing two paper routes. Once, a man he'd brought one to opened it in front of him, and it was stuffed with hundred dollar bills.

What a character, he thought as he drove. Here's a guy selling candy bars and papers yet he buys a new Caddy every other month. Not only that, he owns an eighteen-room house in Mt. Kisco, a twelve-room home around the corner from the stand, a place in Coral Gables, and a duplex in the east 80s; the latter was reserved for his extracurricular activities. He also owned a 38-foot sport fisherman named the IBETCHA that he kept docked next to Guy Lombardo's mahogany speed-boat in Freeport, Long Island.

Joe Joe could well afford his lavish life style seeing how, among other things, he was the largest policy bank in New Your City, probably in the entire state—and he did it from a newsstand. The fact that he was a first cousin to one Alfonsa Ponzinno helped him financially as well—Harry was sure of that.

At times he would have a half dozen people jammed behind the counter with him answering a battery of phones which never stopped ringing.

Joe Joe may have looked and sounded like he'd taken one to may left hooks, but he had the mind of an NYU math professor.

Today was his son's eighteenth birthday, and he'd asked Harry to pick something up for him to give to his son. It was a new item in the Santronics' line—an AM/FM stereo tape deck that could be slipped in and out of a bracket mounted under a car's dash. The kid had seen it someplace.

The sanders hadn't bothered to come out yet and the roads were getting bad, so he was glad there wasn't much traffic. If he was going to slide around, he thought, better he should do it by himself.

When he got to Coney Island Avenue, he noticed the headlights of the car in his rearview mirror getting off behind him. At Kings Highway it turned left when he did. Now he realized the driver of the vehicle was pacing him, speeding and slowing when he did. Normal New Yorkers didn't drive like that. They either raced by you, or sat six inches off your bumper.

Not that he was paranoid, but he was sure he was being followed. There was a traffic light two blocks ahead. If he ran the light and the guy behind him did too, he'd know if he had a problem.

When he got to within thirty feet of the intersection the light went from green, to amber, to red. He'd been warned by the dealer when he bought the car about jackrabbit starts on wet pavement, "You have a lot of horses under there so be careful," the salesman had said. Before the gas pedal was halfway to the floor, the car was screeching and fishtailing through the light. Fighting to regain control, he looked in the rearview mirror and as the clouds of mist and smoke began to clear, he saw the other car right behind him.

"Son of a bitch, who the hell is this guy?" he asked himself as he slammed on the brakes to avoid crashing into the car ahead of him. Hoping it was just some smart-ass drunk, or maybe a couple of punks out joyriding, he tried to think of what to do next. The newsstand, there were always plenty of people around, coming down off the train station and going into the late night deli.

Parking in a no loading zone directly in front of the stand, he watched in the rearview mirror as his stalker pulled into the curb seven or eight stores behind him on the same side of the street. Its driver turned off the lights but left the engine running evidenced by the plumes of exhaust vapor billowing into the damp, night air. There was enough light coming from the pizza parlor opposite from where it had stopped to afford him a good look. It was a four-door sedan, beige, or maybe light brown in color with black-wall tires, much like the car Peter Longdon, his so-called drinking buddy had shown him in the parking lot behind the Bavarian House.

He'd read someplace that taking deep breaths helped calm the nerves, but it wasn't doing a thing for him. He was shaking like he had a bad hangover. Not only was he being followed, but he'd come close to killing himself drag racing through the light. For the time being, he was safe. This was Joe Joe's place of business, his neighborhood. If anyone was going to get jammed up it would be whoever was following him.

Trying to act nonchalant, he got out and walked back to the trunk for the tape deck, glancing over his shoulder as he bent. A hand flipped a lighted cigarette out the passenger side window of the sedan, so there were probably at least two of them, he thought. Closing the trunk, he took the carton and slowly walked to the stand.

"Hey, Harry, *come stai?*" his friend asked in a deep gravelly voice. Joe Joe was the original Mr. Five-by-Five and barely fit behind the counter. His head was the size of a basketball and still covered by a thick rug of healthy, jet-black hair. Even in subfreezing temperatures, he worked in his shirtsleeves. Harry liked to call his appearance "unique" except for the unlit, foot-long, black cigar he constantly chewed on, and the trace of dark dribble always present in one corner of his mouth—a sight Harry called disgusting.

"Good, Joe, good, I'm fine," he replied. "Thanks. And you? How's the family?"

"They're good. They're all over at the house, we gotta little party tonight."

"Here, I hope it fits," Harry said, handing the carton to his friend. "All the hardware is supposed to be in there, but if he's missing anything let me know and I'll get it for him. How is Sally anyway? I haven't seen him in awhile. He's 18 now, right?"

"Forget about it," Joe Joe replied, spitting a big garb of black, slimy cigar juice out onto the sidewalk. "Yeah, he's 18, but he don't got no smarts. Harry, the kid is bad! I don't know what I'm gonna do with'm. I got'm the Lincoln for his birthday and already he's out bangin' every broad in the neighborhood. He's gonna make me a grandfather again if he doesn't knock it off. Or get shot. One or the other. You know, Harry, he likes you. Maybe you could talk to him, kinda tell'm to straighten out."

"I really wouldn't know what to say to him."

"Sure you would, Harry, you're a college guy. Stuff like, be good, maybe go back to school, that kind of stuff—you know how to talk good."

"Well," he said reluctantly, "I guess I could try."

"Thanks, Harry, thanks a lot. Like I say, he likes you. He won't listen to me, but he'll listen to you. By the way, what's the tab for this?"

"It's taken care of, just wish him a happy birthday for me. Tell him if he wants, he can call me at the office and I'll take him to lunch—maybe over in the city."

"Hey! He'd like that, goin' to a nice place to eat an' all. You know, Harry, a lot of people like you. You know why? Cause you know how to do the right thing. You know how important that is? You got respect for people too. Remember when you were a kid, even then you knew how to show respect. Too bad you ain't Italian, you could marry my sister and get her out of my house."

"There is one thing you could do for me," Harry said, stepping in under the overhang, closer to his friend.

"Yeah, sure, whatever, you got it."

"Don't look right at it, but do you see the brown sedan across from the pizza parlor?"

"What about it?"

"It's been tailing me."

"What makes you say that?"

Harry explained he'd first noticed it when he got off the Parkway at Coney Island Avenue, but it was possible it had followed him all the way up from Carmine Tebello's place in Sheepshead Bay. He also told Joe Joe about his car being broken into and about the business at the traffic light.

"You got problems with any of those guys down there?"

"No, not that I'm aware of. Carmine was there. He spoke to me. If any of his people were lookin' at me, he would've said somethin', no?"

"Yeah, you're right. If you had a problem with him, you'd know, that's for sure."

Joe Joe picked up one of the wall phones and dialed. As he waited, he reached under the counter, brought up a .25 caliber handgun, chambered a round, and rolled it up in a copy of the *Daily Racing Form*.

"Yeah, Tommy, it's me. No, no problem," he told his brother who owned the pizza place. "What time you comin' by the house? Eleven? Good. Just make sure you bring the pastries I put downstairs in the walk-in.

"Listen, Tommy, you see that brown car out your window? No!? Wipe the flour off your glasses and look again. Yeah, now you got it, the one with the engine runnin'. You ever see it before? They in by you getting' a pie or somethin'? It's nobody we know, right? That's what I figured.

"Harry's here. He says it tailed him from maybe Tebello's place. Anybody around down there?

"Nicky's there? Anybody with'm?

"Good. Tell Nicky I want he should take some people across the street and see who's in the car.

"You put those things downstairs I gave you?

"OK. Tell Nicky to get 'em, but listen, Tommy, make sure you get 'em all back—the silencers too.

"No, not out front, there's too many people around. Make Nicky bring 'em down here to the alley, I wanna talk to 'em.

"Tommy, make sure he searches 'em—the car too. I don't want any fuckin' surprises.

"Sally? Forget about it. Who know where he is. Since he's got the car, his mother and I never see'm.

"Yeah, he's supposed to bring her over the house later for coffee.

"She's Phil Medicci's kid. Adie says she's a nice girl. She sees her sometimes at confession.

"Which one? Brooklyn, or New York?

"737.

"Well, whatta you expect? I told you to box it, buy no, you gottta play it straight cause you're greedy and now you got screwed. Next time you'll listen to what I tell you."

Harry stood in the freezing rain listening. Uncomfortable as he was with being followed, he was getting even more uncomfortable with the way things were developing. Someone was going to get seriously hurt, maybe even killed, and for what? Now he wished he hadn't said anything.

Hearing a door close hard and several men laughing, he turned to look. Five men had come out of the pizza parlor and were crossing the street toward the brown car. Its driver, realizing he had a problem, screeched the tires on the icy blacktop sending up clouds of smoke and water. As it roared away from the curb, it caught the rear fender of the car parked ahead of it, sending a huge jagged piece of metal gyrating into the roadway. Nicky threw himself onto the hood of a parked car to avoid getting hit by it and two of his men had their faces showered with debris from the spinning wheels, but weren't seriously hurt.

With smoke pouring from a rubbing tire, the sedan raced past the newsstand and when it reached the intersection, its driver almost rolled it as he turned into a one-way street and disappeared into the night.

Frozen in place, eyes bulging, Harry could only watch. And then he was aware of a god-awful, stabbing pain in his right ear. It was like someone had driven a pointy stick into it. The smoking barrel of Joe Joe's gun was just inches away from his head. He'd emptied it at the fleeing auto.

"I hate these fuckin' little things," Joe Joe complained, turning it from side to side, examining it like he would a piece of fruit in the supermarket. "I gotta keep somethin' bigger here."

Expecting to find blood, Harry put his hand to his ear, but there wasn't any. So while he couldn't hear anything except a head-splitting buzz, at least he thought, the eardrum wasn't busted.

Once, when he was a kid, he'd stumbled into a thing up on the avenue by his house. A bunch of cops were trading shots with two guys who'd just held up the liquor store. The guns were so loud he got scared and ran home. But tonight, Jesus Christ, this is a nightmare, he thought. I got bullets inches away from my head. And what if the bastards had shot back? I'd probably be dead now.

Joe Joe wiggled his bulky, fireplug of a body back behind the counter.

"Yeah, Tommy, it's me. You see that shit? Sonnsa bitches. No, I don't want anybody goin' after 'em. It's bad drivin' with the ice. Everybody OK? Good. Have the cleanin' kid get that metal out of the street and sweep up the glass before somebody gets a flat.

"OK, I'll tell'm.

"Have Nicky take those things over to the meat store before the cops come, and put 'em in the chop meat. But make sure he puts paper around 'em, the last time he didn't and they got all fucked up. It took me a whole day to clean 'em. You know, he's a nice guy and all, but sometimes he's a real jerk—you know what I mean?

"OK, good. Come by the house when you close, and remember the pastries. That stuff cost me sixty bucks.

"I tell you what. Maybe you should bring a couple of pies. Put anchovies on one, you know, the way I like it."

Hanging up, Joe Joe wrote something down on the corner of the Racing Form, ripped it off and handed it to him.

"Here, one of them got a plate number. You got somebody that can run it? Harry? Are you listenin'? You OK?"

"Yeah, I guess so," he replied, rubbing his ear, still expecting to find blood. "What did you ask me? Oh, yeah, the plate number. Yeah, I think I know somebody."

"Harry, you ain't lookin' so good. How about comin' over the house for awhile? Maybe when Sally comes with his girlfriend you could talk to'm."

"I don't think so. You're right, I'm not feelin' so hot, I better go." The roaring chatter of a train pulling into the overhead station and his bad ear couldn't drown out the unmistakable sound of approaching sirens. "What about the cops?" he asked, wincing with pain and at the same time trying to deal with the knots strangling his chest and stomach.

Joe Joe laughed. "Don't worry, I'll take care of it. A couple of punks tried to hold me up, that's all. No big deal. I got a permit. Maybe you want I should send some people by your house?"

"No, I'll be all right—I think."

As if nothing had happened, his friend sat down, turned on a radio, and opened a newspaper. "Thanks for the kid's present, he'll get a kick out of it. If you have any problems tonight, call me at the house. You got the number, right?"

Three squad cars with lights flashing and earsplitting sirens wailing, raced by him just as he made the turn at the intersection. In his rearview mirror he could see two others already stopped in front of the stand.

*   *   *

Peering inquisitively over the tops of his glasses, the elderly liquor store owner rang up the sale, slipped the pint of whiskey into a paper bag and watched as Harry fumbled in his wallet. Shaking like he had the DTs, he could barely hand the man his money.

"Are you all right mister? Would you like me to call you a cab?"

"No, I'm OK. I got the flu." Harry replied as the owner buzzed him out, and then watched him walk down the block.

Breaking his own cardinal rule about drinking in the car, he gulped down half the pint before putting the key in the ignition. Eyes shut, teeth clenched so tightly he thought they'd break, the pain of swallowing so much booze all at once was excruciating. He sat motionless for several moments with a vicelike grip on the wheel until the pain began to subside, and he felt the comforting warmth of the alcohol sinking into his body.

The trip back to Queens took more than an hour. Each time headlights flashed in his rearview mirror he'd make a turn, or drive into an open gas station, or into a diner's parking lot, or anyplace where there were lights and people. Afraid someone might be waiting for him, he parked five blocks away from his apartment building and used the unlocked service entrance in the alley. It wasn't until he had locked his apartment door and turned on every light that the heart attack he swore he was having, ebbed.

"You're an embarrassment, you know that, right?" he said out loud. "You're acting like some scuzzy street punk."

But he couldn't help it. He was scared. More scared than when he was 13 and the cops caught him baby-sitting a pair of switchblades for some friends. With his mother's permission, they'd thrown him into the local precinct's holding tank for some overnight shock therapy and he'd come close to getting raped.

"Dead soldier," he said, standing in the living room sucking the last of the whiskey he'd bought, and trying to make sense of things. Had the men who followed him mistaken his car for someone elses? Were they the same people who broke into his car? Maybe Joe Joe scared them good and they wouldn't be back. On the other hand, he thought, maybe they were really pissed off now and they'd be back with a vengeance. God, what a mess.

One thing was for certain. Given the events of the evening he would-n't be going out of the house anymore empty-handed. After changing into dry clothing, he muscled the chest of drawers out of the corner by the bedroom windows and climbed up on a chair. The ceiling was com-posed of foot square acoustical panels; standing on tiptoes, he pushed the corner one up.

His imagined heart attack started again when he couldn't find what he was looking for. "Damn. Where is it?" he groaned. Four, expensive, leather-bound encyclopedias from the bookcase extended his reach far enough for his fingers to touch it.

Inside the shoe box, wrapped in an old T-shirt, was a .25 caliber Beretta, less any serial number it had when it left the factory, three empty clips, and three full boxes of shells. Taking everything, along with an unopened quart of whiskey from a kitchen cabinet, he sat down on the edge of the bed. Not that watching TV interested him, but he turned it on anyway. Its noise broke the lonely silence of his nights.

Alternately pushing shells into the clips, and taking hefty swigs from the bottle, he wracked his brain trying to remember if he'd done or said anything to get somebody mad at him, but he couldn't. Even the worst of the people he knew, including actual killers, he got along with. A cou-ple of times they'd even invited him to their kids' birthday parties.

Slipping a loaded clip into the gun and chambering a round, he asked himself, "How in God's name did I get myself into this?"

Gradually the booze began doing its job. Kicking off his shoes, he turned the covers down and leaned back against the pillows. Three more gulps and now he started twirling the loaded gun around cowboy-style on one finger and taking make-believe shots at figures on the TV, complete with sound effects. With the bottle almost half empty, he passed out, his finger still curled around the trigger.

Thrashing from side-to-side, tormented by dreams, his breathing became shallow and he'd utter muffled cries as if he were fighting with someone. Finally, the violent jerking and flailing reached a crescendo, sending what was left of the whiskey, the gun, and the remaining bullets flying across the bedroom floor.

He would suffer more nights like this. A pathetic sight, in a drunken stupor, oblivious to the depths of the cesspool he was being sucked into, he had no way of knowing that people he'd been in contact with that same night, were being murdered.

The late news was starting on channel 3.

"WCKW News time is 11:30 and I'm Ken Terry.

"Our top story, of course, is the resignation earlier this evening of Vice President Stanley Jeffers and the shock waves it's sending through the already soiled halls of government.

"In a tersely worded letter he informed the president that in all good conscience, and with the well-being of the American people in mind, he could no longer support him.

"When pressed by reporters why copies of the letter were simultane-ously hand delivered to all the major TV networks, radio stations, and newspapers, a spokesman for the vice president's office refused to com-ment. This political bombshell comes after months of rumors that there has been a growing rift between the two men.

"A reporter for Reuters International wire service asked the spokesman if there was any truth to the story that the vice president, along with his family, had left Washington because they feared for their safety. The spokesman, before abruptly ending the interview, would only say that the present whereabouts of the vice president and his family was not known.

"Reliable sources inside the White House, speaking on the promise of anonymity, told WCKW News that shortly after receiving the letter at Camp David, the president ordered Secret Service agents to seal the vice president's office and reassign his staff to other duties. At a hastily called news conference, Tony Shelvy, White House press secretary, was asked by our Adriana Browning if it was true that several of the vice president's staff had been detained and questioned by the Secret Service. He admitted there were a few who volunteered to answer questions as to their opinion of what the vice president's problems were. Shelvy also confirmed that Secret Service agents had, in fact, sealed the vice president's office, but only to secure any classified materials it might contain. In addition, he said, several agents had gone to the vice president's home when they learned it was empty.

"Asked about rumors that the vice president and his family had fled the Capital out of fear for their safety, Shelvy said they were ludicrous and had been spread by political enemies of the president. He said the president was already preparing to address the nation and in the meantime, the American people had nothing to worry about.

"In a statement to the press, Speaker of the House, Senator Dan Fells said he had grave concerns about the circumstances surrounding the vice president's resignation and disappearance. He said he was saddened to see a man of his stature and high moral character succumb to the forces of evil. The speaker concluded by saying that the nation would have been better served had the president resigned.

"Earlier in the day, the speaker had again called upon the attorney general to regain her self-respect and appoint a special councel to investigate what he said was the abrogation by the president of his responsibilities, and continued obstruction of legislation that would halt the illegal dumping of certain foreign products into American markets.

"WCKW News reporter Adriana Browing is at the White House and will bring us any late breaking developments in the story."

Part 6

Harry's problem was far more serious than he could've imagined. The men in the beige sedan hadn't mistaken him for someone else. In fact, they had been following him for more than a week. Tonight, desperate for information, they'd gotten too close—that was their first mistake. Their second was not realizing they were on Joe Joe's turf.

They'd gotten sloppy because they were being pressed by their boss, a man charged with heading off the debacle looming before the entire country. The man knew Harry wasn't part of it, but he was running out of time. It was Harry's company he wanted to know about, and about the shadows controlling it—especially about the maniac giving them their orders. That's why Harry was getting jammed-up. There were people who thought he could lead them to the information they wanted. Unknowingly, he had become a pawn in a murderous, multi-sided game of chess.

*   *   *

For the next several days he continued parking in different locations away from his apartment building. If he was going or coming from the office he'd pick a different route each time, and would only enter and leave his building through the service door in the alley. A couple of times he even climbed the chain-link fence at the end of the alley and went out to the adjoining street.

When he needed groceries or gas, he'd go to another neighborhood, but when it came to liquor, the store around the corner was more than happy to deliver since he was one of its best customers.

Keys, wallet, watch, extra clip, gun, that was his checklist each morning. While driving, he kept it on the front seat under a newspaper. At work he put it in the bottom desk drawer, and when he showered, it was within arm's reach on top of the toilet tank.

It wasn't long before the newsstand episode started taking a physical toll on him. Drinking excessively even by his standards, and living on pizza and hamburgers, he started losing weight. At work in the morning, his secretary, Connie, would call over to the restaurant and have them deliver two containers of his special tea. That was the code name for Manhattans. People in the office started noticing the changes in him.

One morning as he walked down the hallway suffering from a particularly nasty hangover, Ira called to him.

"Harry, got a minute? Come in, *wie geht's?* I gotta tell you, you're not looking so hot."

"I know," he sighed slumping into the chair in front of Ira's desk. "I haven't been sleeping well. I think I have the flu or something."

"Have you seen a doctor? If you need a couple of days off just say the word. We can arrange a business trip for you, someplace nice and sunny."

"Thanks Ira, it's tempting, but I'll be OK. Maybe I'll leave a little early today and go and get a shot." Dragging himself out of the chair, jokingly he said maybe what they both needed was to go out together again for a drink.

"Oh, no, my wife wouldn't appreciate it, she got very upset when we did."

"Why? You had one drink and you got home a little later than usual."

"No, it wasn't that. Something happened at the house that really scared her."

Freezing in the doorway, Harry could feel the nerves in the back of his neck tense. Somehow he know what Ira was about to tell him had something to do with him being followed.

"What happened?" he asked.

Ira explained a couple of times during the evening his wife thought she heard a car pull up outside the house, and thinking it was him, went to the front windows. After awhile she noticed a beige sedan parked across the street with its engine running. Whenever she went to the window, it would still be there.

A neighbor called her and said a man had gotten out of it and went into their driveway. Earlier in the evening, Ira continued, his daughter had come home with his car and parked in the driveway in back of her brother. While the neighbor couldn't swear to it, she was pretty sure the stranger had looked in both vehicles and copied down their plate numbers.

"Go on, then what?" Harry asked trying not to show how upset he was.

Ira said that in his temple the congregation had formed a citizen's patrol. Anyone who thought they had a problem at their house could call the rabbi, or that night's designated patrol officer, and then the police. In turn, the rabbi, or the patrol officer would start calling the person's neighbors. It wouldn't take long before a lot of people on the block turned their outside lights on and came out to see what was going on.

"So what happened to the car?"

"Well when the neighbors came out, it left."

"Did you ever see it again?"

"No, and good riddance."

Harry told Ira he was glad everything turned out all right and left.

"Son of a bitch," he said to himself, sitting down at his desk. "Son of a bitch, this thing just keeps getting worse. That means there were two cars involved and God knows how many of the bastards. What the hell do they want?"

Concentrating on work was impossible, and as he sat there his fear gradually changed to resentment.

"Who the hell do these bastards think they are coming around like this? Who needs this crap?" He was more upset and embarrassed with himself now than anything else, and over the way he'd been sneaking around like some cheap, nickel-and-dime thief, afraid to leave his apartment at night.

Chiding himself he said, "O'Day, I think you better start lookin' around for your balls."

Going home that night, he thought about all the chances he had as a kid to get seriously hooked up with people like Joe Joe and with others of his ilk, to be connected, to belong to a crew; they did whatever they wanted. However, given his arrogance, he'd always secretly considered himself above them. Now he wished he was one of them. They would never stand for this kind of garbage, he thought. If some jerk was stupid enough to fool with even one of them, he'd find himself upstate sleeping under a blanket of lime, or taking a beating so bad he wouldn't walk or talk for a month.

Ignoring the fire zone sign, he parked directly in front of his apartment house, and with the safety off, held the gun down to one side as he swaggered to the main entrance. "If you got a problem with me, I got just the solution," he said in a loud, defiant voice, hoping that someone would appear and challenge him. For the first time in awhile he felt good about himself.

Upstairs, he went directly to his mother's Bible on the desk and took out the piece of Daily Racing Form Joe Joe had written the plate number on. He'd been invited to a surprise promotion party for a detective friend down in Rockaway, and if anybody could find out who the plate belonged to, Mike O'Banion Jr. could.

For some time he'd been thinking about asking Diedra out, and now that his divorce was final, there wasn't any reason not to. Mike's party would provide the perfect environment for a first date. Between the people, the drinking, and the dancing, the awkwardness of having to go one-on-one with each other would be minimal.

Along with a little self-respect, some of his appetite had returned, so he threw a mishmash of rather questionable looking coldcuts between two equally questionable looking pieces of bread, grabbed a six-pack and when in to watch TV.

Diedra got off from work at eleven so he waited until just after midnight to call. The phone rang for awhile and he was about to hang up when he heard her voice.

"Hello?"

"Diedra, it's Harry. Are you OK? You sound out of breath."

"Well, hello, stranger. The question is, are you OK? I was going to call you tonight. You haven't been around lately and I was starting to think maybe something happened to you. Your friend Peter was in a couple of times asking if I'd seen you."

"I had the flu so I've been coming straight home at night, but I'm feeling better. Are you sure you're all right?"

"Yes, fine. I had the shower running and when I turned it off I heard the phone. I ran because I thought it might be you. Harry, could I call you right back? I'm standing here naked dripping water on my new rug. Just let me dry off and put something on—it's cold!"

"OK, meanwhile I'll pour us a couple of drinks."

"Good. Make mine a double," she said laughingly.

He couldn't remember if he'd ever heard her laugh before. It was nice, it had a warm sound to it.

Tired of the beer, he got a bottle of whiskey and a water glass from the kitchen and went back to the phone to wait. Diedra had said the word "naked" and it kept repeating itself in his mind. He tried to envision her prancing around her bedroom rubbing her body with a big, fluffy bath towel. He wondered if she ever combed her long, ponytail standing naked in front of a full-length mirror. The phone rank just as he started thinking about stroking something of his own.

They talked for an hour, mainly about money. In addition to her husband's job insurance, and the collection taken by the PBA, it turned out her dead prick of a husband had two life insurance policies, both naming her as the beneficiary. It was the only decent thing the guy had ever done for her. All together, she had received about a million dollars, along with the house and his yellow corvette.

"Harry, I don't know what I'd do without you. It's so much money, it scares me."

"There's no reason to be scared. Just remember what I told you, under no circumstance are you to sign anything unless you have it looked at. You have an excellent lawyer and accountant now, so listen to them. And don't ever say anything to that drunken father-in-law of yours about those two policies, or else he'll be falling all over you trying to get his grubby paws on some of the dough. The bulk of you money is in T-bills and tax-exempt bonds, all in your name, so nobody besides you can touch a dime of it.

"Now, Miss Moneybags, let's change the subject. What are you doing Friday night?"

"I don't know. Why? What's Friday night? I know I'm not working because the new schedule came out and I'm off the next two weekends."

He told her about his friend being promoted to detective second grade and about the surprise party the guy's father was throwing at the family bar down in Rockaway.

"Why Mr. O'Day! Are you asking me for a date?"

"You have a problem with that?"

"No, not at all. On the contrary, I think it's wonderful. But what will the neighbors say? Me being the grieving widow and you a married man?" she asked coyly.

"Not anymore. Not according to the papers her lawyer sent me."

"Harry, I really am sorry it didn't work out for you. You're a nice guy. How are you doing? It must be rough."

"Not really. It was a mistake right from the start. Besides, lately I have more important things to deal with, like you."

"If there's anything I can do for you, anything at all, please, let me help," she said softly.

"Thanks, I appreciate that because I know you're sincere. But you've already done something for me."

"How's that?"

"You've agreed to go out with me."

"Oh but I haven't, not yet anyway," she said teasingly.

"Will you go if I tell you everyone there is going to be Irish?"

"That's different. Why didn't you say that in the first place? Oh my god, I don't have a thing to wear."

"Calm down, calm down, this isn't the Waldorf we're going to, it's a bar in Rockaway. Slacks and a sweater, that's what the rest of the women will be wearing. Anyway, once they get a look at your Irish face and red hair, they won't notice what you're wearing."

"Harry, are there going to be a lot of cops there?"

"A lot? Yes. Almost all the men will be cops. Why? Will that bother you?"

"I don't know."

"Look, if you're worried about people asking questions, don't be. There's more Shannahans in New York City than you can shake a stick at. As long as you don't say anything about your husband getting killed on the job, you won't have a problem. The only thing they'll know is that you're my date."

"If you only knew how good that sounds. It makes me feel like I'm 16 again—I wish."

"How what sounds?"

"That I'm your date. It's like we're back in high school."

"I'll pick you up a 8, OK?"

"Fine, I'm looking forward to it."

Bursting with excitement, she whirled through the house pulling clothes out of closets, scattering shoe boxes around, and posturing in front of the bedroom mirror wondering if she should wear he hair up or down. How wonderful, she thought, here's a rugged, good-looking guy who's always treated me with respect and now he's asked me out. It would be her first social contact with a man since the death of her husband. Who knows, she thought, a party, a drink, maybe a dance or two, and he might ask me out again—it could be the start of something. She was right, it would be the start of something. By going out on what seemed to be an innocent date, she would become part of Harry's world, a world that at times, would border on the insane.

Part 7

The homes on both sides of the street looked exactly the same, like they'd been stamped from the same mold and placed side-by-side, except Diedra's house seemed different. The lights shining through fluffy, white, living room curtains gave the neat, frame structure a warm, cozy appearance. The winter darkness couldn't hide the fact that when the weather was nice, she paid meticulous attention to the shrubs and flower beds surrounding it.

Careful not to go off the concrete and mess anything up, he pulled into the driveway and parked. As he got out he felt the weight of the gun drag on his jacket pocket. "Not such a good idea taking this into a room full of cops," he said to himself slipping it under the driver's seat.

On Wednesday he'd called the florist and made the man swear that he would have two dozen roses ready for him to bring to Diedra. Like the bouquet was made of fragile glass, he lifted it off the passenger seat and walked around to the front door. Fussing with his hair and clothes like he was a gawky 15-year old on his first date, he held the flowers behind his back and rang the bell.

She was wearing slacks with a reddish, brown, tartan design, and a soft-looking, kelly-green cardigan with pearl buttons down the front. The little white lace collar made her appear younger than she was, like maybe she was on her way down to the ice cream parlor, or something.

He took special notice of her perfectly matched, expensive, waist length leather jacket and high-heeled boots. Combined with her long ponytail, the heels gave her body a statuesque, sensual appearance.

Her clothes weren't tight fitting—they didn't have to be. A person would have to be blind not to notice how beautifully shaped her body was. That had been one of her many problems when her drunk of a husband was alive. If he thought another man was looking at her, she caught the beating, not the guy. He didn't have the balls for anything else.

Besides its gorgeous shape, it was the way Diedra's body moved when she moved. It had a slow, gliding motion, free of any noticeable gait, and her beauty was natural, wholesome looking. But at the same time there was a mystique about her, a combination of innocence and allurement.

"Diedra Agnes Shannahan," he said in his best Irish brogue, "'tis a vision of loveliness that I'm seeing to be sure."

"Oh be off with you now, Harry O'Day, you and your blarney," she said laughingly, going along with the charade. "It's all the girls you'd be telling that to."

"Here, seeing how it's our first date and all," he said sheepishly bringing the roses out from behind his back. For a moment she just stood there, looking at them, not saying anything. He could see small tears forming in the corners of her eyes and a slight redness come into her face.

"Now, now, we'll have none of that, Diedra Agnes," he said taking a clean handkerchief out of his pocket and pressing it into her hand.

"Oh, Harry, they're so beautiful, thank you. It's been a long, long time since anyone brought me flowers. I can't stop crying." Disappearing for a moment, she came back with a large, green vase. Carefully, almost professionally, she arranged the ferns and roses, picked-up the few fallen petals, and stepped back to admire the results. Turning, she placed her hand on the back of his neck and slowly kissed him full on the lips. She kissed him again, but this time with her mouth open much wider—he could feel her tongue.

"God, you smell good," he murmured slipping his arms under her jacket and pulling her body tightly against his. He kissed her back several more times the same way.

Finally, they let go of each other. Taking her hands in his, he kissed her palms. "I think we should get going," he said reluctantly.

*   *   *

They were halfway down to Rockaway before there was anything much in the was of conversation between them. Both had been aware for some time that there was a chemistry between them, but given their individual circumstances, they had avoided any open display of emotion toward each other. It all changed with the roses. Their touching and kissing had rocketed the relationship into another dimension, and neither of them was comfortable with it yet.

"Now let me tell you about Michael Patrick O'Banion Jr.," he said in an effort to lighten things up.

"And just who is Michael Patrick O'Banion Jr.?" she asked turning off the radio and placing her hand on his shoulder.

"That's whose party we're going to."

He told her that he and Michael first met when they were 10. It was the beginning of a new school term and all the kids were racing around the yard trying to find the right class line. For whatever the reason the two of them got into a fight. Father Joseph, the gym teacher, finally broke it up, but not before they'd beaten the tar out of each other.

The following morning they got into it again, this time in the principal's office in front of their parents. Mike's father suggested that he "Take the lads into the next room and have a wee talk with them," which he did, only he didn't talk much. Instead, he took off his two-inch wide leather belt and beat them from one end of the room to the other, and then beat them some more for good luck. Harry told Diedra that his mother and the principal were more than pleased with the results. It was agreed that the principal would let Mr. O'Banion Sr. know if at any time during the school term, the boys needed to be spoken to again, in the same manner.

From that day on, he and Mike went out of their way to be nice to each other. They even sat together at mass until the priests separated them, claiming they were disrupting the service. Over time a strong friendship developed, and they often kidded each other about which one of them had cried that day in the principals' office when Mr. O'Banion Sr. beat them.

He told Diedra if it wasn't for Mike backing him up a couple of times in the streets, he might not be taking her to the party.

"I don't know why," Harry said, "but he's like a rabid dog when he gets into a fight. He'll do anything. Sometimes I think he's nuts."

"Nuts?" Diedra asked. "In what way?"

"At first I thought it was just his bad temper, and because he's so damn tough, but then I realized he's not too tightly wrapped."

"So what you're telling me is that this guy, a cop, is missing some buttons off his uniform, and now they're promoting him?"

"Something like that, but don't get me wrong. It's not like he's ready for the rubber room, it's just, well, when he gets mad he changes—like a Dr. Jekyll thing. He snaps."

He told Diedra even as a kid, his friend could be in a nasty fight with someone yet he'd be laughing and making all kinds of stupid faces at the guy. He'd do crazy things like take his pants off and dance around like an indian, but the crazier he got, the more vicious his attack on his victim would become. Then all of a sudden the jerky stuff would stop. His face would go expressionless and he'd start looking around up in the air like he was trying to hear what someone was saying to him. When he got like that it was time for the other guy to run, if he still could, because all hell was about to break loose.

Harry said it was like watching some kind of demonic possession taking place. Mike's face would actually change, become contorted, and he'd start making weird sounds. The biting was the worst part. He'd actually seen Mike get small pieces of a person's flesh in his mouth and spit them out like the end of a cigar.

And then suddenly it would all stop, like someone had pulled the electric cord that made the monster work, and Mike would say something like, "Let's go over to White Castle, I'm hungry."

"Jesus, Mary, and Joseph, with all due respect to your friendship with this guy," Diedra said, "he needs some help, some serious, serious help. Does the job know he's like this?"

"Yeah, they know. They get a lot of complaints about him, but he's probably the best homicide detective they got. He's also got a lot of juice in the department because of relatives. But I have to admit, lately he's gotten worse."

"How come?"

"I'm not sure. It may have something to do with both his uncles getting killed in Belfast."

"What happened to them?"

"Well the Brits told the families they got shot trying to escape from prison."

"Why were they arrested?"

"Who knows? The was things are in Belfast, the Brits don't need a reason to arrest people. If you're Irish, that's reason enough."

"So that's Mike's problem? He doesn't believe the story?"

"Not for a second, neither does his father. When the families got the bodies back, they had them autopsied. The pathologist said they'd been beaten to death and that the gunshot wounds were to the back of their heads."

"God rest their souls," Diedra said making the sign of the cross.

            *   *   *

O'Banion's was a cops' place, and a family place, usually cops' Irish Catholic families. It had been ever since Mike Jr.'s grandfather, an inspector for the NYPD, bought it in the early 1900s. With only two years before retirement, he was gunned down during a bank robbery just two blocks away, but not before killing all three of the bandits. Over the years the locals embellished their own versions of the facts thus creating a kind of folklore about the "Great O'Banion" and the "Great Shoot-Out."

Mike Jr.'s father took over the business and quickly realized that customers, many of them law enforcement officers, were coming from all over the city, some even from out of state, to have a drink in the bar once owned by the Great O'Banion. Not being one to miss out on a business opportunity, he gathered every picture he could find showing his Da with important political figures, police fraternal organizations, and especially the one of him shaking the Cardinal's hand. After proper framing, he hung them along with copies of old newspapers telling what had happened, all over the bar. The headline on one paper read, "HERO COP DIES SHOOTING ROCKAWAY RATS."

The O'Banion ancestral home was further out on the peninsula in Breezy Point, a private section inhabited mostly by firemen and New York's finest. Harry remembered how he would be invited out on weekends during summer vacation since he was Mike Jr.'s best friend and classmate. The time spent with the O'Banion family was special because it allowed an escape, at least for a while, from his miserable situation at home.

At 9:15 they found a parking spot down the block from the bar. Noticing the headlights of the car behind them, and still uneasy about having been followed, he sat for a moment letting the engine run.

"I wanna charge the battery a little," he told Diedra.

Once the car passed and turned the corner, they got out. If he'd sat there for awhile longer he would have seen the same car come back around the block, go down the street and park.

With the exception of a few hardy souls willing to brave the icy wind coming off the beach, and the snow now falling at a steady pace, the avenue was empty. Not like in the summer months when it would be crowded with raucous, young sun-worshippers jamming into hotdog concessions and the bars willing to put up with them.

They'd only gone a few feet and already the sounds of people's voices singing "Irish Soldier Boy," and live pipes, cut through the cold, quiet, night air as if the party was outside the bar.

"Wait, before we go in," he said taking hold of her arm. "They're probably going to take up a collection, so if anybody hands you and envelope, put this in and pass it along." And with that, he slipped several folded bills into the pocket of her jacket.

"That's not a good place, it'll fall out," she said, "here, let me put it in my slacks. God almighty, Harry, this is 500 dollars. What are they collecting for, the national debt?"

"Don't worry about it, it's not important."

"All right, whatever you say. It's your money, but God, Harry, 500 dollars. Remind me to let you take up a collection for me sometime. These people must invite you to a lot of parties."

"One more thing," he said softly, stepping closer, "whatever you hear in there, you can't repeat to anybody. If someone ever asks you about these people, you didn't know them, you didn't get their name, and you didn't hear what they were talking about. OK? Most of all, if anybody ever asks you about the O'Banions in particular, you don't know anything."

"If you're trying to scare me, you're doing a very good job of it. What kind of a place is this?"

"No, no, no, there's no reason to be frightened. It's just that some of these people are, uh, well...some of them are involved in things in Ireland."

"O'Day," she whispered, her lips almost touching his ear, "are we talking IRA?"

"You got it, and that's the last time you wanna say that, tonight or any other time. Are you still scared? Would you rather go someplace else?"

"Not on your life. We're staying right here. I've never been to a place like this before. I'll say one thing, you sure know how to make a first date interesting; I saw a movie like this once."

O'Banion Sr. spotted them instantly. Excusing himself from a group of men at the bar, he made his way towards them through the crowded, smoke-filled room. The man was a giant. Harry figured he weighed at least 300 pounds and probably stood taller than 6' 6". With only a hint of white showing in his thick, strawberry blond hair, just a cursory examination of his overall appearance told anybody that he was still in excellent physical condition. As big as he was his movements seemed effortless, like a well-trained boxer.

The acorn hadn't fallen far from the O'Banion tree either. Mike Jr. was the spitting image of his father both in size and looks. Sometimes when they were working behind the bar together on a busy night, it was hard to tell them apart from a distance.

On rare occasions some outsider would forget to control his liquor and would have to be dealt with. Usually one of the off-duty cops in the place handled it for the owners, but if the jerk was especially abusive, he quickly found himself out back in the alley with either Mike Jr., or Sr., using his face as a punching bag. They rarely had trouble with him again.

"Good lad, Harry, good lad, I knew you'd make it. Mike Jr. was just asking for you." Mr. O'Banion Sr. said in a loud, booming voice. Harry swore he could feel it bouncing off him.

"Thanks for letting me know, Mike, I wouldn't have missed this for the world." The two men shook hands and embraced. "You must be very proud of him."

"Aye lad, that I am, that I am. It's just too bad his mother, God rest her soul, couldn't be here. She would have had a grand cry to be sure."

"Mike, I'd like you to meet Miss Diedra Agnes Shannahan. Diedra Agnes, I'd like you to meet Michael Patrick O'Banion, proprietor and captain, NYPD, retired."

"Welcome, Diedra Agnes," Mike Sr. said in a much gentler voice. "You do my humble establishment an honor. A bonnie lass, Harry, a bonnie lass to be sure. Not since I last laid my tear filled eyes on my dear, sainted Kathleen have I seen such beauty."

"Thank you, sir, you're very kind. Bless all here. Your dear, sainted wife, God rest her soul, was fortunate to have had such a fine figure of a man such as yourself, Michael Patrick, as her husband. And it's at mass this Sunday that'll be lighting a candle for her."

In sixty seconds, Diedra Agnes Shannahan had won the heart of Michael Patrick O'Banion, the toughest retired cop in the Rockaways. She knew, and had said, all the right words.

Bang! went the cellar door up against the wall behind them as Mike Jr. squeezed his massive frame through the doorway holding a case of liquor under each arm.

"Harry, me boy! Glad to see you." his voice as loud as his father's. "Give us a hand now like a good lad."

He helped Mike load the liquor onto a hand truck standing next to the cellar door.

"I just asked Da if he'd seen you. Can you beat this? It's my party and they've got me in the basement working. And who is this lovely young creature you've brought with you?"

"Mike, I'd like you to meet a very special friend of mine, Miss Diedra Agnes Shannahan," Harry said smiling and putting his arm around her waist. "Diedra, I'd like you to meet Michael Patrick O'Banion Jr., detective second grade, NYPD."

"It's nice meeting you, Mr. O'Banion. Congratulations on your promotion."

"The pleasure is all mine lass, and please, call me Mike. I see you've already met my Da. Has he asked you to marry him yet?"

"No, not yet," she answered, a slight blush coming to her face.

"And what kind of a host are you," Mike Sr. reprimanded his son, "not to be offering your guests a wee dram of what you've just taken out of my cellar?

"Never mind," he continued, taking a firm hold of Diedra's hand. "Come with me, lass, we'll go to the bar before we both perish from the thirst."

"Go ahead," Harry told her, "I'd like to talk with Mike for a minute, if that's OK with you Mike. You have some time for me now?"

"Sure, Harry, sure, let's go into Da's office."

Mike Jr. crunched down into a king-sized leather chair behind an equally king-sized desk and listened intently while Harry told him about being followed and about the shooting. He also told him about having his car broken into, and how a vehicle just like the one that had followed him, was scoping out Ira's house the very same night.

"You were involved in that thing down by the train station?" Mike Jr. asked.

"So you already know about it."

"Yes. My partner and I heard the 'shots fired' on the radio, but we were sitting on some skells so we stayed put. I heard it was your friend Joe Joe doin' the shooting, but what you're telling me now is different from what he told the responding officers. He told them a couple of guys tried holding him up. Harry, I told you, watch out for that meatball. Don't get involved with him."

"Why, what's so bad about him?"

"What's wrong with him? You mean besides that he breaks people's heads when they don't pay him? I know you two got a history, but I'm tellin' you, this guy isn't just anybody. He's mobbed up big time. Well, anyway, just don't get obligated. Now, how can I help?"

Harry showed him the plate number and asked if he could run it.

"I can't promise you anything, but I'll see what I can do. Now we'd better go and find those two before Da runs off with her."

For the rest of the night Harry didn't think about being followed, and Diedra didn't think about the beatings her dead husband had given her. Instead, they both enjoyed themselves for the first time in a long while. Laughing, dancing, and having a few drinks, they had fun, but most of all they enjoyed each other's company. Around 1 a.m. the party started to break up when somebody came in and said it had started snowing again.

*   *   *

By the time they got over the second bridge there was already several inches of heavy, wet snow covering the ground. At times, when the wind ripped across the open causeway it became a whiteout and they'd have to slow to a crawl until the gusts subsided. Diedra nervously grasped the dashboard and fidgeted in her seat. She had every right to be scared, the freak storm was intensifying and the car was all over the road.

"Don't you have any snow tires on?" she asked trying her best to keep the inside of the windows clear.

"I was gonna have them put on the other day, but I didn't get around to it. Who knew it was gonna snow like this?"

When they reached the entrance to the parkway, it was blocked by a police car with its lights flashing. One of the officers was nice enough to get out and struggle over to them. He said the parkway was closed all the way to the Cross Island and would probably stay closed until the morning when the DOT could get more plows out.

The officer asked Harry where they were going and when he heard New Hyde Park, he told them to forget about it. He suggested that they either check into one of the motels right in the area, or if they had any friends close by, to stay with them for the night. They thanked him for his help and continued slowly up the boulevard.

"Look Diedra, I'm sorry about this, but there's no way I can get you home. We'll be lucky just to make it to my place. Sorry."

"I don't care where we go," she snapped, "just get me out of this car before we get killed. Your place, a diner, I don't care. Just get me inside. I'll have to call my neighbor and let her know what's going on. She's got to go over and feed my cat."

Squinting to see out the windshield and fighting to control the car, he managed to reach his apartment house. There were several shovels by the entrance and together, they cleared a space large enough to get the vehicle out of the road.

Diedra made a pot of coffee while he put together a makeshift meal from what the refrigerator had to offer, which wasn't much. A few slices of ham, some cheese, three pieces of pizza, and four semidried, stuffed cabbage rolls was the best he could do. While he attempted to resurrect what he'd found, Diedra called her neighbor.

"Marie? Hi, it's me. Yes, fine. How about this? Isn't it something? I'm OK. I'm at a friend's house. Yes, the man I went out with tonight. Yes, it was fun—his friends are very nice. No! I'm not in bed. You're terrible. Look, can you go next door and feed Bartholomew? You know what he gets, and put another light on in the living room. Marie? Wait, take this number in case you need me. I'll call you again in the morning to let you know when I'll be home. Thanks, you're a doll, I appreciate it."

While she had been talking, Harry set up a little buffet on the coffee table complete with an already opened bottle of Chianti, and some cloth napkins with the store's price tags still on them. As they ate, she paid his gourmet cooking skills a few tongue-in-cheek compliments, and they laughed about the events of the evening—especially the ride home. He got up a couple of times to find a weather report on the radio, but instead, settled for some soft music.

"How come you keep working at the restaurant?" he asked as he refilled her wine glass. "You certainly don't need the money."

"Why? I don't know. I hadn't thought about *not* working. You know, when Terrence died, I figured I'd have to give up the house. I didn't know about all the insurance, we never talked about money. He handled everything."

Diedra explained that while she was afraid of losing the place, at the same time she couldn't stand to be in it because that's where she'd taken the worst beatings. Both her parents were dead and she had no friends because her husband wouldn't let her. "Besides you and your wife, my neighbor Marie, was the only other person I knew, and she happened to be the night cashier at the Bavarian House."

"Why don't you come down to the restaurant," Marie said, "they're always looking for waitresses. It'll be good. You'll get out of this place, and you'll make good money."

"So that's how I got there," Diedra said, "and as for why I keep working, what else would I do? Go back to sitting alone in the house?"

"Yeah, I guess you're right."

"Besides, I thought you liked to watch me bending over tables in that stupid costume. I know your friend Peter does."

Harry's ears perked up at that and he asked, "Why? Has he ever said anything?"

"Oh no, on the contrary, next to you, he's the politest guy that comes into the place."

"Have you see him lately?"

"Yes, he was in the other night and he was asking if I'd seen you."

"Was he alone?"

"He was when he first came in, but later, when I took some sandwiches into the bar there were two men with him. I don't think they stayed long though because I would've remembered—they looked so funny."

"Funny? How?"

"I guess because they looked so much alike. They had blond hair, short, like crewcut style. They both were wearing black raincoats, too, and they were both the same height. Even Jerry the bartender was joking about them. He said they looked like pallbearers, or like those men you always see following the president around when he goes someplace. Why are you so interested?"

"Do you remember the first time you met him? Well, when we left that night he showed me his new car in the parking lot. I accidentally found a gun taped to the back of his glove compartment. He gave me some cock-and-bull story about how he'd gotten it and why he kept it like that."

"Harry, believe me, a lot of people have guns in that place. If you bend over enough tables, it's amazing some of the things you see. But you're right, that's pretty weird having it in the car like that."

"It's more than just the gun. How can he afford to dress like that?" I make good money but I couldn't have my suits made. And the way he talks, he sounds like a cop or something. Believe me, he's more that what he says he is."

"So what is he?"

"I don't know, yet, but I'm gonna find out."

He was right, he was going to find out, and it wouldn't be too much longer before he did.

"All right, enough about him" Diedra said getting up. "How about we clean this mess up? It's way past my bedtime."

Being close to her as they worked around the kitchen was enjoyable, and he noticed how fastidiously she did everything. The dishtowels had to be folded a certain way, the countertops had to be perfectly clean, and even the garbage had to be double bagged so it wouldn't smell.

Since he'd gotten used to sleeping on the couch during the last six months of his marriage, he insisted Diedra take the bedroom.

"Besides," he told her, "I don't want anybody messin' up the grooves in the cushions."

It wasn't until she asked for a pair of pajamas and some towels to take a shower, that they both suddenly became uncomfortable with their situation.

"Pajamas! I don't think I have any."

"Well you've gotta give me something to sleep in. It's not exactly a head wave in here."

"Wait, maybe I do have something," he said taking her by the hand into the bedroom. She watched while he rummaged through the dresser.

"Here, how's this?" he asked handing her an old football jersey.

"This label says 3x. Are you trying to tell me something?" she asked with a smile.

"No, of course not, but it's the only thing I have. I'm sorry. I don't think I ever owned a pair of pajamas."

"I'm only kidding. This will do just fine," she said holding it up against her and looking in the mirror. "Not exactly Maidenform, but it'll do. Now, how about a couple of towels?"

Fortunately he had two brand new bath sheets he'd bought but never used. How embarrassing, he thought, if he had to give her the faded, dryer-burned things he used.

"Here's the towels and a new bar of soap, there's a switch on the wall by the door for the ceiling heater in case you're cold, and…" but before he could say anything else, she put her hand gently over his mouth.

"Harry, Harry, it's Ok, relax, I've been in bathrooms before."

Taking the towels, the bar of soap, and the football jersey, she closed the door. He hesitated for a moment and listened for the sound of the lock, but the only thing he heard was the shower water and Diedra singing "Irish Soldier Boy" to herself.

He changed into a pair of Bermuda shorts and a paint-stained St. John's sweatshirt. In case she might be cold during the night he got the heavy, king-sized comforter out of the blanket chest and laid it on the bed.

"Calm down now, calm down," he told himself. If he'd been nervous when he picked her up, he was worse now. "Don't be doin' anything stupid O'Day, what's gonna be, will be," his testosterone factory now in high gear. This wasn't just some weekend bimbo in his shower, he had feeling for Diedra. From the day they first met, he know she was special. Unfortunately he'd already made the mistake of marrying the blight of his life, Martie.

He remembered how pissed-off he'd gotten when he found out how badly Diedra was getting slapped around by her husband. Now and then he'd see her in the supermarket and either her lip would be split, or one, sometimes both of her eyes would be blackened. She'd be wearing big, dark sunglasses, but they couldn't hide the damage. Once she had her right arm in a cast. The day he saw her with all the stitches in her face, he thought seriously about going to people he knew and having her husband's legs broken, but on the way home, he thought about it. Knowing the lousy scumbag he was, Harry knew that when he could walk again, he'd probably kill Diedra.

After doing some emergency dusting and housekeeping, he was making his bed up on the couch when he heard her voice behind him, "Harry, is there any more coffee?"

She was standing in the bathroom doorway framed by a halo of steam, and her skin had a slight, strawberry tint from the hot water. My God, you are luscious, he thought. The jersey barely reached the middle of her thighs and behind her, hanging on the towel bar, he could see her freshly washed underwear. Even without a bra her large breasts stood straight out, enough to hold what she was wearing away from the lower part of her body.

"I've never seen you without your hair in a ponytail," he said, gawking at her. She had his hair dryer and brush and as she groomed herself, she tossed and flicked her head causing her hair to fly every which way, like flashes of fire.

"Harry, you didn't answer me, is there any more coffee?"

"Uh, yes, yes there is. It's on the coffee table," he said, forcing himself to stop staring at her body.

"That's a good place for it," she said with a smile as they sat down together on the couch. When she crossed her legs, the jersey rode up to the tops of her thighs and he couldn't help but stare; more than anything, he wanted her.

"I love your outfit. Very collegiate," she said. "We make quite the elegant couple, don't we? You can tell this is a designer jersey by the way it has 'Property of Greenpoint Mustangs' printed on the front."

Being alone together in his apartment was an awkward situation for both of them, and they struggled to make conversation.

"I like your friends," she said, fixing her coffee. "Thank you for taking me tonight." She said that Mr. O'Banion Sr. had asked her to marry him and that she'd told him, "Just as soon as I can get rid of Harry."

"It was a pleasure taking you," he said. "Maybe we can go out to dinner some night and to a movie."

"I'd like that, I like being with you."

They leaned towards each other and gently kissed. Their lips parting for a moment, they searched for a sign of approval, and then kissed again, but now harder and with their mouths open. In his arms, she could feel his erection pressing against her and his hand moving from her waist down to her bare buttock. Both breathed heavily and she began making low, moaning sounds.

Taking care not to offend him, she slowly pushed away. Kissing his cheek she said, "It's been a long time, I don't know if I'm ready for this. Please, don't be mad at me."

"I'm not mad. It's been awhile for me to. The last thing you need in your life right now is somebody giving you a hard time. Look, it's been a long day. How about we get some sleep and in the morning I'll make you some Irish whiskey pancakes. How's that sound?"

"That sounds wonderful, but please, don't be made at me. I'd hate that."

"Go on, get some sleep. I'll leave a couple of lights on."

Kissing him, she went into the bedroom, but left the door open.

Turning out the end table lamps, he crawled under the covers and took off his sweatshirt and shorts. Watching the snow drive against the windows, he thought how being Mr. Nice Guy sucked. It always had, even back in high school.

"O'Day," he reprimanded himself, "you've got to stop being so fucking noble."

Well, at least you're not a hypocrite, he thought, a half hour ago you were telling yourself not to do anything stupid.

About to dose off, he heard the bed frame squeak and felt the vibrations of Diedra's steps on the living room floor. The snow reflected enough light through the windows for him to see her standing next to the couch. Without speaking, he made as much room as possible. Already hard, he nervously stared while she pulled the jersey up over her head and let it fall to the floor.

"Harry, dearest," she said enticingly while slowly slipping under the blankets next to him, "I've got something to tell you."

"Oh, yes, please, tell me something, tell me whatever you want. You have my complete attention."

Running the tips of her fingers up and down his thigh, she said in a loud voice, "Harry, that's the worst fucking mattress I ever tried to sleep on. Where the hell did you get that thing?"

They broke into hysterics. But afterwards, words like timidity, prudishness, and self-control had no meaning for the rest of the night, and for the better part of the next day.

Part 8

By Monday morning, the city's plows and traffic had reduced the snow to mounds of dirty mush for people to curse at as it got into their shoes. Diedra was anxious to get home to her cat, so by 6 a.m., they were up and on their way. With everything that had been going on he'd fallen behind at work, so after dropping her off, he headed for the office. As he drove, he put the radio on.

"Washington was rocked yesterday by yet another sex-related incident involving the president. While presenting National Achievement Awards to a group of high school students in a White House ceremony, he was punched in the face by Secretary of Agriculture L. Boynton Meller.

"Secretary Meller was immediately subdued by Secret Service agents and taken to an undisclosed location. Other agents assigned to the president's personal bodyguard, picked him up off his knees and led him into a small, adjoining room.

"A White House spokesman told reporters later that the president's personal physician had treated him for a small cut on his lip and that there would be no permanent disfigurement.

"More than a dozen eyewitnesses to the attack, confirmed that as Secretary Meller struck the president, he yelled, 'That's for getting my daughter pregnant, you bastard.' A friend of the Meller family, not wishing to be identified, confirmed Mr. And Mrs. Meller did have a 16-year old daughter and that she was an honor student at one of the exclusive private schools for girls in the Washington, D.C. area.

"Secret Service agents subsequently turned Secretary Meller over to Capital police, who released him on his own recognizance. When pressed by reporters why no charges had been filed given the seriousness of the attack, the president's spokesman had no comment.

"Sen. Samuel Hammond, an ordained Baptist minister, and the most outspoken critic of the president's moral track record, again called upon him to resign. In his strongest denouncement yet, he said the president was an angel of evil and a danger to the country's youth.

"At the same time, Sen. Tracey Lathrid of New York, a long time personal friend of the president, when asked about the allegations that the president had gotten a 16-year old high school girl pregnant, said he was positive the entire nation joined him in thanking the good Lord the president wouldn't have to go through the rest of his life with a scar on his face."

RESERVED-H. O'Day, is what the little, white and red sign read where he parked at work. It was right smack in front of the main entrance and he loved it, so did his ego. Even some of the big shot Japanese executives weren't as close to the building's front door.

"Christ!, I hope it's still there," he said nervously fumbling under the driver's seat for the gun. He'd forgotten about it all weekend. Taking a minute to let his heart slide back down his throat, he put the Beretta and extra clips into his briefcase and went inside. It would be at least an hour before the office staff started to arrive, so he took the spare shirt, tie, and jacket he kept in a closet for "I couldn't make it home" emergencies, and changed in the men's room.

The first thing he always looked at was the weekly Age Trail Balance prepared by the data processing department as of the close of business on Friday nights. It was a report showing how much each account owed, how much was current, and how much was past due, and for how long. Part A of the report covered Ira's Key Accounts and usually he just scanned it. This time, however, one figure in particular jumped off the page and smacked him in the face. The name of the account was Premiums Three, Inc., and they owed $2,227,000, almost every penny of which was past due.

"Son of a bitch, what the hell has this jerk done?" he yelled jumping up from his chair. He'd questioned Ira about the account when it first started appearing on the report and over a period of time, watched the balance steadily grow, but this—this was crazy.

Premiums was one of maybe a half dozen accounts he'd let Ira set up on his own, at least he had made it look that way. In each instance, after Ira had gone home for the day, he rechecked all of the credit investigation work. They were all triple A1 companies, except for this one. "Jesus Christ, how the hell did this get by me? This is bad, bad, bad," he said staring at the figure, "$2,227,000, Jesus Christ Almighty."

Ira had told him Premiums Three had verified contracts to supply Santronics merchandise to be given as prizes and incentives by banks, publishing houses, and local radio stations. He knew the premium business was growing by leaps and bounds so he had no problem accepting the reasoning.

As the balance had grown, he'd asked him about it, but Ira always had some legitimate sounding excuse as to why they weren't taking care of the past due invoices. They either had a lot of returns coming back, or they were in the process of refinancing at their banks, or some other story, which at the time, seemed to make sense.

"O'Day, you're a schmuck," he said to himself, "a number on schmuck. This is a bust out and it's your fault. Good Christ Almighty, $2,227,000 and it's a bust out!"

From day one he'd known his boss was stupid, and he should have been watching him. The credit file was in Ira's office.

Jay Rossbaum was listed as the company's president, and his sons, Aaron and Ezra as vice presidents. A Dunn and Bradstreet report showed them as also being the principals in eleven other companies, all incorporated under the laws of the state of Pennsylvania, and all subsidiaries of Premiums Three, Inc., itself, a Delaware corporation.

He went into accounting and pulled the invoice file, and as he suspected, the merchandise had been billed to the eleven subsidiaries, but shipped to one location, Premiums' warehouse in Long Island City. He even knew the building because another dealer of his had a warehouse right next to it.

The Rossbaums had given Ira financial statements not worth the paper they were printed on, they'd even had the balls to list their own companies as credit references.

"What a joke," he said to himself, noticing in the file that all three of the Rossbaums were certified public accountants. "Shit! What if there's more stuff out for delivery?" he said heading back to his office.

Plenum Trucking handled all of Santronics' merchandise from the time it came off the ships and planes to the time it got delivered to the dealers. Their office was physically in Santronics' warehouse, and the man who ran it, Manny Ostrow, was a good drinking buddy of Harry's.

"Hello? Manny, it's Harry. Yeah, fine, and yours? Good. Listen, you got anything out for Premiums? Yeah, please, if you would, it's important." He could hear Manny shuffling papers and when he came back on the phone he said, "Yeah, I got a full truck out now, he might already be there. Why?"

"A truck!? That's what, maybe fifty, sixty grand? Manny, please, can you stop it?"

"I can try," Manny answered in his usual low, growl of a voice. The four packs of cigarettes he smoked each day made him sound as if he had a throat full of pebbles.

"You sure you know what you're doin'?"

"Yeah, I'm sure all right. Please Manny, we're talking about my ass here."

"OK, OK, hold on, stay on the phone with me."

For security reasons, all of Plenum's trucks were equipped with two-way radios and Manny kept in constant contact with his drivers. Harry could hear him calling the one hauling Premiums' order.

"Yeah, Mario, you do Premiums yet? Good, bring it back. Why? What the fuck you wanna know why for? Did I die or somethin' and leave you boss, you Guinea prick you. Just bring the stuff back. Ten-four."

That's the way Manny talked to some people. After you'd been around him for a while and you got to know him, you realized if he spoke to a person in some other manner, he probably didn't like them.

"OK, Harry, it's comin' back. I hope you know what the fuck you're doin' up there. I still gotta charge Santronics for the freight. Are you sure you're not boozin' this mornin'?"

"Thanks, Manny, I owe you, big time."

It was a safe bet the Rossbaums' lawyers were already drawing up the Chapter 11 papers, in which case Santronics, at best, would get back ten cents on the dollar.

It was also a safe bet that his and Ira's asses were history once the company found out about the $2,227,000. That's the problem of being somebody's protege, he thought, if number one screws up and gets fired, number two usually buys the farm also. Harry could already picture the grin on Max Kiedelman's ugly, little, weasel face when he found out.

"Sons of bitches, who the hell are these Rossbaums anyway?" he asked himself, getting more agitated by the minute. The one person who might be able to give him some quick answers so early in the morning, was someone he really didn't want to call, but he had no choice.

"Hello? Is Pete Longdon there? Please. Hi, Pete, it's Harry O'Day."

"Well, hello, stranger, how are you? I haven't seen you in awhile."

"Yeah, well, you know how it is, busy and all. Look, Pete, I was wondering if you'd ever heard of an outfit by the name of Premiums Three, Inc., It's run by a Jay Rossbaum and his kids, Aaron and Ezra."

"Yes, I've heard of them. How much are they into you for?"

"Right now it's hard to say, but it's a bundle."

"Give me a couple of minutes and I'll call you back."

"Thanks, Pete, I really appreciate it."

By now his secretary, Connie, had come in and he had her call the restaurant across the street to send over two containers of his "special tea."

"It's kind of early even for you boss, isn't it?"

"Connie, please, never mind what time it is, just do it."

His private line rang—it was Longdon. He said all three Rossbaums were presently under federal indictments for income tax evasion and that two additional indictments were going to be handed down in a day or two charging them all with mail and wire fraud. Their MO, Longdon said, was to set up paper corporations and use them to scam manufacturers out of large quantities of merchandise, and then file for bankruptcy.

"Lots of luck," Harry said as his heart sank into his shoes. "Thanks, Pete, I appreciate the information. I gotta go, but I'll call you."

"Yes, if you would, Harry. There's something I need to talk to you about. It's very, very important."

For a moment he sat there after hanging up, trying to gather his thoughts. It felt like he'd been run over by a train. Suddenly it dawned on him. How the hell could Longdon know about federal indictments that hadn't even been handed down yet? The tax indictments might be part of the public record in some courthouse, but how could he find out in just a couple of minutes what was going on in some federal prosecutor's office when it came to the new ones?

Now he was sure Longdon was some kind of a cop, or maybe even a fed. All those questions that night at the bar, the gun under the dashboard, the trips down to Washington he was always taking supposedly on business, and now this thing with the indictments.

"What the hell is this guy up to?" he asked himself.

Normally, Ira would stick his head in the doorway and say good morning when he came to work, but today was different. Instead, he went directly into his office and without turning the lights on, slumped in his chair.

"Easy, Harry, easy, don't kill the bastard," he said to himself as he gathered up the Premiums' file, walked into Ira's office and threw it on the desk. After looking at it for a moment, Ira slowly lowered his head into his hands and began to cry. For Harry, it was like watching a drunk at an AA meeting breaking down and for the first time admitting in public that he needed help.

"Do you have any idea what you've done, Ira? Do you have the slightest idea what you've done to us, you stupid Bastard? The first time I get a good job, the first time in my life I'm paying my bills on time, and you go and fuck it all up."

Ira took his hands away from his face and blubbered, "What are you getting so upset about? It's me they're going to fire. You didn't do it—I did."

"Oh, stop your crying you egotistical bastard, it's making me sick. Do you think they ever once considered you as the brains in this department? It was me they came to when they had a problem. It was me they came to when they needed extra money collected. It was me they came to when they had problems in the other branches. Not you, Ira—me! They're not just going to fire you, they're going to fire me too, you fucking jerk!"

Like a child scolded for a mischievous deed, Ira lowered his head back down into his hands and sobbed.

"Not that it makes any difference at this point, but could you explain why in God's name you kept shipping them after they didn't pay what was past due?"

Ira said he had stopped shipping them, several times, but the Rossbaums wouldn't let him alone. All three of them would constantly call, begging him for more merchandise and promising to clean up the account. They even got his home phone number and would call him at all hours of the night. Finally, they came right out and told him that if he didn't keep shipping they'd simply file for bankruptcy and Santronics wouldn't get a dime.

"I got scared," Ira said. "I didn't know what to do, so I kept shipping."

"Ira, Ira, Ira. Don't you know anything? That's the way they work. They find some schmuck in a company and load up on him. What about this memo from Kiedelman? He warned you two months ago to stop shipping if they didn't pay. This was your way out. You could've told them it was out of your hands, that your boss had turned off the faucet."

"What memo? I never got a memo from Kiedelman."

"This one, right here in the credit file. He couldn't have spelled it out any clearer—NO Money, NO Inventory."

"I never saw that before. He sent for the file about two months ago, but when it came back, I just put it into the cabinet. It says here you received a copy of it, so did Shihoto and Mishimia."

Harry looked at it again and said, "I never got a copy of this thing, I bet nobody did. It's a phony, Kiedelman planted the damn thing."

"I don't understand. Why would he do a thing like that?"

"Why? Because he's not stupid. He saw the file, he knew you weren't gonna get paid, he knew it was a scam. The memo covered his ass. He took himself out of the loop. In fact, he was probably hoping you'd be dumb enough to keep shipping, which you did, you jerk. We've been screwed, good, Ira. First by you, you dumb bastard, then by the Rossbaums, then by Kiedelman, and when this hits the fan, the company will take its turn."

"They want to see us Friday morning, over in the city," Ira said, wiping his eyes. "Shihoto and Mishimia, and I think Kiedelman will be there. Yamatoki called the meeting, it's up by his office at 9 a.m."

"Well, well, well, the big man himself," Harry said sarcastically. "That's the first time we've been invited up to the platform of the gods, right, Ira? The first and the last time if I'm not mistaken."

Part 9

Fifteen minutes after he got back to his office, he saw Ira take his coat and leave. His secretary said he wasn't feeling well.

"Good riddance," Harry said to himself. For the rest of the day, and into the early evening, he struggled to do his work. Not that he thought being conscientious was going to change anything, it was too late for that, he did it for himself. At 8 o'clock he was packing up to leave when the phone rang. It was Mike O'Banion Jr.

"Listen," Mike said, "I've got a bit of news about the plate business we discussed."

"Good, I was just thinking about calling you. Were you able to come up with anything?"

"It's kind of complicated and I'd rather not get into it over the phone. How about having a wee taste at Ryan's, say around 11?"

"OK, I'll be there."

For security reasons, the only way out of the building complex after a certain hour was through Plenum Trucking down at the far end of the building. He had to go see Manny Ostrow anyway to pick up the paperwork on what had been brought back from Premiums Three.

The warehouse was always busy. Trailers hauling merchandise from the piers and airports arrived throughout the night and had to be unloaded. In addition, Manny's people worked at night picking and loading the next day's orders. If you weren't careful, you could get your feet run over by a high-low.

Within the warehouse itself, there was a secured area, a large room, off-limits to all but a few select Japanese. All six of the Santronics warehouse centers in the country had one. He'd asked Ira about them once who said they were for research and development work, which to Harry, explained nothing. Someone else had told him they were working on top secret projects for the United States military.

Whatever they were doing, nobody got into the room except the Japanese technicians and a few of the Do Nothings as he liked to call them, young, muscular men who looked more like they belonged in the Japanese Army than working in an office. As far as he could see, the only thing they ever did was lurk around and watch what the rest of the people wee doing. Ira said they gave him the creeps because of the way they looked at him, like they wanted to hurt him or something.

Personally, Harry had never spoken to any of them, and that was just fine because he thought they were nothing but a bunch of nasty weirdoes.

When Santronics opened its Brooklyn facility, the company contracted with Plenum to do all the trucking and to handle the day-to-day operation of the warehouse as well. Not that Santronics and its parent, Komti, had a choice in the selection of a trucker. If they wanted to do business in New York, they had to use Plenum. That's the way it was. Not much of anything moved by truck in New York unless it was on a Plenum truck, or on trucks belonging to companies owned by business associates of Plenum.

Officially, Camella E. Bissetti was listed as the president and CEO, and her daughter Alida, as vice president. Camella just happened to be the wife of Anthony Bissetti, better known to his friends as Tony Trucks.

Once in awhile when Harry would stop into Manny's office at night for a couple of drinks, Tony would either be there, or he'd come in later on. A hulking, brute, he had steely, cold, black eyes, and there was a charisma about him that would have sent even the Spanish Inquisitors to the mattress.

Harry didn't know their past history together, and he didn't want to, but it was obvious that Manny and Tony were close friends. Manny ran Tony's business with an iron fist and not even the Do Nothings dared stick their noses into the warehouse's operation. If they had, somebody probably would have cut them off.

Bissetti's portion of the city's lucrative trucking business was a reward bestowed upon him by one Alfonsa Ponzinno for services rendered. An alleged capo, Ponzinno was the de facto owner of Plenum.

You had to go through the warehouse and up a flight of metal steps to reach Manny's office. It looked like a big, plate glass box with a floor, hung from the ceiling. He'd brought people in to build it according to his own design, and it allowed him an almost uninterrupted view of the warehouse and the ten loading bays.

The chemistry which had made Manny and Harry fast comrades was undoubtedly alcoholic, but still, they were friends. Manny had once told him, "You know, O'Day, I like you. You're like me. You ain't got too much class, and you drink too much." And they certainly did drink. It wasn't unusual for them to polish off a fifth of whiskey in an hour.

"Hey, kid, come in, have a drink," Manny said, sitting awkwardly, one leg up on the desk, as he tried to fix the strap on his ankle holster. "I got Premiums' paperwork. It came to $53,000, give or take. What the fuck is goin' on with this outfit anyway?" he asked, filling two slightly bent, and slightly soiled coffee containers with booze.

After a few swallows of Manny's rotgut liquor, Harry told him how the Rossbaums had set Ira up, about the phony financial statements, and how the whole thing had been a bust out from the beginning.

"How much we talkin' about?" Manny asked.

"$2,227,000."

Manny choked and spilled most of what was in the coffee container down the front of his shirt. For whatever the reason, Manny had a nervous thing that made him blink and nod his head excessively. When he got upset the affliction became exaggerated, and right now he looked like one of those little, toy dogs people put in the rear window of their cars. The kind where the head bobs up and down every time the car hits a bump.

"Forget about it, $2,227,000! Jesus Christ, you gotta be fuckin' kiddin' me," he shouted as he used the palms of his hands to wipe the liquor off his shirt and pants.

"I wish I was. It would've been more if you hadn't stopped the truck this morning."

"So what's gonna be? You gettin' any dough from these guys? Whatta they tellin' you?"

"They're not telling me anything. I can't reach them. The two phones at that Long Island City warehouse have been constantly busy, and the number where they live is unlisted. Besides, I only found out about this today, just before I called you. Who knows? Maybe they've already skipped."

"What's their name again? Rossboom, Rossbaum? Here, write it down for me, and where they live."

"Can I ask why?"

"Hey! We're talkin' a big load of stuff here, I'm gonna tell my drivers to keep an eye out for anybody tryin' to peddle a lot of Santronics. Maybe we can grab some of it up."

"That would be great," he said, writing the information on a pad, "only by now, it's probably scattered all over the place. I spoke to a friend of mine. He says these pricks have been indicted for tax evasion and that the feds are lookin' at them for some other things. It could be they're in Switzerland. All right, look, I gotta go. I told somebody I'd meet them. Manny, just in case I don't see you, thanks for all the help you've given me. I'm gonna miss our little drinkin' sessions."

"Whatta ya talkin' about? It sounds like you're leavin' the company or somethin'."

Harry told him about the meeting on Friday at Komti's headquarters, and that without a doubt, both he and Ira were going to get fired.

"Nah, don't say that. Look, you never know, somethin' might break for you—you're a good kid. That little prick Ira, I never liked him, but you're a good kid."

As he walked back up to the parking lot, he started laughing. "Maybe Manny is gonna send some of his boys over to see the Rossbaums." He was close. Tony Trucks would send them.

*   *   *

Ryan's was one of a series of bars out along Northern Boulevard that attracted primarily an Irish clientele. He'd been there before and was positive it was another watering hole for wanna-be IRA bad guys.

A few in the crowded room glanced up from their pints and balls when he entered, but given the fact that he had a face as Irish as Patty's pig, they quickly lost interest. It wasn't hard spotting O'Banion's massive body and strawberry blond hair at the far end of the packed bar. He was talking to a couple of Victor McGlauglin look-alikes in three-quarter length leather jackets and peaked caps. They saw him making his way towards them and simply faded into the smoke and maze of people.

"I'm sorry, Mike, I didn't mean for your friends to leave."

"That's OK, don't worry about it. They're just a few of the lads, that's all, just a few of the lads. How are you? You look troubled."

"It's nothing, just some problems on the job." Harry was too embarrassed to say anything about the fact that he was probably going to be fired.

"And how's Diedra Agnes? A bonnie lass, bonnie."

"Fine, Mike, she's fine. And your Da?"

"Like a bull. He gets younger every time I look at him. He says to tell you that if Diedra Agnes and yourself get married, he'll give you a grand reception at the bar, pipes and all."

"Well, I don't think we're at that point yet, but it's a very generous offer. Please, thank him for me."

"Sheamus!" Mike called to one of the three bartenders, "be a good lad and give up a round here, and yourself too."

They finished a half dozen balls and beers and then Mike suggested they move to a small corner table being wiped off by an attractive, young lady.

Harry listened intently to the results of his friend's inquiries.

At 5 a.m. the morning following the shooting incident on Kings Highway, an engine company in the south Bronx had been called to a car fire in an empty lot. After knocking it down, they found what was left of two men in the front seat so they called the marshall. The neighbors had already called the police.

"Were there bullet holes in it?" Harry asked hesitantly, like he was hoping Mike would say no.

"There were a couple of small caliber holes in the trunk, but that's not what killed them. Forensics said they'd each been shot in the head with something heavy, maybe a .45. They were dead before the car was torched."

"And so what are you telling me? The plate number I gave you belonged to that car, and the two guys were the ones following me?"

Mike said the car didn't have any plates, but when the crime scene people got going, they found one at the curb fronting the lot. As a professional courtesy, the detectives in charge of the case let him have the number and it matched the one he already had in his notepad. "And yes, they probably were the men who followed you."

So, whoever killed them took the plates, but dropped one? Jesus Christ, Mike, this thing sucks!"

"Now here's where it gets interesting," Mike continued, leaning closer. "When I ran the plate it came back blank."

"I don't understand. Were they stolen or somethin'?"

"No. What I'm telling you is that they were never issued by any motor vehicle department."

"You're losing me. Whatta you mean, never issued? How could that be?"

Speaking in a whisper, Mike said, "Government people, feds, G-men, use these plates. They're almost impossible to check because of all their damned secrecy bullshit."

"Son of a bitch, this is crazy. What the hell am I mixed up in?"

Mike said that while the NYPD was still working the crime scene, a bunch of FBI agents showed up saying they were taking over and were promptly told to fuck off. One of them called the Bronx chief of detectives who, after some heated discussion, was forced to make his men give it up. Mike said the FBI took everything, the bodies, what was left of the car, the dirt from around it, the license plate, they even made the detectives give up their notes.

"Mike, I can't tell you how scared I am. Look at me, I'm shaking. First it was the shooting, and now this. What the fuck is goin' on!?"

"Calm down, calm down," Mike said, motioning to the waitress who'd cleaned the table to bring another round of doubles. "Someone I know works in D.C. and he's a big fan of our friends in Belfast, so I asked him to check out the plate. He said the men in the car were Secret Service."

"Secret Service!? Jesus, Mike, this thing is like a bad movie. Why the hell would they be interested in me? It doesn't make any sense."

"Aye, lad, that's just what I asked myself," Mike said, finishing his drink and again telling the waitress to bring another round. "Why would they be wanting to follow a fine, upstanding man such as yourself? And do you know what the answer to my question was? Because maybe they weren't lookin' at Harry O'Day. Maybe they were interested in somebody he knew. This thing might not be as bad as you think.

"The way I see it," he continued, "what ever their intentions were, I don't think they were out to physically harm you. The same goes for the people who torched them. If they were going to whack you, you'd probably be died now. I think those poor souls knew their killers seein' how they let them get so close. They were both armed, yet their weapons were still holstered. It could be they even agreed to meet them. What other reason would they have had for being in a rat-infested lot at that hour of the morning? I think you're a secondary player in this. I think the dead men were messing up somebody elses action, or maybe knew too much about something."

Mike's assumptions were amazingly accurate.

"Look," he said, "I'm going to give you two numbers. This one's the precinct. If I'm not there they can reach me. This other one is for the men you saw me talking with before when you came in. If you have a problem you can call either one and somebody will get to you. OK?"

"Thanks, Mike. Just like the old days—you saving my ass."

"Off the record," Mike said, "it wouldn't hurt for you to have something in your pocket, at least until we get a handle on this thing."

"I've already taken care of it," he replied as they put their coats on, and made their was through the crowded bar.

"Don't be afraid to call the other number if you can't reach me right away," Mike said. "They're two of the meanest bastards you'd ever want on you side. I'm gonna call them right now." They shook hands, embraced, and drove off in opposite directions. Harry turned on the radio to try and stop thinking about what his friend had told him.

"We interrupt out regularly scheduled broadcasting to bring you this special news bulletin from our WKYH news desk: The body of L. Boynton Meller, secretary of agriculture, was found tonight by his wife when she returned home from visiting friends. Arlington, Va., police said that pending a full investigation, Mr. Meller apparently died from a single, self-inflicted gunshot wound to the head.

Mr. Meller had been involved in an altercation on Sunday with the president during a White House awards ceremony. He'd accused the president of having gotten his 16-year old daughter pregnant and then struck him in the face causing a slight cut to the president's lip. In a statement just released, a White House spokesman said that Mr. Meller's accusations were outrageous and that the former secretary had obviously suffered some type of mental anomaly. The White House spokesman said both the president and first lady were personally devastated by the secretary's suicide and that the president would issue a statement regarding the entire matter in the morning."

"Self-inflicted my ass," Harry said to himself turning off the radio.

Part 10

Routinely, Bobby Ostrow went out for supper between 9 and 10 o'clock and his father kept an eye on the warehouse until he came back. Tonight, however, it was already after 10:30 when Manny saw his son's car pull back into one of the empty loading bays.

"Where the fuck were you? Around the corner bangin' that broad again?" Manny snarled, not too pleased with things.

"No! I was watchin' the game in the bar and I forgot what time it was," Bobby answered, climbing onto the platform.

"They don't got no clock there? You're so full of shit your eyes are brown," Manny castigated his son. "I told you, watch out for her. You knock her up and she'll never let you alone. You listenin'?"

"Yeah, sure, Pop. You goin' someplace?"

"Yeah, I gotta go by Tony's place. If he calls, tell'm I'm on my way. Tell'm I just left, and make sure you tell'm how come I'm gonna be late, you prick. I'm supposed to be there already. You and that fuckin' broad."

"Listen," Manny continued, "you want me to bring you any of that guinea food?"

"Nah, I had kielbassa at the bar," Bobby answered, watching his father climb down the platform ladder to his car.

"Hey, Pop? When you gonna get a new set of wheels, you cheap fuck? You got more money than God."

Manny didn't answer, but simply made an obscene gesture as he backed out of the bay door.

Leaving his son in charge never worried him. Although Bobby was only 30, he was a natural organizer and not afraid of anything, or anybody. The men in the warehouse knew he'd done hard time for manslaughter and weren't anxious to test his mettle.

*   *   *

Tony Trucks Bissetti owned Annunzio's, a small bistro on Knickerbocker Avenue in Brooklyn. The former owner signed it over when he couldn't make the payments on a loan he'd gotten from one of Tony's many finance companies. Now he was the chef and the food was excellent. The place actually made a profit, but Bissetti's accountants took care of that.

The main dining room had the standard wooden tables covered with red and white checkered tablecloths, and empty wax-covered Chianti bottles served as candleholders. A bar ran the length of the wall to the right of the entrance, and along the left wall, were a series of individual booths. This was the area in which the general public ate.

The adjoining two rooms were of equal size and similarly furnished. Tall potted plants and floor-to-ceiling heavy wooden spindles had been strategically placed between them so as to form dividers. It was the middle room that served as Tony's private dining area and office. Only members of his crew and selected restaurant staff were allowed in it. If someone came to see him on business, two of his men would escort the visitor in, stand off to one side while Tony dealt with him, and then escort the person back out. No "outsider" ever got to see him without being searched.

Manny parked across the street by the fire hydrant. The usual complement of gofers and wise guys were hanging out in front and one of them yelled, "Hey, Manny, what is that? A 1902 or somethin'? Here, you wanna gun so you can shoot it?" Some of the others standing around laughed, mockingly.

"Very funny, you fat fuck," Manny growled. "At least it's not stolen like that pimpmobile you're drivin', you prick."

With his back to the wall, Bissetti was sitting at a table alone in the extreme left-hand corner of the room. In front of him was an enormous dish of spaghetti that he was twirling with a fork onto a tablespoon and pushing into his mouth. As he ate, little particles of red sauce and clams splattered onto the white linen tablecloth.

Several of his personal bodyguards sitting at a nearby table were themselves bathing in large plates of macaroni and assorted meat dishes. As Manny approached they looked up and one of them gave an almost undetectable nod of recognition.

There were some in Bissetti's organization who had no use for Manny Ostrow. Paramount on their list of objections was his close personal relationship with their boss—they were jealous. They didn't appreciate the fact that he wasn't Italian either. But what they disliked most about him, was the way he was openly disrespectful to them, and Bissetti did nothing to discourage it, which got them even more upset.

They'd do a lot of posturing when Manny was around to make themselves feel tough, but if push came to shove, not one of them would have the balls to go up into his face. They might have shot him in the back in a dark alley, but they'd never openly challenge him.

Manny and his older brother, Benny, had committed their first murder for pay by the ages of 15 and 17 respectfully. Rumor had it that over the years, the Ostrow brothers, a/k/a "The Bat Boys" because they always used baseball bats, had whacked at least three dozen people. Allegedly, the majority of the hits were carried out while in the employment of Tony Trucks Bissetti and by order of one Alfonsa Ponzinno. The word on the street was that if you fucked with the Ostrows, you were fucking with Mr. Ponzinno.

"How is it? Manny asked, taking his coat off and sitting down at the table.

"Forget about it," Tony replied, slurping the last few strands of spaghetti into his face, "this guy I got doin' the cookin'" is the best. Remember when we were gonna whack him because he couldn't pay?"

"Right? Didn't I tell ya to keep 'm, that he was a good cook?" Manny replied.

"Come on, have somethin'," Tony insisted. "Try the sausage, they're real hot."

"Are you kiddin'?" If I ate that stuff you'd have to take me to the hospital. Don't you got nothin' American in this place?"

"Hey, you," Tony yelled to one of his men, "go tell the cook I want 'm."

After overcoming some language difficulties, the chef brought Manny a small loaf of Italian bread, several slices of yellow store cheese, and some bologna. "This is more like it," Manny said, "now go and get me some mayonnaise."

"So what's doin'?" Tony asked, sipping black coffee and wiping blotches of sauce off his face and French cuffs.

Manny told him about the Rossbaums and how they'd used Premiums Three to scam Santronics. He also told him about the federal indictments.

"Do we know these Rossbaums?" Tony asked.

"Nah, they're some mutts from Phily. The kid, O'Day, says they've done this before."

"So what are we talkin' about?"

"Two, two an a half mil, give or take."

Tony stopped making little, methodical circles in his coffee cup and carefully placed the tiny spoon down on his napkin.

"So what you're tellin' me is that these three Jews came in here and grabbed up a couple of million dollars in stuff right under our noses, and we didn't know a fuckin' thing."

"You got it. Some balls, no?"

"When you made deliveries, did it all go to the same place, or was it scattered around?"

"It went to a warehouse in Long Island City."

"You think any of its still there?"

"It might be. There was supposed to be a delivery today, but O'Day had me bring it back. Mario took a load there last week. Maybe he saw what was in the place. He's the only driver I send over there."

"Call'm, tell'm to come down here, now. If he's not home send somebody to find'm, but I wanna see'm now."

Manny left the restaurant and went around the corner to use the phone in the gas station. Tony wouldn't let anybody make calls from Annunzio's, except the cook who was allowed to use the kitchen phone to order supplies. Once Tony had come in unexpectedly and caught one of his men using the pay phone up front in the public part of the restaurant. Incensed, he grabbed a bar stool and smashed all the glass out of the booth with the guy still inside.

The purpose of Manny's trip was to inform Tony that the Rossbaums had violated the sanctity of "his" territory. As far as Manny was concerned, the Rossbaums had stolen from Tony, not from Santronics. There wouldn't be any problem if they'd first come to Bissetti and gotten permission to work the scam. He would have told them what the obligatory tribute would be and that would have been the end of it. Unfortunately, they hadn't, instead, they'd elected to show their disrespect for his authority, and now they were probably going to get whacked for their arrogance.

Now, even it they offered to pay they were still going to get whacked—that's the way it had to be. If Tony let them get away with insulting him, what kind of a message would it send to others? Everybody and his brother would be looking to do the same thing. Bissetti would have a revolution on his hands.

It took Mario forty minutes to get there. When he pulled up he saw Manny waiting in his car and parked behind him. They talked for a moment while Manny searched him before going inside.

Mario was accustomed to Manny calling him at all hours of the night to handle certain tasks for him, but this was different. He'd never been summoned to the restaurant by Mr. Bissetti. A lot of times Mario and his wife had eaten there, but that was up front, this would be the first time he would be allowed into the big man's private domain and he was visibly nervous.

Obediently, he followed Manny through the first room and as they approached the entrance to the second, two of Bissetti's goons got up from a table and blocked their path.

"He's OK," Manny said. "He's with me, I checked him, he's clean."

"Yeah, but we still gotta check him," the bigger of the two said with an attitude.

"You gotta fuckin' hearin' problem or somethin'?" Manny asked angrily, his blinking and nodding affliction pronounced. "Here! You wanna check somethin'? Check this," he snarled, grabbing his crotch.

"All right, all right, for Christ's sake," Tony yelled from inside. "Will you please knock off the crap and let the guy in, I'd like to get the fuck outta here sometime tonight. If Manny says he's clean, he's clean. Why the fuck don't you guys listen when he tells you somethin'?"

Staring daggers, and red in the face for having been chastised in front of their peers, Tony's bodyguards stepped aside.

"Thanks for comin' Mario, I hope I didn't cause your family any trouble," Tony said apologetically.

"Oh, no, not at all, Mr. Bissetti. Please, anytime I can be of service to you," Mario stuttered. Sticking his cap into the pocket of his pea coat, he stumbled when told to sit down and knocked over the chair.

"Manny says you were in Premiums' warehouse last week."

"Yes, sir, last week."

"You see a lot of Santronics?"

Mario said the place was jammed with it. "It looks like they still got everything I ever brought them. The pallets still got the straps around them." Mario said they had only one guy working there, a black man who ran the high-low. "He runs the new stuff inside and puts it up against what's already there."

"So last week when you were there, that's what you saw, right?" Bissetti asked.

"Yes, sir, in fact the black guy was bitchin' and moanin' cause he didn't have enough room to work the high-low."

"What about the owners?" Tony asked. "You ever see three guys with suits there?"

"Well, there's this one white-haired guy, he signs my papers. Then there's two others, younger. Yeah, now that I think about it, there's always three of 'em there."

"OK, thanks, Mario, you did good," Tony said, pressing two, crisp hundred dollar bills into his hand. "Please, apologize to you wife for me. Tell her it was important that you and I spoke."

"Please, Mr. Bissetti, you didn't disturb us. Thank you, thank you, very much. If I can help, please, let me know."

"OK, you can hit the road," Manny said, patting him on the shoulder. "You were a big help, and don't be late for work in the mornin', ya prick ya."

"So whatta ya think?" Manny asked, leaning over the table closer to Tony.

"You got someone who can get in there tonight? I gotta make sure I know what I'm talkin' about when I got to Alfonsa."

"Sure, no problem. It may take a couple of hours. You gonna be here?"

"No, I got that thing I told you about. I'll come by the warehouse when I'm finished. How's Bobby doin'?"

"Forget about it. I wish the fuck he'd find a nice girl and get married. Everytime I go to the icebox for somethin' it's empty."

"Kids, right? They're all the same," Tony said, shrugging.

*   *   *

At 3 a.m. Manny was dozing at his desk when he heard the warning buzzer in the warehouse. All ten bay doors were wired into a system that let people know when a truck was entering or leaving. After a quick search, he found his glasses on top of his head, got up, and looked out the office window. Tony's Lincoln was pulling in next to a trailer being unloaded. Four men in a Caddy pulled in right behind him.

Not having consumed his normal quota of alcohol the night before, Manny had a slight case of the whammies, but quickly remedied the problem by downing half a coffee container of high-jacked whiskey.

"How'd ya make out?" Tony asked, flopping into a chair in front of the desk, the grueling length of his workday painfully obvious on his face.

"Good, here, take a look," Manny replied, flipping him an envelope containing several Polaroid pictures.

"You had the guy take pictures!? You're a pisser. How could he take pictures in the dark?"

"He didn't, he put the lights on."

Tony shook his head and laughed. "This is all Santronics?" he asked.

"All of it. Mario was right. The place is jammed. You talk with Alfonsa?"

"Yeah, I explained everything. He says if it's there, to go and get it, but you're not gonna believe this. He wants it brought back here. He wants it to look like those scumbags returned it for credit cause they couldn't come up with the dough."

"You gotta be kiddin'. You pullin' my leg or somethin'?"

"No, he's serious. I asked him if he was sure and he jumped all over my ass for questionin' him. It's got somethin' to do with O'Day. Did he ever mention that he knew Alfonsa?"

"Never! How the fuck does a guy like that have juice with Alfonsa?"

"Beats me," Tony answered, putting his arms up in the air, "but obviously he does. Well, look, that's what he wants and that's what we gotta do. Did the Rossbaums call yesterday when they didn't get their order?"

"Yeah, the father did. He was pissed off. Can you imagine the balls on the guy? He's mad because we didn't give him more to steal. The prick said I cost him money cause he had to pay the high-low guy. He's stealin' a couple of million and he's moanin' about a hundred bucks. I told him the truck broke down and I'd get back to him about reshippin' the stuff."

"Good, call'm and set the thing up for Thursday, 7 a.m. Tell'm we're gonna put an extra man on with a high-low so he don't gotta bring the black guy in. No sense havin' to whack'm too. I hope Mario was right about all three of 'em bein' there. It'll be easier if we don't gotta start lookin' for 'em. Just in case, make sure everybody's got their home address."

"You want me over there?"

"No. Have Bobby take some people and a couple of high-lows over in Mario's truck. When he opens up, they can grab the Rossbaums and start loadin' right away. You stay here and make sure everything goes OK. I don't need Alfonsa on my ass again. Not like last night. I thought he was gonna get nuts on me. You know how he starts tappin' with somethin' and just stares? Well, that's how he was gettin'. It's got somethin' to do with this O'Day guy. Anyhow, tell Bobby to call you when Mario's leavin' so you can start another trailer from here."

Manny said there wouldn't be any problem. "It won't take more than three hours."

"Good, but make sure the trucks don't get backed up over there, we don't want anybody gettin' nosey. As soon as it start comin' in, get the paperwork goin', receiving reports, inventory sheets, the whole bit. It's gotta look legit, like they returned it themselves."

"You know Tony, I was thinkin'. It might be good if we got those mutts to sign somethin', like a letter maybe."

"We're gonna. Tell Bobby and Mario some of my people will be behind 'em on the way over. They'll handle the two kids and the old man after Bobby grabs 'em up. They'll have 'em sign a letter and give it to Mario to bring back here. Make sure he gives it to you."

"I just don't get it," Manny said, shaking his head and pouring another coffee container full of liquid breakfast. "How do you figure this business with Alfonsa and O'Day?"

"Look," Tony said, getting up to leave, "I only work here, but if you want you can ask him yourself Thursday night. He wants you should bring O'Day to my place at 10 p.m. Make sure you have all the paperwork on this with you, and the letter. Go figure, right? Well, I gotta go home and get some sleep. This job is killin' me."

"Tony? What's gonna be with the Rossbaums?"

"Forget about it."

Part 11

The shrillness of the alarm clock ripped through Harry's head like a root canal that had gone terribly wrong. Slowly, and with great effort, he managed to move one arm to turn it off, but instead of finding the clock, he found his fingers in a dish of crusting potato salad, stale pieces of rye bread, and curled slices of dried, Lebanon bologna.

"What the hell? Where am I?" he moaned.

Again, with considerable effort, he got his eyes open and saw he was on the living room couch along with an empty whiskey bottle, several partially filled beer bottles, and a piece of creamed, pickled herring that his weight had smeared over the center cushion. Mercifully the alarm ran out, and as he lay there, he wondered if it might be easier committing suicide rather than making the Herculean effort it was going to take to live through the day's hangover. Once before, when he was a kid, he'd felt like this. His mother had taken him to have his tonsils removed and when he woke up form the ether, he thought he was paralyzed. He couldn't even move his face.

"Oh man, this is gonna be a bad one," he said, stumbling into the kitchen.

If he was going to make it to work, he'd have to start drinking again, and right away because the shakes and sweats had already begun. There was an unopened quart of orange juice in the refrigerator, half of which he poured down the sink and refilled with vodka. The first swallow came right back up, mostly through his nose, but gradually his system allowed enough of the alcohol to stay down and he started feeling better. The secret was to take smaller swallows and to hold your nose.

The hard, stinging bite of the shower felt good hitting him in the face, but it was also letting the memory of the previous day's painful events seep back into his booze soaked brain.

That bastard, Ira, he thought, reaching out of the shower for another swallow. The best job I ever had and it's finished. Wait until the word gets around about how Premiums scammed us, my name will be mud. I'll be lucky if I get a job pumping gas. Well at least I don't have to worry about money—which he didn't. The sale of his mother's house had netted him a nice piece of change thanks to Alfonsa Ponzinno.

If he did get fired, Friday night would be as good time as any to tell Diedra. They were scheduled to go see a movie. Afterwards, he figured he'd take Diedra to O'Banion's for a couple of drinks, and then tell her. Who knows, he thought, maybe between now and Friday, some miracle might happen and he wouldn't have to suffer the embarrassment of telling her she was going out with a flake.

As for telling her about the other things, like being followed, the shooting, and the Secret Service agents being torched, who the hell knew what was going on, so why mention them at all? If she asked him questions he wouldn't be able to answer them anyway. Why bring her into it?

He got a refill and went into the bedroom to dress. They'd been talking about more snow so he put the TV on to get the weather.

"As part of his goodwill tour, the president and first lady seen here, spent yesterday in Tokyo shopping for their daughter's upcoming graduation.

"Before departing on Air Force One, they attended a 65th birthday celebration for Sugomu Nagakura, president and CEO of Komti, Ltd., one of Japan's largest and most diversified industrial companies."

Harry's ears perked up when he heard the name Komti.

"During the celebration, Mr. Nagakura was presented with the World Achievement Award in recognition of his New Suns Foundation's work over the years on behalf of Hiroshima and Nagasaki radiation victims and their families. Mr. Nagakura told the gathering that the foundation's work was to honor his wife, his children, and the sixteen members of his family who were incinerated when the Americans dropped the first atomic bomb.

"The new Suns Foundation provides the victims of both blasts and their families with free medical treatment for life, including plastic and reconstructive surgery for the badly disfigured. Mr. Nagakura's worldwide companies also provide them with jobs, if they are able to work. To date, he said, more than 30,000 people have received assistance and many of the young men are presently employees. He likes to refer to them as his 'New Sun Samurais.'

"Noticeably absent from the festivities were any officials of the Japanese government."

"Well I'll be," he said to himself, turning off the TV, so that's Mr. Komti himself. "Not much to look at."

Finished dressing, he checked the stove, turned off the lights, and left, but not before making sure the Beretta and extra clips were in his briefcase. The one sure cure for a bad hangover had always been greasy bacon and eggs, greasy potatoes, greasy toast, and a half bottle of catsup, so he bought the newspaper and headed for the diner on Queens Boulevard.

Football scores and yesterday's racing results were the only things he ever looked at. Everything else was "dreck", rubbish, trash, as Ira would say. Today however, something at the top of the front page caught his eye. In a little box, surrounded by stars, was a mini prologue to an article by Freddie Sorrinson, one of the city's feistier reporters. It was titled "FUNNY MONEY, KOMTI TO D.C." and it had to be more than mere coincidence that the paper had elected to run it while the president was visiting Japan.

Sorrinson talked about the growing allegations that foreigners had funneled money into the president's reelection campaign through a series of bagmen and bogus organizations. He specifically mentioned the charge made by Americans Together, Inc., alleging the president had personally taken more than $3 million from Sugomu Nagakura, head of Komti, Ltd., and a former colonel in the Imperial Japanese Army during World War II.

In conclusion, Sorrinson urged the American people to contact their elected officials and demand they force the attorney general to appoint not one, but three special prosecutors to a blue ribbon panel to investigate "the stench in the White House."

Directly below the story was an editor's note. "Since Mr. Sorrinson's articles about alleged illegal campaign contributions began appearing in this paper, both he and this editor have received numerous death threats, two of which the New York City Police Department and the FBI consider serious and are presently investigating."

"Just in case you forgot my number," the shapely, mini-skirted waitress whispered as she lay the check down on the table, along with a small, white card, "Ammie, 555 7146." Not being able to recall exactly what had transpired during their last get-together, he mopped up the remaining mixture of egg yoke and catsup with a piece of toast, left a $10 tip, quickly paid the bill, and left the diner before "Ammie" came back.

*   *   *

Not that he thought going over to Premiums' Long Island City warehouse would accomplish anything, but he made the trip anyway. If nothing else, it might give some vent to his feelings of anger and helplessness. What if the prick Rossbaum and his sons are there? he thought. I got the gun. Maybe I could make them pay, or give back the inventory.

The more he thought, the more he realized how ridiculous he was getting, and the harder the finality of the situation slapped at his face.

With the exception of a few early morning deliveries being made to other parts of the huge warehouse building, the section rented by the Rossbaums was closed tighter than a drum. Disheartened and frustrated, he sat staring at the dirty red brick structure and grudgingly accepted the fact that there would be no getting back the inventory, no grabbing the Rossbaums by the throat, no getting paid, and no more job as Santronics.

The only thing left now was to go to the office and call the company's lawyers and break the news to them, then, wait for the ax to fall on Friday.

*   *   *

Before he even turned the lights on, Ira's secretary was in his office saying her boss had called; he was sick and might not be in for the rest of the week.

"Do me a favor, Mary? Call your boss and tell him if he's not at the meeting on Friday I'm coming to his house and I'll tie his miserable ass to the roof of my car. Would you do that for me, please, Mary?"

"Yes, sir! At once, Mr. O'Day." Shocked, she scurried back to her desk.

As difficult and depressing as it was, during the next two days he managed to get a lot accomplished, but all the while feeling like he was attending his own wake. Ira sent a message saying he'd be at the meeting.

Late Thursday he received a copy of a memo from Kiedelman to Ira reminding him to bring all the Premiums' paperwork to the meeting at

Komti. Messrs. Yamatoki, Shihoto, and Mishimia also got copies. Sure, Harry thought, the weasel wants to make sure there's an audience for our execution. What he didn't know was that Kiedelman had already been to his own execution. At 6:30 that morning, two of the Do Nothings had slipped through an unlocked deck door at Kiedelman's Long Island home and dropped a radio into his bathtub.

In the past, Kiedelman had been repeatedly cautioned about over-stepping his authority, and about sticking his nose into places where it didn't belong. However, being the jerk he was, he either wouldn't, or couldn't stop. Now he'd done it once too often.

Kiedelman's demise was a direct result of his excessive, compulsive nosiness, and his arrogant, irritating, Nazi attitude. With deliberate sarcasm, he liked to use the term "little people" when referring to any-one he thought wasn't on his own level of imagined importance. How fitting that his death should have been expedited by a switchboard operator and a $4 an hour clerk, each making a simple error.

Whatever projects Komti's technicians were working on in those well-protected rooms, all of their materials came directly from Japan. It came in sealed metal containers about the size of a suitcase on the same ships as the regular Santronics merchandise. Santronics paid Plenum Trucking an extra fee to pick them up at the piers, or airports in a spe-cial van. Supposedly they contained delicate electronic equipment and parts Komti didn't want getting banged around inside a trailer, or truck. At least one technician and two of the Do Nothings accompanied a van when it was sent to make a pickup.

The five other Santronics warehouse centers in Atlanta, Boston, New Orleans, Chicago, and San Francisco also had research facilities and received the same kind of cases. Again, whoever was doing the trucking provided a special van.

When Komti was still in the process of opening these regional warehouses, Tony Trucks had graciously traveled to each city with company executives and introduced them to trucking business associates of his.

"These are friends of mine," he'd say, "and it would be to your advantage to let them handle things here for you like I do in New York."

The Japanese were not deficient in worldly wisdom. They knew exactly who and what Tony Trucks and his friends were, but they weren't concerned about it. Expediency in establishing warehouse centers in the six major cities, and gaining control of the huge, expanding home electronics entertainment business in America was first on Komti's list of priorities. Banging heads with Tony and his associates would have been self-defeating. Besides, the premium they'd pay to make sure their merchandise was unloaded from their ships, trucked to their warehouses, and then delivered to the point of sale, was a drop in the bucket compared to what they would make.

The financial benefit of such a business relationship was mutual. In addition to the inflated fees Komti paid the trucking companies, the employees of the warehouse centers provided a ready-made market for loan-sharking, numbers, sports betting, the selling of swag, union dues, and access to union pension funds.

*   *   *

Only once had Komti's technicians in New York needed something and for reasons unknown, couldn't wait for it to come from Japan. Contacting an American company on their own, they gave Thermol Vanguard a small order with explicit instructions that any invoice or communication in any form, had to be directed to S. Yamatoki, vice president, corporate accounting.

Kiedelman's fate was sealed when a clerk at Thermol called a few months later about the invoice which somehow had been overlooked for payment by Yamatoki's staff. The clerk, on the job just three days, asked to speak to someone in accounting, and the switchboard operator not yet fully recovered from a weekend roll in the hay with her married boyfriend, gave the call to Kiedelman, accounts payable manager.

The kid explained about the invoice and asked when his company might expect payment. Not having the slightest idea who Thermol Vanguard was, and annoyed that such a trivial matter had been referred to a man of his importance, Kiedelman said, "Look, just send me a copy of the damn thing and I'll have someone take care of it."

A week later he received the copy. Most of the items listed were described in such technical mumbo jumbo that he couldn't understand what the technicians at Santronics in Brooklyn had bought—all except three:

> four (4) radiation badge detectors
> two (2) replacement heads and cords, Thermol geiger counter, model TGI-A1100
> four (4) leadlined radiation disposal cylinders, model RW3-0005

"What could they possibly need this type of equipment for?" he asked himself, and it was then he made the mistake of going to Yamatoki with the copy of the invoice.

"Where did you get this from, Max?" he asked with a smile. "Have you shown this to anyone else?"

"No, I just got it in the mail. Who is Thermol Vanguard?"

"I have a meeting to attend Max, but why don't you come up tomorrow morning. We'll have tea together and I'll tell you all about this. I'm sure you'll find it quite interesting. Leave the invoice with me Max and I'll look it over. Thank you, Max."

Kiedelman never got his tea, instead Yamatoki had two of his Do Nothings give him his own radio.

Part 12

At 7 p.m. his secretary brought in the last of the dictation. "I'm going now boss. Don't stay too late. You don't get overtime like me."

"Thanks for staying, Connie, I appreciate it."

"That's OK boss, only the next time you're gonna have to take me to dinner," she said, trying to make it sound like she was kidding, but he knew she wasn't. Connie often dropped subtle hints that it would be all right if their relationship extended beyond regular business hours, and more than once he'd come close to accepting her offer of some discreet companionship. Fortunately, every time his zipper had tried taking over his brain, he'd managed to talk some sense into himself.

"You're nuts, O'Day, you know that?" he would always tell himself. "You're in a new job, you're married, for at least the time being, the girl is married, and you're lookin' to mess around."

One night her husband came to pick her up at the office and he thought the guy was a real putz. They were going to his mother's house for dinner which they did several times a week. Rather than being home rolling around in bed with her, Putz was drying dishes at momma's place. That was Connie's biggest problem—not getting enough.

Zaftig was how a dealer visiting his office had once described her. Meticulous when it came to her appearance and personal habits, she stood 5' 10" or so in heels and had long flowing, blond hair like the girls in the TV shampoo commercials. Large breasted, and full in the hips, physically, they would have given each other a run for their money in bed. He enjoyed the way she smelled when she sat close to him taking dictation, and the way the aroma lingered for awhile after she'd gone back to her desk.

And he liked the way she knew him. Though not sexual, their relationship was still intimate. She knew when to nudge or reprimand him, and when not to. She knew when he was hung over and in need of some special tea from the restaurant. She knew when he needed a sandwich during the day and what he liked on it. And she knew that whatever went on in his personal life, or in the office, especially what he said to people over the phone, wasn't to be repeated.

If he hadn't gotten serious with Diedra, eventually he would have started up with Connie, married or not. But after Friday, the whole subject of what might have been between them was moot seeing how he'd no longer be employed at the company.

After she left for the night, he started proofreading the letters, but something was bothering him. It had been ever since he'd read Sorrinson's article. Swiveling around to the long, wooden worktable behind him, he took the newspaper out of his briefcase and read it again. He'd underlined the part about Sugomu Nagakura having been a colonel during the war.

"Nagakura? Nagakura? I've seen that name someplace before besides on the TV." he said to himself. Not being able to remember things like that annoyed him. Like when he couldn't think of an actor's name when he was watching an old movie. Invariably, he'd remember at 3 a.m. when he was stumbling to the head.

Engrossed in the paper, he didn't know Manny was standing in the doorway until he spoke.

"Whatta ya gotta do to get a drink around this place?" he asked—his throat sounding like he'd been eating sand.

"Jesus Christ, Manny, you scared the hell out of me," he said, spinning around in his chair. "You'd make a good cat burglar. Whatta you sneakin' around up this end of the building for, Bobby throw you out or somethin'?"

Taking a bottle and some paper cups out of the bottom desk drawer he said, "Here, try something decent for once."

"You like this Bushmills stuff, no?" Manny asked, making short work of what his friend had poured. "I like Carstairs myself."

"Manny, drinkin' Carstairs rather than Bushmills is like drinkin' mouthwash instead of champagne. Whatta you pay for a quart of Carstairs anyway? About 60 cents, or is it less now that they're putting turpentine in it?"

"You know in the old days," Manny said, handing his cup back for a refill, "I used to make my own stuff. My old lady would get pissed off if I spilled it cause it could take the paint off the furniture. I see that prick Ira hasn't been in lately. You don't need him anyway, right?"

"Whether I need him or not isn't gonna matter after tomorrow."

"How come?"

"You know, I told you. I got that thing up at Komti. After that I'm history. So is Ira."

"Yeah, that's what I come to see you about. There might be a way for you to square things with those jokers."

"In your dreams, Manny, in your dreams, It's over, finito, kaput. You don't lose that kind of dough and just get a slap on the wrist.

Manny got up, closed the office door, and sat down in the chair next to the desk.

"First, I gotta tell ya," Manny said, "you're a nice guy and all that, but if you ever run your mouth about what I'm tellin' you, you could get hurt. I mean hurt bad."

Harry was ready to laugh until he looked into Manny's face and knew he wasn't kidding around. His eyes had narrowed and there was a threatening, ominous look about them.

"You know Alfonsa Ponzinno?" Manny asked in a low voice.

"I lived next door to him when I was a kid. In fact, when my mother died I sold him her house. What's this all about?"

"You ever work for him, maybe do a favor for him or somethin'?"

"No. When I was a kid I used to shovel snow by his house, but other than that, I never did anything for him, except like I said, I sold him my mother's place."

"Well, then I don't understand why he'd doin' this."

"Doin' what? Manny, please, what the hell are you talkin' about?"

"You know that I work for Ponzinno, right?"

"No. I thought you worked for Bissetti."

"I do, Tony works for Ponzinno."

"For Christ's sake, Manny, this is startin' to sound like who's on first. Would you please explain what's all this got to do with me."

"Mr. Ponzinno wants to have dinner with you tonight. He's gonna tell you how he might be able to help with this Premiums thing. I don't know why, but that's what he wants to do. Tony's got a restaurant, did you know that? It's a nice place, down on Knickerbocker Avenue. It's gonna be Mr. Ponzinno, Tony, me, and you."

"You're scaring me, Manny, I've heard some things about this guy and, well, I don't think this is such a good idea. I think maybe you should just thank him for me and I'll take a rain check."

"I don't think so kid. You gotta show a man like Alfonsa respect. If he invites you someplace, you go. Besides, I was told to bring you and if you crap out, you'll make me look bad and you don't wanna do that."

"This is no good Manny, I'm gettin' jammed up here. I got enough problems without gettin' involved with people like him. I mean no disrespect, but let's face it, this guy is a heavy hitter."

"Look, kid," Manny said, leaning closer, "how would you like to stick it right up their asses over there tomorrow? I mean show them you're not just some punk."

"To be honest, I'd give my left nut, but how the hell would I be able to do a thing like that?"

"Take my word for it, if you go see Alfonsa, he'll tell ya how. Look, this could be a good deal for you. You don't got no idea how much juice he's got."

"I suppose I don't have any choice now that you've told me all this, right?"

"You got it. Come down to my place around 9, we'll take my car. We don't gotta be there until 10, but it's better we shouldn't be late. You're doin' the right thing, kid; trust me."

*   *   *

When he got down to the warehouse Manny and his son were out on the dock talking.

"You sure Tony took everything before?" Manny asked.

"Everything, the letter too. How many times you gonna ask?"

"Hey, Harry, how's it hangin'?" Bobby asked.

"Slightly to port, Bobby, slightly to port."

"You goin' out with this old fuck?"

"Yeah, he's takin' me to the last supper."

"All right, all right, that's enough bullshit," Manny said as he started climbing down the ladder into the bay. "We'll be at Tony's if you need me. You got two boxes comin' from Newark at midnight and you gotta send the van to LaGuardia for those cases. And listen, if those pricks start breakin' your balls again about not wantin' our guy drivin', tell 'em to go fuck themselves, and don't send it. See how they like that. One of these days I'm gonna have to straighten those jerks out."

On the ride down to Tony's, Harry didn't say much because the lump in his throat was to big, but Manny never shut up. He rattled on about how much he'd lost that day on the horses, his problems with Bobby, whether or not he should buy a new car, and on and on. Harry was almost glad when Manny said, "We're here."

Annunzio's was busy. He could see people waiting in the lobby for tables, and the bar was packed.

Good, he thought, they wouldn't take a chance on killing me with all these people around.

Manny went past the restaurant, made a left turn at the corner and drove halfway down the block to an alleyway that ran behind it. Ponzinno always used the back entrance and his people would block off both ends of the alley with their cars. Such was the case when he and Manny pulled up.

Two men got out of a car and walked over to them. "Hey, Chichi, what's doin'?" Manny asked the behemoth that bent to look into the driver's side window.

"Same old stuff. What's doin' with you? Is this the guy Mr. Ponzinno wants to see?"

When Manny nodded yes, the monster standing on the passenger side pulled the door open and told Harry to get out and put his hands on the roof of the car. Roughly, and with mitts the size of ping-pong paddles, he made sure Harry wasn't carrying any kind of a weapon. "OK, he's clean," he informed his associate as he walked back to the car he'd gotten out of and moved it just enough to let Manny pull into the alley.

The door had been covered with a heavy metal plate, and as they approached he wondered if Manny would have to give some kind of secret knock like in the gangster movies, and all the time, he was shaking like a leaf. Instead, it was opened just as they reached it by a nicely dressed, whit-haired gentleman holding a gun at his side. They'd barely cleared the sill when the man slammed it shut and secured the three large sliding bolts.

There must have been security cameras in the alley because right inside the door, on a small table, were three TVs and he could see Ponzinno's men moving around outside.

The only light in the room came from a dozen or so cheap looking wall sconces designed in the shape of Cupid holding two electric candles. Four men were eating at a table which had been pushed into the opening between the back and middle room—Tony Trucks' private dining area and office. Anyone trying to reach Ponzinno would first have to go through Tony's people, and then through Ponzinno's personal bodyguards.

Behind the men at the table, leaning against the wall in the corner, he could see several sawed-off shotguns. Two of the men had their jackets hanging on the backs of their chairs and they were wearing shoulder holsters.

Bissetti was sitting at a table in the opposite corner with another man who looked familiar, then he recognized him, it was Ponzinno. He was sure of it, he'd seen his picture in the papers often enough.

"Tony, you know Harry," Manny said.

"Yeah, sure, how you doin'?"

"Harry, I'd like you to meet Mr. Ponzinno," Manny said, pulling him ever closer to the table, like a parent trying to get a reluctant child into the dentist's chair. "Alfonsa, this is the guy we've been tellin' you about, Harry O'Day."

Unlike Bissetti's cold, almost hostile greeting, Ponzinno stood, reached across the table and offered his hand. Like a dummy, Harry stood motionless, staring at it. He hadn't expected to be greeted so graciously by a man of Ponzinno's caliber and reputation. Helped by the presence of Manny's heel on his toes, he gathered enough wits and shook the hand of the infamous Alfonsa Ponzinno.

Harry could feel how soaked the waistbands of his shorts and trousers were from the sweat pouring down his body, and the lump in his throat now felt the size of a tennis ball.

Whatever preconceptions he may have had about what a Mafia boss should look like, they didn't apply to Ponzinno. In his early 60s, he couldn't have been more than 5' 8" tall, and might have weighed 150 pounds. No pinky rings, no Edward G. Robinson cigar, no shiny suit— he simply looked like a nice, quiet, mature gentleman. The dark brown business suit fit well and he had a full head of well-groomed, snow-white hair. On his left hand was a plain gold wedding band and watch.

It was the way Ponzinno glared at him that he noticed the most, like he was looking inside him, studying him, trying to calculate his strengths and weaknesses.

"Thank you for inviting me," Harry said nervously. "I'm not sure why I'm here, but it's an honor to meet you. I thought I'd meet you at the closing, only your lawyers took care of everything."

"Please, sit down," Ponzinno said amicably, his voice having a slight Italian accent. "Thank you for coming on such short notice. I thought this might be a good opportunity for us to meet and discuss a few things. I apologize for not being at the closing, but I had to go out of town that day. It was impolite of me not to be there."

"Please, Mr. Ponzinno, it's very gracious of you to say that, but you certainly weren't impolite. I know a man of your, uh, a businessman such as yourself has to do a lot of traveling. I want to thank you for being so generous."

"Your mother's house, it's in excellent shape. Did you do all the work upstairs in the bath and bedrooms?"

"Yes, sir, except for the wiring."

"I understand you are one of the few who can keep up with Manny here when it comes to taking a drink," Ponzinno said, his face showing just the hint of a smile.

"Well, I've been known to take a drink every now and then." It was obvious the comment had embarrassed him. He'd been called a drunk before, but not so eloquently.

"No, no, don't be embarrassed, there's nothing wrong with it. Sometimes it's good for the nerves. You drink Bushmills, am I correct? Would you care for some?"

"Yes, sir, right now I could use a drink."

"Please, relax, there's no reason to be nervous," Ponzinno assured him, "you're my guest, no one will harm you here." He barely moved his hand but it was enough to bring three waiters rushing to the table from what seemed like nowhere, and within minutes, hurried back with whatever it was that each man had asked for. The cook was also summoned to personally explain what was being prepared.

During the next hour he managed to eat enough of his food so as not to offend his host, but given the acidity level of his stomach, and the sight and sound of Bissetti sucking ugly strands of sauce-covered quid into his mouth, it wasn't easy. Manny had the waiter bring him something American—yellow cheese and bologna on white, with mayo.

The conversation was congenial—horse racing, the weather, how Bobby Ostrow was doing a good job in the warehouse, and there was even some discussion about the allegations involving the president's finances and behavior. Ponzinno asked him if he knew what *coruptio optimi pessuma*, meant and he answered no, that he didn't understand Latin.

"Didn't the nuns teach you?" Ponzinno asked.

"They tried to, but after they broke all their rulers I guess they gave up."

"It means the corruption of the best is the worst of all."

"Obviously the nuns had better success with you than me," Harry replied, attempting to pay his host a complement.

It hadn't been the nuns who'd taught him Latin, Ponzinno explained, but a private tutor he'd hired to help his son when the boy was having trouble in school. He had made a point of sitting in on the lessons so that after the tutor left, he'd be able to continue working with the child.

When they'd finished eating, the waiters brought small cups of black coffee, fruit, a sealed box of cuban cigars, and a long-necked dark-colored bottle of something.

"Do you like wine, Harry?" Ponzinno asked.

"I've never been too crazy for it to be honest, I prefer something a little stronger."

"Here, try some of this." Harry watched as his host poured what looked like India ink out of the bottle.

"Wow! I never had wine like that before," he exclaimed. After a second sip, he asked what kind it was.

"It's homemade," Ponzinno said with a smile. "My father, he's 90 and still insists on making it himself, like back in Sicily. We take him up to the market and then he'll come home and sit for an entire day going through every box of grapes before putting them in the press. He says one bad one could spoil the lot. Now it's too big of a job for him, so we all pitch in, but we've got to be careful. It's important we make him feel like he's the boss or else he gets mad."

"God bless him," Harry said, taking another, smaller taste. "Please, tell your father if he needs help with the press to let me know, but he'll have to pay me one bottle."

"That's kind of you to offer, I'll tell him. You've helped my family before, do you remember? When you were young you would shovel snow for my mother, God rest her soul," he said, making the sign of the cross.

"Yes, she was always very kind to me."

Pouring more wine into both their glasses, Ponzinno said, "She would tell me how well-mannered you were, and when she passed away, your mother brought you to the house to pay your respects. Do you remember?"

"Yes, I do. I remember how scared I was. I'd never seen a, uh, I'd never been to a wake before."

"You were going to say that seeing a dead person scared you. The dead can't hurt you, only the living can. Your mother, God rest her soul," and again he made the sign of the cross, "brought a Mass card—thank you."

There was no doubt in his mind that Ponzinno was everything the papers said he was, and then some. But as he sat listening, watching, and talking to this soft-spoken, affable person across from him, he was having difficulty matching the two images.

Ponzinno took several photographs out from the inside pocket of his jacket and handed one to him. "Do you recognize this person?" he asked.

It was a picture of a young man about his age wearing a priest's collar. The heavy scar tissue around his left eye and sagging lid were quite noticeable as was his badly deformed nose. Without the damage to his face, he would have been good-looking.

Up until now, Tony and Manny hadn't been paying much attention to what Harry and their boss were talking about, but that changed the instant Ponzinno brought out the photographs.

"Here's one of him celebrating his first mass." Ponzinno said, looking dotingly at the picture.

"Mr. Ponzinno, is this your son?" Harry asked.

"Yes, it is," he answered proudly. "His name in Alfonsa Arezzo, that's his mother's maiden name. You helped him once too, a long time ago."

"I don't understand. How did I help him?" he asked, studying the photos.

"Your face, it's scarred for life, like my son's. You got them saving his life. Those punks, sons of puttanas, they wanted to kill him, but you made them stop, you beat them, you hurt them."

"Holy mother of Jesus," Harry said slowly, "so that's what this is all about." That day, when he was 16 and he'd caught two mutts beating the kid behind the garages by his mother's house, it was Ponzinno's son he's helped. Shaking his head from side to side, he sat staring at the photos not knowing what to say.

Bissetti and Manny looked at each other, then at Ponzinno, then at Harry, and then back again at each other, their mouths open, shocked by what they'd heard for the first time. For whatever his reason, Ponzinno had never told either of them he knew the identity of the person who had saved the child's life.

"He's blind in one eye," Ponzinno continued, "and his hearing isn't very good, so it was hard for him in the schools. I made him use his mother's name in case people might want to punish him for being my son. They punished him enough because of his disfigurements. At first he refused, he said he was proud to be my son, to be a Ponzinno!, but I insisted. Do you know that at mass, he prays for the souls of the swine that did this thing to him? May they and their families burn in eternal hell."

Unable to control his hatred, Ponzinno raged as he repeatedly drove a small paring knife into the table until the blade snapped and shot across the room like an arrow.

"Alfonsa, stop!" Bissetti yelled as he stood and grabbed for what was left of the knife. "*Basta cosi!* That's enough, don't do this."

After that the only sound was the air rushing through the overhead ventilating ducts. Once Ponzinno's tirade had started, no one had dared to move, much less speak. It wasn't until he'd returned to his chair and they saw the crazed look on his face begin to fade, that his bodyguards took a chance and got the waiters out of the room.

For what seemed like eternity, he sat staring at the box of cigars until finally, motioning to one of his people, he said, "Chichi, give me your knife." The hulking brute from the alleyway reluctantly approached the table and handed him a large, vicious looking push-button. Almost cowering, others present stood silently and watched as he ran a finger up and down the white, bone handle, turning it from side to side like he was deciding how to best use the weapon. When he pressed the release button, the long, bayonet-like blade made a loud snapping sound causing Chichi to flinch. Carefully, Ponzinno slit the seal on the box.

"Do you smoke cigars, Harry?" He asked calmly. "Here, try one of these. They're excellent, and please, have another glass of wine."

Embarrassed by the noticeable tremor in his hand, Harry removed one of the cigars and leaned forward to light it on the table candle. As he did, it suddenly dawned on him. The gracious, soft-spoken, affable gentleman who was his host earlier in the evening had never existed. It had been smoke and mirrors, theatre, a disguise to hide the monster sitting across from his now.

He was scared, and he had every right to be, Ponzinno wasn't just a gangster, he was a cold-blooded, vicious killer. Yet at the same time, he was fascinated by him, awed by the way Ponzinno made the worst of the men in the room cringe. Harry envied him.

There was a collective sigh of relief when Harry broke the agonizing silence.

"Mr. Ponzinno, please, forgive me if I'm wrong, but I'm sure it was you who paid the roofer for my mother, and my hospital bill, too. Thank you, thank you very much."

"Please," Ponzinno replied, once again disguised as the gracious host, "I should be thanking you. My son is alive and I'm indebted to you. I had my personal physician make inquiries as to your condition and he assured me that you would recover."

Fortunately, he was all right. He'd come out of the fight with eighteen stitches, a face swollen the size of a beach ball, and a headache that lasted for a week. The only problem was the scar, it never faded the way the doctors said it would.

Ponzinno's son hadn't fared as well. The emergency room staff took one look at him and called his mother right away. They said it would be best if she got there immediately, and if there was a family priest, he should come, too. The boy had been beaten so badly they weren't sure how long he was going to live. Before leaving the house, she had the presence of mind to call Manny who in turn, called Tony.

For six days, neither man left the hospital. They slept sitting up in the waiting room and washed in the men's rooms and sink closets. They were both Alfonsa Jr.'s godfathers and when he'd made his first communion, they had both stood as his sponsors. Bissetti had also been Ponzinno's best man.

It wasn't until the chief resident swore the child was out of danger, and until Ponzinno ordered them to, that Manny and Tony finally went home.

Given who and what Ponzinno was even back then, the punks responsible for the attack had signed their own death warrants the moment they laid a hand on the kid. Within hours after the incident, every friend and business associate of the Ponzinno family had people in the street looking for the pair. "No cops, they're not to be touched either," they were told. "Mr. Ponzinno will deal with them."

It was only fitting that it should be some of Bissetti's own crew who grabbed them up late one night outside a bowling alley on Staten Island. The owner of the lanes happened to be his brother and had seen the pair trying to peddle an expensive watch to some guy at the bar. Much to their detriment, the brother was present at a family function when Ponzinno gave the watch to his son as a gift for doing well in school.

Manny Ostrow and Tony Bissetti personally transported the pair upstate, jammed in a car trunk, to a farm Ponzinno owned fifty miles west of Utica. They hung them up from a barn rafter and for a day and a half, took turns beating them with baseball bats, but were careful not to kill them.

At 3 a.m. on the morning of the third day, Alfonsa Sr. drove up by himself and went directly to the barn. Without saying anything to Tony or Manny, he spit on the two bloody pieces of pulp hanging from the rafter, and then used a five foot, steel prybar to lay their skulls open.

After making the gesture of dragging the backs of his fingers under his chin, he got back in his car and drove away.

Manny and Tony raised the concrete lid on the cesspool, chopped up the bodies, and threw in the pieces.

*   *   *

Ponzinno took a large brown envelope from under the table and handed it to Harry. "Is this everything? The letter too?" he asked Tony.

"Yeah, that's all of it," Tony answered. "We had to go lookin' for one of 'em, but they all signed it. By the way, they decided to go visit the farm."

"Now it's my turn to help you," Ponzinno told Harry. "Listen to Tony and Manny, they'll tell you the best way to use this."

Harry opened the envelope and read the brief letter in which the Rossbaums thanked him for taking back merchandise in settlement of their account. It was secured to a batch of Plenum warehouse receiving documents.

Bissetti and Manny understood now what Ponzinno was doing. He was repaying at least in part, a debt long owed by the three of them. He'd done the right thing. Their beloved Alfonsa Jr. was alive thanks to Harry O'Day.

"Well, I want to thank you again for everything," Ponzinno said as he stood. "I have to leave now, but I would like you to think about something. *Fatti maschii, parole femine*, the literal translation is, manly deeds, womanly words, but between you and I, Mr. O'Day, it will mean deeds are more effective than words.

Harry read the letter over and over again turning it from side to side like he expected to find some kind of explanation written on the back of it.

"I'm lost, Manny. When did this all happen? This letter, how did you get it?"

"Look, kid," Manny said, "you don't wanna be askin' a lot of question, OK?"

"Where are they, Manny?"

When he asked about the Rossbaums, Bissetti stood and said, "If you're smart, you'll take these papers and do what you're told. Maybe you should be showin' a little gratitude for what Alfonsa has done for you. All right, look, I gotta go someplace. I didn't mean to yell, we owe you now, for the kid. Manny, you're taken him back to the warehouse, right?"

Bissetti put his coat on and left.

Harry didn't need a program to tell him that the Rossbaums were dead, and suddenly, he wasn't feeling too well.

Like with the two Secret Service agents torched up in the Bronx, he was again involved in murder, maybe not directly, but he was involved. Now it was the three Rossbaums. "What the hell is happening with me?" he asked himself as he gathered up the warehouse papers and put on his coat. "One day I'm minding my own business, doing my job, making good money, and suddenly guys are gettin' whacked all around me, I'm sleeping with a gun, and now I'm having dinner with a bunch of gangsters. This is insane."

"Come on, let's get out of here," Manny said, rubbing himself. "My poor ass can't take these chairs anymore. We can talk in the car."

The white-haired man with the gun put his paper down on the table and got up to let them out. As he passed, Harry glanced at the headline. "Wait, Manny, let me look at this."

VICE PRESIDENT AND FAMILY DIE IN PLANE CRASH

by Payton Jarvis

The question of former vice president Stanley Jeffers' whereabouts was tragically answered yesterday when he, his wife, and their three children died in a fiery plane crash. The small military transport which they were on had just taken off from Centennial Air Force Base in Twin Mountains, Okla. when it suddenly lost power and slammed into a hillside. There were no survivors.

In a highly unusual departure from the military's no comment policy, Maj. Gen. Wendell Horner, commander of the base, told reporters that arrangements for the vice president and his family to stay at Centennial had been made prior to his resignation.

Visibly angry, the general said that in addition to the vice president and his family, dead were the pilot, co-pilot, and twelve Marines. When asked why there were Marines onboard, the general said they had been providing personal protection for the vice president. Asked if he thought the plane might have been sabotaged, and if so, how could that happen on a military base, the general shot back, "Look, the vice president's death is just a small part of a big, stinking can of worms, and now the lid is starting to come off it. You guys had better get your asses back to Washington and start asking some of those politicians why they're sitting on their hands while the country is being put up for sale. You tell them for me that they got a couple of foxes in the hen house and we're not gonna sit around much longer before we turn the coondogs loose."

Asked if he was threatening the United States Government with sedition, the general replied, "Boy, you listen, and you listen good. The American people are the government of the United States and no one else. If they decide to get rid of a bunch of lowlife, backdooring, fornicating pieces of waste, that's not sedition, that's their right guaranteed by the constitution."

*   *   *

On the way back to get his car, Harry listened to Manny's "suggestions" about how and when to use the letter and warehouse receiving
reports, only they weren't suggestions. They were Ponzinno's explicit
instructions as to what he wanted done at the meeting.

"You know what I feel like, Manny?" Harry asked, staring out the
foggy, rain-covered windshield. "You ever see one of them puppets with
all the strings tied to it? That's what I feel like, with you and Tony and
Ponzinno all jerkin' on them."

Inside, he was still fuming over the way Bissetti had talked to him. "If
you're smart," he'd said, "you'll take these papers and do what you're
told," like he was some kind of two-bit, street punk.

How many times had his friend, Mike O'Banion Jr., warned him,
"Harry, you may think it's smart hangin' around those characters, but
believe me, they're like quicksand, they're gonna pull you down and
you're never gonna get out."

Harry had no doubt that Ponzinno was sincere when he'd expressed
his gratitude for having his son alive. Certainly the recovery of
$2,227,000 in stolen merchandise was proof positive of that. Only now
as he listened to Manny, it was becoming clear that Ponzinno had other
things in mind besides the settlement of a debt. The recovery of the
inventory was the beginning of something, not the end.

For his personal benefit, Ponzinno had begun a process that would
establish Harry as a man to be shown respect by the people in charge at
Santronics, a person who had powerful friends, a person not to be tri-
fled with, and if anyone did, there would be retribution.

"This think keeps gettin' deeper and deeper, Manny. I don't know if I
have the balls to go through with it tomorrow." Manny would have
agreed with him about how deep things were getting had he known of
Harry's involvement with Secret Service agents, but he didn't, and
Harry wasn't about to tell him, not if he wanted to stay alive.

"Listen, kid," Manny growled as he threw the roach of one Camel out
the car window and lit another, "these mutts you work for are lookin' to

cut you loose. You really think they give a rat's ass what happens to you? You make good money, right? You got a nice car, a nice apartment. Well, it could be a hundred times better, believe me. All you gotta do is what Alfonsa is askin'. Just go in there tomorrow and do like I explained. A chance like this isn't gonna come along again. Besides, the last thing you wanna do is refuse his friendship."

"I assume that's a polite threat."

"Whatever. Just remember, you're in this thing whether you like it or not. Don't go and do somethin' stupid and fuck everything up."

"Hey, that's nice," Manny said as he pulled along side Harry's car in the deserted parking lot, "you got your own reserved spot. Listen, I didn't get a chance to thank you back there."

"For what?"

"For the kid. Me and Tony never knew who helped him. We didn't talk to the cops that day in the hospital, and the only thing Alfonsa told us was that he'd been beaten up. The kid's his whole life."

*   *   *

He hadn't eaten much at the restaurant and now that his stomach wasn't stuck in his throat anymore, it was talking to him. The deli on Queens Boulevard was still open.

"That looks good, put some gravy on them," he said, watching his friend, Bernie, load brisket onto the sandwiches he'd ordered. Standing at the take-out counter, Manny's words kept echoing in his ears. "You're in this thing whether you like it or not. You're in this thing whether you like is or not."

"Harry! Wake-up," Bernie yelled. "You want french fries or not?"

"Uh, yeah, please, one order. Sorry, Bernie, I got a lot on my mind."

This is the way they worked, he thought to himself, he'd seen it happen often enough—to others. Somehow they'd obligate a person and at a later date, and depending on their needs, would call upon him to perform a service. If he refused, they'd kill him. Manny hadn't said that in so many words, but the inference was loud and clear.

So let's assume, he thought, that I do what they want and I don't get fired, then what? Now I'm bought, now I'm Ponzinno's mole. What next?

"Harry, Wake-up. What's with you?" Bernie asked as he rolled a whole pickle in wax paper and put it in with the sandwiches. "Are you OK?"

"Yeah, fine, sorry, Bernie. How much do I owe you?"

"Nothing, you're the last customer."

The cab, with its driver and passenger pulled away from the curb when he did. Engrossed in his thoughts, he didn't realize he was being followed, again.

*   *   *

"God! What a day," he said, slumping down on the couch. The phone startled him when it rang. "Damn, who the hell can that be?"

"Harry, it's Ira. I've been trying to reach you all night," he said excitedly. "Harry, Kiedelman is dead."

"What? What the hell are you talkin' about?"

"It's true. He's dead. This morning at his house."

"How do you know?"

Ira explained that Kiedelman's nephew called the company. He told them he'd gone to the house like he did every workday to drive his uncle to the train station. When he didn't answer the bell, he went around back and found the deck door open. His uncle was in the upstairs bathtub. Somehow he'd managed to pull a radio into the water while it was playing.

"Oh, Harry, I feel so bad."

"Bad!?" Harry screamed. "What are you, some kind of schmuck? This guy was ready to cut our balls off and you feel bad he's dead?"

"Yes, but…" Ira started to say something.

"Yes, but, your ass! Straighten up and get a hold of yourself. While you've been hidin' in your house, I've been out tryin' to save our jobs."

"Oh!? Saving our jobs?" Ira asked, sounding a little bit less interested in lamenting the loss of his landsman.

He told Ira about the letter and how Plenum had picked up the merchandise.

"Oh my God, Harry, that's fantastic! I can't believe it. What did they say at work?"

"They don't know yet. I'm saving it as a surprise for tomorrow."

"Harry, this is great, now everything can go back to normal."

"Not so fast. If I can save our asses, there's gonna be some changes. You're gonna be the new vice president of the Special Products Division, and I'll be taking over your job, and we'll both be making more money. But as far as things goin' back to the was they were, forget about it, it'll never happen. If I pull this off, you and I are finished, understand? I don't want anything to do with you."

"Harry, I swear, I never meant for you to get involved like this. What happens if they still fire us even after you tell them about the merchandise?"

"That's a good question. You're not as dumb as I thought. You remember two years ago during the dock strike when they had no merchandise to sell? Remember how much they lost? It was millions."

"Yes, they took a terrible beating. In fact they're worried now because there might be another strike. But what's that got to do with us?"

"What if I could guarantee that if there was a strike, they could still get their stuff unloaded and off the piers?"

"They'd probably laugh, or they'd tell you to prove it."

"And if I could, then what?"

"They'd give you whatever you wanted."

"That's right, and there's only one way to find out. Make sure you're at Komti in the morning. When I start talking try and look like you know what the hell is goin' on, but keep your mouth shut, understand? You're in this thing whether you like it or not. Besides, if you get fired, where would you get the twenty grand a year for your kids' tuition?"

He didn't wait for Ira to answer, but just hung up.

By now the grease from the french fries and sandwiches had soaked through the bag. "Boy! Does that smell good," he said, unwrapping everything and dumping it on a plate. "Pickle, mustard, catsup, salt, we're ready." Along with a bottle of liquor and a water glass, he went back to the phone.

"Any snowstorms on the weather report?" he asked as soon as Diedra picked up the phone. He was making reference to the night they'd slept together, thanks to a snowstorm.

"They didn't say anything, but who knows?" she teased.

"I thought I'd check to see that we're still going out tomorrow night."

"Of course, sweetheart, I'm looking forward to it."

They talked for about ten minutes and said goodnight.

While eating his late night grease, he went through the warehouse receiving reports, and every so often, he glanced at the newspaper in his briefcase, the one with Sorrinson's article about illegal campaign contributions.

Nagakura, Sugomu Nagakura, the name wouldn't let him alone. Oh well, he is the president of Komti, he thought, I probably saw it at work. Exhausted, he set the alarm, turned off the light and lay down on the couch.

*   *   *

"Son of a bitch! Son of a bitch!" he kept yelling, as he jumped up and rammed his toes against the leg of the coffee table. The luminous hands of the clock said 4 a.m. "Son of a bitch, that lousy rat bastard," he screamed again, turning on the light and hurrying to his desk. One by one, he ripped through the contents of the drawers until he found what he was looking for. It was Mr. Prior's letter, the one he'd written to his mother after the war, the letter that told how her husband had been murdered, and by whom.

Frantically he turned the hand-written pages until, there it was, the name of the person who ordered the butchering of his father in the prison camp, and then stood by and watched—Col. Sugomu Nagakura, murder, and Sugomu Nagakura, president of Komti, Ltd., his boss, were one in the same.

His entire body trembling with uncontrollable anger, as he lowered himself into the chair next to the desk.

In the early morning false light, he could see the big, fluffy snowflakes hitting and melting against the window. With the backs of his hands he wiped the tears from his eyes and said, "God, if you're really out there, please, I beg of you, help me kill this bastard."

If he'd had the slightest hesitance about giving Ponzinno what he wanted, it was gone. He would do it no matter what the cost. The best chance he'd have of killing Nagakura and revenging his father's murder would be from inside the company.

Part 13

At last, he was out of the tunnel. Now all he had to do was fight his way across town to 8th Avenue, past a hundred or so double-parked trucks.

Komti owned the eighty-five story building on 34th street, but occupied only the top five floors. The rest of the building they either leased or rented to a variety of businesses. Underground parking was a concession, but Komti had arranged for its employees to park free whenever they brought their cars into the city, so that's where he headed.

Two huge, glass doors was the first thing people saw when they stepped out of the express elevator on the 85th floor. The top halves were etched with Komti's logo, a flock of birds flying around the earth, and behind the globe were the slanting rays of the sun.

The second thing they saw through the clear, bottom halves were Laurie's legs—she was the receptionist. A long mahogany table, minus any kind of a modesty panel, served as her desk. Looking from the front, it was impossible to tell if she was wearing anything from the waist down because she always wore miniskirts and short dresses.

"Good morning, Mr. O'Day," she said in her very best Brooklynese.

"Good morning, Laurie, how are you?"

"Just fine, Mr. O'Day, thank you. New suit? You're looking very sharp," she said, leaning just far enough over the table so he could get a better view into her black, push-up bra—not that she needed any pushing up.

He'd never been able to have any real conversation with her because invariably his mind and eyeballs would always become preoccupied with her body. Today, however, was different. Getting little Miss Brooklyn under the covers was the furthest thing from his mind.

"Ain't it a shame about poor Mr. Kiedelman?" she asked.

"Yes, Laurie, it's a real tragedy, we're all going to miss him," he answered, trying hard to sound remorseful.

By now she'd pushed her chair away from the table so he could examine the rest of her. The yellow, knit dress she was almost wearing was so short he could see the crotch of her panties. Laurie kept her job by being "friendly" with several of the company's executives.

"I see by my appointment book that Mr. Senowitz and yourself have a 9:30 meeting with Mr. Yamatoki."

"That's right, Laurie. Has Mr. Senowitz come in yet?"

"Oh yes, he was here when I came in. You might look for him in the cafeteria. He said something about needing a cup of coffee."

As he turned, he saw a man get off the elevator and walk into the lobby. "I'll be damned," he said under his breath. He recognized the guy. It was the white-haired man with the gun from Annunzio's, the one who'd opened the backdoor for him and Manny. Without saying anything, the man handed him a small, folded piece of paper, turned, went out through the glass doors, and disappeared back into the elevator.

> Edgar Maru unloading now, San Fran, pier 12,
> but that could change if you want it to.
>
> M

Cryptic as it was, he understood the message. Manny had already provided him with information about one Komti ship, but was now giving him an insurance policy.

"Hi, Harry," Ira said as he walked up in back of him.

"Good, I was just coming to look for you," he said, pulling him to one side by the arm. "Remember what I told you last night, keep your mouth shut and let me do the talking. We're either gonna come out of this smellin' like roses, or we're history."

"Hello?" Laurie said when one of her phones rang. "Yes, they're both here. Yes, right away. Mr. Senowitz, that was Mr. Yamatoki's secretary, you and Mr. O'Day can go in now."

The "platform of the gods" as Harry called it, was a luxuriously carpeted, slightly raised area with a three-foot high, spindled railing across the front of it. Since it was a corner location, one wall was all glass and the view of the city was impressive. Along the other wall were offices for executive secretaries, and a conference room in which their meeting was to take place. On the platform itself, were six magnificent, mahogany desks, one of which belonged to Yamatoki.

Mishimia and Shihoto were already seated at the long, polished table when he and Ira walked in. Both had yellow legal pads in front of them covered with a lot of numbers and some kind of symbols, and were busy pushing the little beads of their abacuses around. They never came to a meeting without them. At one point, he had become so fascinated by what the devices were capable of, that he'd considered learning how to use one—for handicapping horses.

The way the table had been arranged, it was going to be the Japanese at one end and he and Ira at the other. As they entered, nobody spoke, there was just the customary smiles and head nodding, which was the way all the meetings between the Japanese and their American colleagues started.

The moment Ira sat down he began fidgeting and tapping on the table until Harry kicked him in the leg.

Yamatoki was the last to arrive as usual. Mishimia and Shihoto snapped out of their seats like two jack-in-the-boxes and bowed so low Harry thought they'd hit their heads on the edge of the table. Yamatoki wasn't alone, he'd brought one of the Do Nothings with him. This particular one Harry had seen before hanging around the research room at Santronics' warehouse in Brooklyn. How could he forget him? The guy's face was covered with scars, like he'd been badly burned, and he was missing fingers on both hands. Just like all the other Do Nothings, "Scarface" stared at him and Ira like he wanted more than anything else in the world to cut their throats.

Irritated by the clown's presence, Harry was going to say something, but decided there were more important matters at hand. What he found interesting was the way Scarface obediently held Yamatoki's chair when he sat down. That was the first time he'd seen a Do Nothing show respect for one of the elder Japanese executives.

Shihoto began by reading a brief, matter-of-fact statement about how the company was going to miss Max Kiedelman, and how he'd been a loyal employee. Harry glanced at Scarface who was grinning.

Once the formality and hypocrisy of the eulogy had been dispensed with, Shihoto got down to the order of business.

"As you know, the purpose of this meeting is to review the unfortunate, but avoidable mistakes made by the credit department in the handling of the Premiums Three matter, and the $2,227,000 loss the company has sustained because of those mistakes."

Seething over Shihoto's patronizing, arrogant tone, Harry mashed his teeth and continued embellishing the doodle he'd created on his pad. It was the word "PRIOR" in large, three dimensional letters surrounded by what looked like strands of barbed wire. He remembered saying something to Manny the night before about not knowing if he'd have the balls to go through with Ponzinno's suggestions, but listening to this wiseass, this crony, this Yamatoki stooge, he laughed.

"Excuse me, excuse me," he interrupted, "that's not correct. There is no loss. Ira and I have recovered sufficient merchandise to clear the balance of the account. It's already been picked up by Plenum." As he spoke, he handed out copies of the warehouse receiving reports and the letter signed by the Rossbaums. The three Japanese sat silently staring at the pile of papers in front of them. He'd caught them by surprise and they didn't like it. Things were not going the way they'd orchestrated them. Pissed off best described the expression on Yamatoki's face, not so much at Harry, but at his "boys" for not having known about the return.

Clearing his throat, Yamatoki said, "While the company appreciates your effort…" but Harry cut him short, no longer able to contain his rage now being fueled by the mental image of his father's bloody body.

"I think it's time the three of you woke up. You may think all the people you're doing business with are honest, but they're not, some are crooks, professional thieves who will go to extraordinary lengths to steal from you. The Rossbaums were, I mean, are such people."

Yamatoki snapped something in Japanese to Scarface. Responding with a crisp, abbreviated bow, he distributed copies of Kiedelman's memo.

How do you explain this Mr. Senowitz?" Yamatoki demanded with the attitude of a prosecutor. "Mr. Kiedelman warned you about the account's delinquency yet you continued shipping. Please, if you would, explain that to us, Mr. Senowitz."

"Ira never saw the memo," Harry shot back, "nobody did, it's a phony. Kiedelman planted it in the credit file to cover himself. He could have stopped any further shipments then and there, but he didn't. He's the guilty party here, not us."

"It doesn't excuse the irresponsible manner in which you both handled the account," Yamatoki yelled, scattering the pile of papers in front of him onto the floor. "Regrettably, under the circumstances the company has no choice but to let both of you go."

"Not so fast," Harry said, his face fire red. "What is regrettable is your arrogance and the way Ira and me are being treated. You brought us here to humiliate and insult us, and I demand an apology."

Yamatoki trembled with anger. Mishimia and Shihoto were dumbstruck by what they considered to be Harry's Western insolence. Reacting to the verbal fireworks, Scarface, who'd been sitting off to one side, sprang to his feet and stood next to Yamatoki, like an attack dog trained to come to his master's defense.

Reason having failed, Harry took delight in explaining the terms of the quid pro quo much to the consternation of his openmouthed audience.

For having recovered the Premiums inventory, and for future services, he and Ira were to receive promotions and substantial increases in salary.

Yamatoki and his cronies snickered and spoke among themselves in Japanese. They were mocking Harry and it infuriated him. For a moment, a vision of the three prison guards driving and twisting their bayonets into his father's tormented body flashed before his eyes and he wanted to smash the grins off their faces, to maim them, even to kill them.

"I'm glad you think this is funny," Harry said, sneering and looking at his watch. "I hope you think it's funny when I tell you that fifteen minutes ago the Kara Maru ran into some labor problems at Port Newark and now none of your inventory is being unloaded.

"Fortunately, Mr. Yamatoki," he continued, making every effort to sound sarcastic, "I'm in a position to help you—again. Would you like me to help you, Mr. Yamatoki?"

If looks could kill, Ira and Harry were dead. Yamatoki grunted a command to Scarface who made a brief phone call. When he nodded affirmatively, Yamatoki broke the pencil he was holding sending pieces of it flying in different directions. Even more than Harry's belligerent behavior, it was the fact that the Kara Maru was carrying two of Yamatoki's precious metal containers for the research facility in Brooklyn that had him so furious.

"And just how would you go about helping us solve this problem, Mr. O'Day?"

Harry walked to the phone. Scarface was still standing by it, blocking his access. "Get out of my way!" he yelled. After some posturing,

Scarface stepped aside, and Harry dialed a number Manny had given him the night before.

"Manny, it's me. Yeah, pretty much like you said. OK, I'll call if I need the other one."

Returning to his seat, he told Yamatoki to have his "boy" wait ten minutes and then call to see if the dockworkers had started unloading again.

"While we're waiting," Harry said, "the three of you might want to reconsider my offer, the one you all thought was so funny before. If you don't, there's a good possibility the Edgar Maru now being unloaded in San Francisco could run into some labor problems."

"I caution you, Mr. O'Day," Yamatoki said, slowly rising from his chair, "you are interfering in very serious matters, I warn you, don't do this," and with that, he and his entourage left the room.

"Is that it?" Ira whispered, loosening his shirt collar and wiping the sweat off his face. "I don't understand what's happening. Harry, they're really upset. Are they coming back, or are we fired?"

"They'll be back," he replied, himself opening the top button of his shirt and drying his face with some tissues. "They're in there playing their stupid games, makin' us wait, the sons of bitches. God, how I hate them."

Thirty long minutes later Shihoto came back into the room. "In recognition of your services to the company, we have decided to agree to your, uh, proposal. Your promotions and salary increases will become effective on Monday, and the other warehouse centers will be notified accordingly." That was it, short but not sweet. He'd won, at least for the moment.

Stunned, shaking his head, Ira pushed himself up out of his chair. "I can't believe it," he said, "I just don't believe what's happened here. Did you see the way they looked at us? How in God's name did you know about those ships? Harry? Who's doing this for you?"

"Ira, what I do is m y business, it doesn't concern you. Just be thankful you have a job, and a better one at that—thanks to me. Remember, don't call me, don't come to my office, and whatever you do, don't ever tell anyone about what went on here today. Got it? You never tell anyone about this meeting."

✳   ✳   ✳

The elevator doors closed and he slumped against the wall like he'd been punched. It felt as if every muscle in his body was hurting and twitching from the tension they'd been under, and slowly the enormity of what he'd done began to register. Not only had he succeeded in staying in the company with a promotion and big increase in pay, but more importantly, he'd done what Ponzinno had wanted and was now in a position to ask for his help in killing Nagakura.

But along with his victory had come something else. Yamatoki and his "boy" were now a couple of serious enemies and somewhere down the line, Harry knew they would have to be dealt with, before they dealt with him.

He jumped when the elevator bell rang announcing that he'd reached the parking level.

✳   ✳   ✳

"Let me kill the swine," Scarface pleaded.

"Not yet," Yamatoki said as he repeatedly slid the razor sharp blade of the samurai sword letter opener in and out of its scabbard. "He's obviously found some powerful friends who are in a position to hurt us. No, we'll let this Mr. O'Day enjoy his little game for awhile. But once he's outlived his usefulness, I want you to have our American contacts handle it. In the meantime, do what's necessary to find out who his new acquaintances are."

"What about the jew?"

"Have them both killed, but not until I say so. Soon we won't have to deal with any of these dogs. Now, go and see that the cases get to the warehouse safely."

Part 14

By the time he managed to fight his way back through the tunnel to Queens, it was already 2 p.m. and he decided he'd had enough of Komti and Santronics for the week. Besides, Diedra was expecting him to pick her up at 5 p.m. for dinner and a movie. Also, if the line at the car wash wasn't two blocks long as it usually was on a Friday afternoon, he could stop before going home to shower and change.

Amazing, he thought, as he pulled in, a short line. The guy on the vacuum was very thorough so he took the Beretta with him when he got out. Given what was happening lately, he'd thought about getting a different kind of gun, something powerful, maybe a .45. He could ask his friend Joe Joe about it tonight because Diedra wanted pizza after the movie and he was taking her down to Joe Joe's brother's place in Brooklyn.

"Take it easy! Take it easy!" he yelled at the shabbily dressed, young man who'd just raced his car from the guy with the vacuum to the mouth of the wash, "That's a new car."

As he watched the soapy tentacles begin to do their job, he thought about the wacky twists and turns his life was taking. He was actually living in two worlds. In one, he was indirectly involved in murder, first the Secret Service agents, and now the Rossbaums. He himself was planning to kill someone. In a matter of just a few short hours, he'd gotten a major promotion and increase in salary, made some serious enemies, and done the bidding of a Mafia boss.

In the other, the softer, gentler world Diedra was creating for him, he had to be careful not to involve her in things and not to scare her by saying anything about what was going on. Deep in his heart though, he knew eventually both worlds would come crashing together and he would have to tell her everything, if for no other reason than her own safety.

Of course, the collision could be avoided by either him walking away from Santronics, his vendetta, and now Ponzinno, or by walking away from Diedra, but he had a problem. He'd fallen in love with her, and if he tried walking away from Ponzinno, he'd probably be killed.

"For God's sake, it's about time," he mumbled as the two giggling teenage girls finally got out of the phone booth in front of the car wash office.

"Manny? Yeah, it's me. No, I'm outside in a pay phone. You were right, they bought the deal. What's next? OK, so I'll see you Monday and we'll talk.

"Ira? No, you don't have to worry. I told him I'd break his head if he ever said anything about what went on at the meeting. Besides, he's so damn scared of not having a paycheck.

"Manny, I can't believe how they folded—you were right. They did exactly what you said they would, but they're pissed.

"Me? I'm all right. A little shook-up, but I'm OK. I gotta tell you though, I wouldn't want to do it again.

"OK, look, I got a couple of kids breakin' my balls to use the phone. I'll talk to you Monday."

"Hey! Mister, your car is ready," one of the five men drying it yelled. Stuffing $5 into the tipbox, he drove out of the wash.

"Let's see what the weather is," he said with a smile.

"This has been a WKYB skywatch traffic update, and now the news.

"Japan's prime minister arrived in Washington today accompanied by representatives of several of his country's major industries. They are here for talks with both the secretaries of State and Commerce. This is after his government took the unprecedented action of filing a formal complaint with the U.S. Department of Justice against the president of the United States. The complaint alleges that he, along with other yet unnamed U.S. officials, colluded with individuals in Japan to allow Komti, Ltd. unfair trade advantages.

"In a brief statement, the prime minister vehemently denied accusations that his government funneled illegal money to the president's campaign. He said the idea of helping someone intent upon harming the Japanese people was 'asinine'. On the contrary, he said his government was fully aware of the identity of the person guilty of having passed the funds, and who, in fact, was still doing it. The prime minister said his efforts to rectify the situation were taking longer than expected due to the guilty party's vast wealth and influence among certain members of his government.

'He warned the American people to take care, that their welfare would be better served if a handful of men at the highest level of their government were to resign. When asked to name names, he refused. He did say, however, that he would be reminding the State Department that leases on certain strategic American military bases located on Japanese soil were due to expire shortly and it was questionable whether or not they'd be renewed.

"Turning to local news, Riverhead police have now labeled the death of Max Kiedelman, former executive at Komti, Ltd., as suspicious. Originally, they had called it an accident. Somehow police said, the deceased had managed to pull a radio into his bathtub while it was playing. However, homicide detectives assigned to the case now say new evidence found at the Kiedelman home indicates the possibility of foul play."

Even with a coat on and the windows rolled up, a sudden chill ran up his back. He knew Yamatoki had Kiedelman killed. Why? Who knows, and Scarface was probably the one who did it. He thought about Yamatoki's warning, "I caution you Mr. O'Day, you are interfering in very serious matters." And he realized there was a distinct possibility that he himself could have an unfortunate accident.

*   *   *

Diedra was standing on the porch with a coat over he shoulders talking to another woman when he pulled into the driveway.

"Hi, sweetheart," she said, kissing him as he walked over to them. "I'd like you to meet my neighbor, Marie, she's the nice lady who took care of my cat the night of the storm. Marie, this is the man I've been telling you about, Harry O'Day."

"Goodness, he's a big one, and handsome too," Marie said, in a high-pitched, squeaky, nerve-grinding, horrible voice. She stood maybe 4' 6" tall and looked like a mouse.

"Harry, I have to finish up in the kitchen, then we can go. Would you excuse us, Marie?"

"Oh? Do you have to go already?" Marie pleaded. "Maybe you could come in for coffee. I just made a tray of brownies."

By now Diedra had moved around in back of her friend and was giving Harry the finger across the throat sign indicating that if he valued his sanity, he shouldn't get into any kind of conversation with the woman.

"Well, it's a pleasure meeting you," he said, "but we've got to be going or else we'll be late for the movie."

Reluctantly, Marie let them escape into the house.

"Thank God," Diedra said after closing the door. "She's a wonderful, wonderful person, but she doesn't know when to give up. Let me hang your coat up."

"I love your outfit," he said, taking her in his arms and kissing her several times. "You look great."

She was wearing an expensive looking, tailored, black pants suit, white turtleneck, and high-heeled, black leather boots.

"It won't take me long, there's just a couple of dishes and I have to give the cat some water. I better take my jacket off before I slop it up."

With her back to him, she slipped it off and hung it on one of the kitchen chairs. It wasn't until she turned around looking for a dishtowel that he noticed her breasts. The sweater was a lot tighter fitting than the cardigan she'd worn the night they'd gone to Mike O'Banion Jr.'s party, and she must have had on a softer bra because her nipples were quite pronounced. Her breasts seemed larger too, and when she moved, they bounced and quivered.

"God, you are beautiful," he said.

"Do you like my sweater?" she asked coyly, placing her arms around his neck and leaning into him.

"I can't begin to tell you how much I like it," he said softly, pulling her body tightly against his. She could feel his growing erection and began to slowly move her crotch from side to side. They kissed with their tongues and ran their hands over each other's body.

"Did you ever do it on a kitchen table?" he asked, the thrusts of their tongues and kisses becoming more violent.

"No, but I think I'm about to." she panted.

Nervously, they fumbled with each other's zippers and buttons until he had her nude sitting on the table. "Wait, wait," she said, "pull the shade down, Marie will see us."

The whole thing lasted fifteen minutes and it was better than when they'd made love on his couch, and it was the first time they'd used the words, "I love you" during sex. Afterwards, they showered together.

"We still have some time before the movie starts," he said, holding the car door for her, "so if it's all right, I'd like to stop and take care of something."

"I thought you just did," she said teasingly.

"Be serious now," he said. "Look, this may sound strange after I've just finished ravaging you, but do you know anyplace around here that sells religious things? You know, like for the Catholic Church?"

"Why? Have you suddenly developed a need for religion? Is that what having sex with me does to you?" She was in a good mood and was having fun needling him.

"Miss Shannahan, you're breaking them. What would Sister whatever her name was say if she heard you talking like this?"

"Am I getting you mad?" she asked.

"No, on the contrary, I like when you laugh and fool around. It's good. You're very sexy when you do it."

"Sweetheart, are you serious about the religious store?"

"Very. Someone did me a good turn at work today and his son was just ordained, so I figured it would be nice if I got him something."

"That's a very thoughtful gesture. I like that. You're a good person, and yes, I do know a place. It's called Romano's. I just bought a rosary there the other day for a girl at work. You know the little shopping center just before you get to the movie? Well that's where it is."

Diedra was right, it was a nice place—and big. There were two connecting stores and both were jammed with all kinds of religious articles. It looked like a warehouse for the Vatican.

A short, middle-aged woman dressed in black came over when they entered. Obviously she knew Diedra.

"Everything OK with the rosary?"

"Yes, fine," Diedra answered. "She loved it. She's going on a retreat and I wanted her to have it. Thank you. I have a customer for you. He's looking for a gift for a newly ordained priest."

"Oh how wonderful," the owner said. "I have a brother who's a priest. Did you have something special in mind, or would you like to look around? There's so many beautiful things to choose from."

"No, I know what I want. I'd like you to make three sets of vestments for him. One for daily mass, one for Easter services, and one set for Christmas mass. The chalice and Host plate over there in the case, are they gold plate, or solid?"

Struggling to find her tongue, the owner said, "Uh, yes, the chalice is plated, so is the Host plate."

"OK, when the vestments are done, I want them sent to this person," he said, handing her a piece of paper he'd gotten from Manny. On it was printed, Father Alfonsa Arezzo, Our Lady of Precious Blood, Lac Saint-Jean, Quebec, Canada, 5' 11", 170 pounds. "I want the chalice and Host plate to go with them."

The woman smiled, looked at the paper, then at him, then at Diedra, cleared her throat and said, "Yes, but Mr., uh, I'm sorry, I didn't quite get your name."

"O'Day, Mrs. Romano," Diedra said, "Harry O'Day," herself trying to figure out if he was serious.

"Yes, well, Mr. O'Day, with all due respect," the owner said, "these vestments are all handmade, and the chalice and plate, all these things are very expensive."

Annoyed by her patronizing attitude, and the insinuation that he was unable to afford them, he said, "Look, rather than standing here telling me how expensive they are, why don't you find a pencil or something and come up with a ballpark figure for me."

"Please, Mr. O'Day, I didn't mean it to sound that way."

"Yes, I'm sure you didn't. Do you want the business or not?"

"Yes! Of course. Please, why don't we go back into my office?" Mrs. Romano suggested, suddenly displaying a more congenial attitude.

"May I offer you both something? A glass of wine perhaps, or maybe a cup of tea?"

As they walked to the rear of the store, Diedra yanked on his arm. "Do you have the slightest idea of what you're dong?" she whispered through her teeth. "Is this a relative or something that you're looking to spend so much money? Do you have any idea how much these things cost?"

"I don't have any relatives."

After flipping through a series of catalogs, price lists, and making several phone calls, Mrs. Romano pushed the total key on the adding machine. "Well, Mr. O'Day, including the Host plate, chalice, vestments, insurance, shipping, oh yes, and the tax, we're talking approximately $15,000—give or take."

"Good. I'll give you a check now and when my bank opens on Monday, you can take it over and have it certified. How long is this gonna take? It's important that it's done right away. Do we understand each other, Mrs. Romano?"

"Completely, Mr. O'Day, completely. I can assure you that the work will start immediately and that I'll personally stay on top of this from start to finish—you have my word."

"Fine, I'm gonna hold you to that. If you need more money, here's my office number, call me and I'll send you a check."

On the way back to the car, Diedra, bursting with curiosity, stopped him "Harry, if you don't tell me who this guy is, I'm going to smack you."

"A person who's life I saved a long time ago."

"And you're buying *him* a $15,000 gift? Shouldn't it be the other way around?"

"Not really. This is an investment. I'm gonna have business dealings with his father and the gift is like an insurance policy that everything goes OK. The father is a great believer in people doing the right thing and showing respect."

"Well I gotta tell you, Mr. O'Day, this is certainly some kind of respect you're showing. What kind of business dealings?"

"Nothing for you to be concerned about. He's a very important man and I'm going to ask him to help me with something I want to do. To him, $15,000 is lunch money."

"You're a strange guy, but I've fallen in love with you." They kissed and got into the car.

"Do you know that the movie started twenty minutes ago?" she asked.

"Oh, damn, I'm sorry."

"That's OK," she said, placing her hand high up on the inside of his thigh. "Look, how about we just go for a pie at that place you were telling me about, and then we go back to my house and watch TV or something?"

"That sounds nice." Jokingly he suggested that they invite her neighbor, Marie, over with a plate of her brownies.

"Are you sure you want to do that?" she asked, moving her hand higher.

"Oh well, sorry, Marie, maybe next time," he said, moving Diedra's hand even higher.

*   *   *

Kings Highway was always a busy place by Joe Joe's newsstand, especially on Friday nights. When Harry didn't see him squeezed behind the counter, he double-parked and asked the guy cutting open bundles of Sunday's inserts where he was. The young man said he was having supper down at his brother's pizzeria.

Pizzeria was a misnomer, the word didn't do the business justice. Restaurant or rosticceria would better describe the type of establishment it was.

When his brother, Tommy, was getting the place ready for its grand opening, he reluctantly let Joe Joe pay some artist to paint scenes of the

Sicilian countryside on all the walls. Unfortunately for Joe Joe, the artist had a fixation with donkeys and painted hundreds of them into the murals. Harry remembered being there the afternoon Tommy and his wife came back from a Vegas junket and saw the walls.

"Jesus Christ!, watta you crazy?" he screamed at his brother. "What the fuck is with you and these donkeys?" Tommy was so infuriated he threw Joe Joe out and wouldn't let him back in for a month.

Although he begged Tommy to let him have the walls repainted, Tommy refused. "No, no," he said, "now I want them there. Every time you come in to feed your fat face, I want you should have to look at them. You're just like them," Tommy told him, "an ass!"

The ovens, showcases, and take-out counter were in front by the windows, and the rest of the place was a long, wide room with booths running the length of both walls. Down back were the bathrooms and an immense kitchen.

"Hey! Harry, what's happenin'?" Tommy yelled as he flipped an ever growing circle of floury dough over his head.

"How are you, Tommy? Tommy I'd like you to meet a very special friend of mine, Miss Diedra Shannahan. Diedra, this is Tommy Bonaveddia, better know as King of the Brooklyn pizza makers."

"Hi, Tommy." Impressed with his talent, she asked, "Could you teach me to do that?"

"It's all in the wrist," he answered, tossing the dough even higher, but being careful not to let it get sucked into the big exhaust fan.

"Harry, I gotta tell ya," Tommy said, "you do my place an honor by bringin' such a beautiful woman to it. *Una donna di essezionale bellezze.* Just in case you don't speak Italian, Diedra, that means you're an exceptionally beautiful woman."

"That's very nice of you, Tommy, thank you," she said, her face turning crimson. "It sounds so romantic when people speak Italian."

"He's down back eating with his pals," (the donkeys), Tommy said, using his head to point to the rear of the restaurant. "Tell him his bail of hay is almost ready."

Sidestepping a steady flow of customers and teenage waitresses carrying trays of dishes, they were just about to his table when Joe Joe looked up from his paper and saw them. Quickly wiping the spaghetti sauce and bread crumbs from his face, he struggled out of the booth. "Hey! Good to see you. What's doin'?" he asked, still wiping at his face with a napkin.

"Sorry we're interrupting your super, Joe," Harry said apologetically.

"Nah, it's OK. I was finished—no problem."

"Joe, I'd like you to meet Miss Diedra Shannahan. Diedra, this is an old friend of mine, Joseph Bonaveddia. His only claim to fame is that he's the brother of Tommy Bonaveddia. Other than that, he's a bum."

"Oh, Harry, that's a terrible thing to say," Diedra admonished him. "It's a pleasure meeting you Mr. Bonaveddia."

"The pleasure is mine Miss. Please, excuse me for staring, but you're very beautiful, and call me Joe. Harry, I didn't know ugly guys like you knew people like this.

"Please, sit down." Joe Joe continued. Forgive me, where are my manners?" he said, attempting to wedge his huge body back into the booth. "You wanna see a menu of somethin'? How about a nice glass of Chianti?"

"We're just going to have a pie," Diedra said, "but I think I would like to have something to drink, thank you."

Joe Joe kept them company while they finished off most of a house special pizza and a small bottle of wine. Afterwards, Diedra said she had to use the little girl's room.

"Rose, got a minute?" Joe Joe called to Tommy's wife. On weekends she helped out on the tables, but mostly she was there to keep an eye on the young waitresses and their underage friends who would come in looking to have a beer with their pizza.

"Rose, I'd like ya to meet Diedra, she's a friend of Harry's, why I don't know, but anyway, they're together. How about takin' her upstairs and lettin' her freshen up. OK?"

Rose and Tommy lived up over the restaurant, something Harry never could understand given the fact that he and Joe Joe were probably rolling in money. It wasn't until Tommy took him upstairs one day and showed him the place that his curiosity was satisfied. It was like a palace—nothing but the best, everything from antique, French provincial furniture, to walls full of original oil paintings. Tommy said he'd gotten everything at a discount.

After the women left the table, Joe Joe asked, "You ain't sayin' much, what's up? Those guys again, the ones who followed you? They come back?"

"Those guys," Harry whispered, "turned out to be feds, Secret Service no less. At least they were until somebody torched them the morning after that thing at the stand. Up in the Bronx."

"You gotta be fuckin' kiddin'."

"I wish I was."

"So what were they lookin' at you for? You got your ass in some kind of a jam?"

"Not that I know about. The plate number you gave me? I had a friend check it out and he was the one who told me who they were. But he didn't think I was number one on their hit parade."

"So what else did this guy tell you?"

"This sounds crazy, but he thought maybe they were interested in the people I work for."

"The Japs!?"

"Yeah. Don't that beat all?"

"I don't get it," Joe Joe said, leaning as far over the edge of the table as his stomach would allow. "Why would they be interested in them?"

"Maybe not all of them," Harry answered, lowering his voice to a whisper. "There's a small bunch, real whackos. Maybe it's them. If they are doin' somethin', it can't be anything good, why else would the feds be scopin' them out? The other Japanese act like they're afraid of them. I hope to hell the feds don't think I have anything to do with them. And listen to this. My friend things maybe it was their own people that whacked them."

"Hey, forget about it," Joe Joe said, "feds whackin' feds. That's real spy shit—no?"

"Joe, I was wonderin' about somethin'. I need a roscoe, something heavy—maybe a .45."

"Nah! You don't want anything like that," his friend said, like a parent telling a child he was buying the wrong kind of clothing. "You're watchin' too may gangster movies. They make a racket, and besides, it's like walkin' around with a brick in you pocket. Come downstairs. I got some stuff in yesterday—they're nice."

Flabbergasted, amazed, shocked, were all good words to describe Harry's reaction when Joe Joe unlocked the heavy, metal cellar door. Inside was a swag warehouse par excellence. The wall between the restaurant's basement and the one adjoining it had been knocked out and a series of metal expansion jacks strategically placed under the main, steel I-beam to support the upper floors. There was a conveyor belt coming down from Tommy's street cellar door that he used to take in supplies, but additions had been made to it. Like mini train tracks, a series of rollers ran to different parts of the cavernous room so Joe Joe's people wouldn't have to lift anything heavy when they got a shipment.

Rack after rack of men's suits and women's designer dresses lined the walls, all covered with sheets of clear plastic so they wouldn't get dusty. TVs and stereos were stocked first by manufacturer, and then by model. There were even jewelry cases full of watches and rings so customers could look around for what they wanted when they shopped.

"So whatta your think?" Joe Joe asked proudly. "Just like Macy's, no?"

The sight of all the loot made Harry instantly recall a movie he'd seen once, "Ali Baba and the Forty Thieves," except in the picture the thieves had their stash inside a mountain. Tommy and Joe Joe kept theirs in a cellar in Brooklyn.

"We got every brand except Santronics," Joe Joe said, "you gotta see Tony Trucks if you want your stuff. Come on, they're in the box."

The walk-in refrigerator was massive. When it was very hot, Joe Joe would have his brother put a table and chair in it so he could have his lunch there.

Carefully, Joe Joe took a carton marked shredded mozzarella down off a shelf and started emptying it. Halfway down, under a piece of cardboard and wrapped in wax paper, were a dozen snub-nose .38 caliber revolvers and a dozen boxes of shells.

"This guy always gives me good stuff," Joe Joe said, unwrapping one of the weapons and handing it to his wide-eyed friend. "I ordered two dozen, but this is all he had. Feels good, no?" he asked with all the enthusiasm of a shopkeeper anxious to please his first customer of the day.

"How much?" Harry asked, hefting it from hand to hand.

"Hey, for you, no charge. Here, take another box of shells. Thanks for gettin' me the kid's radio. To tell you the truth, I'm glad to see that you're gonna stop bein' Mr. Fuckin' Nice Guy. I told you, you gotta let people know they can't mess with you. Maybe sometime you could talk to Sally, or did you forget?"

"Well, maybe a little, but things have been crazy. I promise, Monday, I'll call you and find out where he is."

"Here," Joe Joe said, handing him a large paper bag. "put all your stuff in here, people will think you got your lunch. And here, take this cheese, it's good. You and Diedra can make pizza at home, but don't tell Tommy I said that."

Part 15

Outwardly, Monday was a routine day at work following Harry and Ira's confrontation with Yamatoki and his henchman, until late in the afternoon when a special messenger hand delivered their official letters of promotion. That was Harry's cue. "Clean out you desk, Ira." He said. "As of tomorrow morning your office is over in the Komti building."

By Tuesday the other warehouse centers received notification of the changes in New York, and his phone never stopped ringing with people offering congratulations. Connie, his secretary, was especially thrilled when he told her to make Ira's office her own. Connie was one person Harry intended to take very good care of.

Overly protective and motherly, at times to a fault, she could be a real nudge, but at the same time, she was fiercely loyal and knew more about what was happening with the company and to the people in it, than anyone. Also, she had mentioned once that her aunt was senior among the private secretaries on the "platform of the gods" and handled all the travel arrangements for the big shot Japanese executives when they traveled to and from the U.S. That might come in handy now that his hunt for Nagakura had started.

He missed Diedra, so he was glad when 5 p.m. came on Wednesday. They were going to see the movie they were supposed to have seen the previous Friday.

*　　　　*　　　　*

It was the worst movie he'd ever seen. Twenty minutes after it started, he knew the number of steps between his seat and the candy counter. If the heroine wasn't losing her sight, she was losing her mind, or her husband, or some other tragedy was befalling her. Diedra loved it, "Oh, Harry, this is so beautiful, isn't it?" she asked, stuffing another used tissue into her purse.

At times, it was so embarrassing he cringed, but he did have one laugh when he though about "dish night". Under the guise of treating him, his mother and father would take him to the movies—no matter what the picture, and on dish night it was usually a crummy one. But they needed the gravy boat of the meat platter or some other piece. The fun came about every fifteen minutes when someone in the theater dropped a dish and people applauded and whistled.

After the movie mercifully ended, they drove down to Irishtown in Rockaway Beach. Wednesday nights at O'Banion's during the winter were something special. What had started out as an attempt to bring in a little business during the off-season, had turned into a pot of gold. Mike Sr. personally cooked corned beef, boiled potatoes and cabbage, and a local woman would come in and bake dish after dish of Irish soda bread. If that weren't enough to attract the local clansmen, O'Banion brought in two. Live Irish bands, complete with drums, pipes and harp, and had them take turns playing while the people ate and drank.

This was a particularly busy night, so Diedra volunteered to help Mike Sr. prepare servings in the kitchen, and Harry did yeoman service washing glasses and beer pitchers behind the bar for Mike Jr. and his bartender.

While delivering a gigantic bowl of boiled potatoes to the bar, Diedra told Harry that Mike Sr. was flirting with her, and that she was enjoying it.

"I'm beginning to have second thoughts about our relationship, Mr. O'Day," she said laughingly, "maybe an older man would be better for me. But then again, with your promotion and all, well, we'll see, maybe I'll keep you." On the way down he'd told her about getting a big increase in salary and a new position, but nothing about the thing with Yamatoki, or about the Rossbaums. Why get her involved?

Many in the bar were personal friends of the O'Banions. In particular Harry recognized the pair of Victor McGlauglin look-alikes he'd see talking to Mike Jr. in Ryan's out on Northern Boulevard. Every so often, someone would come out of the office with beer pitchers needing a refill, and he'd catch a glimpse of them inside talking to several other men.

Harry's real enjoyment that night came from watching Diedra. Not only had the O'Banions fallen in love with her, but many of their friends had taken a fancy to her as well. Gradually it became known she was the wife of a New York City policeman killed on the job. That, plus her name, Shannahan, automatically entitled her to acceptance into their close-knit world.

*   *   *

At midnight they started for home. "My place is closer," he said, waiting for the coins to find their way into the automatic tollbooth machine. "What would Marie say if you called and asked her to take care of your cat?"

"She'd say yes, and then she would ask if I was going to sleep with that nice Mr. O'Day."

"And what would you tell her?"

"I'd tell her it was possible."

In what seemed like not time they were backing into a parking spot across from his apartment building.

"Your football jersey came back from the laundry yesterday," he said, leaning toward her.

"Do I have to wear it?" she teased.

Gently pulling her head back by her ponytail, they began to kiss and fondle each other.

"You get so hard," she murmured, reaching to undo his belt.

"All I have to do is look at you and I get hard," he whispered, enjoying the feel of her touch.

"Wait, wait a minute," he told her, moving her hand away.

"What's wrong? Am I hurting you? I'm sorry."

"No, you're not hurting me, it feels good. It's not that," he said, watching the car that had turned slowly into the block up at the intersection. It parked about a hundred feet in front of them on the opposite side of the street under the light, and he could see it was a four-door sedan, maybe light brown, or beige.

"What's happening? Do you know them?" Diedra whispered as two men in dark coats got out and looked up and down the empty street.

"No, I've never seen them before, but I don't like the was they're lookin' around." He watched as they disappeared down the alley alongside his apartment building.

"Maybe they just moved in or something, and you don't know them yet."

"I don't think so. I've seen that kind of a car before though, down in Brooklyn. And that prick Longdon had one like it too."

"Harry! Look, up there, in those windows," she said excitedly, do you see those lights?"

"Son of a bitch! They're flashlights, and that's my living room."

"Oh my God, they've broken into your apartment. We have to call the cops. Jesus, you were right about them."

"Easy, easy, calm down, they can't hurt us as long as we stay here. Do you know how to use a gun?"

"Yes, Terrence taught me how to fire his service revolver. Why, do you have one?"

"Yes, and don't start askin' a lot of questions, now's not the time, right now we got a real problem. Here," he said taking the Beretta from under the driver's seat, chambering a round, and handing it to her. "You see this? This is the safety, on, off, on, off, got it? And this is how you drop the clip with this little button here. Got it? Here's another clip, put it in your pocket. Be careful, the safety's off the gun."

"I've fired this kind too," she said to his surprise. "Terry had one. He called it his throwaway piece or something like that. Harry we gotta call the cops!"

"We're gonna, right now, from the bar on the corner. Get out and start walkin' down the block, but stay up against the buildings. I'll be right behind you. I gotta get somethin' from the trunk."

"Damn, damn, damn," he said, mad at himself for shaking so badly, but finally managing to get the right key into the trunk lock. Fumbling in the darkness, he found the .38 and a box of shells Joe Joe had given him and started down the block after Diedra. Three bullets fell to the ground as he struggled to load the weapon, but he kept going.

"OK, walk in slow," he told Diedra, "the phone's down back by the pool table. Act normal, I'll order a couple of drinks."

"Normal!? Are you nuts? I'm going into a strange bar full of strange men with a loaded gun in my pocket, and I'm supposed to act normal?"

"O'Banion's, Mike Jr. speaking."

"Mike, it's Harry. Listen, I'm in the bar on the corner of my block with Diedra. There's two guys tossin' my apartment. Yeah, I'm sure. They went in through the alley just as we got here. Yeah, I can see their flashlight behind the blinds."

"OK, lad," O'Banion said calmly, "where's your car? Good, go back and get in it, lock the doors, and wait for me. I'll be there in thirty minutes. If they leave before I get there, don't try and stop them, and don't follow them. See maybe if you can get a plate number."

"Mike, it's the same kind of car those guys in the Bronx got torched in. Should I call the cops from here?"

"No! The only was we're gonna find out who these fuckers are is to grab them ourselves and have a wee chat with them. It'll be best if there's no paperwork just in case things get out of hand."

It was less than thirty minutes when they saw Mike's car pull into the curb up the next block right at the corner. Mike and another man got out of the front, and the two Victor McGlauglin look-alikes climbed out of the back. Both had what looked like heavy sticks which they put under their coats. All four men crossed the intersection and started up the street.

"Don't be frightened lass," Mike said reassuringly as he leaned down and spoke through the driver's side window. "Still up there?" he asked Harry.

"Yeah, I see their flashlights every couple of minutes. They must really be pullin' the place apart. Sons of bitches."

Mike said they'd wait and take them down after they came out and were getting into their car. "If there's any shooting," Mike said, "take off, we'll handle it. Go back down to the bar. I told Da what's happening and he'll know what to do."

Harry and Diedra watched as Mike took a bar of soap from his pocket and drew a large penis and testicles on the windshield of the sedan. Then he picked the lock of the car in front of it and got in, along with his associate. The leather jacketed pair broke into the car behind the sedan, and as they got in, Harry could see the large sticks they'd put under their coats were sawed-off shotguns.

It was only a matter of minutes before the intruders appeared at the head of the alley, looked around, and headed for their car.

"For Christ's sake," the shorter of the two moaned, putting his hands on his hips, "will you look at this." In seconds, Mike and his companion were on them, pushing their weapons hard up against the faces of the bewildered burglars.

"Police," Mike yelled, "move one fucking muscle and you're dead."

Simultaneously, his other two men came up behind the pair and smashed the butts of the shotguns into their backs, sending them sprawling to the pavement. Once down, both were repeatedly kicked. The shorter of the two made the mistake of reaching inside his coat which earned him an exceptionally vicious kick in the face, breaking his nose and cheekbone.

"OK lads, that's enough," Mike said, holstering his gun, "I think we have their attention. Get their guns and cuff them."

"You dumb bastard! Do you have any fucking idea who we are?" the taller one groaned.

"You'll speak with a civil tongue in you head," Mike said, driving the man's face into the dirty pavement with his foot. Now, tell me, who might I be having the pleasure of addressing?"

Barely able to speak with Mike's huge foot crushing his face against the ground, the man said he and his partner were Secret Service agents.

"Ah, and that's a fine job now to be sure," Mike said patronizingly, "and how would I be knowin' you're tellin' the truth?"

"Look in my wallet you fucking jerk." Mike kicked him in the face knocking him unconscious.

"OK lads, we'll each take one. Blindfold them and get them loaded. Let me have their wallets."

Mike walked back to Harry and Diedra and said they should follow him, that he was taking the two men down to a garage on Flatlands Avenue to continue his conversation with them.

*   *   *

With Mike in the lead, the McGlauglin look-alikes in the middle driving the agents' car, and Harry and Diedra bringing up the rear, the caravan came to an abrupt stop in the middle of what seemed like nowhere. Diedra gasped at the sight of several large rats caught in the glare of the car's headlights. Frightened, Harry and Diedra watched as one of Mike's men undid the lock on a high, chain-link gate.

Once inside, they bounced violently along a rutted, muddy road lined with hundreds of junked autos waiting their turn in the crusher. In some spots, they were piled four high, like mountains of dirty, twisted pieces of metal. The O'Banions owned the business, and it was one of may such operations in an area that took up ten square city blocks.

Their final destination was a scarred, dilapidated, cinder block building surrounded by mounds of salvaged tires and bumpers. Mike got out, went through a small door, and activated the motor for the overhead door. Inside, he suggested that Harry and Diedra go and wait in a room that served as an office.

"OK! Now, let's see what we have," Mike said, handing his weapon to his partner.

The McGlauglin twins opened the rear doors of the cars, dragged the handcuffed pair out by their collars, across the greasy, stone floor, and slammed them down on a couple of wooden crates.

"Take the cuffs and blindfolds off," Mike said, reaching into his pocket for his guests' wallets.

"Now, it says here that one of you is Mr. Robert K. Huxley, and that you work for the Secret Service. Which one of you might that be?" The bigger of the pair said he was.

"That's a fine English name Bob. Would you be havin' any relatives in Belfast now? Say in the British Army maybe?"

"Do you have any idea how much trouble you and your jerk-off friends are in?" Huxley asked, still defiant. "Do yourself a favor and tell the leather boys over there to dump those shotguns and let up go."

For a moment Mike looked at him and smiled, and then drove his massive fist into his face splitting both lips and loosening several teeth.

The impact of the punch sent Huxley tumbling backwards off the crate and up against the front wheel of one of the cars.

"Pick him up," Mike said, using a rag to wipe the man's blood from his hand. "I would suggest, Mr. Huxley, that you try and be more sociable. What were you doing in that apartment?"

"Go fuck yourself, Patty," Huxley managed to say even though his mouth and face were badly swollen.

"And it's Patty now that you would be calling me. Tell me, would you be usin' that in a derogatory way?"

"If the shoe fits," Huxley snarled belligerently, trying to stem the flow of blood from his mouth and nose.

"If the shoe fits!? If the shoe fits?!" Mike bellowed, pulling the agent up by the ears and driving his knee into his groin. Huxley's contorting body slid to the cement like melting butter.

"Pick him up."

"You know, Bob, when the Brits drove my great grand Da off his farm and killed his animals, they called him Patty. Did you know that now?"

"You're crazy, do you know that? You're fucking insane," Huxley said, in terrible pain and fighting for breath. "I'm warning you, before this goes too far, let us go, or you're gonna be four sorry asses."

With the flat of his foot, he kicked Huxley in the chest, sending him somersaulting backwards onto the floor and then continued kicking him in the head.

"Don't Mike, not yet," one of the McGlauglin pair yelled, barely managing to pull him off the agent. "Let's see what he knows first."

"Aye, right you are lad, right you are," Mike said, slowly regaining his composure.

"Well, well, well," Mike said as he searched the trunk of Huxley's vehicle, "will you look at what we have here." In plain view, next to an empty gas can, was a license plate. Flipping through several pages of his casenote pad, he found what he knew he would. The number of the plate in the trunk of Huxley's car matched the number Harry had given him. Using evidence bags from his car, he carefully packaged the plate, the agents' .45 caliber weapons, and their wallets, and then used newspaper to wrap around the gas can.

"Now, Mr. Huxley, perhaps you can explain why it was necessary to murder your own people." Mike waited for a reply, but got none. "No? Not talking? Good. I was hoping you wouldn't. Do either of you have pets? I do. I keep them here, out back in the yard for security. Would you like to meet them?"

As he started out the rear exit, Mike told his partner to take the agents' jackets and lay them on the ground next to the door.

"Oh God," the smaller of the two agents cried the second he heard the dogs. Mike's men began to laugh.

Even with his great size and strength, Mike had difficulty restraining the two grease-and mud-encrusted German shepherds fighting each other to get through the door first. Snarling and barking, their faces were covered with dried blood from the rats they'd been eating.

"Easy now, lads, easy," Mike said, "there's plenty for both of you. It's fine English beef you'll be dining on tonight. Here, get a good smell," he said, rubbing the agents' jackets into their snouts.

Horrified by the sight of the creatures, the smaller agent bolted for the door, and Mike let one of them loose. The force of the attack lifted the man off his feet and drove him face first into the closed door. By the time Mike regained control of the dog, it had bitten the man several times on the buttocks, and the backs of his legs. The attack looked worse than it was because of all the blood and shredded clothing.

Whimpering, calling for God to help him, the agent managed to pull himself to his hands and knees, and that's how they let him stay.

"Now, lads," Mike said to the dogs, "come have a taste of this one."

"OK!, OK!, Jesus Christ, man, get them away from me," Huxley pleaded. "Please! Get them away."

With the dogs tied back outside, Mike got a pad and pencil from his car and threw them at Huxley's feet. "Here write it," he demanded. "I want to know who told you to murder those poor souls, I want to know what you were doing in that apartment, and I want the names of any others like you and your friend over there who might be skulking about.

As Huxley wrote, Mike sat down on the wooden crate next to him, and put his arm around his shoulders. "Englishman," he said softly, "it's a grand house you live in, I saw the pictures in your wallet, And the children, they're bonnie. That's why I thought we'd have this little chat. When I read your story, if I should for some reason get the idea that you've left something out, or that you're lying, or if you've even spelled a word wrong, I'm going to feed your rotten British ass to my dogs. Do you understand what I'm saying Englishman? And when they've had their fill of you I'm going to hang what's left in that tree in front of your grand house. In the morning your children will be able to look out the windows at their Da. Mark my word Englishman, you are as close to death right now as you will ever come without dying."

It took Huxley ten minutes to finish. Mike read it, made both agents sign it, and went into the office.

He told Harry and Diedra that the two men out in the garage were also Secret Service agents and had signed a confession admitting to murdering their fellow agents in the Bronx. It was a contract killing, at least that's what the one called Huxley claimed, for their own personal financial benefit. It wasn't an agency-ordered hit.

Mike said they were rogues, recruited more than a year earlier by a stranger in a bus terminal with a briefcase full of money. From then on, they got their assignments by phone from a man who sounded Oriental.

Bewildered, stunned, shocked, pissed-off were good words to describe Diedra's reaction as she listened to things she was hearing for the first time, things that had been going on in Harry's life and which he hadn't told her about.

"Jesus, Harry, what the hell are you mixed up in?" she asked. "Why haven't you told me about any of this?"

"You're right, I should have," he said, ashamedly, "but I didn't want to get you involved. I didn't want you to be scared. Besides, Mike thought maybe it wasn't me they were interested in, that maybe it was some of the people I work for. We're still not sure. It could be that I'm getting jammed up in someone else's problems."

"He's right, lass," Mike said, again coming to Harry's rescue. "The men who followed him might have been interested in some people at Santronics and thought Harry could help them somehow. The fact that his friend Ira's house was being watched the same night makes me think it's true. The Englishman outside, Huxley, said they were paid to kill the people following Harry, that's all.

"But tonight's a different story lad," Mike continued. "Tonight their instructions were about you. They were paid to search your apartment to try and find out who your friends are. Does that make any sense to you? Why would they be interested in knowing who your friends are, other than the ones at work?"

"I don't know," Harry answered, but he did. It was like he'd turned to the last page of a whodunit and suddenly knew the name of the bad guy. Mike's Englishman had tied all the pieces together when he said he and his partner got their instructions by phone from a man sounding Oriental. There were two separate things going on, and he was willing to bet Yamatoki was involved in both, he and his Shadows. That's why the feds had followed him, and why they had been parked outside Ira's place. They wanted Yamatoki.

This other thing, this business of Mike's prisoners being sent to find out who his friends were, it was Yamatoki trying to find out who had helped him cause the work stoppages at the piers.

He felt bad about lying to Mike, by telling him he didn't know why anyone would be interested in finding out who his friends were, but he had no choice. If he told Mike about his dealings with Ponzinno, he'd probably get murdered. What he couldn't figure though, was how Yamatoki had gotten two Secret Service agents to do his dirty work.

True, the agents told Mike they were freelancers, in it strictly for money, but it didn't make any sense. Yamatoki could have hired any pro he wanted. Why Secret Service agents? Then the ton of bricks hit him. What if someone in the government was tied in with Yamatoki somehow?

"Mike, is it possible there's more of these rats in the agency?" he asked.

"Harry, me boy, I've asked myself that very same question. I don't know, but we're all gonna find out real soon. Anything's possible with these people. They may work for the same outfit, but you'd be hard-pressed to find any three of them who knew what the next three were up to. Everything with them is compartmentalized, that's how they manage to get away with things.

"I'm not trying to scare you," Mike continued, "but I want you both to understand the situation. Who's ever behind this has a lot of assets, and it's my guess they'll come at you again, maybe both of you. What ever they were looking for they didn't get here tonight."

"So what are you saying? Diedra asked. "Are we supposed to hide?"

"On the contrary, lass. These people hate publicity, and I'm going to give them a dose of it they'll not soon forget. They're like cockroaches; turn on the kitchen light and they run under the stove."

"What happens with those two outside?" asked Harry.

"I found the missing license plate in their car, and when ballistics checks their weapons it'll tell us which one of them is the shooter—maybe they both are. As of now they're under arrest for murder.

"Lass, would you be havin' a problem with Harry stayin' at you place for awhile? His apartment has become too popular. And if you don't mind, I'd like to put some people outside your house for a couple of days, just to keep an eye on things."

"That's fine with me, Mike," she answered, "God knows, with all this going on, having Harry and the cops around wouldn't be any problem."

"Harry, between the three of us, it wouldn't hurt now for Diedra Agnes to have something with her also. Life is cheap with these bastards."

"I've already taken care of it. She's got my Beretta, and I have a .38."

"Good. Keep them handy. Now why don't you and the lass go and pick up some of your things. I'll have a car at your apartment house and it'll follow you over to Diedra's. I have some work to finish up here, and then it's off to the hoosegow with my guests."

"Mike, what can I say? Thank you. I'm just afraid I've dragged you into something bad."

"It's I who should be thanking you lad. You've probably gotten me detective third grade with these collars. Besides, these bastards murdered their own kind and I'm going to hang their asses out for everyone to see. And as for my safety, I appreciate the concern, but something tells me that by breakfast time, we're all going to have a lot less to worry about. I'm going to buy us an insurance policy. Be off with you now."

After they left, Mike called Brady MacNeice, Bronx chief of detectives, who was still smarting over the shabby treatment he'd received from the FBI when they pulled the torch murders away from him. MacNeice was a longtime friend of the O'Banion family, and a generous supporter of their mutual friends in Belfast.

Mike explained that he was bringing in the men responsible for the Bronx murders, and according to the IDs they were carrying, both worked for the Secret Service.

"Jesus, Michael, no wonder the feds jumped all over this. What the hell are we into?"

He also told MacNeice about Harry working for Santronics and that he thought the company was somehow involved, or at least some of its people were.

"I'll have them up to the 47 in about an hour for arraignment."

"That's fine, Mike. By the way, what kind of shape are they in?"

"Well, now that you ask, they did manage to get a wee banged up resisting arrest, especially the Englishman that likes to call Irish people 'Patty.' Did you hear that now Brady?"

"We've got the makings of a real brouhaha, you know that Michael?"

"Aye, that we do, that we do. It'll be a grand arraignment to be sure." Mike suggested to MacNeice that he call a few of his TV and newspaper friends and have them at the precinct when he arrived with the prisoners.

"We'll make a bonnie time of it," Mike said. "Tell them to bring plenty of pencils and film. And, Brady, you might want to have a table handy for all the things I'm bringing, like the gas can and weapons they used, their IDs, and their signed confession. In fact, we should hand out copies of it before it grows legs and decides to walk out of the property room."

"You know Michael, their lawyers will have a field day if we do this. We're depriving the bastards of due process."

"Aye, that we are, Brady, that we are, and we're doing a fine job of it too. But something tells me that after this gets on TV and in the papers, no one in their right mind will want anything to do with saving their miserable asses.

"Whoever owns them will try and kill them," O'Banion continued, "so we had better find a couple of good lads to sit on them, or else we'll be finding them hanging from a steam pipe."

It may have seemed theatrical, which it was, but what Mike was doing would keep Harry, Diedra, and himself alive, the media would guarantee it. By 7 a.m., millions of people across the country would know that the U.S. Secret Service had in their employ, men willing to hire out as professional assassins, and who, in fact had already murdered other Secret Service agents.

Mike was also going to drop the name "Komti" at the arraignment, and intimate that somehow, the company was involved. If there were people at either Komti, or Santronics up to no good, once the press started snooping, they'd be hard pressed to keep their activities secret.

In the morning, some of the newspaper headlines read; "Secret Service Murders Their Own" "Secret Service Mafia Taking Over Government" "Spy City Takes Orders From Oriental Mystery Man".

Part 16

Diedra woke when Harry got out of bed, and for awhile, she lay there watching him shower and shave. Any other time she would have joined him, but instead, she went down to the kitchen, turned on the little TV on the counter, and made a pot of coffee.

The lead story of course on every morning news program, was the arrest of the two Secret Service agents by a detective Michael O'Banion, for the shooting/torch murders of two other agents. The network anchormen were having a field day with the story, complete with a steady stream of so-called experts on everything from international espionage, to the failure of congressional oversight committees to police America's intelligence agencies.

"Is that on all the channels?" Harry asked, pouring himself a mug of coffee.

"Every one, but at least Mike kept our names out of it, so far. Thank God."

"You gonna be OK here when I go to work?" he asked.

"I think so. I've got the gun over there in the drawer, and Marie's always home if I need her. How about you?"

"I'll be all right. I get the feeling there's gonna be fewer rats runnin' around the city today. Just make sure you keep the gun handy. If you go out, take the safety off and put it under the seat. What time do you have to be at work tonight?"

"I'm not going. I've decided to take some time, at least until this thing calms down. Do me a favor, call me when you get to the office so I know you're all right.

"Harry," she continued, "sit down, there's something we have to talk about. I can't tell you how hurt I am about you not trusting me. You never said a damn thing about any of it. If you and I are going to have a future, you can't shut me out, I won't put up with it again. Terry did it to me and I hated it. It's my life that's in danger too, not just yours. Am I making any sense? God Almighty, if I'm gonna have to shoot somebody, I'd at least like to know why."

"I'm sorry," he said, getting down on one knee. "I can't begin to tell you how sorry I am. I apologize, I don't think I could handle this right now if I didn't have you. As God is my witness, from now on we'll do this thing together. Please, I love you, and I don't want to lose you."

*   *   *

While the painter may have finished putting his new, impressive title on the door to his office, his desk was still overflowing with work.

"Good morning, boss," his secretary said as she brought in the mail. "Is it still OK to call you that, or do I have to call you Mr. O'Day? By the was, you look like hell."

"Thanks, Connie. Remind me to do the same for you some time. How about getting me some tea?"

It wasn't long before the guy from the restaurant delivered it, and after quickly finishing one container, he started feeling better. Connie buzzed him on the intercom and said Mr. Longdon was on line three. Hesitating for a moment, he picked up the phone.

"Harry, it's Pete Longdon. I think maybe it's time for us to talk."

"What about?"

"Well, for starters, about what's all over the TV and in the papers this morning."

"Why would I want to talk to you about that?"

"Because we need your help, we've got to stop these people."

"What people?"

"You know what people, people like Yamatoki and Nagakura, and maybe some others at Komti. They're dangerous, or maybe you've already found that out. Listen, I shouldn't be saying these things on the phone, how about coming over to my office. I've got some people scheduled for a meeting shortly and I would like you to sit in."

"Where's your office today Pete? Washington? Brooklyn? New York? I can never remember," Harry asked sarcastically, "you seem to have so many of them."

"Third and 70th. It's the ugly, dark building right on the corner, the Federal Building. I'm on the 35th floor. You'll have to sign in and get a visitor's badge, and then the guard will send somebody upstairs with you. Thanks, Harry, believe me, you'll be doing a lot of people a big favor. If you're apprehensive about coming, why don't you call Diedra and Mike O'Banion and tell them where you're going. Tell them I called and asked you to come over."

Shocked, then enraged by hearing his friends' names coming out of Longdon's mouth, he flew out of his chair sending it smashing into the long, wooden work table behind him. The water decanter and light that were on it, clattered to the floor.

"You son of a bitch!" he screamed. "You lousy, rat, son of a bitch. If anything happens to those people, I'll blow your fucking head off. Do you understand me? I'll cut your fucking heart out and stuff it in you fat face."

By now, everyone in the outer-office, stunned by the violence of his outburst, sat or stood gawking.

"Harry, Harry, please! Calm down." Longdon begged.

"We're not the bad guys. Those two men in the Bronx, they worked for me. I was the one who had to explain to their families why they died like that. Look, you've got to trust me."

"Bullshit! Why were they following me to begin with? I'm sorry they're dead, but you're the prick that got them whacked. You haven't told me the truth about anything since I've known you, and you want me to trust you? Bullshit! Now I'm gonna ask you once more why they were following me, and if you don't tell me the truth I'm gonna start callin' the newspapers and TV stations and give them your name, and tell them who you are."

"Harry, please, don't do that, don't hang up. Look, my men weren't looking to hurt you or your boss, Senowitz. I was desperate for any information I could get. I thought you and Senowitz might be able to help us."

"Help you with what? What the hell is Komti up to? And what about those two scumbags they arrested? They're part of your crew, right?"

"Harry, please, come over, I'll explain everything. I promise."

"So long, Pete."

"All right, all right, you leave me no choice but to say this on the phone. We know from Navel Intelligence files that Nagakura had your father murdered. Help us, and we'll give him to you, alive or dead, whichever way you want him. Harry? Harry, did you hear me?"

"Where did you say you were?"

"Third and 70th. I can send a car for you."

"No thanks, I've seen enough of your cars."

"You won't regret this, I promise you Harry. How soon can you get here?"

"I gotta make a couple of calls first; maybe in an hour."

He wasn't exactly sure what he'd let himself in for, but the thought of firing a bullet into Nagakura's face had become an obsession. Both

Diedra and O'Banion tried their best to convince him not to go alone, but he insisted that's the way it had to be.

$$\ast \qquad\qquad \ast \qquad\qquad \ast$$

Ugly wasn't the word for it. The building reminded him of the crematorium in the middle of the cemetery his rear apartment windows faced.

After having him sign the register, the armed guard at the desk handed him a visitor's ID badge, picked up a phone, and dialed. "Mr. Longdon, sir, Mr. Harry O'Day is here. Yes, sir, I'll send him right up. Mr. O'Day, Mr. Longdon will be waiting at the elevator for you on the 35th floor. You'll have to come back here when you leave to sign out."

Another armed guard rode up in the elevator with him, and Longdon was standing there when the doors opened.

"Thanks, Harry, thanks for coming. Please, follow me."

They walked down what seemed like an endless, doorlined, gray floored corridor, with the sharp echoes of their steps bouncing off the walls. Conference Room 11A had two young Marine guards outside it. Besides their sidearms, both had automatic weapons. On his way through the door, Harry whispered "semper fi," to the one on the left who broke his stone-faced expression long enough to glance at him and smile.

Inside, a group of men milled about, some talking to each other in hushed voices, while others looked through papers in black briefcases. Two were in uniform. The older one bore the insignia of a four star general, and the other, three stars. Both their chests were heavily laden with battle ribbons. The rest of the men wore civilian clothing. Harry took note of the fact that one of them was Japanese.

"Gentlemen," Longdon said loudly, "may I have your attention? This is the man I've been telling you about, Mr. Harry O'Day. He's come to help us. Harry, I'd like you to meet General Tobber; General Thysen; Henry Kramer, head of the Secret Service; Sy Hasbrook, assistant director of the FBI; Roger Vogel, assistant CIA director; and Ted Gigommi, he's with Japanese Military Intelligence, and he cheats at poker, so watch him.

"OK, gentlemen," Longdon continued, now standing at the head of the long, highly polished table, tapping a ruler on it, "why don't you be seated. We've got a lot to cover."

Longdon turned, looked him straight in the face, and said, "Harry, you're going to hear things that if repeated outside this room, could cause the deaths of millions of people. There's no going back now. If you don't stay and help us, in a short while, there may not be anything to go back to."

Addressing the group, Longdon said, "I know we're holding this meeting earlier than expected, but since the arrests of the two agents last night, and the press getting involved, we have no choice.

"First, I think we owe a debt of gratitude to Ted Gigommi and to his government for supplying us with a lot of the intelligence we'll be looking at today. Secondly, it might be useful if I spend a few minutes giving a brief synopsis of our situation so everyone's up to speed.

"Shortly after the war, Sugomu Nagakura resurfaced in Japan. In hindsight we now know he should have been arrested on the spot and tried for atrocities against Allied prisoners of war held in his death camps, but he wasn't."

"Why wasn't he?" General Thysen asked. "I find it hard to believe that nobody on MacArthur's staff knew who the son of a bitch was."

"I can't answer that, General, no one in the American Government seems to have an answer, or, if they do, they're not saying. It's just too bad someone didn't put a bullet into him. If they had, we wouldn't have to be doing this. Be that as it may, we're faced with the problem of the bastard being alive.

"Almost immediately he started reconstructing his father's manufacturing plants. The first item in your folders is a list of South American holding companies Nagakura Sr. set up during a three-year period just prior to the attack on Pearl Harbor. Attached to it is an accounting of U.S. currency transferred to those companies by Japanese banks on behalf of Komti. Ltd. Obviously poppa had the foresight to know we'd eventually kick Tojo's butt. After the war, the holding companies bankrolled the reconstruction.

"When the factories started making profits, Junior used a good portion of the money to set up and operate his New Suns Foundation, which is nothing more than his private army. According to Ted Gigommi's latest estimates, there are about forty thousand of these elite guards scattered around the world working in Komti companies. They're Nagakura's version of a *Schutstaffel*, which was Hitler's SS, and they're fanatically loyal to him. They're also fanatically anti-American and serve as his personal bodyguards when he's traveling."

"Is that why we've been unable to terminate him?" asked General Tobber.

"That's one of the reasons," Longdon answered. "Another is that as intelligence improved, we realized his so-called research and development operations were much further along in putting his project together. Killing him was no longer a viable option. His death might have escalated the technicians' efforts, or worse, some of his whacko followers might have decided to revenge his death by using one of their toys, assuming they had one ready to go. We couldn't take the chance."

"Pete, if I may?"

"Yes, General Tobber?"

"The thing I'm curious about is during the time the U.S. occupational government was running Japan, did anybody ever try to institute some kind of control over this guy?"

"Who knows? Maybe they figured it would be better for the people to be making radios in one of his factories, than trouble. I do know one thing though, we're dealing with a madman. Believe me, he's missing most of his deck. You'll see what I mean when you read his profile in your folders. His entire family was killed at Hiroshima which didn't help his mental stability, but he was a lunatic even before the war. As a child, he liked to cut up the neighbors' cats."

General Thysen raised his hand. "Pete, getting back to the money. You know, at the end of the war, we were flying sorties twenty-four hours a day over there. Anything bigger than an outhouse got plastered. So to rebuild what he has today, and to bankroll this New Suns outfit, the tin can in the backyard needs a lotta fillin'. Do they really sell that much, or maybe we got a situation where another government is helping him?"

Longdon grinned and said, "General, let me answer your question with a question. Do you have any Santronics merchandise in your home?"

"Well, yes, I guess I do. I got their refrigerator-freezer, and I think the TV and stereo down the basement are theirs also. Come to think of it, the grandkids both have those damn big radios. They look like they're carrying logs around on their shoulders."

"You know, General," Longdon said, "last Christmas I bought my wife a color TV for her sewing room. The salesmen in three different stores told me the same thing, Santronics was the best set on the market, the cheapest, too. Does that answer your question? This country has done more to finance Nagakura than any other country in the world. We use his golf clubs, we bring oil here in his supertankers, and we even put his electronics in our fighters.

"Ok. Next thing," Longdon said, getting up. "What I'm distributing, is a copy of a memo sent to General Tobber by Major General Wendell Horner, commander of Centennial Air Force Base. It has a lot of technical jargon in it, but the bottom line is that the plane the late vice president and his family were on was sabotaged. Horner's people told him they found tiny fragments of an explosive device embedded in parts of the wreckage. I need not remind any of you that there were also twelve Marines aboard.

"Now, the next item in your folders is a copy of the Arlington, Va., coroner's report on the cause of death of the late Mr. Boynton Meller, our former secretary of agriculture. It says, gentlemen, at the bottom of page three, and I quote, 'standard tests conducted on the deceased's hands for the presence of gunpowder, proved negative.' The report describes several other tests he performed, and then we come down to the last sentence, 'These results are inconsistent with a self-inflicted wound.' Mr. Meller was murdered, gentlemen, You might want to pencil in an addendum on your copies that shortly after our people were able to obtain a copy of this, the coroner's office was completely destroyed by a fire of unknown origin. We have a war on our hands gentlemen, and it's right here at home."

The room was silent until Roger Vogel, No. 2 at the CIA cleared his throat and raised his hand. "Yes, Roger. Question?" Longdon asked.

"Yes. Please. I'd like to ask General Tobber something. General, I'm looking at a newspaper article about the crash of the vice president's plane. A reporter asked General Horner a question that got him very angry, and I'd like to read you his response. 'Boy, you listen, and you listen good. The American people are the United States government, and no one else. If they decide to get rid of a bunch of lowlife, backdooring, fornicating pieces of dog waste, that's not sedition, that's their right guaranteed by the Constitution.' My question General, is, how many other high-ranking general officers in our military hold similar views?"

"That I personally know of? Enough to pose a substantial threat to the civilian authorities," Tobber replied.

"According to my information," Vogel continued, "Major General Horner flew combat missions for almost the entire length of the war, both in the Pacific and in Europe by his own request. He holds the

Bronze Star, the Medal of Honor, two Purple Hearts, and he's been awarded more battle ribbons than I've ever seen on a man's record. From what I've been told, he's a down-to-earth type person and practically worshiped by his men. These other general officers, the ones having a similar mind-set, are they of the same caliber as the general?"

"Well, as you pointed out," Tobber responded, "General Horner is an exceptional soldier and I would say that he's well thought of by most of the people he comes in contact with, especially senior military people. Look, Mr. Vogel, sir, I'm not very good at playing semantics, so if you're asking me if the General would have support within the military if he, uh, if he wanted it, the answer is yes, without a doubt, and I would be the first.

"May I tell you a little story, Mr. Vogel? Perhaps it might explain how some of us in the military feel.

"Do you know where the Matanikao River is? It's on Guadalcanal. Ten minutes after we got there, a young Marine walked up to me with a piece of his skull missing. He was using the one hand he had left to cover the hole. He said, 'I'm sorry, sir,' because he thought he'd let his squad, and me down by getting wounded. When he tried to salute, the blood spurting out from the stump of his other forearm went in his mouth and he vomited on me. I didn't hear the round that hit him in the back, but it pushed him into my arms, and that's where he died, looking into my face.

"I can't speak for anyone else, but I owe him, as God is my witness, I owe him, and I owe all the others who died because I had to take them into battle. And I owe their families, I owe them the right to sit in their living rooms as free people, mourning the men I've taken to their deaths."

There may have been a few sitting at the table who heard the faint wailing of an ambulance far below in the street, or the ringing of a distant phone someplace in the building, but they all heard the silence. The aching remembrance of names like Rabaul, truk, Hill 660, and

Mindanao stole back into the minds of some of them and they bowed their heads.

Visibly shaken by the general's comments, Vogel finally spoke. "Thank you, General, you have my gratitude and respect. Thank you for your candor and integrity. I think now we'll be able to make some meaningful decisions here today."

"The next item on our agenda," Longdon said, "is the president's finances. We've managed to trace the transfer of approximately eleven million dollars from bank accounts controlled by the New Suns Foundation to his campaign through a series of phony companies, individuals, organizations, and bagmen. Another five million has been traced to accounts set up in two foreign countries under bogus names, but to which, he has access. In addition, similar accounts have been established on behalf of his wife. At our last look-see, they contained fifteen million dollars."

Sy Hasbrook, assistant FBI director spoke. "So if he's spreading all this money around, he can't actually be planning on using those damn things. He'll only use them to blackmail us, right?

"That would be a logical assumption," Longdon answered, "if it wasn't for the fact that we're dealing with a maniac. He could snap at any moment, and that would be the ball game."

Harry spoke for the first time. "You keep talking about devices, what the hell are they anyway, and how did he get them?"

"General Tobber," Longdon said, "why don't you take Harry's question? Among other things, the general is in charge of our nuclear facilities at Los Alamos."

"They're bombs, Mr. O'Day, atomic bombs, and he's now building them right under our noses in his so-called research and development centers like the one you work down the hall from in Brooklyn. Where did he get the technology and fissionable material? Simple. He stole them, and in some cases, paid huge sums of money to people who could acquire them for him.

"Unfortunately," the general continued, "Komti's success with electronic miniaturization has enabled him to create a device small enough to fit into something the size of a steamer trunk. The only picture we have of one was taken by an operative at Komti's San Francisco facility. He managed to pass it to Ted's people just before he and his family, including their sixth month old daughter, were found with their throats cut."

"Is that the only place they're building these things besides Brooklyn?" Harry asked.

"No," General Tobber answered. "They're building at least one, maybe two, at each of the six Santronics warehouse centers here in the States."

"Roger? Question?" Longdon asked.

"Yes. Do we know how they're getting their materials into the country? I hope to Christ they're not getting anything here from American companies."

"Good, Roger," Longdon said, "that's a meat-and-potatoes question. Ted has some film to show that we should all pay particular attention to. Ted, if you would."

"As far as we can determine," Gigommi said, "only one company here in America ever sold Komti anything that might have been of some slight use to their technicians. A small quantity of geiger counter replacement parts and radiation badges were shipped to Santronics in Brooklyn. As soon as the vendor realized Santronics was part of a foreign corporation, it notified the FBI.

"This particular segment of film," Gigommi continued, turning on a small movie projector, "was shot in the port of New Orleans. There's nothing unusual about the unloading of this Komti ship until here, right here. I'll run this slow so you can get a better look. Right here, see where my ruler is pointing? On top of the pallets of Santronics in the cargo net? They're two silver-colored metal containers about the size of suitcases. OK, now, watch when the net gets to the ground. See the van coming into the picture? It belongs to the company doing the trucking for Santronics in New Orleans, the same way Plenum trucks for Santronics here in New York.

"Each of the six Santronics warehouse centers pay their truckers extra to provide this special van service to pick these cases up. The carriers have been told they contain highly sensitive electronic equipment for their research work that might be damaged if it was put on a regular trailer. Sometimes they arrive by air, as you'll see in a moment.

"We're positive none of the carriers are involved. To use your colloquial English, these guys are mobbed up; if they knew how they were being duped, they'd probably start whacking Nagakura's people, and God forbid they should ever find out what's in them. That would be like your late Al Capone being in charge of the military.

"This next piece of film is the most disturbing. It was shot at the Tokyo airport. This is your interim vice president boarding his plane on the way back to Washington. Here's a different shot from the other side of the airplane taken with a telephoto lens. OK, now watch when the cameraman zooms in. There, right there, see the small truck coming into the picture? The guy in the passenger seat gets out, goes to the rear, takes out to silver cases and hands them up to someone in the craft's cargo hold. You see the three Americans standing there watching? They're Secret Service.

"Since Henry Kramer is the head of the Service, "Gigommi said, "I'm sure he'd like to pick it up from here."

"Thanks Ted. First, gentlemen, let me say that sitting here, listening to this and watching these films, is the most difficult thing I've ever had to do in my eighteen years of service. The men you see here, along with the two arrested last night, and some others are scum, traitors. They've dishonored not only themselves, their country, the Service, but all of the loyal, devoted men who risk their lives everyday. I make a solemn promise to you all that I will personally deal with these renegades. Once this thing breaks, any of them not terminated in the process will be arrested, tried for treason, and will pay the maximum penalty.

"The only reason they've been allowed to remain in their positions," Kramer continued, "is so we don't tip our hand. But I can assure you, anyone, and I do mean anyone, suspected of being involved in this debacle is under twenty-four hour surveillance.

"Now, having said that, we had our cameras rolling when the vice president arrived back in Washington. The film you're seeing now is after he's left the tarmac. The truck marked Sedger Maintenance coming into view has clearance to clean government aircraft, but the two men in it are not employees of the company. They took it from an unlocked garage area. Unfortunately the quality of the film isn't very good, but the three men you see standing next to the plane's hold are the same ones from the Tokyo airport footage. OK, now, watch, the same two cases come down the belt and are put into the Sedger truck. They were then transferred to a private vehicle in the airport's long-term parking lot. Their final destination was Santronics' warehouse in Brooklyn.

"We believe the contents of these cases was of such major importance that Nagakura refused to entrust their safety to even one of his own ships' captains. Instead, he used the security of the vice president's plane to get them here. It's possible they contained miniaturized firing devices. Two of them.

"As you know, the White House provides the Secret Service with an advance copy of the president's travel itinerary. In two weeks he plans to attend the Council of Economic Ministers meeting in Hawaii, and on his way back to Washington, stop in San Francisco, Atlanta New Orleans, Chicago, and Boston, to make speeches. Each of those cities has a Santronics warehouse with a research and development facility. Two days ago, Ted Gigommi received a hand-carried communiqué from Japanese military intelligence via his country's ambassador to the UN. Ted has given me a copy of it and permission to read it to you.

Quote: 'Suspect Air Force One will be used to get additional firing devices into U.S.', end quote."

"So why the hell let them get the damn things on the plane to begin with?" Harry demanded.

"Because," Kramer responded, "we don't have any choice. Since they may have already armed the devices in Brooklyn, if we move against any of them anywhere along the line, they may use them. There's no telling."

"I don't understand any of this," Harry said, frustrated. "I thought you guys were supposed to be so damn smart, but here you are sittin' around on your asses doin' a lot of talkin'. You keep sayin' how this prick is doin' this, and doin' that, but I don't hear anybody sayin' what you're doin'. No wonder this country is so fucked up, pardon the language. If you know those things are at Plenum, why not just go in and take them?"

"Good question, Mr. O'Day," Kramer answered. "The problem is we can't be sure they're still there. They may have been moved. If we bust in and come up empty-handed, we're in trouble. The only way we're going to avoid a holocaust, as difficult as it might be, is to grab all the devices simultaneously, and we'd like to do it within the next ten days."

"Gentlemen, I'd like to thank you for your presentations," Longdon said. "We still have several more items to cover, so if you would care to break for lunch…no? You all want to continue? Good. I'm not particularly hungry either, and I never thought I'd ever hear myself saying that."

The comment brought a muffled laugh from some at the table when a touch of levity was badly needed.

Longdon left the room for a moment and returned with a large roll of blueprints.

"Fortunately, gentlemen," he said, "even madmen like Nagakura make mistakes. What you're looking at is a copy of the original drawings submitted by Komti to the planning boards of all six cities in which they had Santronics warehouse centers constructed."

Longdon explained that Komti had used an architect in Chicago to design the original complex. Komti officials were so pleased with the results, they used the same design for all of them. "We've checked with the six construction firms involved, and I can assure you, the buildings are identical, right down to the placement of the commodes in the ladies' bathrooms.

"Right here," Longdon said, "is our door," pointing to an area in the warehouse section of the drawing. "See? Right here at the end of the loading dock?"

"I don't see any door," General Tobber said. "All I see is a wall."

"That's right, a cinder block wall," Longdon said, "but if you notice, right behind the wall is a space. It's thirty inches wide. Those lines you see in the space are pipes carrying water to the upper floor's sprinkler system. Notice the ducts passing through the space where the pipes bend and go between the I-beams. They're part of the building's main heating and cooling system. They pass through the research and development rooms. According to the engineering firm that installed the systems, there's a series of vents in the sections of the ducts passing through the research rooms."

"Why go through all that?" Gigommi asked. "Why not just pick the locks some night and go in and look around?"

"I wish it was that easy, Ted," Longdon replied, sitting down heavily in his chair. "First of all, the doors are wired into two separate alarm systems, that much we know. But they installed the systems themselves so we can't go to anybody and find out what we'd be dealing with. We do know that there's security cameras in the rooms wired into one of the systems, and that the viewing screens are in rooms up in the executive areas. At least two of Nagakura's people are always watching. As for the other system, we don't have a clue."

"So what makes you think no one's gonna hear or see you knockin' a hole in the wall, if that's what you're plannin' on doin'?" asked Harry, skeptical of everything Longdon was saying.

"Because," Longdon answered, "we're going to have the truckers, like Plenum, back an empty trailer with its doors open up against the point of entry. We'll have people in the box with high-speed drills and cutters. I've seen them work, they're amazing; practically noiseless. We estimate the whole thing, entry, photographing the rooms' contents, and the extraction shouldn't take more than an hour. We'll start at midnight, and just to make sure everything looks Kosher, we'll have the truckers get a mechanic to pull the hydraulic hoses off the box like there was a problem with them. We'll also have the truckers keep these six big exhaust fans going to give us extra noise cover."

"Just like that, right?" Harry asked, smirking. "How long do you think it'll take Nagakura's men watchin' those TV cameras to pick up a phone after your guys drop through the vents?

"Like I said," Longdon answered, "the ducts in the research rooms have a series of grills in them. Our man will be able to photograph everything to his left, to his right, and below. It's a very interesting cam-era—I'd show it to you, but it's secret. Our man will never have to leave the duct."

"So if the things are there, why not just grab them, or bust them up?" asked Harry. "And another thing, what the hell am I doing here? You pleaded with me to come over, that I had to help you, so what is it that I'm supposed to be doin'?"

"Harry, if you'll be patient for just a few more minutes," Longdon answered, "I'll explain how you're going to help us, and believe me, without you, this isn't going to work. To answer your question about grabbing the devices, we can't. The whole idea is to see what's in the rooms without any of Nagakura's people being any the wiser. The rea-son being, if any of the devices have been moved, we can't tip our hand. If any of them have been moved, well, that's a whole new ballgame. It's imperative we get into all six locations at exactly the same time.

"The photos will be transmitted to General Tobber's staff at Los Alamos for analysis, and then gentlemen, hopefully, the ball will be in our court. Then we will kick in the doors and God help anyone who tries to stop us. General Thysen's special units, already in place, will secure the rooms and terminate any resistance. Specially equipped aircraft will then take the devices to White Sands.

"I want to make it absolutely clear that our plan has the approval of the Japanese government, and it has instructed Ted Gigommi to provide us with a list of every suspected member of Nagakurua's cult presently employed either at Santronics or at Komti's executive offices. The list will include their place of residence, and we'll arrange for local police to handle the arrests, that way, there won't be too much of a military presence in the cities. Those who resist will be terminated. The others will be turned over to General Thysen's units, and with Ted's assistance, transported to predetermined military bases for interrogation and processing. At the start of the next business day, the remaining legitimate Japanese employees at Komti's executive offices and at the six regional warehouse centers will be allowed to continue working. However, in each location a military coordinator will be in charge until such time as the Japanese government decides what they want to do with the business.

"As for Nagakura, according to our information, he's scheduled to arrive in San Francisco in a few days to begin an inspection of the Santronics' facilities, and remain in the country for two weeks. Which means he'll be around when we lower the boom. He'll run, but I promise you, he won't get away—not this time."

Impatient, and getting annoyed with Longdon, Harry interrupted, "Pete, you keep sayin' things like the truckers are gonna do that, the truckers are gonna do this, we'll have them do so and so. Have you actually talked to any of them? Have you told them they're sitting on bombs? Have you told Manny Ostrow at Plenum any of this?"

"No, we haven't," Longdon said, "that's where you come in, that's how you're going to help us."

Harry looked at his quizzically. "And just what is it you think I can do?" he asked.

"I want you to arrange for me to meet with Alfonsa Ponzinno."

Without hesitating, Harry asked, "Who's Alfonsa Ponzinno? I never heard of him."

"Yes, you have. You've known him for most of your life. When your mother died, you sold him her house. You had dinner with him recently at a place called Annunzio's, and you and Ostrow went in through the back door. Shall I continue Harry? I could, but we really don't have time for this."

"All right, so maybe I met him one or twice," Harry said indignantly. "That doesn't mean I can drop a dime and ask him to have coffee. A guy like that lets you know when he wants to see you, not the other way around."

"Harry, please. We've gone as far as we can with this thing," Longdon said, the tone of his voice sounding more contrite. "Now it's up to you. But I'll tell you this, if you don't, we all might as well go and find ourselves an empty pew and start praying. That's how bad things are."

"So what do you think Ponzinno can do?" asked Harry.

"We want him to arrange things with his associates so we can set up in their warehouses. This isn't going to work without all of them helping."

"You're crazy, you know that? What makes you think I can arrange a meeting? You have any idea who this guy is?"

"The question is, do you have any idea who he is? Next to the president, he's probably the most powerful man in the country. Those men, the ones who do the trucking for Santronics'? Ponzinno's their boss, the *Cap di tuti capo*. They owe their allegiance to him, they do what ever he tells them."

"Look, Pete, it's not that I don't wanna help. This stuff I'm hearing scares the hell out of me. I had no idea. But you're gonna get me killed. The first thing he'd ask is how come the feds knew to send me, and then it's one behind the ear and I'm in the weeds someplace. You're asking me to sign my own death warrant."

"I'm not so sure about that," Longdon said, as he took a file folder out of his briefcase and examined its contents. "when you were sixteen, you saved the life of an Alfonsa Arezzo in Queens according to these police and hospital records. Is that right? No, Harry, I don't think he'd harm you, not after saving his son's life.

"That was a big thing you did for him, and you have a chance to do another big thing for him, and for all of his associates."

"You're losing me."

"What I'm saying is that if Nagakura starts pushing the buttons, his son, his associates, along with everything they control, go up in a bright light—him too. His families make God knows how much money just off Santronics, and that's pocket change compared to the income from all their other enterprises. You think he wants some screwball blowing it up? Don't you think he'd be indebted to the person who camw and let him know what was going on right under his nose? That if he didn't do something he'd lose everything?"

"So why don't you go to him yourself?"

"Be practical. Half the budgets of the Justice Department and the FBI are spent investigating and prosecuting his people. We just put one of his nephews away for racketeering. If we told him we wanted him to do us a favor, it would be two months before he stopped laughing. No, you're our best chance of talking with him. You've got to be the inter-locutor."

"I don't know, Pete, I don't know about going to him."

"You don't go to him directly, you go to Manny Ostrow. You tell him we've been looking at several people, including yourself, who work for Santronics, trying to figure who might be able to help us reach out to Plenum's management. You say we told you about some bad things a few of the Japanese were doing, like building bombs in the research rooms. That they're doing it in all the Santronics' warehouses.

"You tell Ostrow it's now a matter of national security, and if we can't get things straightened out, and quick, the military will be forced to come in and shut all the warehouses. Tell him the agent who spoke to you, a Mr. Longdon, wants to meet with him and Mr. Bissetti before things get any worse, and that he has some films to show them that will explain everything. Say the United States government will pay twenty-five million dollars simply for meeting with them, and that Mr. Longdon would have the money in the trunk of his car when he came to the meeting."

"Get out of here," Harry said laughingly. "Are you serious? Twenty-five million dollars?"

"Deadly serious, because that's what we're all gonna be, dead, if they don't meet with us and give up their help. You see those three cloth cases over there? They each contain one million dollars cash. One case is for Ostrow, one's for Bissetti, and the third one is yours."

"Yeah, sure," Harry said with a smirk, "tell me another one."

"I'm serious, but don't get too excited, you and the rest of us might all be ash before you could spend a dollar of it."

"What about Nagakura? You said you could help me? Is he part of the deal?"

Longdon turned to Ted Gigommi and asked, "The thing we talked about before, any problem with your government?"

"None whatsoever," Gigommi replied smiling. "In fact Mr. O'Day would be doing them a favor."

"OK," Longdon said, "you have our word, he's yours. I'll have someone take the cases down to your car and stay with you until you get home. Here, take these phone numbers. This one's my private line, this one is the main switchboard, and this is my home phone. Give them to Ostrow too. Please, I'd like someone to get back to me tonight."

Part 17

Diedra picked the gun up off the coffee table when the car pulled into the driveway, but relaxed when she heard her squeaky voiced neighbor, Marie, say, "Hello, Mr. O'Day, you're home early, aren't you?"

"I'd better go and save him," she said to herself, putting on her coat and going outside into the chilly afternoon air.

"Hi, sweetheart, what's with all the luggage?"

"I'll tell you inside. Do me a favor, close the trunk and get my briefcase off the front seat."

Struggling with the heavy weight of all three bags, he dropped them just inside the kitchen door. "Do we have anything to drink?" he groaned as he covered his face with his hands and slumped down onto a chair.

"Yes, what would you like? Scotch, whiskey?"

"Whiskey, a glass full, and some ice. Thanks."

Getting a bottle and two glasses from a cabinet, she sat down next to him. "Sweetheart, you're scaring me. I've never seen you like this before. Please, what happened over there?"

"Don't worry, I'm OK. I'm just glad to be with you and out of that place. It was like being in a coffin. I love you. I love you very much, do you know that?"

"Of course I do, and I love you the same way," she said, moving her chair closer and brushing the hair out of his eyes. "You were gone so long, I was worried. I didn't know if I should try and call there, or if I should call Mike, I even thought about driving over. Would you please tell me what the hell it was all about? You're getting me crazy."

They sat for the better part of three hours while he told her the entire story. About Nagakura building the devices at all the Santronics' warehouses, and what Longdon and his group were planning. He told her who Ponzinno was and how he'd saved the life of his son a long time ago. Finally, he told her about the three cases of money, two of which Longdon wanted him to take to Ostrow and Bissetti in hopes of buying their help.

The only thing he didn't tell her was that when the opportunity presented itself, he was going to kill Nagakura.

By now it was dark in the kitchen. Diedra turned on the lamp hanging over the butcher's block and said, "How about I fix us something? We'll feel better. There's some cold cuts and I can warm up some soup if you'd like."

"OK. Now that you mention it, I am a little hungry, but no soup, just a sandwich."

He got up, refilled his glass, and went and stood next to her at the counter. "Maybe it would be best if I just left," he said.

"What do you mean, leave?"

"You know, maybe it would be better if you didn't get any deeper into this thing. Maybe we should stop seeing each other."

"Wash your mouth out, Harry O'Day! Don't ever let me hear you say that again. We're in this together and I'm not about to let you just walk out of my life." Grabbing him by the collar with both hands, she said, "Either you gangster friends are going to help Longdon get those damn things back, and I'm gonna have a million bucks to spend, or we'll all go bang. Whatever happens, we're gonna do it together. Is that clear enough, Mr. O'Day?"

"Speaking of money," he said, "can you put one of those bags some-place? I've got to take the other two over to Manny . Christ, I'm draggin' millions of dollars around like my laundry."

"Oh, please, not tonight. Don't go out anymore. Do it tomorrow. Please, stay with me."

"I have to, I don't have any choice. It's gotta be tonight. Who knows what's gonna happen with this crazy bastard running around."

After finishing his sandwich and another drink, he called Manny at the warehouse and said he was coming over, that it was very important they talk.

*   *   *

"I hope you got plenty to drink here because we're both gonna need it." Harry said, laboring to get the heavy sacks through the doorway, and onto the office couch.

"What's doin' kid?" Manny asked, breaking the seal on a quart of his favorite cheap whiskey. "You sounded all bent out of shape on the phone. Takin' a trip?"

"They're presents." Harry answered, sitting down in the chair in front of the desk. After gulping most of what Manny had poured him, he went through the entire scenario.

Manny broke into laughter. "What the fuck you talkin' about?" he asked, watching his friend's face for a giveaway sign that he was fooling around. "Here, you better have another drink. You jus see this shit on TV or somethin'?"

"I'm serious, I saw the films. I was sittin' in a room full of feds and generals."

"Yeah? And when the feds were tellin' you all this, what were you tellin' them?"

"Nothing, I swear, I didn't tell them anything. I just said that I knew you from work, that's all."

"You know what I think? I think the booze has finally messed up your brain."

"I wish to God that's all it was."

"Get out of here. You're bullshittin' me, right?"

"Manny, I swear on my mother's grave, it's true."

"Yeah, sure it is, and I'm supposed to go to Tony and say, 'Hey, Tony, O'Day says the Japs are buildin' atomic bombs in the warehouses.' You know what would happen? Some of his goons would take me to one of them places where they got rubber on the walls. Enough already, kid. Tell me what you wanted to see me about."

Harry got the two, heavy cloth bags, unzippered them, and put them on the desk. "Here, take a look at this and then tell me I'm fucking around."

"Holy sweet mother of Jesus!" Manny yelled, jumping up from his chair. "how much dough you got here? This is real, no?"

"In both bags, two million, and yes, it's real. That's what they sent, just like I told you. One million for you, one million for Bissetti, and I got a million at home. There's another twenty-five million for Ponzinno if he meets with Longdon. Can you believe this shit?"

"These are all fuckin' hundreds." Manny whispered, fanning the individual bundles like decks of playing cards. His nervous eccentricity of squinting and nodding was so exaggerated, he could hardly keep his glasses from falling off.

"Jesus, Harry, will you look at all this fuckin' dough. You were serious. I gotta go see Tony."

Tripping over his own feet, Manny was halfway out the door when Harry yelled, "Manny! Take the money."

"Oh, yeah, thanks. Can you believe this shit?" he kept saying as he struggled to get the bulky cases through the doorway. Harry watched from the office window as he dragged them down the metal steps, across the loading dock, and with difficulty, wedge them into the trunk of his car.

"Hey, Pop, you gonna be gone long?" Manny's son, Bobby, yelled, raising one of the big bay doors to let his father out.

"Call Tony, Tell'm I'm on my way over, and he should wait for me," Manny shouted. "Tell'm it's very very important." Screeching his tires, he disappeared up the darkened street.

*   *   *

He tried to be quiet when he used the key Diedra had given him to the back door.

"Harry? Are you all right?" she asked from the living room. She waited to hear his voice before putting the gun away.

"Hi, yes, I'm OK. I didn't think you'd still be up," he half-whispered, sitting down next to her on the couch.

"I was afraid to go upstairs, I kept hearing noises, so I got a blanket and came in here."

"Anybody call?" he asked, pulling the cover up around her.

"No, no one. What did Manny say? I bet he was shocked when he saw all the money."

"He went nuts. I thought he was gonna blink himself to death."

"When will he tell the other two?"

"Tonight, in fact, he's probably telling at least Bissetti right now. Wait until Ponzinno finds out. If I were some of those Japanese, I'd start looking for my passport."

"Sweetheart," Diedra said, laying her head on his lap, "can't we just take the money we have and go someplace? You know, someplace safe where we could forget all this."

"I wish. I wish I knew a place where this madman couldn't reach us," he said apologetically, slowly stroking her hair.

They both jumped when the phone rang. "Let me get it," he said.

"Harry, it's Manny. Call this guy Longdon and tell'm to be at the ticket booth for the Cyclone in Coney Island at midnight. Tell'm no guns, no wire, and no tails. If he fucks around, he's gonna get hurt. Tell'm that good. I'll wait here at this number until you call me back, I wanna make sure he's comin'. Harry, tell'm to have the dough."

"What's going on?" Diedra asked after he hung up.

"I'm not sure, but they want to see Longdon tonight.

"Is Peter Longdon there? He told me I could reach him at this number. My name is Harry O'Day."

"Oh yes," A woman with a soft, refined voice answered, "could you hold on a moment, I think he's down in his workshop." After relaying Manny's instructions, he said, "Look, Pete, don't mess around with these people. No smart mouth, no stupid tape recorder stuck in your sock, and I suggest you try and show some respect. Don't be a wiseass, not with this bunch, or you'll get hurt."

"Thanks, Harry." Longdon said. "Maybe we have a chance. Wish me luck."

"Pete, wait! Do you really have twenty-five million dollars?"

"I will have after I make a phone call."

He called Manny back and said Longdon was on his way.

✳   ✳   ✳

The only sign of life on the street fronting the Cyclone, was an occasional drunk falling into, or out of, the dingy-looking bar opposite the ticket booth. As he waited, Longdon kept the engine and defroster running to keep the freezing rain from blocking his vision. He watched in his rear-view mirror as the car pulled up behind him, and a white-haired man in his fifties, got out.

"You Longdon?" he asked gruffly. "You're supposed to have some films. You got them?"

"Yes, they're on the back seat with a camera."

With a hand jammed menacingly into a pocket of his heavy overcoat, the white-haired man ordered him out of the car just as another vehicle with two, younger men in it, pulled along side. The man on the passenger side got out, and told Longdon to toss him the trunk key. Inside were several heavily loaded mail sacks, one of which, he opened.

"*Mica!* Can you believe this? These fuckin' bags are full of dough. Hey, Chichi," he yelled to the man who'd been in the car with him, "come take a look at this shit."

"Never mind, never mind," the white-haired man commanded, "just put them in your car and come over here and search this guy, the car too. If he's got a piece, break one of his arms. Chichi, get those films and the camera out of the back seat."

Blindfolded, and squeezed down onto the floor in the back of a car, Longdon was taken to meet with Manny Ostrow, Tony Trucks, and Alfonsa Ponzinno someplace in Brooklyn.

*   *   *

He knew there were several people in the room besides himself, but with only the projector's flickering light to see by, he couldn't tell how many. During the two hours he was there, they allowed him to show his films and to explain the facts as he knew them, but he wasn't allowed to ask any questions. When he was finished, he was again blindfolded, and taken back to his car in Coney Island, minus the money and the films. It would be several days before he'd hear from anyone about the meeting.

Part 18

It was bitter cold, and the snow had been falling steadily since late afternoon. To keep warm, the three well-dressed men had retreated to the comfort of the small, heated, Tudor style guardhouse, where they took turns emptying a bottle of expensive Scotch whiskey.

Every so often, one of them would examine the semiautomatic shotguns sitting in a wall rack to the left of the door.

When a car pulled up to the high iron gates, they momentarily argued over whose turn it was to go outside. Finally, one of them would reluctantly brace himself against the bone-chilling wind and struggle through the snow. Once he'd verified the legitimacy of its occupants, the heavy gates would be swung open, and closed behind it to await the arrival of the next guest. Before the night was over, the men would have to repeat the task more than twenty times.

Ponzinno had bought the four hundred-acre estate shortly after the birth of his only child, Alfonsa, and it was a place where his young family would come to play and enjoy themselves in the summer. The stables were kept just as they were when his beautiful wife and son had gone riding together early in the morning before breakfast, only now, no one went riding. Yet the grooms would wash and brush the horses daily, clean their tack and stalls, and then walk two horses along the same paths his wife and son had ridden on.

Likewise, Ponzinno's instructions to the house staff required that all the linen and towels in the bedrooms and baths be changed daily, even though most of the rooms were never used. When there were no fresh flowers to be had on the estate because of the weather, he had them delivered each morning from local florists. They were for the rooms his wife liked to spend her time in while she was dying.

In her memory, he had a chapel constructed which was an exact replica of the one she'd fallen in love with the first time they'd gone to Lachine, a small town in Quebec. It was in this chapel where she rested, and it was here, with his pride, that he allowed himself to be exposed to the frailties of emotion.

Tonight was different. Tonight the house was alive again. He'd invited his business associates from Atlanta, New Orleans, Chicago, Boston, and San Francisco to eat and drink with him, and to make plans. Tonight he could, for awhile at least, allow himself the luxury of relaxation, and be "en famile," at home with his new family.

These were the men who trusted and respected him, and in some cases, feared him enough to have chosen him as their leader. These were the men who benevolently allowed the so-called corporate icons of American industry to stay in business. These were the men who, tonight, would determine the political future of the country, and ensure its safety.

While they enjoyed the best foods and wine he could offer, Ponzinno would explain how the United States government had sent this Longdon, the *maiale*, (pig) to him, whimpering and begging for protection from its enemies. He would explain how Longdon had insulted them and shown such *mancanza di rispetto*, disrespect, by sending bribe money.

"They thing we are common street whores," he would tell them, "who will do their bidding."

"After all the harassment," he would say, "after all the indictments and imprisonments of you family members, they now come like scared children."

Finally, he would tell them if they wanted to ensure their own personal safety and that of their families, and guarantee the future success of their businesses, they would have to take certain immediate steps.

*   *   *

The little numbers in the clock radio's illuminated window had just flashed 1:33 a.m. when the phone rang on Sunday morning.

"Hello?" Diedra whispered.

"Is Harry there? It's Manny."

"Sweetheart, wake up, it's Manny."

"Listen, Kid," Manny said, "get this Longdon guy and bring'm down to Annunzio's right away, we wanna talk to'm and you too."

"Yeah, sure, right away. What's happenin'?"

"Never mind. Just get'm and come down here. Understand?"

"No problem, I'll call him right now."

Now wide awake, Diedra waited until he hung up and asked, "Harry are they going to help?"

"It looks that way. They want me to bring Longdon down to Tony Trucks' restaurant."

"Now!? Tonight? Harry, please, be careful," she said, grabbing him tightly around the neck, "I don't know what I'd do if anything happened to you."

Gently, he lowered her arms and pulled the blanket around her before calling Longdon at his Valley Stream home. "I'm pretty sure it's Ponzinno who wants to see us," he told him. "Meet me at the diner on Rockaway Boulevard in back of the airport as soon as you can. And Pete, the same as the last time, no wire, no gun, and no company."

In less than fifteen minutes, Harry was showered, dressed, and on his way to a meeting, the outcome of which, not even Solomon in all his wisdom could have predicted the outcome of. A meeting that would provide the nucleus of his eventual status and power. Power that would last as long as his association with a Ponzinno lasted.

When he arrived at the diner, Longdon wasn't there yet, so he went in for coffee. Standing at the register waiting for the girl to finish with the drunk in front of him, he saw Longdon's beige sedan pull into an empty spot right outside the front door.

"Here, take these and push over, I'll drive," he said, handing him the two containers.

Annunzio's was dark except for a few dim lights in the bar. Harry recognized Manny's car and parked behind it. One glance at the three black Lincolns sitting across the street, each with several men in them, and he knew that at least Bissetti, and possibly Ponzinno, were already inside.

"No back alley, Manny?" he asked quietly as the three of them met in the middle of the street.

"Nah, those jerks got it dug up again. Some crap about the sewer pipes bein' old. They're always diggin' around here, they must think it's a fuckin' cemetery of somethin'. I hope nobody's got nothin' on'em, if you do, dump it."

Both Longdon and Harry assured him they weren't that stupid. Manny searched them anyway.

The inner lobby door had barely closed behind them when four figures got up from a table at the end of the darkened bar, one of them being the older, white-haired man. "Put your hands up," he snarled at both Harry and Longdon, and then watched carefully as his three gunsels searched them.

"OK, they're clean," the one named Chichi said.

"Wait here," the white-haired man ordered, before disappearing into the middle section of the restaurant which served as Bissetti's private dining room and office.

Someone must have been still cooking because the smell of garlic and burnt meat was very strong. That, plus the toxic odor of whatever they'd mopped the floors with, was making Harry nauseous.

They stood silently for what seemed like eternity until finally, the white-haired man appeared beckoning for them to follow him. Harry didn't know about Longdon, but he himself was fast developing a full-blown anxiety attack.

Just outside the entrance to Ponzinno's sanctuary, he and Longdon were searched again by two of his personal bodyguards. Bissetti and Ponzinno were sitting at a corner table sipping black coffee. Neither of them looked up, but kept quietly talking.

"Wait until he tells you it's OK to come over," Manny said in a low voice, his head nervously nodding and eyes blinking.

"Something's wrong," Harry said to himself after noticing Manny's condition. "What the hell is he so nervous about? These are his friends." He was right, something was wrong, and he'd only have to wait a short time to find out what it was.

Deliberately, Harry suspected, they were made to stand there for more than ten minutes while the men at the table finished talking. With a flick of his head, it was Bissetti who motioned for them to come forward.

"That's it, go on over," Manny said, nudging them both in their backs, "but don't sit down unless someone tells you to."

Harry remembered how scared he'd been the first time Manny brought him to meet Ponzinno, and tonight was no different. In fact, it was worse because he'd seen firsthand the anger Ponzinno was capable of, and from one look at the man's face, Harry knew he was about to see it again. The expression too on Bissetti's face, was a giveaway. All of a sudden the atmosphere became hostile, like everybody knew there was going to be a bad fight, but weren't sure when the first punch would be thrown.

"Sit down, Gentlemen," Ponzinno said, his eyes never leaving Longdon's face. "Would either of you care for coffee, or maybe a glass of anisette?"

"Mr. Ponzinno," Harry asked hesitantly, "by any chance, would there be any of your father's wine left?"

"Ah! Good, you remembered," Ponzinno said, half smiling. "You've taken my advice and stopped with that Irish whiskey. What is it called? Bushmills? The wine is better for you. I told my father about your generous offer to help with the press. He wanted to know if you are strong. And how about you, Mr. Longdon, may I offer you something?"

"Thank you, yes, I'd like to try the annisette."

With a hand gesture, Bissetti summoned a waiter and spoke to him in Italian. Within minutes he was back with Longdon's drink, and the dark, unlabeled bottle of homemade wine.

"My son called me today, Harry," Ponzinno said. "He wanted to know if I was the one who sent the vestments and the chalice and plate. I told him no, but that I was fairly certain I knew who had. It was you, wasn't it?"

"Yes, sir, I thought they might be things he could use," he answered, trying to look and sound as if he was humble. "I kept thinking about him after you spoke to me, and, well, I wanted to celebrate his ordination with him. Please, if I was out of line, I apologize."

"On the contrary, it was a very thoughtful and splendid gesture. It also showed that you have respect for people, and that you know the importance of doing the right thing. He'd like to meet you. In fact, it would please me if the two of you got to know each other, and perhaps spend some time together."

"I'd like that," Harry answered, "I'd like that very much."

"Is that the way it is with your people, Mr. Longdon?" Ponzinno asked, the tone of his voice laced with hostility. "Do they know how to show respect and the importance of doing the right thing?"

"I'm not sure I understand your question," Longdon answered cautiously, sensing the ominous overtones of his host's inquiry. Ponzinno glared at him like a hungry mongoose cornering a rat. With a nod of his head, two of his men got up and left the room.

They returned dragging the money laden mail sacks the white-haired man had taken from the trunk of Longdon's car. The one called Chichi made a second trip, this time coming back with the two, bulky, cloth sacks Harry had brought to Manny's office.

Ponzinno stood, grabbed one and unzipped it. "Is this how you show respect, Mr. Longdon!?" he screamed, dumping the million dollars onto the table and throwing the bag into his face. Longdon went to stand, but quickly changed his mind when Bissetti pulled a gun and drove the muzzle almost into his mouth.

"Do you think showing respect means sending my people bribes?" Ponzinno continued, his face flushed with anger.

"Do you think by sending these bags of money we're going to become your lackeys? Is this the kind of people your government thinks it's dealing with? Is this how you get people to bare false witness against our families, by giving them money, you bastard, *stupido*, fool." Now, in a rage, Ponzinno picked up one of the mail sacks as if it was weightless, and threw it across the table. Manny and Harry jumped from their chairs and backed away.

With a heavy impact, the bag found its mark; it opened and bundles of money bounced off Longdon's chest.

"Mr. Ponzinno, please," Longdon begged, his voice trembling. "The government sent this money as a good faith offering, certainly not with any intentions of insulting you or your people." Even in the poorly lit room, you could see how the profusion of sweat had darkened

Longdon's shirt, and his cloth napkin was soaked from mopping his face.

"Do you understand Latin, Mr. Longdon?"

"No, sir, I don't."

"*Timeo Danaos et dona ferente.* It means I fear the Greeks even when they bring gifts. It's too bad this waste who passes himself off as your president and the rest of you didn't learn that as children. If you had, your enemies would not now have you all by the throats. I curse you all."

"Mr. Ponzinno," Longdon said haltingly, "with all due respect, the vast majority of the people in our government had no knowledge of what he was doing. They're not responsible for this terrible situation."

"*Non dire stupidita*, don't talk nonsense. They did know!" Ponzinno yelled, slamming his fist on the table with such force that most of the glasses and cups giggled and bounced to the floor. "If they were deaf and blind, or if they were retarded, then, Mr. Longdon, they might have an excuse for letting this renegade, this fornicator, to remain in office."

"Please, Mr. Ponzinno, whatever you may think of us you've got to help us get into those rooms."

Calmly, Ponzinno adjusted his tie and instructed the waiter to clean up and replace what had fallen.

"There's no need for me to help you," he said, "we've already been in them."

Sitting bold-upright, and tilting his head quizzically to one side, Longdon, almost whispering, said, "Pardon?"

Ponzinno leaned over and asked Bissetti something in Italian, who nodded affirmatively.

To their amazement, Harry and Longdon listened while Ponzinno explained how, at 11:15 p.m. that very same night, his men had driven high-lows through the doors of the research rooms at all six of the Santronics warehouse centers and stripped them of their contents.

"You what!?" Longdon shouted, jumping to his feet.

"Sit down, you prick, before I kick you face in," Bissetti demanded as he pulled Longdon back into his chair.

"Please, Mr. Ponzinno, this is terribly important. You've got to tell me what you did with the contents of those rooms."

"You got to? You got to? You gotta learn some fuckin' manners," Bissetti growled as he smashed the barrel of his gun up against the side of Longdon's head. "Please, Alfonsa, let me teach this fat prick some manners."

"In time, Tony, in time," Ponzinno replied, "right now we have need of Mr. Longdon. He's going to be our messenger boy. "To answer your question, Mr. Longdon, "by now what was in those rooms is scattered over who knows how many states. I guarantee your people could look for a lifetime and never find any of it."

"But what about Nagakura's men in the security rooms, and there was a second alarm system too?" Longdon asked, now close to being frantic. "And why would you want to keep the devices?"

"To begin with, Mr. Longdon, the second alarm is a silent one, and it rings in a company I own. As for Nagakura's TV watchers, they're gone."

"Gone?" Longdon asked, trying to stem the flow of blood from the side of his head.

"Yes, gone. They're no concern of yours. If I'm correct, by morning when the rest of this Nagakura's people learn what's happened, they'll be gone too. At least you won't have to kill them. Isn't that what you planned on doing, Mr. Longdon? Perhaps you can explain something to me. When I'm required to deal with my enemies, you call it murder, but when you, what is it you call it? When you terminate people, you call in being patriotic. Can you explain that to me, Mr. Longdon?

"And as for me keeping the devices, we'll get to that.

"Now, to save us all a lot of time," Ponzinno continued, "I'll do the talking, and I don't want to be interrupted, do I make myself clear?"

He reached into his jacket pocket, took out an envelope containing several photographs, and threw them across the table at Longdon.

"These are Polaroids of the equipment and of the two devices we took out of the room here in Brooklyn. I'm sure they'll be of some interest to your scientists. As you can see, they have been fitted into steamer trunks. Three of Komti's technicians were still in the room working; the two who decide to live told us they had just finished installing the firing mechanisms, so we got there none too soon. We provided them with a comfortable place to live—for the time being, just in case we should have future use of them.

"I'm told, Mr. Longdon, there were two of these things in each of the other five warehouse centers, but from the way they were described to me, apparently they're not as near to completion as the one's your looking at. Whether they had firing mechanisms, we won't know until my own experts examine them. I'll have photographs taken of everything we've put into storage for your government and sent to you; you'll be able to make your own determination. Eventually, we'll give most of them back to you.

"Now, as for the Santronics business. Without his toys, Nagakura is *spazzatura*, rubbish, and the whole Komti operation becomes a dog without a head. There was never any stock issued in the new company, there is no board of directors, and as long as he is alive, no one within the company will dare make a move against him, but the Japanese government will. Once it realizes what is happening, it will nationalize his assets.

"It might interest you to know that Nagakura is in San Francisco, one of his little friends was kind enough to let us know before...before he had to go away. We have a good idea where he is and it won't be long before we locate him.

"Now, in exchange for the contents of the rooms, including most of the devices, you are going to sell us Santronics. The sale will include the physical assets of all six warehouse distribution centers here in America, and the trade name Santronics, along with all inventories presently in the warehouses, all inventories presently on route to them, and all dealer accounts receivable are to be assigned to us. In addition, you will sell us the five Komti factories in Japan presently engaged in the manufacturing of Santronics product.

"For this, I will pay exactly twenty-eight million dollars. These mail sacks contain twenty-five million, the two cloth bags another two million, and Harry here will see that you get the bag he has home. That, Mr. Longdon, adds up to twenty-eight million dollars.

"Both the governments of Japan and the United States will endorse, in writing, the legitimacy of the sale, and the endorsement will stipulate there are to be no taxes of any kind due either government for a period of ten years. There are to be no import of export tariffs for a like period of time, and the Japanese government will agree that Komti Shipping, Ltd., will transport, free of charge, all merchandise manufactured at the five plants in Japan, to the United States during the same ten-year period.

"Finally, Mr. Longdon, there are fourteen names on this list I'm giving you. These individuals are to be released from prison within ten days, and receive full pardons signed by whoever the next president of the United States is going to be; not by this one.

"Effective immediately, Mr. Harry O'Day, is the new President and CEO of Santronics America, Inc., and of Santronics Japan, Ltd., which will control the five manufacturing plants.

"That, Mr. Longdon, is what you're going to do for me in exchange for the devices. If you decide you don't want them, that's fine too. I'm sure we'll have no difficulty selling them. There are people, say in Belfast for instance, who have an 800 year-old score to settle. I'm sure they would be most interested in getting their hands on one. But we'd make sure the British government knows how the United States could have prevented them from getting hold of it.

"What about the Jews, Mr. Longdon? Perhaps they might be interested in one? Or maybe the Arabs? Perhaps both countries would like one? How about the North Koreans? Would that worry the Japanese, having one of these things in their own backyard?

"Any questions, Mr. Longdon?"

Drained of color and sitting in a puddle of sweat, Longdon spoke. "Sir, you said we'll be getting some of the devices back. With all due respect, I don't understand what you mean by some."

"That's simple," Ponzinno answered. "When we have a signed agreement, and our friends have been free, you'll get them all back except the two from Brooklyn. Those we'll keep in a safe place for your government."

Painfully aware of Bissetti's presence behind him, Longdon struggled to control his usual arrogant attitude, and his newfound hatred of the gangster dictating to him. "But, Mr. Ponzinno, they're the most important ones—they're armed."

"Exactly, Mr. Longdon, exactly. *Si vis pacem, para bellum*, if you wish peace, then you have to prepare or war."

"The two from Brooklyn? Do you have any intention of giving them back at some future time?"

"We'll see, we'll see."

"Mr. Ponzinno, we have no power with the Japanese government. We could never force them to agree to something like this. There's nothing we could offer that would induce them to make such a deal."

"On the contrary, you have a great deal to offer. To begin with, you can get rid of this president of yours for them, and make sure nobody like him ever gets into the White House again. You can also guarantee Nagakura will no longer be a thorn in their side, I'll see to that. You'll point out to them how they automatically become the sole possessor of billions of dollars of his assets. All they have to do is walk in and take them, less, of course, what is being sold to me. They might even be interested in having one of the devices themselves. They have some very unpleasant neighbors.

"Tony," Ponzinno continued, "why don't you have Mr. Longdon and his money taken back to his car? And Tony, for his safety, have your men escort him right to his front door. That way if we should ever want him, we'll know exactly where he lives.

"Before you go, Mr. Longdon, let me give you some advice. It is unwise to let your enemies know the extent of your hatred of them. I've been watching your eyes, and I can tell you've thought about having me killed, and if you could, all this would go away, and you could force my people to give back what I've taken from you. I can assure you, it will never happen. Tell your government that.

"You may think you know who we are, where we are, and what we're doing, but the truth is, you know nothing. With all your hidden cameras, and tapped phones, and yes, even with your stupid microphones in the wheels of automobiles parked outside our businesses, you still know nothing. There are people involved in this who's names you will never know, so if anything happened to me, it wouldn't change a thing, except of course that you and your family would be murdered also. Your government would try and hide you, but it wouldn't take long to find you, or your two sons and their families.

"I can guarantee that if anything happens to me, not a ship in any port in this country will get loaded, or unloaded. Any truck driver taking the chance of hauling anything would suddenly find himself with a broken arm. Every major construction site in the nation would start having unexplained catastrophes, that's assuming of course any of the men bothered to show up for work. The airlines would be lucky if they got 10 percent of their flights off the ground.

"Should I continue, Mr. Longdon? Are you prepared to use the military to keep the country from chaos? Then again, you'd be dead, so it wouldn't be your problem.

"I expect an answer from you within ten days. Do you understand me? And from now on, you're to deal with Harry. Now get out of my sight."

After Longdon and the money were taken away, Bissetti, Manny, and Harry remained at the table, and in a somber, almost surreal atmosphere, listened while Ponzinno explained things. Evil was in the process of replacing evil.

Harry asked timidly, "Mr. Ponzinno, why me? With all due respect, there must be thousands of men far more capable of this. I'm afraid I might be in over my head. I may not be able to give you what you want."

"I'm told, Harry," Ponzinno began, "That you know this business better than anyone around. That you work some kind of magic to get people to do what you want. The important thing is that I trust you. Tony and Manny, they trust you too. You also know the importance of showing respect, and having loyalty to your friends, to protect their confidences. You're not just anybody, you're capable of doing whatever you put your mind to, and doing it well. I have great plans for you. Believe me, you are going to be a powerful man.

"No, I don't think I've chosen the wrong person, besides, you'll have plenty of help. My lawyers and many others who are already working on this, have been instructed to give you their complete cooperation. But always remember, you are the boss, no one else. Listen to what they have to say, but then you must decide. Once you've told them to do something, never second guess yourself, it's a sign of weakness. It's better that men should fear and respect you, than pretend to be your friends and flout their disrespect behind you back. Men like that you must deal with harshly.

"Have you ever read Machiavelli?"

"Yes, in college."

"What did you think of him?"

"I think he would have made a great manager for the Yankees."

"Very good, Harry, very good. I have to remember to tell that to my son. He's a great fan of Niccolo."

"Mr. Ponzinno, if I may," Harry asked. "There's something I'd like to mention. It's very important to me personally." He explained how his father had been murdered in a prisoner of war camp run by Nagakura, and how the body had been desecrated. He told Ponzinno that he'd taken an oath on his mother's grave to avenge his father's murder, but that he would need help doing it.

"You shall have it," Ponzinno said, coming from around the table and putting both hands on his shoulders. I promise you. I make your vendetta mine.

"Tony, when our friends find that trash, I don't want him touched. Tell them Manny is bringing someone to deal with him. Ask them to have whatever they might need ready when they get there."

*   *   *

It wasn't the same Harry O'Day who drove back to Queens that Sunday morning. Somewhere between the time he'd met Longdon at the diner, and now, a metamorphosis had taken place.

Everything was different now. He was different. It was no longer simply a case of enjoying being around, "those people." Now he had to be around them.

Ponzinno's charisma and power were like narcotics, and overnight, Harry had become an addict. "Those people," had made him privy to their awesome strength, and as long as he did what they told him, he'd be part of their thing with rewards beyond imagination and with permission to use their power against his enemies.

As he drove, he thought about what he'd tell Diedra. Until now she'd begrudgingly accepted his explanations of what was happening. Her concern had been for their personal safety. Once things started calming down, if they did, he was sure her fears would be redirected, and she'd ask a lot of questions. So it would be important how he explained what was about to take place. He certainly couldn't tell her Ponzinno was a super gangster blackmailing the U.S. government, or that he'd probably had the Rossbaums murdered. Nor that he was going to help him kill Nagakura.

Instead, he would tell her there had been a dramatic change in things for the better. That Ponzinno was in the process of brokering a deal that would allow the government to take possession of the devices. As for Nagakura and his cohorts, most of them were trying to flee the country, and Longdon's men were looking for the few who'd gone into hiding. He would tell her as part of what was happening, Ponzinno was looking to buy Santronics and run it as a legitimate business. Furthermore, Ponzinno would be putting together a team of American businessmen to run the operation both here and in Japan, and incredibly, had asked him to be the man in charge.

Hopefully, he thought, she'd believe him, that the explanation sounded plausible. It would be important because he didn't want her doubting his integrity when he asked her to marry him.

Part 19

"Don't be scared, it's me," he said, trying not to make the bedroom floor squeak.

"No, it's OK," she said, taking the gun out from under her pillow and putting it into the night table drawer. "I heard your car and looked out the window. Are you all right?"

"A lot better than when I went out," he replied, sitting on the edge of the bed, and starting to undress.

"You were gone so long, what happened? Are we going to get blown up?"

"Well, I'll tell you. First of all, you can stop worrying. No, we're not going to get blown up. Secondly, how about getting me a cup of coffee? I'll take a quick shower and we can talk. OK?"

As she stood, the bright rays of early morning sunlight streaming through the blinds, danced over he nude body. Her red hair seemed longer than ever as it hung down her smooth white back almost to the middle of her buttocks. He watched as she stretched both arms over her head and made a groaning sound.

"Forget the coffee," he said, "I want you to help me with something in the shower." Quickly, he finished undressing and took her by the hand into the bathroom They hadn't been together for awhile, but made up for it under the shower's hot driving water, and afterwards, on the bed.

"Well, Mr. O'Day, I'll say you're feeling better. So am I. Do you still want the coffee?"

"Yes, and if you have a bagel or something. I'm starved."

They sat on the bed talking while he emptied the breakfast tray she'd brought him, and after hearing the story he'd composed on the was home, she seemed genuinely relieved, much to his delight.

"Thank God," she said. "You know, in school, the nuns used to make us practice where to go in case they dropped an atomic bomb. Do you know how many times in the last week I've gone around this house trying to figure out the best place to hide? Sweetheart, are you really going to be in charge?"

"That's what they tell me, Mr. Harry O'Day, president and CEO, hows that grab you? We'll have to give the money back, but I guarantee, if this works, we'll be rich. Can you imagine, giving back a million bucks and not thinking it's a big deal?"

"Harry, this whole thing is so crazy, I'm afraid to hope."

"I'm telling you, stop worrying. After last night, everything is gonna be all right."

"Sweetheart, it's too late now, but next Sunday, could we go to mass together?"

"Funny you should ask that. I was thinking about that on the way home."

"About going to mass?"

"Something like that, but more along the lines of you and I going to church to get married."

"Oh my God! Are you serious?" she screamed. "O'Day, don't be kidding around about something like this. Are you really asking me to marry you?

"As sure as I'm naked."

"Oh, yes, sweetheart! Yes! Yes! Yes! Of course I'll marry you," she cried, pushing him down on the bed and straddling him. "I love you. When?"

"As soon as possible. We just have to wait a bit to make sure this deal Ponzinno's working on goes through. It would be nice to know that we weren't gonna get blown up on our honeymoon."

"I can't believe it, I'm so happy, sweetheart," she murmured, tears starting to run down her cheeks. "Harry, I just thought of something. We probably can't get married from the altar because you're divorced. I can go over after Father Grimaldi finishes noon mass and ask him, but I don't think we can."

"Would that bother you if we couldn't?" he asked.

"No! Not in the least. I'd marry you naked in Macy's window if that's the only way I could do it."

"What would you say if I told you I'm thinking about asking Mike O'Banion to be my best man?"

"I'm sure he'd be honored. He's been your friend for a long time, and after the way he's helped up, I think it would be a nice thing to do. You know his father said that if we got married, he'd let us have the bar for a reception."

"We'll see. I was thinking more like a place in the country, you know, with a lot of trees and flowers. We might not be getting married for awhile, by then it'll be nice and warm."

"Oh God, I just thought of something. My maid of honor, I need a maid of honor."

"So? What's the big deal?"

"The big deal is that I don't know anyone well enough to ask them to do a think like that for me. It's not cheap."

"What about Marie? She'd probably turn herself inside out if you asked her. It's obvious she likes you."

"Oh she does, she does. The problem is sometimes she doesn't know when to give it a rest. She's a wonderful, goodhearted person, and I care for her dearly, but, well, you met her, you see what she's like. It's because she's alone in that house too much, like I was here in this place.

"If you and your wife weren't home, I'd go to her after Terrence had beaten me, especially if I couldn't stop the bleeding. I'd wear one of her ridiculous housecoats if she had to wash the blood out of my clothing."

Diedra's voice trailed off, and staring into nothingness, she began to cry. It was like she was collapsing inwardly, cowering at the nightmarish memories of the savage beatings her dead prick of a husband had inflicted upon her.

"No, no, no," he said tenderly, "that's over with, let it go, you're safe now. No one's going to hurt you anymore."

She began shaking, and he grabbed her tightly. He'd seen her like this before. Sometimes at night she'd jump awake screaming, and then slowly sink back down using a pillow to muffle her cries. When it happened, he'd hold her and stroke her hair until, exhausted, she'd fall asleep. Even then her body would continue to jerk and tremble.

In the morning, he'd ask her about it, but she wouldn't have any recollection.

He got an idea of how bad the beatings must have been when they were in the park one day fooling around. He raised his hand, not even in a threatening manner, but by conditioning, she fell to the ground in a fetal position and protected her face and head with her arms.

"OK," he said, drying her face with tissues, "let's see if I can tell you something funny enough to make you laugh. Picture this, Marie and the priest fighting over how our wedding ceremony should be arranged and you and I taking bets from the guests on who's gonna win. How's that?"

She smiled and he kissed her salty cheek.

"Thank you," she said, wiping her tears on the blanket. "I hate for you to see me like this, but sometimes, I can't help it. You know, when he was beating me, I would ask God to let me die so that it would be over with. Harry? Did you ever kill anybody? I almost did. One night, after he got drunk and passed out, I got his service revolver. I was going to kill him and then myself, but I was afraid of going to hell."

Lovingly, he held her head against his chest.

"Look," he said, "how about we get some sleep and then we'll go up to the park and ride the merry-go-round? I'll buy you some of those greasy french fries in a paper cup you like. They probably haven't gotten any fresh beer since last summer, but who cares."

"Oh could we? I'd like that. We could spend the afternoon together, and there might even be some snow left up there."

She slipped off her robe and pulled him down next to her. "You know, Mr. O'Day, if we keep doing this, I'll have to buy a maternity wedding dress. Would that bother you?"

"Not me, but it might bother your friend, Father Grimaldi when he was marrying us."

*　　　*　　　*

The moment he pulled into the parking lot he knew it was going to be a different kind of Monday morning. "one, two, three empty spots. I wonder where they could be?" he asked himself, smirking. He was looking at spaces reserved for some of the Japanese big bosses. For as long as he'd worked in the building, no matter how early he got there, the spots were always filled.

"Let's see what else is different," he said, taking his coat and briefcase off the front seat before heading down to the warehouse section of the complex.

The smashed, heavy, metal door to the research and development room had been left hanging by one hinge, and the two gaping holes made by the fork of the high-low, looked as if armor piercing shells had been fired through it. The room itself was empty, not even a wastebasket.

Noticeably absent were the few, sneering Do Nothings who were always lurking about the place. The Japanese behind the parts department security fence, and the four in the print shop didn't look up when he passed by, which was totally uncharacteristic for them. To the man, they had always smiled and given him a little bow whenever he went by, and he would do the same. It was like a game they played with each other. But today, they wouldn't look at him.

Then he noticed Manny standing behind the big, plate glass window up in his office. With a Chesire cat smile, he pointed to the remains of the door with one hand, and with the other, gave an exaggerated military salute.

Connie, his secretary had two containers of his special tea waiting when he got to his office. That was standard Monday morning procedure. "good morning Boss," she said, "got a minute?"

"Sure, come in, and bring you book." They'd been together long enough for him to know by the sound of her voice when something was bugging her.

"What the hell is going on around here this morning?" she asked, standing so close that for the first time, he noticed the small, heart shaped mole on the inside of her left breast.

"I don't know, you tell me, I just got here. You mean there's something happening around this place that you don't 'now about? I though you knew everything. Weren't you the one who told me your girlfriend and that Cheri in the order department were getting it on?" He was playing dumb because he wanted to hear what the office scuttlebutt was saying about the missing Japanese, and about the door.

"Yes, but that's everyday stuff. This is real weird stuff going on."

"Weird like how?"

"Like all those creepy guys you call Do Nothings. They're all gone, not one of them came in. I've never seen that before. And some of the other Japanese men aren't here either. Even their desks have been cleaned out, at least that's what I hear."

"Excuse me, Connie," he said when the phone rang. "let me take this call and then we can talk. "

"Harry, it's Ira. I know you told me never to call you, but I thought you'd like to know, Yamatoki is dead."

Like a holy revelation, he knew in an instant that his suspicions about Yamatoki had been correct. The Do Nothings had taken their orders from him. It was Yamatoki who had Kiedelman whacked, he was sure of it, and it was Yamatoki that ordered the two Secret Service agents to search his apartment, the same two guys who had torched their own people in the Bronx. "Rest in hell you bastard!" he said to himself.

"What happened?" he asked Ira calmly.

"The cleaning people found him this morning at his desk. He stabbed himself with that stupid sword letter opener he was always playing with. They said he did it to himself in the stomach and the blood and everything was all over."

"Are the police there?"

"Quite a few. Someone said the FBI is here too. All the women are crying and want to leave, but the police won't let them. They want to ask them questions."

"Listen, Ira, and listen carefully. You don't say a word about that meeting. Understand? Not a word. What about Mishimia and Shihoto, are they around?"

"No, I haven't seen them. And all the creeps are gone, even the one with the scars. Harry? What's going on? Did you hear anything about all the warehouses being robbed?"

"No, I didn't hear that. Look thanks for letting me know. Remember, not a word about our meeting with Yamatoki."

"Of course, Harry, anything you say, you can count on me. Harry? Are you still mad at me?"

"We'll talk about it," he said, and hung up.

He knew that what was happening in Brooklyn, was also happening in the five other Santronics warehouse centers. Once Ponzinno's people had smashed into the research rooms, the news spread like wildfire among Nagakura's henchmen and they ran. Where they'd all gone to was anybody's guess, but one thing was for certain, not one of them was about to call the police to report a robbery.

Ponzinno had been right. Once their toys had been taken away, they were dead meat. They couldn't complain to the cops, they couldn't complain to the American government, and they couldn't even complain to their own government. They were now pariahs, on the run, with a lot of people out looking to kill them.

As far as work was concerned, the day was a waste. The suspense of not knowing Longdon's situation was unnerving to say the least. Maybe, Harry thought, when Longdon went back to his people with Ponzinno's ultimatums, they laughed and were getting ready to arrest everyone connected to the scheme. Maybe Manny had heard something, he thought, as he got up and made the long walk down to the warehouse.

Manny and his son Bobby were sitting with their feet up on the desk eating sandwiches and doing a good job getting rid of a bottle of liquor. "Hey, Harry, what's doin'?" Manny asked, obviously feeling good from the booze. "Or should I call you Mr. President? Here, have a sandwich. Whatta you want? Tuna, or ham and cheese? And get yourself a cup and have a drink."

"Just the drink, you can keep the sandwich."

"How you like the way we left the door?" Manny asked with a big grin. "Just in case any of those fuckers are still around, we figured it would be a good message."

"You're a pisser Manny, a real pisser. What happens if Longdon busts in here with a bunch of feds and arrests us all?"

"Harry, Harry, don't worry so much, you'll get ulcers. Relax, here, have another drink, you'll feel better."

"Hey, Harry," Bobby said, "when you take over, how about gettin' Tony to fire this old fuck here and makin' me boss?"

"Why you little prick you," Manny told his son, "if it wasn't for me, you wouldn't know what end of the fuckin' box to put the stuff in."

"I can't believe you two. This whole think is a joke."

"Harry, take it easy," Manny said, "everything's under control. We're only breakin' your balls a little. Tony says for you to sit tight. You're gonna hear somethin' real soon, maybe even today. There's a lot goin' on. How's that girl of yours?"

"Fine. It just so happens I asked her to marry me."

"Hey, that's great. Here, have a drink. Alfonsa will like that. Wait until he hears. He thinks married guys got more stability. He'll probably ask you how many kids you're gonna have."

On the way back to his office, he wondered if Manny had personally been involved in murdering the Rossbaums.

*   *   *

By Thursday afternoon, he was down to biting his nails. Even at home, Diedra was becoming a nervous wreck herself from watching him.

He'd just gotten off the phone when Connie raced into his office with a small radio jammed against her ear.

"Boss! Listen to this. Oh my God, this is terrible!" she cried.

"…interrupt our regularly scheduled broadcasting to repeat this special bulletin. The White House has confirmed that the president was aboard Air Force One when it disappeared from radar while enroute from Guam to Manila International Airport. A massive sea and air rescue operation is now under way, but so far, there have been no sightings of wreckage.

"A spokesman for the headquarters of Rear Admiral Jason Murotie at Pearl Harbor stated that every available rescue plane and ship have been dispatched to the area. However, due to deteriorating weather conditions and the immensity of the possible crash area, their efforts were being severely hampered.

"The president was scheduled to attend memorial services for American and Allied servicemen who died during the Bataan Death March, and in Japanese prison camps.

"Also onboard were General Hale Andrunn, head of the Joint Chiefs, and several of his staff. In addition, two members of the cabinet and a number of the president's key advisers were traveling with him.

"The Philippine government has informed the U.S. State Department it is prepared to extend all possible assistance to the search effort. It pointed out, however, the shark-infested waters in that part of the ocean are more than eight thousand feet deep, and at present, the seas there are running abnormally high due to an approaching typhoon.

"As we get more information about this possible tragedy, we will interrupt our programming at once. This has been a special news bulletin from WKCC news headquarters. We now return you to the program already in progress."

"My God, boss, " Connie moaned, "this is so bad. Do you think they're dead? Can you imagine? Being eaten by sharks. What happens if they can't find him?"

"Then the vice president takes over, but something tells me he's not gonna want the job."

"What makes you say that?"

"Oh, nothing. Let's just say it's a premonition."

"Are you very upset, boss?"

"Yes, Connie, I'm speechless, absolutely overwhelmed."

"You don't look or sound like it."

"You know me, Connie, I try not to show my emotions."

She left to join the others in the outer office who by now, had gathered into small groups and were either listening to radios or watching the TV coverage. From time to time they would turn to each other and make muffled comments about something.

Out of the corner of his eye, Harry saw Manny come through a door-way and drop a load of completed orders onto a clerk's desk. As he turned to leave, he snapped off a salute and grinned.

Gradually the commotion among the workers subsided. Every so often someone would say, "Hey, did you hear the latest," but for the most part, once the staff had absorbed the initial shock of the not so dynamic president's unfortunate accident, it was business as usual. In the days and weeks ahead the spin doctors, much to their dismay, would find it impossible to sell the accident as one of the great calamities of the century.

At 4 p.m. Connie came in. "Hey boss, guess what? There's a priest out in the reception room and he's asking to see you."

"A priest? What the hell would a priest want to see me for? All right, look, we can't just let him sit there, go and get him.

"Oh, no," he said to himself, "this is some of Diedra's work." He fig-ured she'd gone to see Father Grimaldi about him being divorced and whether or not they could get married from the altar, and now the guy had come to talk to him about it, at the office no less. "For Christ's sake, why the hell did she send him here?" he asked himself.

"Right this way, Father," Connie said as she ushered a rather young looking priest into his office. Harry knew Father Grimaldi and this was-n't him.

"Father, this is Mr. O'Day," Connie said, taking his coat. "Father, isn't it terrible about the president and all those people?"

"Yes, it's a tragedy," he answered, making the sign of the cross. "Now they're in God's hands. Are you a Catholic?"

"Yes I am, Father."

"Then go to your church on the way home tonight, and light a candle for their souls."

While the two of them were talking, Harry noticed the priest's face, and how badly scared and disfigured the left side of it was. Suddenly the priest turned. "Hi" my name is Father Alfonsa Arezzo, and I've been waiting a long time to meet you." Taking hold of Harry's hand and shaking it vigorously, he asked, "May I close the door and sit down?"

"Yes, of course, where are my manners," Harry answered. "Father, do I know you? You look familiar, and you name, Arezzo, I've heard it before."

"As a matter of fact we do know each other. We met many years ago when two misguided souls decided to beat the dickens out of me."

Harry leaped to his feet and yelled, "Well I'll be dipped in shit, you're, oh, please, excuse the language, but you're Alfonsa Ponzinno's son, aren't you?"

"Yes, and don't worry about the language, I had pretty much the same reaction last night when my father told me that after all these years of looking, he'd managed to find you. I'm down here for a seminar and he told me you worked in the same building as Uncle Manny. So I just had to stop by and thank you. Isn't it wonderful, how God let my father find you?"

"Yes, it's incredible. Can I offer you something? Maybe a soda? Coffee? There's a restaurant across the way, we could go over and have something if you'd like. Or we could have them send something over."

"No, thank you anyway. I've already had lunch, besides, a priest friend of mine is waiting outside, I promised him I'd go visit his parents. I also have to go see Uncle Manny. If he finds out I was here and didn't say hello, he'll be mad. Do you know him?"

"Quite well. In fact, lately we've been spending a lot of time together."

"My father is giving a small dinner party Saturday night at our home upstate, and it would please him greatly if you would come. If my suspicions are correct, you and I may end up being the centerpieces. He was going to contact you himself, but I asked that he let me invite you. Uncle Manny and my Uncle Tony are going to be there, along with some of my father's business associates. Do you know Uncle Tony?"

"Yes, I had the pleasure of dining with him, your father, and your Uncle Manny just recently. He's a fine man."

"Good, then it's all set. It'll be like one big family. My father would be honored if you brought your fiancée. Uncle Manny told him you were getting married. That's wonderful, congratulations. Will the wedding be soon?"

"Yes, very soon, especially if things keep going the way they did today."

"Things have gone well today, haven't they? Now, I've drawn this little map here to help you find us, I hope you can understand My hieroglyphics."

"I appreciate the invitation, and please, thank your father. Tell him it's very gracious of him to ask my fiancée and myself to your home. Tell him I'm honored."

"Oh, I almost forgot," the priest said, taking a large, brown envelope out of his briefcase. "My father asked me to personally hand this to you. He'd appreciate it if you would look over the contents and then maybe Saturday night, the two of you could get together.

"Well, Harry, I can't tell you how glad I am that we finally met. Is it all right to call you Harry?"

"Of course! And may I call you Alfonsa?"

"By all means. You know, it's not like we're strangers. We've actually known each other for years. It's like we're long lost brothers. My father even said something to that effect last night as dinner.

"Now, just one more thing," the priest continued, "the vestments, and the chalice and plate. You know when the package came, some of the other priests kidded me. They said when His Holiness the Pope, found out I was dressing better than him, he'd excommunicate me. They cost a great deal, didn't they?"

"That's not important," Harry answered, glad to see that the fifteen grand he'd invested in the gifts might just be starting to pay off.

"Would you mind telling me why you sent them?"

"I guess after your father, uh, found me, and explained it was his son I'd helped, and that you had just been ordained, I started thinking. I remembered the look on those bastards' faces when you were on the ground and they wouldn't stop kicking you. They were trying to kill you, you know that, right? They were looking to do a number on me too, but I got lucky. I went back to the hospital a couple of days later, but they said you were critical and nobody could see you. They wouldn't even tell me your name."

"Yes, they really hurt me. The doctors had to remove my spleen and I've had a lot of reconstructive surgery."

"I went back a second time and they said you had been transferred to a private hospital. After that, I could never find out what happened to you, until your father, uh, until your father found me. I felt like I knew you and I wanted to do something. Are you upset about the vestments?"

"No, not at all. They're a gift to God, and it's in his name and glory that they're being used. Well, again, thank you for everything. I'd better go see Uncle Manny before my friend outside leaves without me. I'm looking forward to meeting your fiancée, so is my father. *Dieu vous garde*, God keep you."

*   *   *

The brown envelope contained a twelve-page letter typed on expensive parchment stationery from the Washington law firm of Spellman, Digbe, Conrad, Mellon and Associates, and was addressed to Mr. Harold L. O'Day, president and CEO, Santronics America, Inc.

It was an overview of how the two new corporations would operate, and what his responsibilities would be in each. The first ten pages were a lot of legalese, but then he came to one short subparagraph titled, REMUNERATION, and that read crystal clear.

He was to receive 1 percent of the initial number of shares of common stock issued by each corporation, and a combined annual salary of $6,500,000. He and Diedra were set, they were going to be rich. The fact that he was now owned by murderers didn't even enter his mind. If it had, he would have said, "so what? It's too bad people are dead, but I've got nothing to do with any of that stuff."

At first his salary and stock deal sounded like a fortune. But after doing some rough figuring, he estimated that with Santronics' assets in America, the five Japanese manufacturing plants, tax and tariff breaks, existing inventories, free shipping, and a few other items, Ponzinno had picked himself up a two billion dollar business for nothing.

The lawyers' letter went on to say that shortly, it would be necessary for him to attend a series of meetings to be held in their Manhattan offices. For his convenience, a limousine service had been instructed to provide him with transportation on an around-the-clock basis, and that a suite had been permanently reserved for him at the Regis should he decide to stay in town overnight.

"Enough," he said, standing and stretching, "time to get out of this place." He'd already turned out the office lights when the phone rang.

It was Diedra. "Harry, could you get my dresses from the cleaners?"

"Sure, no problem, I have to stop for something on the avenue anyway. Listen, how about going down to O'Banion's for sandwiches and a couple of beers? If Mike is there, I'm going to ask him about being best man."

"That sounds like fun. By the way, I told Marie we're getting married, and I asked her to be my maid of honor. I thought she was having a nervous breakdown the way she started to cry and jump around."

"So did she say yes?"

"Of course! In fact, we're going to start making up lists of things we have to do. She says a friend of hers sews wedding dresses. Wouldn't that be nice? Having my dress made?"

"OK, let me get out of here," he said. "I love you. I'll be home in two hours, but if it's a little longer, don't be worried."

"Harry? Have you been listening to any of this business about the president?"

"Yeah, some, but I've been so busy here today, we can talk about it when I get home, OK?"

Before leaving for work that morning, he'd pilfered Diedra's birthstone ring from her jewelry box. She wore it on her left ring finger so he was taking it with him to shop for an engagement ring.

After putting her dry cleaning in the car, he went next door to Resnick's Jewelers.

"Harry! *Wie geht's*?" the elderly man behind the counter asked with a smile.

"Fine, just fine. And by you and your lovely wife?"

"Thank God, much better. Her sisters in Fort Lauderdale want her to come and stay with them for a couple of weeks so she can get the sun."

"I'm glad she's better, she's a nice lady. Mr. Resnick, I have a ring here and I'd like to buy and engagement ring the same size, something nice."

"You're getting married!? *Mazal tov*. When's the wedding?"

"Soon, that's why I was hoping you'd have something I could take with me now."

They spent the next half hour examining every engagement ring in the display case, but nothing struck Harry's fancy.

"Wait," Mr. Resnick said, "I got a couple of consignment pieces this morning. They're still in the safe. There's one piece you might be interested in, but it's a little expensive.

"So whatta you think?" Mr. Resnick asked as he opened the black velour ring box and handed it to him.

"My God, that's what I call a rock, this is more like it!" Harry exclaimed, holding the ring under the bright light of the counter lamp. "it's incredible!"

He was looking at a one and a half caret, blue marquise diamond in a white platinum setting, with a large baguette on each side of the stone, they were sixty-five points each. Harry watched as the jeweler carefully used a sizing iron to check it against Diedra's birthstone ring.

"Perfect! The exact same size," he said excitedly, realizing that he might very well have a sale. "Harry, believe me, you wouldn't find another ring like this. Look at the workmanship."

"How much?"

For what seemed like an interminable period of time, the jeweler scribbled numbers on a pad, added them, subtracted them, crossed them out, wrote new ones, tapped the pencil on his head, and finally, drew a circle around a figure.

"Since I don't have to do anything except clean it, I can let you have it for $6,700, and I'll do something with the taxes as a wedding present. How's that?"

Without hesitating, he said, "Ill take it."

*   *   *

When he got home, Diedra was already dressed and waiting for him in the living room.

"I won't be long," he said, on the way upstairs. "I'll take a quick shower and change."

She had the TV on when he came back down. "Sweetheart, come watch this."

"… has now confirmed earlier reports that a Philippines Coast Guard cutter has located the wreckage of Air Force One, three hundred miles east, northeast of Manila Bay. There were no signs of survivors.

"WCCY TV News has learned that interim Vice President Mason Hallstrow, informed Representative Sanford Feldon, the Speaker of the House, that due to health problems, he will be unable to assume the duties of the presidency. When asked if he was prepared to take the job, the House Speaker assured reporters that he was ready, willing, honest, and able. He said a change in the country's leadership was long overdue, and that the American people should only know how close the nation had come to disaster.

"He concluded his statement by saying that certain members of the late president's inner circle would be well advised to find themselves a good lawyer, one that specialized in treason.

"Pressed for an explanation, the Speaker said that his first official act as President would be to sign an executive order instructing the FBI to make public their intelligence relating to the criminal and treasonous activities of the president's reelection committee, as well as that of certain government officials.

"In financial news, the Dow reached a new high today as it experienced the greatest one-day gain in its history. Rayfield Mead, chief market analyst for Gregory Trust Securities, could not explain today's binge buying. He said the death of this particular president would have so significant effect on business in general.

"That's enough of that," Harry said, getting up and turning off the set. "Thank God we're rid of those two."

"Now is that anyway to talk about our late president?" Diedra asked glibly.

"Before I forget, Miss Shannahan, here's a little something I picked up for you at Resnick's."

"Yes! Yes! Yes!," she squealed as he handed her the small package. "I knew you were up to something, I knew it!"

"How?"

"Because my birthstone ring was missing out of my jewelry box this morning, and you're the only one beside the cat who could have taken it. And then when you said you had to stop on the avenue, you hate going up there when the people are coming from work. That's when I knew you were going to Resnick's."

"Well, why don't you open it?"

"I hate to mess it up, look how beautifully he wrapped it, and look how my hands are shaking."

In a second the bow and wrapping were on the floor.

"Jesus, Mary, and Joseph, will you look at this? It's enormous! Sweetheart, I've never seen anything like it. Look at the color, and the baguettes, they're huge! Oh, Harry, please, put it on me."

"With this ring I thee wed," he whispered, slipping it onto her finger.

Silent for a moment, she put her hand against his face, gently kissed his lips, and said, "Thank you, thank you for teaching me how to laugh again. The only thing I'll ever ask of you is that when you're hurting that you'll let me help you."

If he was uneasy it was because he was embarrassed by Diedra's genuine sincerity and unselfishness, qualities he was void of.

*　　　　*　　　　*

On the way down to O'Banion's, he told her about being visited by a priest at work who turned out to be Ponzinno's son.

"How many sons does he have?"

"Just one."

"So the person you saved became a priest?"

"Right."

"He's the one you bought the vestments and chalice for?"

"Right."

"Is this how it all started, your relationship with Ponzinno?"

"Pretty much so, plus the fact that I lived next door to him when I was a kid. I used to shovel snow for his mother. And then when my mother died, I sold him her house."

"Small world."

"Isn't it?"

"So the priest found out from his father that you were the one who saved his life?"

"Right."

"And then the father told him where you worked?"

"Right."

"Can you beat that?" she said.

"Wait, it gets better. His Uncle Manny happens to be Manny Ostrow and his Uncle Tony is Tony Bissetti, Ostrow's boss. They're his godfathers and they both work for guess who? Alfonsa Ponzinno."

"So Ponzinno owns Plenum Trucking?"

"Among a lot of other things."

"My God, Harry, can you imagine, being a priest and having a man like him for a father?"

"He uses his mother's maiden name, Arezzo, Father Alfonsa Arezzo. He seems like a nice guy, but then why shouldn't be, he's a priest, right?"

"How did you save his life?"

"He was getting mugged, worse than that, the two guys were trying to kill him."

"And?"

"And I stopped it."

"Is that when you got that scar, and the broken nose?"

"Yes, one of my broken noses. But he was really hurt. They fractured a lot of bones in his face and now he's partially blind and deaf."

"That's horrible."

"Yeah, it's too bad because other than that he's a good lookin', young guy. You'll get a chance to meet him Saturday night. Ponzinno has invited us to a dinner party at his place upstate. Ostrow and Bissetti are gonna be there, and some of Ponzinno's business friends."

"Oh, now wait a minute, not so fast. I don't know about this. I hope you didn't say we'd go."

"It's important we go."

"Harry, I don't know any of those people, I'd feel funny, and besides, this Ponzinno, he scares me. I never even met the man and he scares me. The papers keep saying he's the head of organized crime. Is that true?"

"Of course not, he's a businessman. All that stuff is a lot of garbage they print just to sell papers. Wait until you meet him, he's a real class guy. Besides, his son is a priest, how bad could he be?

"Now, let me ask you a question, how would you like to be rich?"

"We are rich," she said, referring to her dead husband's insurance money.

"I mean rich, rich. Big time rich. A summer house in the Hamptons rich."

"I haven't the slightest idea what you're talking about."

"You remember I told you Ponzinno was working on a deal to get the devices back for Longdon, and if he could, the Japanese would sell him Santronics? Guess what? It's happening. I'm pretty sure that's what this thing Saturday night is about."

He told her what was in the lawyers' letter, but she didn't say anything.

"Hello, are you in there?" he asked, gently poking her with his elbow. "Nothing to say? I thought you'd be excited. What's wrong?"

"I'm not sure," she answered, "but something isn't right. Maybe it's because everything is happening so fast. One day we're praying we don't get blown up, and the next day, we have a million dollars sitting on the kitchen floor. It's crazy. Aren't you worried that we might end up getting hurt with this thing? I know I am."

"No!" he said emphatically. "We've both paid our dues and now that things are breaking our way for a change, we should let them."

"Harry, you know what I don't understand? How come after all these years, Ponzinno decides to reward you? Didn't he know all along you were the one who saved his son? Why now? How come now he decides to make you a millionaire?"

"I don't know. Maybe he always intended to do something for me. Who knows? What difference does it make? The important thing is that it's happening."

Diedra's intuitive mind wasn't clogged with visions of grandeur like Harry's, and she'd asked the important question, "why now?" The answer was simple. Ponzinno had a plan he'd been contemplating for a long time, but he needed bodies, respectable bodies to implement it. Harry, the Rossbaums, the merchandise they tried to steal, and finally, Longdon's stupidity in telling him about the devices, were factors which had combined to produce the main, respectable body, and that was, Mr. Harry O'Day. For now, Ponzinno was concentrating on making Harry even more respectable, a little more refined, a little more executive leader type. A young, dynamic person, running a multimillion dollar international operation, with his beautiful and gracious, young bride standing at his side. The fact that Harry was apolitical and enjoyed being openly insulting to what passed as elected officials, was icing on the cake.

"Look at it this way," Harry said, "It'll be a great opportunity to show your ring off."

"I never thought about that. All right, we'll go. If it's as important as you say it is, we'll go. But in the future, I'd appreciate it if we could talk about things like this before you say yes to anybody, especially when it involves people I don't know."

"I promise."

"Now all I have to do is figure out what I'm supposed to wear to something like this. I saw a beautiful two-piece, black suit the other day. It has white piping on the pockets and lapels, and the skirt has a little slit in one side. If they have it in my size, would something like that be OK to wear? I have a set of double strand cultured pearls and broach that would look great with it."

"Perfect, but I gotta tell you, no matter what you wear, you look beautiful. You're beautiful too, when you don't wear anything."

*   *   *

The O'Banions were overjoyed when told of the engagement, so much so that on the way home, both Diedra and Harry complained of sore ribs from being hugged by the two Irish giants.

At one point during the evening O'Banion Sr. yelled, "Champagne for everyone," which prompted Mike Jr. to stop in his tracks behind the bar and say, "The man's gone daft I tell you." When Harry asked him to be his best man, he couldn't tell if the mist in Mike's eyes was from emotion, or from the boilermakers he'd been throwing down behind the bar.

Only once during the evening did Harry's previous encounter with the rogue Secret Service agents come up. "Anymore rats running around your place?" Mike asked. He was now aware that Longdon was conducting an investigation into the spying activities of certain Komti/Santronics executives, and incorrectly assumed he was FBI. Harry wasn't about to tell him Longdon was actually the hatchet man for a cabal of high-level civilian and military officials within the government looking to exorcise the presidency. Nor could he tell O'Banion about the devices, or his involvement with Ponzinno. Eventually he'd have to tell him something, like, "Mike, I didn't know my friend the priest was Ponzinno's son when we asked him to marry us."

Part 20

In took three hours to drive upstate. Fortunately the roads were clear and the prediction was for only light snow.

Diedra had been right. She looked exquisite in the tailored, black suit, like one of those sleek Sunday New York times models. Her sensuality constantly aroused him and tonight was no different. Since the death of her sot husband, he'd noticed a gradual change in her, especially after they had become intimate. Ever so slowly, she was beginning to unwind, to loosen up. It was most evident when she was in with the crowd down at O'Banion's. At one point during their impromptu engagement party, he watched while she got into a couple of gigglefests with some of the other woman. With very little encouragement, she'd even gotten up and held her own doing some Irish toe dancing. In fact, he was amazed at just how good she was.

Between the two of them, Father Arezzo's map, and one trip up a snowy, muddy road to ask directions at a farm house, they managed to find Ponzinno's estate.

"Sweet Jesus, will you look at this," was Diedra's reaction when she saw the place. "It looks like the Museum of Natural History."

She was close. The gray stone three-story structure was massive, and if it weren't for the many light being on inside, it would have resembled a scene out of Poe's *Fall of the House of Usher.*

Like they had set off a silent alarm, a burly man wearing a belted, camel hair coat came out of the stone guardhouse just as they stopped at the pair of high iron gates. Coming to the driver's side window, he bent and said, "Oh, Mr. O'Day, how are you? Good evening, Miss. Go right in, Mr. O'Day, Mr. Ponzinno is expecting you. You can pull up to the circle in front and somebody will park your car." After ogling Diedra's long legs, the man opened the gates wide and waved them through.

Harry recognized the ape. His name was Chichi and he'd been in the alley behind Annunzio's the night Manny had taken him to meet Ponzinno for the first time. Chichi looked the same, but his attitude was certainly different. It had done from, "Is this the guy Mr. Ponzinno wants to see?" to, "Good evening, Mr. O'Day, go right in, Mr. Ponzinno is expecting you." Obviously, between the alley and here, someone had told the ape who talked through his nose, that Mr. O'Day was a person to be shown respect, a person of some stature, a person who got invited to dine with Alfonsa Ponzinno.

Like the glow of deers' eyes caught in a car's headlights, Harry's high beams discovered every gun barrel, every cigarette lighter, every pinky ring, and every flask along the tree-lined driveway leading up to the house. Now and then he'd catch a glimpse of one of the small army of faceless men transported from the city to guard the festivities. Their white roll collars and six inches of white French cuff sticking out of black overcoats, acted like beacons and betrayed their presence. Like Chichi said, a young Rudolf Valentino met them at the massive front steps, opened the door for Diedra, came to the driver's side, and drove off with their car.

The vestibule, if that's what it was called was the size of Harry's entire apartment. Its walls were paneled with mahogany veneer and the floor was inlaid marble, presumably Italian. Two young attractive dark skinned women neatly dressed in black and white uniforms, politely asked for their coats, and a distinguished looking black man in a well-fitting tuxedo suddenly appeared and requested that they follow him.

He escorted them into "the great hall," as they would later refer to it. "I could fit my whole house in here," was Diedra's reaction. There were two enormous staircases which began on opposite sides of the cavernous room, and curved upwards until they met at an upper landing. The banisters and spindles looked like dark mahogany and had a soft lush appearance from years of being painstakingly rubbed with oil.

Hanging from the high domed circular ceiling of the chamber on a long, heavy chain, was the biggest chandelier either of them had ever seen. "You know what that thing reminds me of?" he quietly asked Diedra. "It looks like the one Claude Raines cut down in the 'Phantom of the Opera.'" The dome itself had a series of religious frescos painted on it, but it hurt their necks to look up at them, and the red rug was so plush they left deep impressions in the pile as they walked. Two servants carrying linen and tableware came through a blind door in one of the paneled walls, and Harry wondered if maybe the entire house wasn't full of secret passageways.

They were led through a pair of heavy oak doors which opened into a sitting room of gigantic proportions; Manny, Tony Trucks, and Father Arezzo were standing just inside helping themselves from a tray of hors d'oeuvres held by a waiter wearing white gloves and jacket. Further in, Ponzinno was talking to a group of men. Harry took special note that one was the white-haired man with the gun who had opened the back door for him and Manny at Annunzio's. He obviously enjoyed a close relationship with Ponzinno because he had his arm around his shoulders and they were laughing.

"I'm so glad you could make it," the priest said as he walked over and took hold of their hands. "And this, of course, is your lovely fiancée. Please, introduce her to us." He motioned for Manny and Bissetti to come over.

"Gentlemen," Harry said proudly, slipping his arm around her waist, "I would like you to meet Miss Diedra Agnes Shannahan. Diedra, this is Father Alfonsa Arezzo, Mr. Ponzinno's son, his uncle, Manny Ostrow, he works in the same building as I do, and Mr. Anthony Bissetti. Mr. Bissetti is also Father Arezzo's uncle."

To say that Manny and Tony were smittened by Diedra's beauty and elegance would have been an understatement. Sensing the awkwardness of two men who thought nothing of chopping people up, she said, "It's a pleasure meeting you all. Does anybody know what the rent is on a place like this?" That broke the ice and even Bissetti smiled. For a change, everybody was in a good mood.

When Harry introduced her to Ponzinno, it was a different story. On his best day, Douglas Fairbanks Sr. couldn't have been more suave and gallant. Much to Harry's surprise, Diedra seemed perfectly at ease with him also, given her earlier fears about him being some kind of mass murderer.

After they'd been formally introduced, Ponzinno asked to see her ring.

"Of course, I love showing it to people," she said, extending her hand.

"Its beauty is surpassed only by that of your own," he said, gently placing his other hand on top of hers, and momentarily leaving it there.

"That's most gracious of you, thank you," she said. "Your home is exquisite."

"I'm pleased you like it. When my wife was alive she took great joy in caring for it. I've not allowed anything to be changed since her death, she would have wanted it that way. You remind me of her. She was also a beautiful woman, and her hands, they were fine and delicate like yours."

Amiably, Diedra touched his arm and said, "I'm going to start a novena tomorrow for our marriage, and when I go to church, I'll light a candle for her."

Harry could see by the expression on Ponzinno's face that Diedra's sincerity and genuine respect for the memory of his dead wife had touched him. The man is human, Harry thought.

Appearing from nowhere, the butler announced dinner was about to be served, and Ponzinno asked Harry's permission to escort Diedra to the dining room.

There were forty-five people seated at the massive table, most of whom Diedra and Harry couldn't see because of the giant candelabras and huge floral arrangements running down its center. Never in his life had Harry seen such a luxurious display of silverware, china, linen, and glassware.

All but a dozen of the men at the table looked like they were either lawyers or bankers, and the woman accompanying them, at best, were generic in their appearance. These were the men Ponzinno had charged with the responsibility of setting up the new corporations. The dozen men who'd kept to themselves prior to dinner, had no female companions; for them, the evening was strictly business.

They looked like gangsters because they were gangsters, and represented the five families each of which, would receive one of the Santronics warehouse centers from Ponzinno for past and future services, much the same way a medieval king would bestow fiefdoms upon his warrior barons.

Regardless of what the papers of incorporation would say, they were the owners of the centers, and Harry would be responsible for the centers' profitability. He would be one of the biggest "earners," in the Ponzinno conglomerate with every cent of income legitimately made by legitimate businesses.

So in part, the dinner would give everybody a chance to get acquainted. Before the evening ended, Ponzinno would take Harry to each of the families and they would talk for a time. Later, Harry would tell Diedra that to a man, they had the warmth and charm of cadavers.

When everyone had been seated, Ponzinno tapped on the table and asked for their attention.

"Ladies, gentlemen, I want to thank you all for coming tonight, you do me a great honor. This is a very special occasion for me. Besides having you as my guests, I also have my son with me, Father Alfonsa Arezzo. For those of you who are staying over, he will be offering mass in the family chapel tomorrow at 8 a.m.

"He's here with me tonight because a long time ago, someone was brave enough to stand up and do the right thing. When my son was being attacked by scums, and they wanted to kill him, this person took the blows for him and drove them away. To this day, he carries the scars of the attack on his face, like the scars on my son's face."

Walking from the head of the table to where Harry was seated, Ponzinno put both his hands on his shoulders and said, "*Grazie, Ti sono eramento grato*, I am most grateful to you, you are a friend of ours.

"Those of you who are working on our new enterprise know that Harry will be in charge and I would like you to give him your cooperation. He speaks with my approval in all matters relating to it.

"This enchanting young lady sitting next to him is Miss Diedra Shannahan, his fiancée. Please, it is important to me that you make her feel comfortable."

As he walked back to the head of the table, he stopped next to his son who was sitting on his immediate right. Gently touching the priest's head, Ponzinno bent and almost whispering, spoke in Latin, "*Experto credite, audense fortuna juvat*, believe one who has the experience, fortune favors the bold."

The white-haired man with the gun and Tony Bissetti were close enough to have heard what Ponzinno said, but they didn't need to understand Latin to know the significance of the gesture. Both nodded their affirmation. "*Va bene!*" Tony said.

Within seconds after Ponzinno sat down, a column of servants streamed into the room from all directions carrying large soup terrenes, massive platters of antipasto, bowls of green salad, and platters of shrimp boiled to a bright reddish pink. Others came with baskets of breads wrapped in fine white linen napkins. Still others went quietly around the table pouring water and wine from beautiful, cut crystal decanters that sparkled when they caught the iridescent glow of the table candles.

Kink Louis XVI would have felt right at home in the baroque ambiance of the gathering.

For the next two hours Ponzinno's guests gorged themselves on lobster, pasta, several different kinds of meat dishes, stuffed artichokes, and calamari. When they'd finished, some retired to a series of drawing rooms for coffee and liqueurs, while others went downstairs to watch a motion picture in Ponzinno's private theater.

These were people who enjoyed the excitement, the element of danger they perceived was involved in associating with a man like Ponzinno, as long as it could be done under the cover of darkness, and a three-hour drive from New York City. They were more than willing to accept his hospitality as long as it didn't weaken the façade of bogus respectability they'd cloaked themselves in, and they were perfectly willing to accept the gigantic fees and commissions he paid them in unmarked envelopes for their various services. They were people for whom Ponzinno had no respect—he didn't have to, he owned them. He owned their banks, their law firms; he owned their very souls and they were too bourgeois to care.

*   *   *

Diedra and Harry were standing in front of one of the many fireplaces in the house talking to some guests when Father Arezzo walked up. He apologized for the interruption, and asked if he could speak to them privately. Excusing themselves, they followed his out into the vestibule.

"My father thought you might like to see the chapel, it's very beautiful at night, especially in the winter with the candles and snow. He's waiting for us, but you'll need your coats, the temperature has really dropped."

The chapel was a domed, circular structure made of thousands of intricately fitted pieces of dark gray fieldstone. Its pews could easily accommodate a hundred people.

One was immediately struck by the sixteen stained glass windows that ringed the walls, two of which were directly behind the altar. One depicted Christ's crucifixion, and the other, the Virgin Mary holding the baby Jesus. The fourteen remaining windows told the story of the Stations of the Cross, and a music system provided the appropriate, continuous Gregorian chants to give the place a proper sanctimonious atmosphere.

Ponzinno was on his knees praying at a small side altar. The intruders blessed themselves with holy water, knelt, and sat down to wait.

"It's quiet here," he said sitting down in the pew in front of them and putting his rosary away in a small gold box. "I like to come here whenever I can. My wife and I talk like we used to."

"Diedra, Harry," Father Arezzo began, "my father and I have been talking and we have a special request to make of you. We would be honored if you would agree to be married here in the chapel, and I would consider it a privilege if you would allow me to perform the ceremony. You don't have to answer right away, I'm sure this must come as a surprise to you. Take some time and think about it, but it would please both my father and me greatly,"

Stunned, her eyes darting between the three men as if she expected one of them to tell her what to do, Diedra parted her lips to speak, but nothing came out. Harry wasn't experiencing the same difficulty. Before the priest had finished asking the question, he knew the answer, yes!

Can you imagine, he thought, the prestige of being asked by a man like Ponzinno to be married in his family's private chapel, and his son the priest performing the ceremony? God, would that ever impress people.

"Sweetheart," Diedra finally said, "what do you think?"

"Look," Father Arezzo interrupted, "let's say you get married in June or July. The weather would be nice and we could set up some tents. We'll have a small band, a buffet after the…" but he wasn't able to finish the sentence.

"Wait, wait, wait, Father," Diedra said excitedly, "we were thinking of having something small. Harry's friend owns a bar in Rockaway."

"Beauty such as your, my dear," Ponzinno broke in, "doesn't belong in a bar in Rockaway on your wedding day. It belongs here among other beautiful things. Please, do me this personal favor."

"Harry," Diedra said, "I just thought about something. What about Mike being your best man?"

"Oh, man, I didn't think about that," he answered. "Mr. Ponzinno, I've asked someone to be my best man, we've known each other since we were kids and he's always been a loyal and trustworthy friend. But he's a detective for the NYPD."

Ponzinno studied Harry's face for a moment, and then spoke. "Friendship of such quality is rare, and a man should consider himself fortunate to have it. It should also be protected and rewarded. I'm certain when you asked him he was honored. I trust you, and I know that you would never bring someone to my home who would look to harm my family, or myself, or to cause me to have problems elsewhere. I believe that, so I have nothing to fear from this person, do I Harry? Would you ever do anything to harm my family, or myself? Would you dare betray my confidences?"

"No, sir, never, I swear to you." Harry answered. Ponzinno's message was clear: "If you vouch for this person and he interferes with me, you will pay the price first."

"Sweetheart," Diedra said smiling and taking hold of his hand, "I guess we're going to have a country wedding after all, just like you wanted. Won't it be wonderful? We'll be able to take pictures in the gardens."

Ponzinno laughed as he stood, "You remind me of someone I knew a long time ago. She also was young and beautiful like you, so full of life. You'll excuse me, I have to see to my other guests. Alfonsa, before Diedra leaves, take her to see Sofia. Sofia has been our housekeeper for twenty-five years. The two of you can work out the details. But try not to upset her, or she'll throw all of us out into the street. Once I made a mess in her kitchen and she refused to feed me until I promised not to do it again."

After Ponzinno left, Father Arezzo asked if they'd like to see the grotto his father was having built.

"I'd love to," Diedra answered, pulling the oversized, fur collar of her coat up around her cheeks.

Leading them through the small grove of trees separating the chapel from the grotto, the priest turned and said, "I want to thank you both, you've made my father happy. There's never been a wedding on the estate, and I've never married anybody before. Harry, I'm going to wear a set of the vestments you sent me, and just remember, it's customary to slip the priest a few dollars."

"Oh God," Diedra gasped, "Harry, what about your divorce? We never went and found out about it. Father, Harry was married before, he's divorced."

Embarrassed, Harry said, "Alfonsa, I'm sorry, it's not that I wasn't gonna tell you, it just slipped my mind."

"I'm sure you were. Did you get married in the Queens archdiocese? Did you ever talk to anyone there about getting an annulment?"

"I got married in Jackson Heights, but I never even thought about getting an annulment."

"All right, don't let it upset you," the priest said, "let me speak to my father."

*   *   *

At midnight, they thanked their hosts for the evening and especially for the invitation to be married on the estate. Ponzinno asked Diedra if she'd met Sofia the housekeeper.

"Oh yes, I certainly have," she replied, looking up in the air and rolling her eyes. He then asked if they would like to stay over, but Harry had his own ideas as to how they were going to spend the rest of the night. He'd never taken a girl to a motel before, and Diedra had never been taken to one.

Part 21

Longdon was standing next to the small sign that read, RESERVED-H. O'Day, when Harry pulled into Santronics' parking lot Monday morning.

"You always hang around parking lots, Longdon?" he asked sarcastically. It was twenty-five degrees, yet the sweat was pouring off Longdon's face like it was a hot afternoon in July.

"I don't have much time. Tell your buddy Ponzinno we're putting his deal together."

"Yeah, I know, I saw it on TV—terrible accident."

"One more thing. The Japanese want us to actually see Nagakura's body. Have you found him yet?"

"That's Ponzinno's department, why don't give him a call?"

"You're turning into a real smart-ass, O'Day, just like you guinea pals."

"Fuck you."

"Well, that's the deal. We get the body and the devices, and Ponzinno gets his agreement. I assume he still intends to keep the two he grabbed out of this place, right?"

"That's Ponzinno's department, why don't you give him a call?"

"You got my number, use it," Longdon said angrily as he screeched his tires on the way out of the lot.

It was important that Manny get a message to Ponzinno about what Longdon had just told him.

Manny was on the phone when he walked in. "Yeah, OK, I got it. Give me the flight number again. Yeah, in fact he just walked in. Wait a minute, he's askin' me somethin'."

"Who's that you're talkin' to?"

"Tony."

"Good, tell'm Longdon was in the parkin' lot just now. He says the deal is good if they get the devices, and they wanna see Nagakura's body."

"Tony? You hear that?" Manny asked. "OK, then we're all set. I'll let you know how things go. You got people meetin' us, right? OK, good, I'll talk to you."

"They found the prick," Manny said, hanging up the phone.

"What prick?"

"Nagakura, he's hold up with a couple of his rats in the Hollywood Hills. Some fancy house. Here, have a drink."

"So what happens now?"

"So now you and me go and whack him. There's tickets for us at the airport, but we gotta go right away or else we'll miss the plane. Somebody will pick up out there."

"I gotta tell you, Manny," Harry said, handing the paper cup back for a refill, "just between the two of us, now that this is really happening, well, I don't know, I never did anything like this."

"I thought you hated the scum bag?"

"I do, but…"

"But your balls. The prick killed your old man. You remember what you told us? How he wouldn't let you pop's buddies take his body away? You ever see a dead body after it's been in the sun a couple of days? I have, plenty of them—in Germany. They swell up like balloons and the maggots get in'em. Well, that's how your old man looked after this fuck had'm whacked."

Harry put down the drink, sat, and lowered his head almost to his knees. "Was that really necessary?" he asked.

"I don't know, you tell me kid. You better toughen up between here and the coast or else this guy might end up puttin' you away. Look, you owe it to your mother, God rest her soul. Remember tellin' me how she got? This prick did it to her. Besides, I'm tellin' you, you owe Alfonsa."

Before boarding the plane at LaGuardia, he called Diedra and told her some problems had come up in the San Francisco warehouse, and he'd asked Manny to fly out there with him to see what had to be done.

"I'll pick up a shirt and whatever else I need someplace if we gotta stay overnight. Don't be afraid to call Mike if you need him. His numbers are in the book by the phone. I love you, take care."

*   *   *

Manny insisted on the aisle seat so he could watch the stewardesses, "wiggle their little asses," as they walked up and down. Breakfast was served, but Harry couldn't look at it, so Manny ate them both, and then asked the stewardess for a bottle of beer and a sandwich.

The combination of watching Manny stuffing his face, the turbulence, and wondering what it would be like killing a man, made the flight a nightmare, at least for him.

For Manny it was a different story. Much to Harry's embarrassment, he found out Manny considered himself a ladies' man. The only bright spot came when Manny said, "Oh, I almost forgot, I got a bottle in my case."

But of all the people Ponzinno could have sent with him, he was glad it was Manny. Manny reminded him a lot of Mike O'Banion Jr. Outwardly, both men displayed a gregarious, sometimes mischievous disposition, but underneath that seemingly friendly exterior, they were capable of ripping the eyes out of their enemies' heads and thinking nothing of it.

After a while, the monotonous drone of the plane's engines and a half a quart of whiskey put them both to sleep.

*   *   *

"Excuse me, gentlemen," the stewardess said, "the Captain has turned on the seatbelt sign, and we'll be landing shortly."

"Shortly," turned into forty-five minutes because of traffic ahead, according to what the captain kept telling the passengers. It took another fifteen minutes to reach the gate after touchdown.

No sooner had they entered the terminal than a heavyset man in his fifties, with graying brown hair, and black horn-rimmed glasses, yelled.

"Hey, Manny, you big prick, over here!" The resemblance between the man with a voice like the airport's public address system and Manny was unmistakable. He even blinked and nodded like Manny. When they embraced and pounded each other's backs, it looked like some kind of ritual courtship dance in a bird sanctuary.

"Harry," Manny said, "I'd like you to meet my brother, Benny."

"I hear good things about you," Benny said as he shook Harry's hand. "Did shithead here embarrass you with the stewardesses?"

"No, he was pretty good, most of the time," Harry answered.

"How's Josie and the kids?" Manny asked his brother.

"Great, just great, they love it out here. She even made a garden in the backyard. Can you beat that? She says you and Harry gotta come by the house before you go back, and when I told the kids you were comin' out they went nuts."

"Be honest, you miss Brooklyn?" Manny asked his brother.

"Yeah, sure, who wouldn't. We keep sayin' we're gonna go and visit, but we never seem to have the time. We don't got no Coney Island or stuff like that, but still, like I said, it's good out here, especially for the kids. Once in awhile we shoot over to Vegas for a couple of days. You know, they brought Freddie Chimenti and some of his people out to run a couple of things over there."

"Yeah, so I heard. He's a good guy," Manny said.

"Well, we gotta get goin'," Benny said, "We got some work to do."

A black Lincoln Continental was waiting for them in a no loading zone outside the terminal's main entrance. Benny got in next to the driver, and Manny and Harry climbed into the rear. Another Lincoln with several men in it was parked directly behind them.

"You remember Carlo, right Manny?" Benny asked.

"Yeah sure, from Ozone Park. You used to drive for Chubby Boy. How you doin'? You still got those two racehorses?"

Carlo laughed. "Nah, now I got the insurance money."

Carlo's enormous body took up half the front seat of the big car. In his early thirties, and jammed into a white muscle builder's shirt, he looked like a gorilla. Minus anything resembling a neck, the portions of his upper body not covered by his shirt, instead, were covered with short curly hair, including the backs of his hands. His face was the exception; it had a dark grayish look from being freshly shaven.

Before the day was over, Harry would know two things about him. First, that Carlo had the IQ of a handball, and secondly, that he owed Carlo his life.

Manny told his brother Mr. Ponzinno sent his regards to his boss, and thanked him for the accommodations.

"Hey, forget about it," Benny replied. "Whatever Mr. Ponzinno needs, Mr. G is honored to help. He says we gotta do the right thing by you guys while you're out here. That Mr. Ponzinno, he's somethin' else; he was the one who spoke to my boss and got me this job. He even sent the kid a savings bond for his first communion. Is that class or what? How's thing's goin' with Bobby? He gettin' married yet?"

"I wish he was," Manny answered. "Don't get me wrong, he's a good kid, and he takes care of business, but when he's home, he make a fuckin' mess out of everything. I told him if he doesn't start washin' the dishes after he eats, I'm gonna throw the damn things out, then he can eat off paper plates. So now he says I gotta buy a dishwasher. Some balls, no?"

"Harry, you ever whack a guy before?" Benny asked.

"Uh, uh, no…no I haven't," he answered haltingly, the question having caught him by surprise.

"It's not bad," Benny said encouragingly. "I understand you got a real hardon for this mutt. Personally, I like it when it's like that. If you want, me and Carlo can really fuck'm up good before you hit'm."

Benny noticed Harry kept glancing out the rear window at the car that had followed them out of the airport.

"Don't worry, they're with us," Benny assured him.

Carlo pulled off the main road and into the sleazy remains of what looked like an industrial park. All the buildings were vacant and rundown.

"This isn't exactly Hollywood and Vine, is it?" Harry commented.

"No," Carlo said, "around here we put more than people's hands in cement. Manny and his brother laughed.

There was still enough peeling paint left on the sign to tell Harry they had pulled up to what once had been the Treager Laundry. Carlo blew the horn and someone inside raised the large overhead door to let the two vehicles enter. The small window in the center of it had been painted over so no one could see in.

"Jimmy, how much more you gotta do on those vans?" Benny asked a young dark haired man. "That shit's gotta by dry before we can use them."

The toxic smell of sprayed paint in the cavernous structure irritated Harry's throat and nostrils, and out of the corner of his eye, he caught a glimpse of several small ugly things scamper behind the skeletal remains of a machine.

Jimmy carefully pulled long strips of masking tape off the sides of one of the vans and assured Benny both of them would be dry in twenty minutes, give or take. He'd just finished painting the name, Bouyer Pool Service on them. Two other men were busy replacing the existing license plates.

"Let's go in the office," Benny said, "before this stuff kills us."

The office was worse than a pigsty. There were several banged-up metal desks the tops of which were littered with the moldy remains of takeout containers, and empty beer bottles. The three remaining swivel chairs had minute traces of padding still clinging to them, but no wheels, and what had once been a bathroom was still being used as one, even though the plumbing hadn't worked in a long time.

Using a stick to avoid contact with the roaches not yet finished dining, Benny pushed everything onto the floor. "OK, let's see what we got," he said taking several sheets of folded notebook paper out of his back pocket.

There's five of them in the house. It's a rental up in the hills, and we know one of them is your guy cause we see him with the binoculars. It's the same mutt in the newspaper pictures you sent. He comes out on the balcony in the morning and does some kind of crazy exercises, but other than that, we've never seen him leave the property. There's only one that does, and he goes down to a shoppin' center for food and the papers in the afternoon. Once he puts the stuff in the car, he goes back and uses the pay phone; they gotta be long distance calls cause he pumps change into it like he's playin' the slots."

Harry interrupted. "He's probably tryin' to find out if any of their rat friends are still around, maybe somebody who could help get their sorry asses out of the country. But why doesn't he use the phone in the house?"

"It ain't turned on," Benny answered. "We told our people in the phone company not to. The same way we had them listen in on the pay phone calls, but the guy talks Japanese all the time. Also, we know the numbers he calls—here's a list." We got people ready to grab him up when he gets into his car.

"After that, we'll start with the two who stay outside most of the time. It's the same every day, one stays up front by the gate, keepin' an eye on the things, and the other usually walks around down back. They both got Roscoes cause we see 'em shootin' squirrels; they're pretty good too, so watch yourselves. Oh, yeah, they got a couple of rifles stashed around the property.

"Carlo's driven' the lead van with me up front, and you two guys on the floor in back. When we get to the gate, we'll say we gotta clean the pool. If he breaks our balls, we tell 'm it's on a contract with the owner, and if we don't do it, we lose the account."

"What happens if he doesn't open up?" asked Manny.

"I take 'm out, but quiet so we don't tip off anyone, especially the one down back; we wanna go lookin' for him, we don't want 'm lookin' for us.

"Jimmy and the people behind us from the airport will be in the second van. Once we're in, he'll go past the gate and send two of them up into the woods along the property line in case someone tries takin' a walk out the back. Then he'll drive in by the pool and start pickin' up the bodies.

"That'll leave Harry's guy in the house with the mutt that's always taggin' around after him, the one with all the scars."

"Scars?" Harry asked.

"Yeah," Benny replied, "I've seen him a couple of times with the glasses. His face in all fucked-up, like he got burned or somethin'."

Harry knew it was Yamatoki's gofer—his "boy."

"What about cops?" Manny asked.

"It's a development," Benny answered, "and the homeowners pay for a private patrol, but we own the security company, and they've been told we're comin'."

"The other houses up there, are the close enough for anyone to see or hear us?" Manny asked.

"No, the house is surrounded by a lot of woods, and when we go in, we're gonna start a generator we got on the truck to make plenty of noise."

"You know what this reminds me of?" Manny asked his brother. "The time we whacked that slob out in Long Beach? Remember how he tried to swim away when he saw us comin' in his backyard?"

"Yeah, that was funny," Benny said, smiling. "Harry you shoulda seen it. He had on a pair of trunks that hadda be size 100, and everytime I put one in'm, he'd go under, but then he'd pop up again. He looked like one of those things you put on the end of a fishin' line."

"Benny, tell Harry what you and Josie did that night," his brother interrupted.

"Oh, yeah, me and the wife took the kid to see an Esther Williams movie, and then we went out for seafood in Rockaway."

Harry watched as Manny and his brother laughed so hard they had tears in their eyes. They laughed even harder when Carlo started making swimming motions with his arms, and a face like a blowfish sucking and exhaling air.

Sick bastards, he thought. This is a game with them, killing people was a game, a sporting event. How in God's name did they ever get like that? Even at this late date, when it came time for him to face Nagakura and murder him, he didn't know if he could do it, regardless of how much he hated him.

"Right off the boat," Benny said, dumping the contents of a shopping bag onto the desk. Harry counted eight semi-automatic handguns, four silencers, and twenty-four loaded clips.

"OK, everybody gets two pieces, a silencer, and three clips. Just in case they got somethin' heavy in the house, Jimmy strapped a BAR up inside each van. Manny, you still know how to use one?"

"Ask all those dead Krauts in Germany," Manny replied proudly. "I told ya, I got 15 in one day."

"There's a box of coveralls outside," Benny said, "so everybody try and grab a pair that fits. Any questions? Good. Let's go."

"Wait, Benny," his brother said, "we gotta leave Harry's guy there, you know that, right? The feds wanna see the body."

"Yeah, but I'll remind Jimmy just to make sure. He's gonna take the rest of them over to some guy we know who dresses out deer; he'll grind 'em up for us."

*   *   *

"Harry, you remember to bring Longdon's phone number?" Manny asked as they sat opposite each other in back of the van.

"Yes, I have it."

"Good. As soon as we're finished we'll stop someplace and you tell'm where to look. You OK?"

"Yeah, fine," but that was a lie. His stomach was trying to come out his mouth, at least that's the way it felt, and he was sitting in the dampness of his sweat. Thoughts and images raced through his head as he fought hard not to be sick. Is this how people feel sitting on death row? What if Diedra finds out I murdered someone? If I get shot, will I die? If I get killed, will Manny ship my body home, or make Jimmy take it over to that guy? I wonder if it hurts when you get shot? What happens if the cops find out and I go to jail?

"OK, we're here," Carlo announced. Both Manny and Harry crept forward to look out the windshield, but the only thing visible were trees. A gust of wind conveniently moved a few branches and Harry saw the stone pillar and hinged gate attached to it. He jumped when the police car suddenly appeared from behind a small grove of trees. Slowly it drove past them and its driver, a member of the Hilltop Security Company, gave Carlo the thumbs-up sign.

"Good," Carlo said, pulling the van into the driveway as far as the closed gate would allow, "they grabbed the one in the shoppin' center."

Jimmy stopped a short ways past the driveway and sent two men up into the woods, each carrying a scoped rifle.

The house was set back another two hundred feet on a circular driveway and was an ugly cream-colored stucco monstrosity with red Spanish tiles on the roof; a lot of them had been replaced, but not with the same shade red. Someone with a grotesque sense of style had stuck pink wrought iron flamingos all around the property, and if the house weren't already a culture shock, the sun bathing area to the left of it, as well as the pool, had been painted shocking pink.

At ground level, there were three sets of sliding doors allowing ample access to the place. A balcony ran the full length of the structure's second floor and was connected to the pool area by a pink, stone staircase. The house had a third floor too, and when they were pulling up the driveway, Carlo said he'd seen someone behind the curtains in one of the rooms.

A young, muscular looking Japanese man wearing a white windbreaker and tan slacks stepped from behind a bunch of tall bushes, walked to the gate, and in perfect English asked, "Can I help you?" Benny got out and spoke to him. After some convincing acting, the young man opened the gate; " "I must check what is inside your truck," he said.

"Sure, be my guest," Benny said with a big smile, "we only got our equipment back there, but you're welcome to see for yourself. Here, take a good look," Benny said as he reached around him with his right hand and opened one of the van's doors. Whether by instinct or training, the man started to react to the sound of Benny's switchblade, but it was too late. Benny grabbed him around the throat and repeatedly rammed the blade into the small of his victim's back. Traumatized, Harry could only stare in horror as Manny reached out through the open door, pulled the still moving body inside, and slipped a plastic bag over the man's head.

"Here, wrap some of this tape around his neck," Manny yelled.

"I…I can't," Harry stuttered as a pool of dark red blood spread out on the floor of the truck.

"Do it, you fuck!" Manny yelled louder, "do what I tell you."

Harry wanted to jump out, to scream, to run someplace where this horror was happening, but he couldn't. It was like he was mesmerized by the acts of brutality he was witnessing, and taking part in.

"Do it, you prick," Manny demanded.

Forcing the vomit back down his throat, he wound the tape tightly around the young man's neck while Manny held him down. Still alive, the man's eyes bulged and pleaded for them to stop. Every time he tried breathing, he'd suck some of the plastic into his mouth.

"Hey, Benny!" Manny yelled, "what the fuck you standin' around out there for? Don't be shy, get in here and finish this prick."

Still holding the bloody knife, Benny climbed into the van and plunged it several more times into the center of his victim's chest. It was over.

Amused, Carlo had been watching from the driver's seat. Lighting a cigarette he said, "You know what you guys look like back there? You look like the fuckin' Three Stooges. That's the worst fuckin' job I ever saw."

"Up yours," Benny snapped back. "Come on, we're wastin' time. Pull the van up next to the pool and start the generator."

"I'll take the next one," Manny said, disgusted by the fiasco he'd just participated in. "I don't need any more of this crap. For Christ's sake, look at my pants, I just bought the damn things."

The generator made a terrible racket. With an extension cord and a few power tools, Benny made it look like he was doing something with the braces holding the diving board in place. Meanwhile, Carlo had gotten a long pool with a net on the end of it down off the roof of the truck and was busy scooping leaves out of the pool.

As Harry and Manny watched through the windshield, another Do Nothing appeared at the corner of the house, and cautiously approached Carlo and Benny. With his hand in his pocket, he demanded to know where his companion was. He kept staring at the van and finally, started toward it.

"Where's he now?" Manny whispered.

"He's on your side," Harry answered, his heart pounding so hard against the wall of his chest it hurt. "I think he's right out back here." The words weren't out of his mouth when the Do Nothing, gun in hand, ripped open one of the doors. For a second, all three men stared at each other until Manny shot him three times in the face. The impact of the rounds knocked the guard backward and as he lay with small geysers of blood hemorrhaging out of the holes in his face, Manny jumped down and fired four rounds into his chest.

Jimmy drove up with two other men.

"Are they all set in back?" Manny asked.

"Yes sir, ready and waitin'."

"OK, then we can start in the house. Get these two jokers in your truck, and then stay put. If our guy comes out this way try not to kill'm, but if you gotta, you gotta. Benny, you and Carlo take the ground floor. Me and Harry are gonna go up to the second."

Methodically, room by room, closet by closet, they began searching for the murderer of Harry's father.

"Check these rooms along here," Manny told Harry. "I'm gonna take a look upstairs. Be careful, you lintenin' to me? You gotta look everyplace; you hear somethin' in a closet, shoot through the door. You hear what I'm sayin'?

An inch at a time, Harry opened the door, it was a bathroom and it was empty. He was so nervous it took both hands to steady the gun in front of him. Even though it was too small for a man to fit into, he checked the narrow linen closet anyway just like Manny had told him to do.

"Ooooh, fuck!" he groaned when he heard the little shower curtain rings slide across the support bar. Before he could turn and fire, Scarface kicked him in the back sending him sprawling out into the hallway on his hands and knees; his gun clattered up against the wall. Scarface kicked him again, harder, this time in the throat and face.

Half in and half out of consciousness, he saw his attacker's hand reaching for his weapon and he knew he was going to die. He wondered if he would actually hear the explosion. Instead, he heard a whooshing sound, then a dull thud and Scarface was on the floor next to him, his head shattered like a pumpkin dropped off a building. Pieces of what looked like blood covered cauliflower—Scarface's brains—were splattered everywhere.

Trying to regain his senses, Harry shook his head, and with considerable difficulty, managed to drag himself to his feet. Carlo was standing there holding a bloody baseball bat at his side.

Having heard the commotion, Manny came flying down the stairs and along the hallway. "Carlo, is he hit?" Manny yelled, seeing the blood all over Harry.

"Nah, he's OK," Carlo answered nonchalantly. "Dickhead here made the mess," and with that, he kicked the dead man in the testicles.

"What the fuck happened?" Manny demanded. "Carlo, go see if there's any towels."

While Harry cleaned the pieces of brain and bone splinters off his face and clothing, he explained how Scarface had been in the shower stall.

Manny got very upset. "Didn't I tell you? Didn't I tell you!?" he screamed. "You fuckin' jerk, you gotta check everywhere. You're lucky you're alive. Carlo, I thought you were helpin' my brother?"

"I was, but Jimmy came in and Benny said I should come up here and keep an eye on Harry."

"Where did the bat come from?" Manny asked.

"Benny found a whole load of stuff in a closet. He says he's gonna take it for his kid's Little League. You should see some of it; catcher's masks, hats, a couple of first baseman's mitts. He's gonna be pissed when he sees how I fucked up this bat. See, over here? Wait, let me wipe some of the crap off. See? Right here—Joe DiMaggio! This thing is expensive."

All right, look," Manny told Carlo, "go tell Jimmy to get this piece of garbage outta here. Harry? You got somethin' you wanna tell Carlo, like thanks or somethin'?"

"Yeah, sure, of course, forgive me, I'm still a little groggy. Carlo, what can I say? Thanks, I owe you, big time. You saved my life."

"Forget about it," Carlo said, using a towel to finish cleaning off the bat, "I was just afraid I'd fuck up my shoulder again when I hit the prick; it's been givin' me a lot of trouble lately."

Benny yelled from the foot of the stairs, "Front and center, we got'm." All three raced downstairs to where Benny was now looking out a sliding glass door leading onto a rear deck.

"He went in that little shed over there," Benny said.

"You sure it's the right guy?" his brother asked.

"Positive, when he got to the steps, he turned around and looked at me. It's the mutt in the newspapers."

"Did he have a gun?" Harry asked.

"A gun!? He had a fuckin' sword!" Benny exclaimed. "Can you beat that? He had a fuckin' sword."

"OK, Harry, you're up." Manny told him.

By the time he reached the shed door, he could hardly breathe, and he had to keep wiping the palms of his hands against his pants. The right side of his face was badly swollen and throbbed terribly from Scarface's attack.

The flimsy, slatted door fell in from the force of his kick and he could see Nagakura standing at the rear of the dimly lit room. What light there was, came through a small window and like a spotlight, one ray glistened off the blade of the samurai sword Nagakura held with both hands over his right shoulder. He wasn't very tall and had an oversized head covered with a thin layer of white peach fuzz hair. His stance and the kimono made him look like a statue in a curio shop.

His speech badly slurred because of the swelling of his face, Harry demanded, "Do you know who I am?"

"Yes," Nagakura snarled, "You are the American swine, O'Day," and then he spit in Harry's direction.

"Good, just so you know," Harry said, raising his gun and emptying the clip. One round caught Nagakura in the shoulder knocking the sword from his grasp. Another took off the tip of his nose, and a third grazed his side. The rest splattered against the cinder block wall behind him.

The rounds that did hit, knocked him against some packing crates, and clutching his chest, he slowly slid to the floor making a moaning sound. He stayed like that and Harry thought he'd killed him.

"Whatch'm!" Manny warned. "He's still movin'. Use your other gun—shoot'm in the head."

The handle of the second weapon snagged in the pocket of his coveralls and as he fumbled with it, Nagakura managed to pull himself up into a sitting position with his back against the crates. Harry suddenly realized that for the first time since his nightmare started with the plane ride out, his hands weren't shaking and sweating, and the constant sensation of having to vomit had left him.

"Do you know why I'm doing this, you bastard?" he demanded as he freed the gun and chambered a round. "It's important to me that you should know before I empty this thing into your stinkin' face."

Tenacious even in the face of certain death, Nagakura indignantly replied, "Because you are scum like the rest of your kind. The only thing you know is to kill and destroy what other men cherish."

"I cherished my father, you bastard," Harry screamed, "but you destroyed him, you murdered him, in your fucking camp. You destroyed my mother! Now I'm going to destroy you."

"Is that what this is all about...your father?" Nagakura scowled. "He was in the war? I spit on his grave; I spit on all their graves. May their souls rot in eternal hell—they were worthless cowards and I should have killed every last one of them."

By now, Harry's right eye was completely swollen closed, and he was barely able to see out of the other because of his sweat and tears. Turning, he took a few steps to the shoulder high window and wiped his eyes and face with the back of his hand. Taking a deep breath, he looked up into the clear deep blue sky. It reminded him a photograph he'd found in his mother's house, a picture of his father wearing dress blues standing aboard ship in some distant place he would never know the name of. On the back his father had written, "Dearest sweet Carry, you and our son are my life."

For a moment more he stood looking out the window, then laid the gun on the ledge. Calmly he turned, picked up the sword and stood directly over Nagakura. Looking into his eyes. He raised it over his head with both hands and with all the strength he could muster, brought the heavy razor sharp blade crashing down alongside Nagakura's neck. The force of the blow split the upper half of his torso in two. Leaving it embedded, Harry spit on him, and walked out of the shed into the sunlight and blue sky.

*   *   *

"I tried to get the same kinda stuff you had on," Benny said as he unpacked the clothes he'd bought them. From experience, his wife knew enough not to ask questions, like how come he was burning the things Manny and Harry had been wearing.

"Oh, please, can't you stay even for a little while?" she pleaded. I have two big trays of lasagna in the oven." But out of compassion for Harry, Manny made some excuse why they had to get back to New York.

On the plane going home, neither of them spoke much. Harry decided to explain his face by telling Diedra they'd been involved in a minor automobile accident, but he'd been checked out and it was nothing.

Once he got up to use the lavatory, and once the stewardess brought him a drink which he didn't touch, the rest of the time he looked out into the darkness and thought about his mother and father, and about the merry-go-round in the park where they had taken him so long, long ago.

Benny Ostrow was right, he thought, if you hate someone enough, it's easy to kill them.

Part 22

In the days and weeks following his trip, business took precedence over everything, except Diedra. More and more he needed to be near her. No matter how busy, or how long the day, he made sure they spent at least the evening meal together, and some time afterward as well.

Between them, they could afford to do pretty much whatever they wanted to, but their favorite retreat was still the merry-go-round up in the park by his old apartment. To them, a couple of burned hot dogs, a stale beer, and a paper cone of heavily salted french fries while watching the old wooden horses sail by, was the greatest thing in the world.

The world could do nothing to them while they were there. It was their place and always would be. They had an understanding. If either of them was in trouble and couldn't get to the other, he, or she, was to come to the merry-go-round, and stay there until the other came.

Unfortunately, the demand on his time constantly increased and their private moments at the park grew fewer and fewer. Once Longdon had passed the word to the new clique in Washington that Nagakura was dead, Ponzinno got everything he'd demanded.

In one thirty day period, Harry made two trips to Japan. The first one to familiarize himself with the five manufacturing plants, and the second, with Ted Gigommi of the Japanese Military Intelligence, to weed out any remaining Do Nothings, or anybody else who might try and cause problems for the new owner.

Diedra accompanied him both times, but soon grew tired of sitting around hotel rooms, or shopping with her Japanese interpreter. Besides, as the date of their wedding grew closer, she and Marie had more important things to do at home.

Diedra even made several trips up to Ponzinno's estate to work on wedding details with his tyrannical housekeeper, Sophia. The first time she went, she brought Marie with her, and that was also the last time. Apparently, busybody ball breaking Marie got into such a confrontation with Sophia that the housekeeper threatened her with *moloccio*, the evil eye, if she ever dared to come back.

For obvious reasons there could be no link whatsoever between Ponzinno and the new corporations. There were a couple of dozen people in the government aware of it, but for everyone else, it wasn't any of their business.

Accordingly, the lawyers for the enterprises served as interlocutors. If Ponzinno wanted something done, he'd tell his personal attorney, his *consigliere*, who would tell the corporation lawyers, who in turn would tell Harry.

Not that Harry wasn't in the loop, far from it. In fact Harry was rapidly becoming the center of it. That's the way Ponzinno had planned it; Harry had to be kept "sanitized."

But if something was of such major importance that it required a face to face sit down between him and his mentor, it always took the form of a small dinner party and Ponzinno would insist Diedra accompany him. It was obvious he'd grown fond of her, and surprisingly, she of him. Manny Ostrow, Tony Bissetti, Ponzinno's *consigliere*, and the white-haired man with the gun were always in attendance. This was the inner circle when it came to matters pertaining to their new interest. But now a new face had been added to the group.

Ever since the gala affair at Ponzinno's estate, Father Alfonsa Arezzo had become a member of the select group. He'd listen intently, and from time to time, speak quietly in Sicilian to his father, or to the white-haired man who would sit directly behind them.

It was sharp-eyed Diedra who pointed out to Harry that the white-haired man always arrived with the young priest, and always left when he did.

Harry couldn't have been more pleased that she accompanied him to these soirees. They helped get her accustomed to the people he was now dependent upon for his future. Gradually, she even stopped referring to them as "your bent nose friends," and began calling them by their first names, with the exception of Ponzinno. She always referred to him as, Mr. Ponzinno.

An invitation to such a gathering was delivered to Harry's office one afternoon.

"Boss," his secretary Connie said, "that priest is outside."

"well don't let him just sit there, go and get him. Listen, he's a very special friend of mine, from now on if he comes, bring him right in, understand?"

"All right, all right, you don't have to bite my head off."

"Connie, if is wasn't for the fact that I'd be lost without you, I'd fire you."

"Peace be with you," Father Arezzo said as he walked in.

"This is a surprise," Harry said, "I didn't know you were in town."

"It's a surprise for me, too. Guess what? I've been transferred. You're looking at the new assistant to Cardinal Siengenza."

"Congratulations! That's fantastic," Harry said, reaching across the desk and shaking the priest's had. "I guess in your outfit that's considered quite a feather in your cap."

"Oh it is, it is, and talk about being surprised, when they told me to pack my bags and where I was going, I almost fainted. My father is very happy. He says I might even be able to help him with a few things. He's not getting any younger, but don't tell him I said that.

"Harry," the priest continued, "my father is giving a small dinner party for a few business friends tomorrow night and he would like to know if you and Diedra can come. It's at Giandolla's on Lexington Avenue, they have excellent food, I like to eat there whenever I'm in the city. How's eight o'clock sound? My father and I are looking forward to seeing Diedra again."

"That's fine. I know she'll be pleased to see you both, and wait until I tell her about your promotion."

"Now, my father gave me a message for you. He says to have Longdon give you a location where he'd like the steamer trunk items and equipment delivered to, and an exact date and time, then you're to tell Uncle Manny. Does that make any sense to you?"

"Yes, it makes a lot of sense. Please, tell your father I'll take care of it at once, and thank him for the invitation. I'm looking forward to seeing him."

*   *   *

Giandola's was the king of place that had no prices on its menu, if you had to ask how much you didn't belong there. It was the kind of restaurant where, before you had your fly zipped, some guy in the men's room wearing a tuxedo was brushing the dandruff off your shoulders, whether you had any or not, and anything less than a five dollar tip would have offended his stockbroker.

"You know, sweetheart," Diedra said as they pulled into the curb, "we're not exactly poor, but I just can't get comfortable eating in places like this."

"I know what you mean, but can you picture guys like Bissetti and Ponzinno down in O'Banion's stuffing potatoes in their faces? Listen, before we go in," he said, leaning over and kissing her shoulder, "we have this suite at the Regis. How about using it tonight?"

"Can we have sex? And can I steal the ashtrays?" she asked mischievously.

He laughed. "Before or after you take the ashtrays?"

"How about before and after?" she whispered running her wet tongue across his lips.

They both jumped when a young parking attendant knocked on the passenger side window and pointed to the door lock button. Diedra pulled it up and the man held the door for her. Her dress had ridden up during the trip and as she swung her long, shapely legs out of the car, several male passersby became so distracted by the view, they walked into a young couple coming from the opposite direction.

"You've outdone yourself tonight," he told her as they walked to the entrance. Her hair was pulled back is a bun and secured with small curved red combs. The expensive black sheath she was wearing combined with the plain red cloth choker gave her a regal look, and the black Spanish lace shawl draped around her shoulders was shear enough to highlight the beauty of her soft, white skin.

The interior was gaudy by anyone's standards. Looking more like a brothel for the Romanov elite, everything in the place, with the exception of the people, seemed to be covered with either gold leaf, or crushed red velour. "I have to remember not to order fish," Diedra whispered in his ear. She was referring to the huge marble spouting fountain complete with foot long goldfish in the center of the lobby.

"*Bounsaera,*" the tall, tuxedoed gentlemen with the graying, razor cut hairdo said as he walked up to them.

"Yes, Mr. Ponzinno's party, please," Harry said as he palmed Mr. Continental a twenty dollar subway.

"Oh, yes, Mr. O'Day, Miss Shannahan, we've been expecting you."

It was happening more and more frequently, and now with Diedra, too. People who they had never seen before knowing their names and going out of their was to be respectful. It was one of the many fringe benefits of being associated with Ponzinno.

"Please, follow me," said the matre'd as he led them to a small elevator. By now, Harry had gotten to know most of Ponzinno's personal bodyguards, and he recognized the one holding the elevator door.

"Hello, Chichi, how are you? You remember Miss Shannahan."

"Yes, sir, of course, nice to see you again Miss. Mr. Ponzinno is upstairs, I'll ride up with you."

The private dining room was as garishly decorated as the lobby, but at least there were no goldfish. Manny, Tony Trucks, and Father Arezzo were sitting around a black marble, pedestal coffee table having some kind of drinks, and the white-haired man with the gun was sitting a few feet in back of the priest. All four got up immediately when they saw Diedra step off the elevator.

Ponzinno had been standing across the room talking to several men in business suits smoking long black cigars.

"Exquisite my dear, absolutely exquisite." He said as he walked over and took hold of her ring hand. "You're going to make a beautiful bride. What is it now? Three weeks? Harry, you're a lucky young man."

"You make me blush," she said, leaning forward and gently kissing his cheek. Excusing herself, she walked over to the three men who had been sitting at the coffee table.

"Father, Manny, Tony, it's nice to see you all again, please, sit down. The white-haired man with the gun brought her his chair. After answering some questions about her wedding preparations and congratulating Father Arezzo on his promotion and transfer, she rejoined Harry and Ponzinno.

"Before I forget, my dear," Ponzinno said with a grin, I've spoken to Sophia about Marie, your maid of honor. As a personal favor, she's promised to remove the curse. But like troublesome children, you and I will have the task of keeping them separated.

"Now, I'd like you both to meet my other guests. Raising his hand like a conductor telling his orchestra to stand, the three men he'd been talking with obediently moved forward.

"Gentlemen, this is the young couple I've been telling you about, Miss Diedra Agnes Shannahan, and Mr. Harry O'Day. They've agreed to do me the honor of being married at my home in three weeks, and my son will perform the ceremony. Please, make them feel comfortable." He proceeded to introduce them.

Mr. Lyle R. Sanderling, president of Ambassador Select Publications. Through a series of paper corporations, his company controlled several hundred magazines and newspapers.

Mr. J. Malcolm Stone, president and CEO of Beldon Enterprises, Inc. His companies controlled TV and radio stations in every major city.

Mr. Stamford Parker, president of Fiduciary International Investments, Inc. He had two specialties, lending money to people who for whatever reason couldn't get it from legitimate banks, and laundering hundreds of millions of dollars each year for Ponzinno.

Harry wasn't the least bit impressed with any of them. Like so many other "important" people Ponzinno had introduced him to, they were nothing, and had nothing. They were button men in pinstripes, and Ponzinno owned them and their fancy companies lock, stock, and barrel. With a wave of his hand he could make them disappear as fast as he'd made them appear to begin with. He allowed them to wallow in their self-importance, and paid them exorbitant amount of money because he needed the legitimacy of their operations.

What did impress Harry was seeing just how deeply Ponzinno's tentacles reached into all kinds of businesses, especially the media. Although, nothing should have surprised him anymore, not after getting a letter from some Vatican honcho telling him his annulment had been approved. That was shortly after he told Father Arezzo that he'd been divorced.

After dinner, Ponzinno stood, picked up his glass and said, "Sometimes it is difficult to combine business with pleasure, but Diedra, Harry, seeing how tonight the two of you are our business, the task is made so much easier. A toast, may God give you the warmth and happiness of each other's love for many, many years. *Buona fortuna*!

"Now, these gentlemen want me to ask Harry a question. How would you like to be the next United States senator from New York?"

The demitasse cup Diedra had been holding made no sound when it hit the plush rug, and Harry gasped a couple of times fighting to clear the wine that had gone down the wrong pipe. Gathering his composure he said, "with all due respect, what I know, or even care about politics could fit into this glass. To be honest, I've had a bad taste in my mouth most of my life when it comes to politicians. I think it's a disgrace what they do to the American people. Pardon my French but I think they're whores. I'm not ashamed to tell you that I've never voted, I couldn't force myself to be that much of a hypocrite. I know that you never say things you don't mean, and I have the greatest respect for you, but in this case, I'd be doing you a disservice."

"Mr. Ponzinno, may I speak?" Stone, the newspaper man asked.

"Harry," he said picking a fleck of tobacco off the tip of his tongue, "you just gave yourself several good reasons why you should think seriously about this. There's millions of young, hardworking people out there, just like yourself, who don't participate, they've written their government off. Why? Because they're fed up reading and hearing about the trash that's taken over down in Washington. Their elected officials have become too much of an embarrassment so they've simply turned to what's important to them, their kids, their homes, jobs…things, hopefully, they can do something about.

"It's going to get worse, now the slimeballs know the majority of the voters don't care what they do. All it takes in a handful of their blood-sucking cronies and they're back in office for another four years. The first place they head for is the people's wallets—if there's anything left."

Mr. Parker, the dressed-up loan shark put his two cents in. "Harry, may I call you Harry? The people Mr. Stone is referring to, people such as yourself, have had their rights abrogated by men whose agendas are totally self-serving. Not only have they lost their rights, but in a little while their children are going to be fighting a war in some godforsaken jungle for who knows what reason, and a lot of them won't be coming back. Harry, the American people are being ambushed. Is that what you want?"

"No! Of course not," Harry answered belligerently, "but I thought after this mutt killed himself in his plane, and his stooge turned the job down, things were supposed to get better."

"Not really," Parker said. "Those two and the ones who've been arrested, or have resigned were the visible part of the cancer. Some serious cutting will be required to get the rest. Besides, it's only a matter of time before the money people buy themselves another president and give the snake a new head."

Mr. Ponzinno," Harry said, "I can't think straight anymore. What about Santronics? I thought you wanted me to handle it?"

"I do! I do!" Ponzinno insisted. "I could not be more pleased with the way things are going."

"But wouldn't I have to give it up?"

"On the contrary. While you were campaigning, the fact that you are a young, self-made man in charge of two major corporations with a beautiful new bride, would only add to your appeal. Diedra can play an important roll in this. We're counting on it.

"As for the bad taste in your mouth, let it out. We're going to teach these people a kind of street politics they've never experienced before, and they're not going to like it.

"We want you to be openly disrespectful to your opponents, because they deserve no better, challenge them. Embarrass them into telling the American people the truth. If they refuse, we'll do it for them. We're going to print who and where their mistresses are, if their wives are alcoholics or adulteresses, if they're stealing from their firm's clients, if they've cheated on their income tax, and if their children are taking drugs. We're going to destroy their family businesses and we're going to destroy them politically.

"We'll start with the worst of them, these so-called party leaders and the committee heads. If they think Mr. Hoover's files are a threat, wait until we start feeding excerpts from the ones our people have put together on them to Mr. Sanderling and Mr. Stone here. If one of them dares to run for reelection, one of our candidates will be right there, demanding he publicly deny what's being printed about him. The fact that he can't, will finish him.

"You don't have to give me an answer now," Ponzinno continued. "Think about it, there's time. Besides, I'm sure your wedding is the most important thing on your mind right now, as it should be. When you return from your honeymoon we'll talk."

"Mr. Ponzinno, is that possible?" Harry asked hesitantly. "Can you really destroy them…their businesses too?"

"We shall see, Harry, we shall see. Times change and so must we to protect ourselves from the fools of the world."

*   *   *

They stayed overnight at the Regis, but it wasn't the kind of evening they'd planned. They talked until dawn.

Of the tens of thousands of words spoken at Giandolla's, Ponzinno had said everything with just four of them, "One of our candidates."

"I'll be damned," Harry said to himself, lying there, staring at the morning's false light, "this Ponzinno, this Machiavellian clone, is going to have his own government." Harry had no way of telling how long he'd been concocting his plan, but given the fact that he had vultures like Stone and Parker and Sanderling lurking in the background, he'd obviously been at it for some time.

Nagakura had planned on taking control of the government with his devices. Ponzinno was going to do it with handpicked people legally elected, and their opponents, legally destroyed, both politically as well as financially. And it would be bankrolled in part by the two billion dollar Santronics operation the jerk Longdon had handed him.

Ponzinno would also keep Nagakura's two steamer trunks containing the armed devices as insurance against anyone in the government having second thoughts about the agreement. In time, the Ponzinnos wouldn't have to worry about things like that, because so many of the elected people in the government would belong to them.

The difference between the powerful money men Parker had mentioned, and Ponzinno, was that Ponzinno was by far, smarter than all of them, and the embodiment of everything evil.

For himself, Harry thought, he had no illusions about being some kind of political messiah. He wasn't the only young, hard working executive type being courted. But he was the only one of them who had saved the son of Ponzinno from being beaten to death. And he was the only one who was about to marry a beautiful young woman who Ponzinno swore was the reincarnation of his dead wife.

There was no doubt in Harry's mind that if he ran, he'd be elected, Ponzinno would make sure of that. So would anyone else be elected with his backing. In time he'd have what him and his associates wanted, their own government.

Part 23

"And who gives this woman in marriage?" Father Arezzo asked.

"I do," Ponzinno responded as he kissed Diedra lightly on the cheek, turned, and stepped to one side of the chapel's altar. Ponzinno had been right. Her beauty did belong there on his estate among the magnificent floral arrangements, and the brilliant sunlight streaming through the stained glass windows.

Mike O'Banion Jr. was Harry's best man and his only other invited guests were Mr. O'Banion Sr., and his long time friend, Joe Joe and his wife.

Diedra's neighbor was her maid of honor. The remaining guests were Manny Ostrow, Tony Trucks Bissetti, his wife, Camella, and Ponzinno's housekeeper, Sophia.

The white-haired man with the gun was someplace in the house, but he didn't come to the chapel or to the reception.

Every detail of the wedding and small gathering, had been meticulously attended to by Sophia and Ponzinno himself—they wouldn't have had it any other way, and when the people took communion, Father Arezzo, looking most pious in his new vestments, used the chalice and Host plate Harry had given him.

Radiant would not have described the way Diedra looked. Wearing a simple, white, empire dress trimmed with pearls, and her long, red hair slipped through a small, plain ring of flowers, she looked almost saintly coming down the aisle on Ponzinno's arm. Harry's first glimpse of her came when the organist began playing. He turned, and looked over his shoulder toward the rear of the chapel. Ponzinno had stepped aside for a moment and she was standing alone in the stone doorway framed in an aura of sunlight.

On the way down the aisle, Mrs. Bissetti gave her a small, lace handkerchief in case she needed it, which she did.

As for the groom, he looked like a scared schoolboy waiting outside the headmaster's study not sure what was in-store for him. But once he heard the priest say, "I now pronounce you man and wife," he was better. He was even better after several shots of his beloved Bushmills.

"Well, how did I do for my first wedding?" Father Arezzo asked when he and Diedra were alone for a moment.

"Alfonsa, how can we ever thank you and your family for everything you've done for us?" she replied, still dabbing at her eyes.

"I've had this rosary since my first communion," he said, handing her a small, violet, colored pouch, "please, I'd like you to have it. It was blessed by the Pope."

"Oh, no, I can't take it, it must mean a great deal to you."

"Please, I want you to have it. Take it as a celebration of your wedding, and my friendship for you both."

"Father? This business of Harry running for the Senate, have we made the right decision?"

"Yes! There's no doubt in my mind, nor in my father's. In fact, he said something just the other morning about Harry being a man capable of doing extraordinary things. 'Who knows?' he said, 'Maybe with the right people behind him, he might even be the president some day.' "

When it came time for the bride and groom to leave, they changed, and Ponzinno had Chichi and another of his personal guards drive them to a small private airport.

"Good luck, *buon viaggio*, have fun," the guests yelled. And so, as man and wife, the important part of their life together was about to begin.

Epilogue

Blowing on a thermos cap of steaming coffee, the young man asked, "Papa, you sure they're coming?"

"Don't worry, they'll be here," he answered, noting by his watch that they were already a half hour late. "Remember what I told you, he's not just you cousin anymore."

In the opinion of many, Albert Ponzinno was the finest stonemason in Sicily. Accompanied by his son, this was their first trip to America. For the last six days, they'd been working down at the grotto on the estate in miserable, hot weather, and were anxious to finish the job and go home.

At his brother Alfonsa's request, he'd gone to a quarry near his village and personally supervised the cutting and polishing of the marble slabs they were using, and had traveled on the same plane when they were transported to America.

Albert and his son turned at the sound of the truck's gears grinding and watched as the small flatbed came out of the tree line and made its way toward the grotto. Father Arezzo and the white-haired man with the gun got out, climbed up, and pulled the tarp off the two wooden packing cases.

Using crowbars, they carefully removed the tops and sides and pushed the steamer trunks onto the power tailgate. Once they were lowered onto dollies, the four men had little trouble sliding them into the sarcophaguslike marble benches Albert and his son had constructed directly in front of the grottos' altar. The only thing left now was to fit and seal the end slabs into place and they could return to Italy.

Ponzinno had designed them himself. Now when anyone came to the grotto to pray, they would have a place to sit and rest.

The four men stood talking for awhile in the already oppressive morning air, and then both Albert Ponzinno and his son kissed the young priest's hand and cheek before going about their work.

Corruptio optimi pessima, the corruption of the best is the worst of all.

Printed in the United States
39993LVS00005B/227